"Buoyed by an abundance of deliciously tart wit, spiced with a generous amount of incendiary sexual chemistry . . . and graced with a cast of captivating characters, Gray's impeccably crafted debut romance . . . is a complete triumph."

—*Booklist* (starred review)

"A smart, witty tale that introduces readers to a marvelously unconventional, eccentric cast of characters and an enchanting Italian setting." —*RT Book Reviews* (Top Pick)

"Charming, original characters, a large dose of humor, and a plot that's fantastic fun . . . Prepare to be captivated by Finn and Alexandra!" —Jennifer Ashley, *USA Today* bestselling author

"Fresh, clever, and supremely witty. A true delight."

—Suzanne Enoch, *New York Times* bestselling author

"Shakespeare meets *Enchanted April* in this dazzling debut . . . The best new book of the year!"

—Lauren Willig, national bestselling author

"Extraordinary! In turns charming, passionate, and thrilling—and sometimes all three at once . . . Juliana Gray is on my auto-buy list." —Elizabeth Hoyt, *New York Times* bestselling author

"A delightful confection of prose and desire that leaps off the page. This romance will stay with you long after you have turned the final page."

—Julia London, *New York Times* bestselling author

"Juliana Gray has a stupendously lyrical voice . . . The story feels tremendously sophisticated, but also fresh, deliciously witty, and devastatingly romantic."

—Meredith Duran, *New York Times* bestselling author

Berkley Sensation titles by Juliana Gray

A LADY NEVER LIES
A GENTLEMAN NEVER TELLS
A DUKE NEVER YIELDS

The Princess in Hiding Romances

HOW TO TAME YOUR DUKE
HOW TO MASTER YOUR MARQUIS
HOW TO SCHOOL YOUR SCOUNDREL

How to School Your Scoundrel

Juliana Gray

BERKLEY SENSATION, NEW YORK

THE BERKLEY PUBLISHING GROUP
Published by the Penguin Group
Penguin Group (USA) LLC
375 Hudson Street, New York, New York 10014

USA • Canada • UK • Ireland • Australia • New Zealand • India • South Africa • China

penguin.com

A Penguin Random House Company

HOW TO SCHOOL YOUR SCOUNDREL

A Berkley Sensation Book / published by arrangement with the author

Berkley Sensation Books are published by The Berkley Publishing Group.
BERKLEY SENSATION® is a registered trademark of Penguin Group (USA) LLC.
The "B" design is a trademark of Penguin Group (USA) LLC.

For information, address: The Berkley Publishing Group,
a division of Penguin Group (USA) LLC,
375 Hudson Street, New York, New York 10014.

ISBN: 978-0-425-26568-0

PUBLISHING HISTORY
Berkley Sensation mass-market edition / June 2014

PRINTED IN THE UNITED STATES OF AMERICA

10 9 8 7 6 5 4 3 2 1

Cover art by Alan Ayers.
Cover design by George Long.
Interior text design by Kristin del Rosario.

To readers of romance,
who make the world a lovelier place to live.

ACKNOWLEDGMENTS

There are mornings when I wake up and can't quite believe how lucky I am to write stories for a living, and I cannot imagine undertaking this adventure without the support of my agent, Alexandra Machinist, and the energetic professionals at Janklow & Nesbit. You make my life better with every book.

My most profound thanks are also due to the wonderful team at Berkley: my marvelous editor, Kate Seaver, Katherine Pelz, Courtney Landi, and all the talented people in marketing, production, art, and sales who bring good stories to great readers.

As usual, I owe a great debt to the creators of stories before me. Readers of my earlier books will recognize the Earl of Somerton and his personal secretary, Mr. Markham, from *A Gentleman Never Tells*, which was inspired in part by the love triangle in Giuseppi Verdi's opera *Don Carlo*. I had King Philip very much in mind in the creation of the troubled Earl of Somerton, and the late-night scene in the library, where Somerton plays his cello, echoes a deeply moving scene in the king's study in Madrid, when he confronts the truth that his wife never loved him. Somerton may have been my most difficult character to write, but as I worked my way through that scene, his character was illuminated for me. I hope it does the same for readers.

Finally, I am forever grateful to the readers and writers of the romance community, who are so filled with love and laughter and encouragement. For every morning filled with happy wonder, I occasionally wake up to mornings of sheer terror, when

I wonder how on earth I'm going to finish the book. Your messages, tweets, emails, and hugs pull me out of every death spiral, and remind me, every so often, that I'm doing something important.

PROLOGUE

Holstein Cathedral
Holstein-Schweinwald-Huhnhof, Germany
October 1889

The undertaker, hastily summoned, had mixed up the shoes on her husband's feet, and Luisa longed to switch them back.

Poor Peter, to go into his eternal rest with the right shoe on the left foot and the left one on the right. But it was fitting, in a way. That was Peter exactly. Tall and spindly, large-eared and bespectacled, he kept his nose in his books and never—at least until they were married, and Luisa hired him a proper valet—wore two socks of the same color. His necktie drooped perpetually in his soup, his right cuff dipped perpetually in his ink, and on their wedding night in June he had actually . . .

Well, never mind that. He had figured it all out eventually, after consulting a book of anatomy. Regardless, he was her husband, he was the posthumous Prince Consort of Holstein-Schweinwald-Huhnhof, and he deserved a little more dignity than a corpse that looked as if its legs had been hacked off and reattached on the wrong ends.

Luisa turned and made a quiet signal to the priest.

"Yes, Your Highness?" he whispered respectfully.

"See to it that the Prince Consort's shoes are switched to the correct feet before the public viewing begins."

The priest looked in horror to the pair of caskets lying in

state on the altar of Holstein Cathedral. "Yes, Your Highness," he gasped.

With Peter taken care of, Luisa turned her attention to the other casket, the one containing the mortal remains of her father, the legendary Prince Rudolf of Holstein-Schweinwald-Huhnhof: legendarily handsome, legendarily vigorous, legendarily unable to produce a legitimate male heir despite his own tenacious efforts and those of his three wives, each one younger than the last. Side by side, he dwarfed his son-in-law as Goliath dwarfed David: his shoulders twice as broad, his neck twice as thick, his thighs twice as massive. Even his nose thrust into the air with decidedly more assertiveness. His burial robes were trimmed in ermine, and his shoes were manifestly on the correct feet.

Wake up. Luisa's stern mind willed the words toward the two caskets. *Wake up, the both of you. You can't possibly be dead. Two days ago, you were prancing on your horses in the courtyard, you were sipping your last from the stirrup cups, you were galloping across the new-fallen leaves into the Schweinwald. You were stalking stags, you were breathing the good clean air, you were alive.*

Alive.

But the men didn't move. Not a flutter from an ermine-trimmed chest, not a flicker of a sleeping eyelash. The two grave faces remained as still as wax.

From somewhere to Luisa's right, one of her two sisters suppressed a tiny sob. Stefanie, probably, youngest and by far the most impetuous. Emilie would be kneeling in quiet dignity, thinking her mysterious inner thoughts.

Another sob rose up, rather less suppressed, from a female throat in the ranks behind her.

Two more sobs, both at once. One of them belonging unmistakably to the Baroness von Spitzberg, of whose five children only two were commonly known to be sired by her husband, the Baron.

Like a dam strained to bursting, the tears broke out among the ladies of the household and the court. A tide of weeping rose to its flood, echoing endlessly along the soaring nave of Holstein Cathedral, as Prince Rudolf's lovers, mistresses, and convenient instruments of carnal relief lamented his loss to heaven above.

Luisa crossed herself and rose. She was the ruler of Holstein-Schweinwald-Huhnhof now, and someone had to take charge of this undignified display of emotion.

She nodded to the priest and walked up to the caskets.

A low chord issued from the massive pipe organ at the rear of the cathedral, a gift of the Duke of Olympia, the brother of Prince Rudolf's English first wife—Luisa's mother—on the occasion of her marriage. Luisa came to a stop in front of her father's proud nose. How was it possible that this pile of sculpted flesh, which so perfectly resembled Prince Rudolf, no longer contained his soul?

"*Auf Wiedersehen*," she whispered softly, which was an odd choice, because they all spoke English to one another within the family. Prince Rudolf had been sent to school in England, her mother was English, they had often spent much of the summer visiting English relatives.

But the final farewell came out in German.

Auf Wiedersehen. Until we meet again.

Her sisters were behind her, waiting to pay respect. Luisa moved to the next casket.

Peter. Her old friend, her new husband. Over the winter, following the death in childbed of his third wife, Prince Rudolf had called Luisa into his library and told her that he had given up hope of a male heir, that he would have her created Crown Princess in a state ceremony, and that she would be married at the same time to reassure the people of a strong leadership, a secure succession, and a damned good party.

After all, what loyal subject doesn't love a royal wedding?

Her father had chosen Peter for her, and she hadn't objected. She'd known him all her life, the son of the Prince of neighboring Baden-Wursthof, more agreeable than most gentlemen and rather handsome, really, when he could be persuaded to endure the attentions of a valet. Why object? She was a princess, after all. She had always known that her body belonged to the state, to the people of Holstein-Schweinwald-Huhnhof, and not to herself. That was the price one paid for privilege. It was her duty. She might as well complain that she had to rise and dress in the morning, or that, in order to live, she had to trouble herself to breathe.

Now she gazed on Peter's still face, on his spindly body dressed in its rich burial clothes, and a cold anger rose up in her chest. Peter had only been doing his duty, too. He had married her in a tedious three-hour ceremony, he had moved to Holstein Castle, he had plunged without complaint into all the responsibilities of the consort to a ruler-in-waiting.

And for this, he had been ambushed in a forest, shot like a dog, and left to die.

Next to her, Stefanie was sobbing quietly into a white lace-edged handkerchief. Emilie's shoulders heaved.

But Luisa felt no desire to cry. She had no wish to waste her time on useless mourning.

"*Auf Wiedersehen*," she said softly to Peter, and then she turned and walked down the center aisle of the cathedral, looking neither right nor left, while her sisters and the church officials hastily assembled themselves to walk behind her.

The air was chilly, crisp with the promise of autumn. In the distance, the white-tipped peaks of the Alpine foothills rose like an echo above the jagged rooftops. Thousands of people thronged in the cathedral square, their red-rimmed eyes gazing at her in eerie silence. Were they quiet out of grieving respect for their fallen Prince, or because they disapproved of their new ruler? Was it sympathy that lay so heavy on the cobblestones of the Kirkenplatz, or an outraged discontent?

A column of carriages stood waiting, and Luisa walked toward the first one, the state coach of the Prince of Holstein-Schweinwald-Huhnhof, now hers by right. It was two hundred years old and gaudily baroque, gleaming with the gold leaf applied lovingly each spring by the master coachman and his assistant, and sumptuous with purple velvet upholstery renewed by the castle's own seamstresses. A footman opened the door and handed her inside. She settled into the cushions, alone.

Not quite alone. From the corner of the seat opposite, Quincy raised his head and whined at her. His small tail thumped against the cushion.

"What's the matter, then?" She held out her arms, and the corgi leaped into her lap. "You're shaking, poor boy. It's all right."

The carriage lurched off. Through the windows, Luisa watched her two outriders jog solemnly alongside, wigs curled and gold braid glittering in all the right places. The autumn sun cast a watery glow on the bricks and stones of her beloved Holsteinton, the houses and shops she knew by heart, the stern Roman columns of the town hall, the elegant white marble facade of the new Grand Hotel Holstein . . .

She straightened in her seat and craned her neck toward the window. On her lap, the trembling Quincy whined again, and let out a nervous yip. Her hand dropped to his head.

The Grand Hotel Holstein was on the Badenstrasse.

The Badenstrasse led away from Holstein Castle, not toward it.

She rapped on the roof. "Hello! Hello!"

There was no response.

She rapped again.

The coach was gaining speed. Outside the left window, the outrider had pushed his horse from a dignified jog into a canter, and for the first time Luisa noticed the rugged profile beneath his white wig and ceremonial hat.

She did not recognize that face.

"What's happened, Quincy?" She looked down at his anxious face and back out the window.

Quincy lifted himself to his feet in her lap and barked at the window.

In one continuous motion, Luisa enclosed Quincy's warm body with her one arm and reached for the door handle with the other, and as her fingers touched the smooth wood, the coach made a careering turn around a corner. They were headed for the outskirts now, toward the open highway and the broad forest of the Schweinwald, where her father and husband had been killed.

Or so went her last thought, before the force of the turn sent her flying across the coach, and the back of her head struck an ornamental gold-leaf scroll carved into the ceiling.

ONE

London
November 1889

The Earl of Somerton leaned back in his chair, steepled his fingers into an imaginary cathedral before his nose, and considered the white-faced man standing at the extreme edge of the antique kilim rug before the desk.

Standing, of course. One never made one's underlings too comfortable.

He allowed the silence to take on a life of its own, a third presence in the room, a roiling thundercloud of anticipation.

The man shifted his weight from one large booted foot to the other. A droplet of sweat trickled its lazy way along the thick vertical scar at the side of his face.

"Are you warm, Mr. Norton? I confess, I find the room a trifle chilly, but you're welcome to open a window if you like."

"No, thank you, sir." Norton's voice tilted queasily.

"A glass of sherry, perhaps? To calm the nerves?"

"The nerves, sir?"

"Yes, Mr. Norton. The nerves." Somerton smiled. "*Your* nerves, to be precise, for I can't imagine that any man could walk into this study to report a failure so colossal as yours, without feeling just the slightest bit"—he sharpened his voice to a dagger point—"nervous."

The Adam's apple jumped and fell in Mr. Norton's throat. "Sir."

"Sir . . . yes? As in: Sir, you are correct, I am shaking in my incompetent boots? Or perhaps you mean: Sir, no, I am quite improbably ignorant of the fatal consequences of failure in this particular matter." Another smile. "Enlighten me, if you will, Mr. Norton."

"Sir. Yes. I am . . . I am most abjectly sorry that I . . . that in the course of . . ."

"That you allowed my wife, a woman, unschooled in the technical aspects of subterfuge—my *wife*, Mr. Norton, the Countess of Somerton—to somehow elude your diligent surveillance last night?" He leaned forward and placed his steepled fingers on the desk before him. "To escape you, Mr. Norton?"

Norton snatched his handkerchief from his pocket and dabbed at his temples. His narrow and unremarkable face—so useful in his choice of profession—shone along every plane surface, like a plank of wood left out in the rain. "Sir, I . . . I . . . I most humbly suggest that Lady Somerton is . . . she has more wits in her possession than . . ."

Somerton's fist crashed into the blotter. "She is my *wife*, Mr. Norton. And she slipped through your grasp."

"Sir, in all the weeks I've kept watch on Lady Somerton, she's traveled nowhere more suspicious than the home of her cousin, Lady Morley . . ."

"Who is undoubtedly complicit in her affairs."

"Oh, but sir . . ."

"And she has followed *me*, on occasion, has she not?"

"Yes, but . . ."

"Which means she has neither the good sense nor the propriety of a common shopwife."

Norton's massive jaw worked and worked. His gaze fell to the rug. "Sir, I feel . . ."

"You *feel*?" Somerton barked. "You *feel*, Mr. Norton? Allow me to observe that your *feelings* have nothing to do with the matter at hand. My wife, the Countess of Somerton, is engaged in an adulterous liaison with another man. It is my belief that she has carried on this sordid correspondence throughout the entire duration of our marriage. Your object—the task, the sole task for which I hired you, Mr. Norton, as the best man in London for clandestine work—your task was to obtain proof of this affair and bring it to me. You are not paid to have *feelings* on the matter."

"Sir, I . . ."

"Look at me, Mr. Norton."

Erasmus Norton, the most stealthy and deadly assassin inside these British Isles, known to have killed at least one mark with a single silent tap to the skull, lifted his dark eyes carefully upward until he met Somerton's gaze. For an instant, a flutter of pity brushed the inside wall of the earl's thick chest.

And then, like the butterfly snatched by the net, it was gone.

"Believe me, Mr. Norton," said Somerton, in his silkiest voice, "I understand your little predicament. She is a beautiful woman, isn't she? Beautiful and full of grace. You wouldn't think, as you watched her smile in that gentle little way of hers, as you watched her float about her daily business, that she would be capable of dishonoring a pet mouse, let alone her husband. I can see how you've fallen under her spell. I can hardly blame you. I fell myself, didn't I, in the most catastrophic manner possible. I married her." The word *married* came out in a growl.

"If I may say, sir . . ."

Somerton rose to his feet. "But you are paid to set aside these tender notions, Mr. Norton, these misguided ideas of yours, and see to your business. Otherwise, I shall be forced to consider, one by one, the various means by which your *feelings* may be forcibly exhumed from your incompetent breast." He leaned forward and spoke in a low voice, just above a whisper. "Do you understand me, Mr. Norton?"

Norton hopped backward from his perch like a startled brown-haired parakeet. "Oh, but sir! She's innocent, I'll stake my life on it . . ."

"Innocent?" The low simmer of fury in Somerton's brain, the fury he had battled all his life to control, flared upward in a roar of heat. "Innocent? By God, Norton. Do I hear you correctly? Are you actually saying I'm mistaken about my own wife?"

Norton's white mouth opened and closed. "Not mistaken exactly, sir, that's the wrong word, I . . ."

Somerton walked around the side of his desk. Norton's eyes followed his progress, while his words drifted into a wary silence.

Somerton came to a stop next to the edge of the rug, mere inches away from Norton's blunt and unlovely figure. They were of about the same height, he and Norton. In fact, taken both together, they made a pair of brothers: tall, dark-haired, brute-boned, thick with muscle, crowned by faces only a particularly adoring mother could admire.

Not that the woman who had given birth to Somerton was that sort of mother.

"Mr. Norton," he said, "I find this conversation has dragged on long enough. Either do your duty, or I shall exact the usual forfeit. There are no other choices. We've done business together before, and you know this fact as well as any man on earth."

Norton's dark eyes blinked twice. "Yes, sir."

"You may go."

Norton turned and dashed for the door. Somerton waited, without moving, until his black-coated figure had stepped off the rug and reached gratefully for the handle.

"Oh! There is one more thing, Mr. Norton."

The man froze with his hand on the knob.

"As I observed, you have allowed Lady Somerton to follow me about my business in the evening, from time to time. A dangerous occupation, that."

"I have kept the closest watch on her, sir. As close as possible without revealing myself," Norton said to the door.

"Let me be clear. If a single hair on Lady Somerton's head, a single *eyelash* belonging to her ladyship's face, is harmed, you will die, Mr. Norton. I shall perform the deed myself. Do you understand me?"

Norton's hand clutched around the knob, as if struck by the actual cold-blooded wind of Somerton's voice.

"I understand, sir," he whispered.

"Very good."

Lord Somerton returned to his seat without another look. The door creaked slightly as it opened and closed, and then there was silence, profound and merciful silence, except for the rhythmic scratch of Somerton's pen as he finished the letter that Norton's entrance had interrupted.

A double knock struck the study door.

He signed his name, considered it carefully, and blotted the ink on the page before he answered.

"Come in," he said.

The footman stepped cautiously through the doorway. "Mr. Markham is here to see you, sir."

"Mr. Markham?"

"For the position of secretary, sir." The footman's voice lifted just a single nervous trifle at the word *sir*, turning the statement into a question. Servants and peers alike performed a similar vocal trick when engaging Lord Somerton in conversation. He couldn't imagine why.

"Send him in."

Somerton folded the letter, slipped it inside an envelope, and addressed it himself in bold strokes of black ink. A wretched and time-consuming chore, that. He did hope this current secretarial prospect would prove capable of the position, but the hope was a faint one. For some reason, he had the most appalling luck with secretaries.

The footman dissolved into the darkness of the hallway. Somerton consulted the list he had prepared an hour ago—another damned chore he was eager to relinquish—and made a small check next to the word *Ireland*. Two more words remained: *Secretary* and *Wife*.

He was about to take care of the first, anyway. He preferred not to think about the second.

A coal popped in the fireplace nearby. The London air had taken a turn for the chillier this week, and the usual miasma of yellow fog had thickened like an evil enchantment about the streets and buildings of the capital, as millions of chimneys put out millions of columns of coal smoke into the damp English atmosphere. In another week, the household would retire to Somerton Hall for the Christmas season. Hunting every day, drinking every night. His wife's uncomplaining mask at dinnertime; his son's brave *Yes, sir* and *No, sir* to the few questions Somerton could stretch his adult imagination to ask.

In short, the usual jolly old Yule.

The door opened. Somerton flexed his fingers.

"Your lordship: Mr. Markham," said the footman.

A young man stepped through the doorway.

"Good morning, Mr. Markham." Somerton glanced at the clock on the mantel. "I hope the hour is not too early for you."

"Not at all, your lordship. I thank you for taking the trouble to see me." Mr. Markham moved into the lamplight, and something stirred in the pit of Somerton's belly.

Indigestion, no doubt.

They were all young men who came to interview for the position of personal secretary to the Earl of Somerton, but this young man seemed younger than all of them. He could not have been more than eighteen. A suit of plain black wool covered his coltish limbs a little too loosely. His face was smooth and unlined, without a single whisker; his dark ginger hair was slicked back from his head with a stiff layer of pomade. In the symmetrical architecture of his face, there was a trace of almost delicate beauty, a lingering evidence of boyhood.

But there was nothing childlike about the way he moved. He squared his thin shoulders, propelled his lanky figure to the center of the rug, and went on, in a firm, rich alto, "I have come to interview for the position of secretary."

Somerton set aside his pen in an exact perpendicular relationship to the edge of the desk. "So I am informed, Mr. Markham. I read over your references last night. Astonishingly fulsome, for a man so young."

"I hope I have given satisfaction, sir." In a voice that knew full well he had.

Cocky little bastard.

Not that cockiness was necessarily a fault. A secretary should approach his work with confidence. That cockiness could shove open more than a few doors in his employer's service; it could accomplish what timid self-effacement could not.

Just so long as the two of them were quite clear: That cockiness should never, ever, direct itself toward the Earl of Somerton himself.

Somerton raised his most devastating eyebrow. "No doubt, Mr. Markham, you gave the—er—the attaché of this beleaguered ambassador of Holstein-Schweinwald-Huhnhof the very utmost satisfaction. I presume you left his employ because of the political revolution there?"

A slight hesitation. "Yes."

Somerton shook his head. "A shocking state of affairs. The

ruler murdered, the heir snatched away from the funeral itself. Is there any news of the missing princesses?"

"None, I'm afraid," said Mr. Markham. "One hears they escaped to relatives in England with their governess, but it's only a rumor. Likely a false hope."

"My sympathies. Regardless, I should warn you that my standards are perhaps a trifle more exacting than those of a backward, corrupt, and regicidal Germanic principality."

Ah. Was that a flare of indignation in Mr. Markham's warm brown eyes? But the lad smothered it instantly, returning his face to the same pale symmetry as before. Another point in his favor: the ability to control emotion.

"That unfortunate state," he said icily, "is nonetheless most exact in its notions of ceremony and diplomatic procedure. I assure you, I am well versed in every aspect of a secretary's duties."

"And I assure you, Mr. Markham, that the duties required of *my* secretary will soon prove unlike any you have encountered before."

Markham's eyelids made a startled blink.

"We will, however, begin at the beginning, so as not to shock your tender sensibilities. I start work directly after breakfast, which you will enjoy on a tray in your bedroom. I dislike company in the morning, and my personal secretary does not take meals with the household staff."

"I see."

"You will report to this room at half eight. We will work through until ten o'clock, when coffee is brought in and I receive visitors. Your desk is there"—he waved to the small mahogany escritoire set at a right angle to the desk, a few feet away—"and you will remain in the room, taking notes of the meeting, unless I direct otherwise. You can write quickly, can you not, Mr. Markham?"

"I have recently learned the essentials of shorthand notation," Mr. Markham said, without the slightest hesitation.

"We will take lunch here in the study, after which your time is your own, provided you complete your assignments by the time I return at six o'clock. We will work for another two hours, after which I dress for dinner. I invariably dine out. You may take your evening meal in the dining room, though you will likely find yourself alone. Her ladyship dines in the nursery with my son." Somerton congratulated himself on the absence of expression in his voice.

"Very good, sir. Do I understand you to mean that I have met with your approval?" Mr. Markham said. His face tilted slightly against the lamplight, exposing the curve of his cheekbone, prominent and graceful, in perfect balance with the rest of his face. His arms remained crossed behind his back, his posture straight. Almost . . . regal.

What an extraordinary chap. The thought slipped without warning between the steel columns of Somerton's mind.

He rose to his feet. "Approval, Mr. Markham? Nothing of the kind. I am in want of a secretary. You, it seems, are the only man daring enough to apply for the position."

"Rather a tight position for you, then, sir."

The words were said so effortlessly, so expressionlessly, that it took a moment for Somerton to process their meaning.

What the *devil*? Had the fellow *actually* just said that? *Rather a tight position for you.* The cheek!

Somerton's shoulders flexed in an arc of counterattack. "You have one week, Mr. Markham, to prove yourself capable of the position. A position, I hardly need add, that no man has held for longer than two months together. If you succeed in winning my—what was your word, Mr. Markham?"

The young man smiled. "*Approval*, Lord Somerton."

"*Approval*." He sneered. "You will be compensated with the handsome sum of two hundred pounds per annum, paid monthly in arrears."

Two hundred solid English pounds sterling. A fortune for an impecunious young man just starting out in his profession, clinging by his claws to the first rung of the professional ladder; twice as much as his wildest hopes might aspire to achieve. Somerton waited for the look of startled gratification to break out across Mr. Markham's exquisite young features.

Waited.

A small curl appeared in the left corner of Mr. Markham's round pink upper lip.

"Two hundred pounds?" he said, as he might say *two hundred disemboweled lizards*. "I no longer wonder that you have difficulty retaining secretaries for any length of time, your lordship. I only wonder that you have tempted any to the position at all."

Somerton shot to his feet.

"I beg your pardon! Two hundred pounds is impossibly generous."

"You will forgive me, Lord Somerton, but the facts speak for themselves. I am the only applicant for the position. Evidently two hundred pounds represents not nearly enough compensation for an ambitious and talented young fellow to take on such an overbearing, demanding, bleak-faced despot as yourself." He uncrossed his arms, walked to the desk, and spread his long, young fingers along the edge. "Allow me, if you will, to make you a counter-proposition. I shall take on the position of your personal secretary for a week's trial, beginning tomorrow morning. If the conditions of employment meet with my approval, why, I'll agree to continue on for a salary of three hundred pounds a year, paid weekly in advance. My room and board included, of course."

Mr. Markham's eyes fixed, without blinking, on Somerton's face. That unlined young face, innocently smooth in the yellow glow of the electric lamp, did not twitch so much as a single nerve.

"By God," Somerton said slowly. The blood pulsed hard at the base of his neck. He sat back in his chair, took up his pen, and balanced it idly along the line of his knuckles. His hand, thank God, did not shake.

"Well, sir? My time this morning is limited."

"You may go, Mr. Markham." He waved to the door.

Markham straightened. "Very well. Good luck to you, sir." He turned and walked to the door, at that same regal pace, as if leading the procession to a state dinner.

Somerton waited until his hand had reached the knob. "And Mr. Markham? Kindly tell my butler to arrange for your belongings to be brought over from your lodgings first thing tomorrow and delivered to the suite next to mine."

"Sir?" At last, a note of astonishment in that imperturbable young voice.

Somerton took out a sheet of blank paper, laid it on the

blotter, and smiled. "I suspect you shall suit this overbearing,
demanding, bleak-faced despot very well, Mr. Markham."

L uisa closed the door to the study and leaned back against
the heavy carved wood.

Her heart still thudded inside her ribs at an alarming speed,
as if she'd just finished a footrace around the shore of the sparkling clear Holsteinsee. Thank God for starched white collars
and snug black neckties, or else that man—that Somerton, that
predatory prizefighter of an aristocrat with his keen black eyes
and his impossibly thick shoulders—would have detected the
rapid thrust of her pulse against her skin.

Her tender female skin.

He would have seen right through her mask of male bra-
vado. He would have annihilated her.

How her chest had collapsed at the words *You may go*, as if
the world had vaporized around her.

And then *unpacked in the suite next to mine*, the point at
which her heart had resumed beating, with this alarming and
reckless patter of . . . what? Fear? Relief? Anticipation?

When Luisa was younger, before her skirts were length-
ened and her hair arranged in elaborate knots and loops under
a jeweled tiara, her father used to take her out in the Schweinwald to stalk deer. They would set out at dawn, while the grass
still breathed out rings of silver mist, and the thud of the
horses' hooves rattled the autumn silence. In those quiet
mornings, Luisa learned how to hold herself still, how to be
patient, how to listen and watch. She would study her father's
movements and replicate them. She was Diana, she was the
virgin huntress, wise and ruthless.

Until that October day when her horse had gone lame and
she had fallen behind, unnoticed, and the familiar trees and
vines of the Schweinwald had become suddenly and terrify-
ingly unfamiliar. She had hallooed softly. She had whistled.
She had called out in mounting alarm, panic mottling her
brain, and as she stood there with her hands gripped around the
loops of her horse's reins, a black bear had wandered into view
among the trees and come to a stop about twelve feet away.

They had stared at each other, she and that bear. She knew, of course, that you weren't supposed to stare. You were supposed to look away and back off slowly. But she couldn't remember all those rules of engagement. She couldn't leave her lame horse. She had nothing to fall back on, no rear position in which to shelter. So she stared back, for what seemed like an hour, and was probably less than a minute.

She still remembered the absolute blackness of the bear's fur, except for a small patch of rufous brown where a miraculous ray of sunlight penetrated the forest canopy. She remembered the dark watchfulness of its eyes, the fingerprint texture of its round nose. She remembered the syrupy scent of the rotting leaves, the chilling handprint of the air on her cheek.

She remembered thinking, *I am going to die, or I am going to live. Which is it?*

"Sir? Are you going to see my father?"

Luisa opened her eyes and straightened away from the door.

A young, dark-haired boy stood before her, examining her with curious black eyes so exactly like those of the Earl of Somerton, her heart jumped an extra beat for good measure.

"I beg your pardon?" she said.

"My father." The boy nodded at the door. "Are you going in to see him? Or has he tossed you out?"

"I . . . I have just finished my interview with his lordship." Luisa heard herself stammering. Children made her nervous, with their all-seeing eyes and their mysterious minds, occupied with infant imaginings Luisa could no longer even attempt to guess. And this one was worse than most, his pale face poised upward with unsmiling curiosity, his eyes far too reminiscent of that pair she'd just escaped. She scrambled for something to say. "You are Lord Somerton's son?"

The boy nodded. "Philip. Lord Kildrake," he added importantly.

"I see."

"I guess he's tossed you out, then. Well, buck up. That's what Mama says. Buck up and try again later, when he's in a good mood."

"I see."

Young Lord Kildrake sighed and stuck his finger in his hair, twirling it into a thoughtful knot. His gaze shifted to the door behind her. "The trouble is, he never is. In a good mood."

From the entrance hall came the sound of feet on marble, of the butler issuing quiet orders. A woman's voice called out. The boy's mother, probably. Lady Somerton, summoning her son.

He never is. In a good mood.

In the end, that long-ago day, Luisa had lived, but not because she had stared the bear down. The thunder of avenging hoofbeats had filled the forest, and Prince Rudolf had appeared on his white charger. He had risen in his stirrups, dropped his reins, lifted his rifle, and shot the bear dead without a break in the horse's stride.

Luisa looked down at the little boy. He had lost interest in her now. He let out another long sigh, turned, and ambled back down the hallway, still twirling his hair.

Her father was dead. Her husband was dead. Her sisters, her governess, all scattered to the winds of England.

She was alone.

Luisa straightened away from the door and shook out her shirt cuffs. She had better get on with it, then, hadn't she?

TWO

On the occasion of his fifteenth birthday, the Earl of Somerton's father had taken notice of him at last. "Getting to be a man, aren't you, Kildrake, my boy?" he'd said, in his rough-edged voice. "Look at the shoulders on you."

Somerton—then merely Leopold, Viscount Kildrake—had beamed with embarrassed pride. He had returned home from school just the day before for the summer holiday, and apart from the butler, who had made the arrangements for his journey, nobody in the house seemed to have noticed his arrival. "Yes, sir," he said.

"You're rising fourteen now, aren't you?"

"Fifteen today, sir."

"Today! By God!" The earl's red-tipped nose had dipped toward his. "Been having a go at the housemaids, have you?"

A bolt of pure fright went through young Leopold's body, as if his father had just read his thoughts. Not that he'd attempted a single housemaid—he hadn't dared to poach on his father's established turf—but he'd admired them from afar. Plump bosoms and round arses and . . . He folded his hands behind his back and dug his fingers hard into his skin, because his unruly young adolescent body was already responding to the mere suggestion of female flesh. "No, sir!"

"No?" A perplexed scowl. "Well, then. Come along with me."

It was ten o'clock in the evening, and Leopold had been on his way upstairs to undress for bed, after a solitary dinner in the family dining room. (His mother was attending three different balls that evening and took the usual tray in her dressing room during her two-hour preparatory toilette.) "Yes, sir," he'd said, and walked outside to the waiting carriage with his father. They had proceeded to his father's favorite brothel, where Leopold had lost his virginity to a plump forty-year-old whore in one room while the Earl of Somerton had expired of a stroke in another.

In the curious way of memory, he recalled little of the carnal act itself, or how he had come to be lying in mingled shock and shame atop the wide white belly of his companion, veins still throbbing, at the vivid instant when his father's two strumpets had burst naked through the doorway screaming, *He's dead! He'd dead! God save us!* He was still wearing his shirt, and his trousers were tangled around his ankles; he remembered that, because he had tripped off the bed and fallen on his face, and the whore had laughed. "Why, then, you're the earl now! And I've got your mess in my cunt this instant, bless me! Ha-ha!"

He'd turned red with humiliation at the words *mess* and *cunt*; he'd turned black with horror at the words *He's dead*, which the other two prostitutes were still screeching, over and over. Eventually the proprietress had swept through and sorted out the bedlam, arranged for a discreet visit by a friendly pair of police inspectors, apologized profusely to the new Earl of Somerton and hoped he would continue to favor Cousin Hannah's with his custom.

He had.

In fact, Cousin Hannah sat before him now: a different and younger Hannah, in the way of things, but just as efficient. Her violet skirts pooled on the chair about her, and her copious bosom was buttoned up to the throat, because it was daytime. By some miracle of corsetry, her waist appeared almost as narrow as her neck.

She released the stopper of a slim bottle of brandy, allowed a luxurious splash into the teacup below, and stirred with a dainty spoon of well-polished Sheffield plate. She motioned the bottle in Somerton's direction. He shook his head patiently.

"To answer your question, sir," said Hannah, though not

before taking a sip of tea, "his lordship has frequented my humble establishment a number of times in the past fortnight, but never in company with your wife."

"You have examined all his companions? She would, of course, have disguised herself."

Hannah sent him a look of patient indulgence, a look he particularly loathed. "Yes, sir. As I did the previous fortnight, and the one before, and all the others."

Somerton's cup of tea sat untouched before him. A last thin gasp of steam rose upward from the surface and dissolved into the air. He leaned forward. "Obviously she's been too clever for you."

"With all respect, sir, she hasn't." Hannah returned his gaze squarely. She spoke firmly and slowly, as she always did, taking care to avoid the telltale pronunciation of her East End roots. Before taking over the business from the original Hannah, she'd been the best girl in the house, a true good-natured whore who actually enjoyed her work, gentle with newcomers and abandoned with regulars, dropping her haitches and her knickers with equal enthusiasm. Now she only slipped a consonant after her third glass of sherry, and only took on a customer if he was a virgin. (Defloration of the young and nervous was her particular specialty.)

Somerton smacked the table with his open palm. "She must have! What about the other houses?"

"Nothing, sir. Now, Penhallow, he makes his round about the bawdies, regular as clockwork, sometimes two or three houses a night. But he hain't . . . he *hasn't* brought a lady with him in ever so long. He brings his friends and takes his pleasure with the girls here, like any honest gentleman." Just as she finished the last sentence, her eyes dropped to her tea. She lifted the cup and took a studious sip.

The air sharpened in Somerton's ears. He had interrogated hundreds of people—usually in far less amicable circumstances than this—and he knew when his opposite number was hiding an important fact.

Or rather, *attempting* to hide. Because Somerton always ferreted out the truth.

One way or another.

He stretched out one long leg and adjusted the razor crease

of his trousers until it peaked precisely in the center of his knee. Every sense was alert; every muscle relaxed with latent power, ready for use. "Brings his friends, does he? Takes his pleasure with the girls here?"

"Yes, sir."

"Every night."

"Not every night," she said hastily. "P'rhaps three or four in the week."

"Regularly, then. Regularly enough that he's a good customer, isn't he? A customer you wouldn't want to lose."

Hannah shrugged. "I has enough customers."

Somerton's brain fastened for an instant on that telling grammatical slip. "But I suspect a generous youth such as Lord Roland Penhallow pays better than most, doesn't he?"

"He pays well enough." Hannah's mouth formed a tight line, as if straining to contain something inside. She grasped the teapot and tilted it over her cup.

A half second before the liquid appeared from the spout, Somerton reached across the low table and plucked the delicate porcelain from its saucer. He held it up to the gaslight.

"A very fine cup," he said. "Very fine indeed. Your business is doing well, isn't it, my dear Hannah?"

"Tolerably well, thank you."

He replaced the cup beneath the shaking teapot. "Excellent. I'm glad to hear it. I presume my little contributions have added in some small way to your store of treasure."

"Why, sir." Bravely. "I hope I've given you full value for your money."

"Full value, my dear Hannah?" He laughed, the sort of laugh that had once made the man sitting across the interrogation table—a fit, hale, hearty, bloodthirsty fellow—roll his eyes back and slither down the wooden seat to the floor below with a resounding thump.

For an instant, Hannah looked in danger of doing just that. She recovered herself just enough to squeak, "Yes, sir. I've told you all I know."

"Have you, Hannah?" Somerton picked up the teapot, removed the lid, and peered inside. "But that's not what I asked for, is it? I asked for evidence—solid evidence, of the sort allowable in a court of law, should the need arise—of my wife's repeated acts of criminal conversation with her lover, Lord Roland Penhallow, brother to the Duke of Wallingford." The very words tasted bitter on his tongue. An image arose in his head: Lord Roland and Elizabeth swirling about a London ballroom over six years ago. The look of adoration on her beautiful face as she gazed upward to her Adonis; the smug look of satisfaction Penhallow returned to her. Elizabeth had worn pink. He remembered that, because of the rosy way it had shimmered in the light of the Duke of Wallingford's ballroom chandeliers as Penhallow swirled her through the open French doors and into the intimate seclusion of the veranda outside.

Hannah said, "But no such evidence exists, sir. I've made my own inquiries. They've not seen each other, not once. His lordship . . ."

Somerton shot to his feet, sending the chair tumbling down behind him.

". . . his lordship has his own friends, sir. I've watched him closely, these past weeks." Hannah glanced down at the fallen chair and back to Somerton's face. Her voice had steadied, her back had straightened.

The subtle exchange of power made his throat throb. "You're in his pocket, aren't you?"

"He pays me for his time, like any honest gentleman."

"You're hiding something for him."

A flush appeared on her cheekbones. "I keeps his secrets, like any customer. Those that hain't got to do with you."

"You admit it!"

She rose, in that awkward straight-backed way of a woman wearing a corset laced too tight. "Lord Roland Penhallow is not meeting your wife, your lordship, not here nor at any other house. That's fact."

He wanted to hit her. His fist clenched at his side, with enough force to crack a walnut. In his mind, he saw a hand swinging and swinging, pounding and pounding, and he heard his mother crying, *Stop, Philip, stop*, and his father saying, *You're a whore, a whore, fucking him in your own bedroom, you whore, you whore*, and he was paralyzed, the slim boy in the corner whom nobody noticed, watching and hurting and powerless, feeling his father's blows on his own body, feeling his mother's sobs in his own chest.

Hannah watched the progress of his rage. No doubt she was used to that, dealing with men in a passion. "There, now," she said. "It's good news, isn't it? Whether you believe it or not."

"You're a fool," he said. The swell of rage subsided. He opened his fist and stretched out his fingers, one by one.

She shrugged. "One of us is a fool, at any rate."

Somerton sucked in his breath. Above his head, the floorboards groaned, over and over, and a man's voice called out in time with the wooden rhythm, repeating a word Somerton couldn't quite make out. Hannah's confident face blurred before him.

"There, now," she said again. She walked around the tea table and picked up the chair behind him. "Go on back to your lovely old house, sir, and talk to her. By all accounts she's a dear lady, and true. She'll love you again, if you let her."

Somerton walked to the door and opened it. "She never loved me," he said, and he strode out into Hannah's crimson hallway and the dank London November beyond.

The painful electric lights of the Aerated Bread Company tea shop forced Luisa to pause and blink as she stepped through the doorway, earning her a hard shove to the backside.

"Oy, move along, ye bleedin' half-wit!" someone snarled in her ear.

She stumbled aside. Her nerves were already jangling from the cramped Tube ride, from the unwholesome, greasy air of the Mansion House station, from the pushes and shoves of her fellow cheap-suited humanity. A man rushed past her, the *Daily Telegraph* fluttering impatiently beneath his elbow, to join the queue at the counter. Luisa wrinkled her nose at the inescapable steam-thickened scent of warm bread and cheap tea; it enveloped her like a hood.

A chair scraped loudly against the tiled floor. "My dear Mr. Markham. Come, have some tea. You look shattered."

Luisa swiveled her head in the direction of the voice. A slight-boned man stood expectantly at a nearby table; to his right sat a large-boned dowager under an extraordinary hat, bearing at least three different types of papier-mâché fruit. The man wore a large smile. The woman appeared disgruntled.

Luisa drew in a deep sigh, clutched her umbrella to her side, and approached the table. "Mr. Dingleby," she said, removing her hat and placing it upon the table. "And Mrs. . . . Mrs. . . ." She coughed. "I beg your pardon, ma'am."

"Mrs. Duke," the woman announced, in a high-pitched strangle of a voice. Her lips were painted a startling shade of mulberry red.

"Mrs. Duke. Of course." Luisa made a little bow to disguise the smile that would insist on curling its way to the corner of her mouth, despite her dark mood.

She'd been against this plan from the start. She simply couldn't imagine her uncle could pull it off. She hadn't quite believed it could be done, that the august Duke of Olympia, that grand puppeteer of human affairs, that towering figure with his glowering ducal face, had actually transformed himself into a woman. A large-hatted, large-figured, large-featured woman who'd layered her face in enough paint to supply a Gilbert and Sullivan troupe for an entire summer's tour, and embalmed her hair in enough red dye to color a warehouse full of Christmas mittens.

The effect *was* rather amusing, she had to admit.

"I see we are not above attracting attention to ourselves," Luisa observed, as she took her seat next to the Duke of Olympia, and immediately found herself asphyxiated by a mouthful of immense purple-feathered boa.

"Hide in plain sight, that's what I've always said." Mrs. Duke settled her boa and lifted her teacup with one gloved pinkie delicately outstretched.

"The tea looks marvelous," Luisa said placidly.

Mr. Dingleby delivered a firm elbow to Mrs. Duke's corseted middle. "Madam?"

"Oh!" Mrs. Duke set down her cup and reached for the pot. "Dear me. Where are my manners? Cream or sugar, Mr. Markham?"

"Both, if you please."

Where on earth had Olympia found a pair of ladies' gloves to fit those enormous hands? Luisa watched in fascination as the tea fell into the cup, as the splash of cream and the dash of sugar bravely followed.

Mr. Dingleby coughed. "So, my dear fellow. I am given to

understand that your recent interview was successful, and you will shortly begin service in a certain Belgravia household?"

"Yes, indeed." Luisa accepted the cup from Mrs. Duke's thick gloved fingers and stirred briskly. "So good of you to refer me to such a friendly and kind-hearted employer. I'm in your debt."

"Now, Mr. Markham," said Mrs. Duke, in a splendid hushed falsetto, tinged with East End. "Remember a powerful employer is always the best employer. You're certain to get ahead with his lordship."

"*Get ahead?*" Luisa pursed her lips. "I beg your pardon. *Get ahead?* What sort of phrase is that? American?" She suppressed a shudder.

"It's a business term," said Mr. Dingleby. "The sort of phrase that an ambitious young man—a man like yourself, for example—might take to heart."

"I see." Luisa cast a deadly gaze at her former governess, whose neat black suit and thin shoulders contrasted with Mrs. Duke's extravagance like a sheet of newspaper next to one of those impossible new French paintings. "Speaking of which, have you had any news of my brothers? Are they getting on well? *Getting ahead*—am I using the phrase correctly, Mr. Dingleby?"

"Oh, quite." Mr. Dingleby picked up his bread and buttered it thoroughly. "Our studious Tobias has taken to tutoring his spoiled young charge with aplomb, and our sprightly young Stephen, if you can possibly believe, has settled down to the gray old practice of British law like a prodigy. I couldn't be more pleased."

"And their employers? What sort of men are they?" The words slid out a little more sharply than Luisa had intended.

Mr. Dingleby smiled a secret smile, a cat's smile. "Oh, I daresay your brothers are well looked after. Well indeed. You needn't worry yourself a bit."

"Mr. Dingleby. I'm the eldest, the . . . the head of the household. Of course I worry. I've always worried. I can hardly stop now, can I?" Luisa stared at her shirt cuffs, white and starched, studded by unremarkable pewter cuff links that absorbed rather than reflected the light from the multitude of gas lamps along the walls. The old weight sank down about her shoulders again: the responsibility for her sisters, the responsibility for her people. And she was powerless now. Powerless to help them, powerless to do anything except grieve. Grieve, and bide her time, while the duke of Olympia and Miss Dingleby—her onetime governess, now a trained agent under her uncle's command—tracked down her father's murderers. Her husband's murderers.

She swallowed her tea and ground the cup back into its saucer.

It was intolerable. The entire situation, intolerable. She, Princess Luisa, biding her time as a common clerk. Paddling about aimlessly in her makeshift life belt, while Olympia and Dingleby manned the helm and righted the ship.

"You are too valuable," said Mr. Dingleby, very low.

Luisa looked up. "What's that?"

"The three of you, but *you* especially, my dear Mr. Markham. It's why we've hidden you like this, as young men, where no one would think to look for you." Dingleby's eyes were soft with compassion. Luisa shifted her gaze to the tranquility of tea before her.

"We are trained professionals, my dear boy," said Mrs. Duke, in a comforting falsetto undertone. "Trained professionals. You must trust us."

"Trained professionals?" Luisa allowed her gaze to travel over the papier-mâché fruit, the abundance of mulberry lip rouge. "Trust you?"

Mrs. Duke's voice shifted a fraction lower. "Since before you were born, my dear. I do know my hacks from my handsaws."

"When the wind is north by northeast," added Mr. Dingleby, with a cryptic pop of buttered bread into rosy mouth.

Luisa shook her head, drained her tea, and stood. "I don't know what the devil"—how surprisingly liberating it was, to use such words!—"what the devil you're talking about, but I do know this: I shan't be able to endure his lordship's company for longer than a month. One of us is certain to murder the other by Christmas, so whatever it is you do, the two of you . . ."

Mr. Dingleby shot to his feet. "Excellent, excellent! I see we are all quite in accord, Mr. Markham. Glad to hear your prospects are looking up at last." He popped a brown felt bowler hat upon his head. "And now, if you'll be so good as to escort your dear old aunt . . ."

"Old?" screeched Mrs. Duke. She patted the stray red curls at the nape of her neck. "Old? Not a day over forty, you insolent wretch."

"Aunt?" said Luisa, rather faintly.

". . . Your charming aunt back to her lodgings," went on Mr. Dingleby, quite placidly, patting his pockets, "I should be very much obliged. Various business appointments. Must be off."

Luisa looked at Mrs. Duke in some alarm. "Your lodgings, ma'am?"

"Battersea, my dear boy. That nice, snug little house I bought with your dear uncle's insurance, God rest him." Mrs. Duke hoisted her magnificent frame from the chair and held out her boa-constricted arm to Luisa. "The very latest in hygienic plumbing. An entire water closet, all to oneself, and a genuine porcelain Crapper for . . ."

"My dear Mrs. Duke." Mr. Dingleby snatched one large gloved paw and pumped it vigorously. "A pleasure to see you again, ma'am. Mr. Markham?" He turned to Luisa and repeated the *snatch, pump* with equal vigor. "Good day."

"Good day," Luisa began, but Mr. Dingleby was already bumping his way outward among the close-packed tables, black umbrella hooked over black forearm, setting teacups to rattle cheaply in their saucers.

Mrs. Duke looped her arm around Luisa's elbow. "Well, then, dear boy! Don't just stand there, catching flies. Find us a hackney. I've a few matters to discuss with you." She bent her fruit-bedecked head toward Luisa's ear. "In private."

Y ou want me to *spy* for you?"

Luisa spoke in a hushed voice, mindful of the hackney driver hovering above the roof, but with all the necessary intensity.

Mrs. Duke—the Duke of Olympia—reached underneath the brim of her hat and scratched vigorously. "Damned wigs. Itch like the devil. Impossible nuisance, but there it . . ."

"Uncle." They were flying down the Embankment in a hackney, dank November wind whistling across their ears, and Luisa was happy to let the disguise drop.

Olympia sighed heavily and replied in the same low tones. "*Spy* is such a common word, my dear. A word for vulgar minds and sensational newspapers. Altogether lacking in nuance. I say, I should sincerely appreciate a glass of brandy at the moment, wouldn't you?"

"Whatever you want to call it," said Luisa. "I can't possibly go searching through Somerton's papers in the dead of night, and peeping through the keyhole, and whatever it is. For one thing, I haven't the smallest amount of training in such matters . . ."

"All the better," said Olympia. "No one smokes out an amateur. It's the professionals who get kil . . . that is to say, caught."

". . . And for another thing, unless Somerton has something to do with the band of vile assassins who have taken over my country, I refuse to waste my time on your affairs. I want to find out who murdered Father and Peter, I want to deliver the most thunderous justice upon them, not to idle my days away in some Belgravia town house, sneaking about in search of . . . of whatever it is . . ." She slammed her fist into the hard leather seat between them.

"Such an outburst, my dear," said Olympia. "And so very much out of character for you."

She rubbed her aching knuckles. "I'm angry. I'm frustrated. You won't tell me a thing, and I *know* you know more about all this . . ."

"I know very little. When your mother died in childbed all those years ago, God rest her dear soul, I thought it best to send someone I trusted to watch over your interests. I sent Miss Dingleby—one of my best agents, mind you—to guide the three of you . . ."

"Yes, yes. You told me all this when we reached England."

"Indeed. And it was she who soon detected the presence of a group of anarchists, members of the Revolutionary Brigade of the Free Blood, a damned filthy pan-European organization, quite sophisticated in its structure and methods, and which as you know is responsible for countless attempts at coup and regicide, not to mention that dreadful ferry bombing in the North Sea last year, and . . ."

"And *I* say to you now, just as I said to you in your study when you first explained: If we know all this, why aren't we back in Holstein-Schweinwald-Huhnhof, bringing them to justice?" A sharp pain dug into her palms. Luisa looked down. The fingers were curled into angry black balls of leather.

Olympia spoke calmly. "Because you would be assassinated within the day. They have already set up a puppet government, for which Free Blood's members act as a secret police. They're led by a ruthless chap, a local Holstein chap with some sort of chip on his shoulder, probably slighted by your father at one time or another, and even Dingleby couldn't discover his identity. There are agents here in England, looking for you. It's quite impossible. No, you're much better off here. Somerton has his faults, the old devil, but he looks after his own. Dingleby and I have a plan, never fear. When the time comes, we'll bring you in. But not before, my dear. You are the prize queen in this most valuable game, and we can't risk you." His breath struck out in a large cloud of white. "Yet."

"Oh, indeed. I'll be much safer as I poke about the Earl of Somerton's private affairs." The hackney lurched around the corner of Westminster Bridge, and Luisa grabbed for the leather strap an instant too late. She crashed into Mrs. Duke's immense false bosom, cushioned in purple feathers, and imagined Somerton's hard black gaze penetrating her skull, to seek out the guilty thoughts within.

"Mind yourself." Olympia plucked her free with an affectionate pat. His silk-skirted bulk had hardly shifted an inch; he was like the Dover cliffs, impervious to time and tide and lurching hackneys. "In any case, you won't be poking. Nothing of the kind. Simply keep your ears open and your wits about you, as you go about your . . . er . . . secretarial duties. Report anything of particular interest to me."

"Report to you? When? How?"

The hackney crested the gentle rise of Westminster Bridge, and for an instant all London spread out around them, coated in gray: the winding rows of houses, the steeples thrusting heavenward, the milky Thames below, speckled with shipping. The bright-colored air of a German October seemed like another world. Another life.

And it was only a month ago.

"My dear boy." Olympia adjusted his gloves with a frightful wiggle of thick fingers. "You're in London now. A member of the professional classes, an ambitious and upstanding young chap. And every dutiful nephew goes to visit his dear auntie in Battersea on his weekly half day, doesn't he?"

THREE

The Earl of Somerton's butler was aghast.

"A dog, sir?" he gasped, eyebrows straining toward the ceiling. An ambitious goal, for the entrance hall of Somerton House soared upward some twenty feet to meet a trompe l'oeil sky trimmed in intricate creamy plasterwork.

Quincy wiggled himself more deeply into the crook of Luisa's elbow and voiced a single disapproving bark. "A corgi," Luisa said. "His name is Quincy. I shall care for him myself, of course, but I will require the assistance of the kitchen for his meals. He's rather particular."

"The kitchen!" sputtered the butler.

"Yes. The staff at the Holstein-Schweinwald-Huhnhof consulate were quite up to the challenge. I hope your establishment is equally efficient?" She raised her voice doubtfully on the last syllable.

"I assure you, my staff are more than capable of . . ."

"Good, then. I believe my portmanteau and my books were delivered this morning, according to his lordship's instruction. You may show me to my room, which I believe is directly adjacent to that of his lordship. We will be in close fellowship, you understand." She swept toward the stairs, leaving her valise behind her on the gleaming marble floor.

Confidence. From her earliest days, she could remember her father reminding her of its importance. *Whatever your chosen action, act with decision,* Prince Rudolf would tell her. *People follow the confident. Doubt is the arsenic of leadership.*

Well, she wasn't leading anything now, except perhaps Quincy. But the principle applied to theater as well, and she was acting the part of her life.

The butler hastened past to lead her up the stairs. She lifted her finger and stroked the silken crown of Quincy's head as they climbed upward, past the first-floor landing and the fleeting glimpse of silk-papered drawing room and book-lined library, and on to the second floor where the principal bedrooms would be found.

Luisa had understood English married couples to subscribe to the quaint custom of interconnecting rooms, so she was mildly surprised to find that the Earl of Somerton, when he had pronounced *the suite next to mine*, had really meant it. Surely this was intended as the countess's room, grandly proportioned, sumptuously upholstered in blues and cheerful yellows, overlooking the back garden, fitted with a dressing room and its own modern bathroom en suite, to say nothing of a pair of paneled doors leading suggestively to the other bedchamber. But her portmanteau and her trunk of books sat unmistakably in the center of the rug near the fire. The butler made way and watched her as she prowled about, inspecting the weave of the silken bed hangings and the polish of the Chippendale highboy, and didn't say a word.

"It will do," she pronounced. "Though the colors are not so much to my taste as those in my chamber at the embassy. Have you hot water taps?" She nodded to the bathroom door.

"Of course," said the butler indignantly. What was his name? She used to be good at remembering servants' names, but now she couldn't find the word. Round syllables. Something solid and commonplace. Roberts?

A footman strode through the door, bearing her valise. She smiled at him, and then at the butler.

Johnson. That was it.

"Excellent. Thank you, Mr. Johnson. No, no, my good man." She waved the footman away. "I'll unpack myself. I have some particularly delicate objects I should not wish to hazard."

"Very good, Mr. Markham." The footman straightened and backed away.

Mr. Johnson was still glowering near the door. "Will that be all, sir?"

"Quite. Thank you terribly."

He bowed, as stiffly and slightly as possible, and turned to pass through the doorway. "Your ladyship!" he said, from the hall.

A woman's quiet voice answered him. Luisa strained her ears, but she couldn't make out the words. She crossed the room and glanced through the doorway, just before Johnson closed it, and in that quarter of an instant an image flashed before Luisa of perhaps the most beautiful woman she'd ever seen, including her second and final stepmother, God rest her soul. Her hair was dark and her eyes were . . . well, Luisa couldn't see the color, but they were large and appealing, and her lips a perfect rosy bow, and her figure . . .

Luisa found herself staring at the closed door. Quincy jumped from her elbow and scurried to the crack of daylight beneath it, whining and scrabbling at the dark floorboards.

"Men," Luisa muttered.

When Luisa crossed the doorway of the Earl of Somerton's private study at ten minutes to six that evening, she was surprised to see its owner already seated behind his desk, scribbling furiously. He looked up at her entrance, and the scowl on his magnificent bleak face made her breath clog in her throat.

"Sit down." He indicated the small desk near his own and returned to his work.

Luisa stalked to her station and dropped into the cane-backed chair. A small envelope lay before her, on which the word *Markham* was written in plain italic letters. She drew a wicked silver letter opener from the implements laid out neatly to the right of the leather blotter and sliced across the envelope's top.

A single ten-pound note lay inside.

"Your weekly salary, paid in advance," said Lord Somerton, without looking up, "with an additional allowance for ordinary expenses. Cab fare and the like. My business will require it from time to time."

"Very good, sir." Luisa placed the note beneath the blotter

and dropped the envelope into the wastebin at the side of the desk. "Shall we begin?"

There was no answer. Somerton finished his writing with a distinct absence of flourish, folded the paper in two, slid it inside a waiting envelope, and set it aside.

"Close the door, if you will, Mr. Markham," he said.

Luisa rose and went to the door, which was open the merest half inch of a crack. She pushed until the latch clicked softly shut.

"Lock it," said Somerton.

She turned the lock.

"You will find, Mr. Markham, that I will require you to close and lock the study door at the beginning of every session. You'll save yourself considerable effort if you remember to perform these tasks upon your entrance."

"Yes, sir." Luisa returned to her seat.

"Now then, Mr. Markham. We will begin with a tedium of ordinary correspondence, I'm afraid, but that is the human lot." He spoke crisply, without dropping a single syllable, sending the final *t* in *lot* pinging about the room. "The first letter goes to my solicitor, in reply to an inquiry of the ninth instant, which you will find at the top of the stack before you. Date, the twelfth of November, eighteen hundred and eighty-nine . . ."

"Sir, today is the fourteenth of November."

"So it is. We shall, however, date it the twelfth. *Dear Mr. Townes. My most fervent apology for the delay in replying to your letter of three days ago. I am sorry to say that I know nothing of the matter you had the goodness to communicate to me, and furthermore I suspect that your complainant may harbor motives which do her little credit. I therefore instruct you to dismiss her complaint in the strongest possible terms, and if this letter should reach you too late to prevent this unfortunate crisis to which she alludes, you may represent our doubts to her nearest living relatives. I remain, etc., Somerton.* Have you any comment, Mr. Markham?"

Luisa laid down her pen and stared at the plain black words before her. "None, sir, except that it is very brief."

"I have little time to waste, Mr. Markham. You may pass the letter to me for signature. The next several items on your desk—invitations to this or that—you may answer in form with regrets. That done, you will proceed to the Foreign Office and obtain a list of all steamships entering this country from the Baltic states during the past year, and . . ."

"I beg your pardon?"

Somerton looked up. "A list of all steamships entering this country from the Baltic states. We will say, from January the first onward. A straightforward instruction; surely there can be no confusion?"

"I only wish to know why . . ."

He lifted his right index finger. "Yours not to question why, Mr. Markham. Yours but to do or die."

The earl's face was a perfect mask, betraying nothing, except perhaps a trace of acerbic surprise in the raised eyebrows. Surprise, no doubt, that Luisa should be so bold as to question him in the first place: an expression with which she was quite familiar. Her own father had worn it on a number of occasions, facing down councilors, secretaries, heads of state, wives, and wayward daughters.

An expression that assumed total control over the person to which it was directed.

For an instant, a tiny streak of imperiousness raced across Luisa's chest. For an instant, she imagined ripping off her necktie and her starched white collar, and telling this upstart earl, this cliff-faced tyrant with his condescending eyebrows, that she had once commanded an army. (A small one, to be sure, but certainly enough to storm a single London town house and vanquish its arrogant owner.) She glanced down at her right hand, which was wrapped about her pen as if to squeeze the ink from beneath its enamel shell.

The instant passed, and the imperious streak dissolved.

"Of course, sir. Your motives are your own business. I shall, however, reserve the right to refuse any request I suspect to be immoral or illegal."

"There is nothing illegal about a perfectly legitimate request to a perfectly legitimate agency of a democratically elected government." His voice held a certain ring that might have been amusement or annoyance.

She looked back up at him. "Of course not. You are a peer of the realm, Lord Somerton, not a criminal. I daresay you've never harbored a wicked thought in your life."

"And *I* daresay, Mr. Markham, you should see about those invitations," snapped the earl, and he returned to his work.

The Foreign Office was, of course, closed.

This was something she ought to have known. The ordinary man knew as he knew the shape of his own chin that you could not simply saunter up to the door of a government office at half past seven o'clock on a November evening, let fall the knocker, state your name and your business, and be ushered inside. Luisa stared up at the acres of magisterial white facade, the rows of stern sash windows, and felt as if she'd been cheated somehow of this common knowledge. To the vast mass of humanity, government was not a thing that could be summoned to your room at any hour of the day and told to account for itself.

"Can I help you, sir?" said a voice at her elbow.

Luisa spun so quickly, she nearly tumbled down the steps.

A small man stood on the stair just below, bundled in dark wool against the chill. A faint tendril of London fog curled around his hat, which was pulled so low upon his forehead, she could scarcely see his eyes.

He put out a hand, not quite touching her arm. "Steady on. Didn't mean to surprise you, sir."

"Not at all." She felt rather foolish—foolish, the Princess of Holstein-Schweinwald-Huhnhof, before this small and nondescript fellow!—and straightened herself. "Can you tell me when the office opens again in the morning?"

"Opens in the morning, sir?" He opened his mouth and breathed out a misty chuckle. "Are you coming from Lord Somerton, sir?"

She hesitated. "How do you know that name?"

The man reached into his pocket and pulled out a small square of paper. "This is for you."

"But I . . ." She looked down at her right hand, into which the man was pressing the note. "But how did you . . ."

He was already turning, tipping his hat, walking swiftly down the pavement to dissolve like a shadow into the shroud of yellow fog. Luisa forced her stunned limbs into movement. She made a step or two to follow him, but he was already gone.

She lifted the hand that held the paper and pried apart the edges with her thick leather-gloved fingers. The sulfurous glow of the gas lamp illuminated a black scratch of handwriting:

11 Ponsonby Place
Cab at the corner of Horse Guards Road

She held the paper closer, sniffed it, examined again the shape of the letters. Somerton's handwriting? Possibly. She couldn't tell for certain.

Horse Guards Road. She peered down the pavement, clogged with fog, where Horse Guards Road should be. She looked down again at the note. What on earth did this mean? Some sort of spy work? Hardly suitable for a princess. Hardly suitable to a private secretary, for that matter. She ought to strike straight off back to her well-appointed room in Chester Square, cuddle Quincy close to the aching hole in her chest, and go to sleep.

On the other hand. She couldn't help but feel a certain sense of . . . what was it? . . . something to do with cats.

Curiosity. That was it.

What awaited her at 11 Ponsonby Place? And, more importantly, why would the Earl of Somerton involve her in it?

Yours not to question why.

Luisa folded the note back into its original square, slipped it into the pocket of her overcoat, and walked off briskly down the street, where the unmistakable outline of a hansom cab soon materialized through the darkness. Her heart struck with a pleasurable quick beat against her ribs.

Yours but to do or die.

FOUR

At first, Luisa thought there must have been some mistake. Nothing about number 11 Ponsonby Place distinguished the house from its row of narrow brothers: All were dressed in the same tired stucco, chipped here and there to reveal the underlying brick; all were fronted by the same modest portico and the same dull black door, flanked by a single sash window.

The street was quiet, thick with acid fog that burned her lungs. She turned to tell the cabman to wait while she rapped the knocker, but the hansom's wheels were already clattering against the pavement, as he hurried off down the road in search of a busier district.

Luisa stared with open mouth at the departing flash of wheel against cobble. The adventurous rhythm of her heartbeat turned a trifle hollow.

She had been rash, hadn't she?

How had that happened? She was Luisa. She was the measured one, the regal one, the responsible one. She had never committed a rash act in her life.

She glanced down at her black masculine clothes. Well, up until a few weeks ago, at any rate. Until she'd been kidnapped in her own state carriage, until she'd only just managed to flee by coshing her guard over the head with her state scepter. Until she'd raced back to the palace to concoct a plan with Miss Dingleby, and stolen across Europe with her sisters, and agreed to her uncle Olympia's mad scheme for disguise.

What had happened to her life? Her royal routine, her road map of duty, stretching out with perfect regularity unto eternity?

Luisa filled her lungs with foggy air and strode up the steps to the door of number 11. She let fall the knocker with a decisive clang that echoed down the entire length of Ponsonby Place.

There was no answer.

She knocked again.

Her foot tapped against the stone step. She craned her neck to the window to peer at the crack in the curtains.

For an instant, she pictured herself returning to Chester Square, standing before the huge square shoulders of the Earl of Somerton, and informing him that no one had been home, and her errand was still unperformed. That this test of her mettle—of course it was a test—she had utterly failed.

She reached for the knob.

To her surprise, it turned without a whisper.

No. Surely she wouldn't actually walk through that door like a common housebreaker, like a burglar in the night. Surely she hadn't forgotten herself that far.

Luisa pushed the door open and stepped into the dark hallway.

From his point of vantage in the dining room, within the shadow of the half-open pocket door, the Earl of Somerton watched the slim black-clad figure ease into the hallway and crane his head, first rightward and then leftward.

The sharp uptick of his pulse surprised him. Something stuck in the back of his throat, a slight paralysis. Perhaps it was the innocence of the young man, his sinuous and wary grace as he stood there, backlit by a distant streetlamp, foolishly brave. Not even knowing what he didn't know. When was the last time Somerton had beheld something so guiltless? A deer, perhaps. A wild animal, caught unaware of human observation.

His wife, the first time he'd seen her. Or so he'd thought at the time.

He made a signal with one hand.

Erasmus Norton stepped forward from the doorjamb and wrapped his left arm around Mr. Markham's slender neck.

To his credit, the young fellow didn't scream. His body stiffened, his hand grabbed for Norton's thick arm, and then he let out a long and silent breath and relaxed. As if he'd been expecting this.

"Who are you?" he demanded.

"Well, now," said Norton. "Seeing as your pretty little neck is about to be snapped by my good left arm, I think I might be so bold as to turn that question around, lad. Who the bloody hell are you?"

"My name is Markham."

"State your business, Markham." He shriveled his voice menacingly on the *Markham*.

An instant's pause. "I'm looking for a shipping list."

"A what, lad?"

"A list of shipping entering British ports from the Baltic states during the past year." Markham's voice rang out with confidence, despite the lethal forearm pressed against his neck.

Norton tightened his arm and gave Markham a jiggle. "Are you having a go at me, you bloody squeaker? Shipping?"

"I am not. I was at the Foreign Office to inquire after my list and received a message to come here instead, on behalf of my employer."

"Who's your employer?"

"That's none of your business."

Somerton was trained in the art of holding himself precisely still, of keeping each flicker of muscle under exact control. Yet the shock of those clear and unexpectedly loyal words hit him like a blow. He flinched, a tiny tension of his shoulders. Norton caught the movement and glanced into the darkness of the living room, to the half-open pocket door beyond.

But he didn't hesitate. He lifted his right hand. "This knife"—the tip caught the feeble light in a silver gleam—"says it's my business."

"And I say it isn't," said Markham. "So if you haven't got

this list, we have nothing further to say to each other. Release me at once."

"I'll release you when I feel like it, lad." Norton hauled him up close. "Is it Somerton who sent you?"

"Release me at once."

"No need to struggle, Markham. You'll only hurt yourself, and wouldn't that be a pity."

"You can't hurt me. My employer will kill you if you do."

"So it *is* Somerton, isn't it?"

"I have nothing to say to you." Markham dug his fingers into Norton's arm and twisted his body.

"Stop yer wriggling, for God's sake. We don't want any accidents, does we?"

"Let go!"

"Now, now. You listen to me a bit, nice and steady. I know you come from Somerton, right enough. Whatever he's paying you, I'll double it. Just stop by for a pleasant little visit, every so often, right here at this house. Let me know what he's up to. Bring me copies of his letters, the names of the coves he sees."

Markham's body stiffened.

A strange weight pressed against Somerton's chest, as if a small but deadly mortar had been accidentally dropped on his ribs. He stood without moving, counting the solid knocks of his heart.

Waiting for Markham's answer.

Damn the lad. Why the devil should Somerton care if he were loyal or not? Another secretary would be found, and another. They lay thick about the London streets, these eager young clerks, desperate for a position with a powerful patron.

But this one. His cheek so smooth in the dimness, his constricted breath rough in the cold hallway. His eyes so warm and brown in Somerton's study. His brave young frame now swallowed by Norton's aggression.

Somerton closed his eyes.

A laugh broke out from Markham's throat, short and incredulous. "Go to the devil."

"Triple, then."

"Not tenfold. Not for any amount. What do you take me for, you stupid ox? Release me this instant, or you'll rue the day, by God."

"Rue the . . . *ugh!*" Norton's last words were swallowed in a grunt. Somerton's eyes flew open. A blur of movement, of Markham's twisting body. The knife flashed in Norton's hand.

No. In Markham's hand.

An almighty thump rattled the bones of the house, as Britain's most notorious assassin dropped to the wooden floor.

"Bloody hell," he whispered.

Markham leaned down and pressed the tip of his knife against the middle of Norton's throat, against the round lump of his Adam's apple. "Just a little something I learned from my father."

"Me balls," Norton groaned.

"They'll be quite all right, I assure you, though I suggest you apply a cold compress when you return home."

Somerton opened up his gloved fist and laid it flat against his thigh. The heat of his own body surprised him. He'd felt so cold, frozen solid against the frail wood of the pocket door, watching the scene unfold.

"Which I suggest you do immediately, sir. Return home, I mean. Unless you happen to have a list of Baltic shipping upon your person, in which case I beg leave to lighten you of the burden." Markham spoke with quiet assurance, perfectly calm. As if the Almighty himself stood behind his shoulder, nodding in approval.

In the first few seconds of the struggle, Somerton's every instinct had pitched him forward to Markham's aid. Only the strictest self-control had held him in place, the confident logic that Markham was right: Norton didn't dare harm the lad.

Because Somerton would kill him if he did.

And now? Somerton gazed at the dim-lit scene in quiet astonishment. Erasmus Norton felled like an oak by a lowly secretary.

By God, the pluck of him. The damned clean-scrubbed ferocity of him. The avenging angel, fighting the good fight.

"That I haven't," hissed Norton, "or I'd wipe your scrawny arse with it."

"How fortunate for me," said Markham. "In any case, I'm off. And I'll be taking this"—he twirled the knife in his hand—"along with me."

He tucked the knife inside his jacket, stepped elegantly over Norton's prostrate body, and walked out the door.

The hearty slam of wood and brass echoed about the walls.

Somerton detached himself from the shadows and stepped along the direct line through the front room. Norton lay in the passage, his torso in the room and his legs sticking out into the hallway. Somerton stared down. "Dear me. Are you quite all right, my good fellow?"

Norton lay stiff. "Going to be sick."

"You should have been more careful. The young ones are agile."

"What sort of gentleman sticks another man in the marbles, I ask you? It ain't on the level. There's a code, sir." He turned on his side and vomited onto the worn wooden floor.

Somerton removed a handkerchief from his pocket—plain white linen, no identifying marks—and dropped it on Norton's chest. He lifted his chin and gazed thoughtfully at the door. "What gentleman, indeed?"

"It ain't right." Norton lay on his side, doubled over. "He might have ruined me forever."

"Oh, buck up." Somerton stepped around the body and reached for the doorknob. "You're a hired assassin, not a curate. It's no more than you deserve, after all."

Before Norton could reply, he opened the door and strode down the steps, just in time to see a black shape emerge from behind an area gate at the end of the street and lunge silently upon the departing figure of Mr. Markham.

Luisa couldn't precisely say when she detected the presence of the Earl of Somerton in the Stygian depths of the Ponsonby Place front room. No particular movement, no particular sound caught her attention. It was the sense of him, breathing quietly in the shadows. His heavy gaze observing her.

Observing her, and also guarding her. She knew, in that instant, she'd nothing to fear from the thick-armed ox holding her throat. Somerton could call him off with a flick of his fingers.

She'd had only to play her part.

As she strode down the pavement, overcoat swinging, fog stinging her face, she smiled at the recollection of her attacker's surprise. His heavy grunt at her unexpected maneuver, his body crashing to the floor. For an instant, she'd turned the tables. She'd taken control again, she'd gained the upper hand.

The exhilaration still surged in her veins, making the smoke-scented gloom around her a bit less grim. A bit less threatening. A bit . . .

Her ears registered the sound of footfalls an instant too late.

She whirled about, arms raised. A pair of dark shoulders flashed before her, a menacing face, bared teeth, and her body flew backward to slam against the iron posts of an area fence.

Another test, she thought frantically, but the rush of panic in her veins told her this was real. No hired thug, no careful control.

Breath panted across her face, hot and foul. Something hard and cold laid itself against the tender skin of her neck.

"Empty yer pockets, lad," growled a voice near her ear, and she realized she'd squeezed her eyes shut.

"I haven't got any money!"

"Empty yer pockets, afore I does it for ye!"

Luisa forced her arms to move. She shoved her hands into her coat pockets and drew out the empty lining. "You see? Nothing."

It was true. She wasn't carrying any money. It hadn't even occurred to her. A few shillings and sixpence sat on her drawer chest, back in Chester Square, along with the Earl of Somerton's crisp ten-pound note. But the practice of holding and spending money was still too new, too foreign to have become habit.

Stupid, of course. How had she expected to get herself home, without any coin? Every ordinary man, woman, and child knew that.

"Take off your coat!"

"I'll do no such . . ."

A sharp pain pierced her neck.

Luisa fumbled with her buttons.

"Faster!"

The coat was off. The man's hands yanked at her jacket; she heard the rip of thread and lost her balance. She crashed to the pavement, hitting her head a glancing blow on one of the iron fence posts. Dimly she felt the man's weight fall upon her, his legs straddle her, his fingers scrabbling at her clothes.

"And what has we here, ye fine cove? A gold watch!"

"It's not . . ."

But he was already pulling at the chain. Luisa's head swam. The man's face blurred above her, pinched and hungry, a ghastly yellow gray in the feeble, faraway gaslight. She tried to haul herself upward, but the man's hands pushed her back. He was fumbling roughly in her waistcoat pockets now. Oh, God! He was going to find . . .

"Blimey!" he breathed.

"Give that back!"

"You wee little liar. Going to keep this hidden away from old Ned, was ye?"

Luisa gathered her breath. "Help! Somebody help! Thie . . ."

"Quiet!"

"Thief!"

The knife pushed at her throat again. She flailed for his arm, and watched in horror as his other arm lifted, the hand drawn into a large, meaty fist, elbow poised near his ear.

She threw her body against the prison of his weight. "No!"

The fist descended.

She shut her eyes and turned her head, and for a brief flash her father's face appeared in her head, looking at her with sad and disappointed eyes, his salty beard clipped into a sharp point at the end, as it had been when she was little.

An instant later—it seemed like a minute, the whole world seemed to have slipped into a sluggish old gear—the weight lifted away from her hips like a sack of grain.

A dog howled, a piercing and miserable howl cut short by a series of deep thuds.

Luisa opened her eyes and struggled upward.

No. Not a dog. A man, the thief, who dangled from one of the Earl of Somerton's large hands while the other fist beat a tattoo into his jaw and ribs.

"Good God," she whispered. Her collar was wet against the night air. She looked down and saw a neat red half circle staining the linen.

The thudding stopped. Somerton let the man drop to the

pavement, as he might rid himself of a sack of ash, should an earl ever have had cause to do so himself.

A faint groan issued from the broken bundle of humanity at his feet.

Somerton straightened his cuffs. "Be grateful you're still alive."

"Good God," Luisa said again. She braced herself on a fence post and hauled her aching body upward.

Somerton turned to her. "What an unfortunate misadventure. Are you still whole?"

His voice was calm, almost icy. She couldn't see his face, couldn't see his expression. Couldn't tell if he were sympathetic or angry, or some mysterious emotion private to himself. His large black outline blocked out what little light shed upon the street: a shadow upon shadows. At his feet, the thief now seemed pitifully small.

"Still whole," she said. She put a hand to the back of her head, which was throbbing but dry of blood. A small mercy.

Somerton's face tilted downward. "Spoils of war," he said, and in a quick motion of his long arm, he scooped up the watch and the ring that the thief had plucked from her pockets. "By God, it looks as if you're not his first victim tonight. A damned fine ring. The watch is inferior, however. Is it yours?"

"Yes." She held out her hand.

"There you are. My hackney is around the corner. We shall be home in half an hour. The housekeeper will see to your injury; I daresay a mere bandage will do. It's stopped bleeding, at any rate." He unfastened the first two buttons of his overcoat and slipped the ring into some hidden pocket next to his body.

In the presence of his matter-of-fact words, Luisa's heart began to slow. She placed the watch and the broken chain into her waistcoat pocket and picked up her overcoat from the damp pavement. She willed her hands to stop shaking.

Somerton waited, without moving, as she buttoned her coat and settled her round bowler hat, now somewhat battered, back on her head. As if she'd simply stumbled and fallen while walking, instead of having nearly been murdered by a London street thief. As if this were all very ordinary.

For Somerton, it probably was.

"Can you walk?" he asked at last, when she was ready. He didn't spare so much as a glance for the thief, who still lay on the pavement, issuing groans from time to time. He didn't even wait for her reply; as soon as the question left his lips, he turned on his heel and began walking down the street, booted heels cracking smartly against the pavement, greatcoat swirling about his legs.

Luisa's cheeks flushed hot against the cold air. She forced her bruised limbs into a run to catch up. "If I *can* walk, it's no thanks to you!"

"I beg your pardon. I believe I just saved your life, young man."

"The least you could do, after you arranged this entire absurd drama tonight."

He turned the corner of Ponsonby Place onto Causton Street. Ahead, a hackney sat patiently by the curb. "I apologize for the austerity of the conveyance. A crested carriage is something of an inconvenience on such errands."

"Errands? This was an errand to you?"

"Tut-tut. All's well that ends well." He reached the hackney and rapped upon the side. The driver started, nearly losing his hat, and sprang open the doors. "After you," said Somerton, with an absence of flourish.

For an instant, Luisa considered delivering a parting shot and stalking off down the street.

"For God's sake, Markham. Don't be such a woman." Somerton pulled his gloves from the pocket of his overcoat— he had evidently removed them in the struggle—and tugged each one over his hands.

Luisa cast him her haughtiest glance and climbed into the hackney.

He swung in behind her at once, making the vehicle stagger under his weight. The doors clanged shut, the whip twitched briskly, the driver spoke. With a weary sigh, the horse leaned forward in his harness and started off from the curb.

"I see you're not going to apologize," said Luisa, after a moment's damp silence.

"Apologize?" The earl's voice was genuinely incredulous. "For what?"

"For nearly having me killed!"

"You were never in any danger."

"And yet there is a great deal of blood on my collar, my head hurts like the devil, and I daresay I shall carry a multitude of bruises well into next week."

"Trifles." He folded his arms against his massive chest.

"I suppose they're trifles to you. I suppose you do this sort of thing on a nightly basis, God knows why, but I refuse to submit to such barbarous treatment again."

A pause settled into the rhythmic motion of the hackney, the close intimacy of their two bodies held together beneath the iron doors. Luisa thought of her ring, tucked inside Somerton's waistcoat, and flexed her fingers.

How the devil was she going to get it back?

"In that case, I assure you, you will come to no further harm in my employ," Somerton said quietly.

"How on earth can you promise that?"

"I promise it."

She couldn't think of a reply to that solemn low voice, that intensity of conviction. His sleeve was next to hers; his enormous leg lay against her own, like the trunk of a hundred-year oak next to a seedling. He radiated heat, almost smothered her with his energy.

Her father's ring. The ring of state, the ring held by the Prince of Holstein-Schweinwald-Huhnhof, as a symbol of his marriage to his subjects. She'd kept it close to her body, as a talisman to keep her safe. What a fool she'd been. A sheltered little fool of a princess, who never thought to consider the common dangers of a London street at night.

Luisa turned her head to watch the sooty buildings slide by, darkest Pimlico giving way to Belgravia. In another few minutes, they would be back at the Earl of Somerton's town house, encased in safety and luxury. Another peculiarity of London, that wealth and squalor lay together as bedfellows. You were never far from one or the other.

She had to get the ring back, before Somerton examined it more carefully. Saw the Holstein crest engraved on the band, the unique arrangement of diamond, sapphire, and ruby.

She drew in a deep breath. Stay calm. Wait for opportunity. Emotion achieves nothing.

Victoria Station passed quietly by. The traffic was growing, hackneys and carriages, a single late omnibus, nearly empty.

The driver turned a corner, and suddenly all was stately and grand, lit by energetic gas lamps. The world she knew, through different eyes, in a different time.

"I suppose this means you intend to keep me on?" she said.

Somerton roused himself. "Keep you on? Yes, of course."

"But I didn't pass your test."

"I beg your pardon. I don't quite understand you."

"Your test. Your test of my abilities. The Baltic shipping list, which, as you see, I have failed to deliver."

Somerton rapped against the roof. The trapdoor slid open. "Pull over. We'll walk from here."

"Very good, sir."

The hackney swerved to the curb and came to a stop. Perhaps she could fall against him when she climbed out, and pluck the ring from his pocket in the resulting confusion.

But his overcoat remained buttoned, and the jacket beneath that. Besides, she was no trained pickpocket.

Somerton reached inside his coat for the fare. In a moment, they would be back on the pavement, back in the house. She might not see him again until the morning.

The cabbie took the fare. The doors fell open.

Luisa braced her hand on the side of the hackney. "Well, your lordship? Don't say you're willing to overlook my failure."

"My dear fellow. The Baltic shipping list is neither here nor there." He sprang to the pavement and turned to face her.

She rose to her feet and stumbled deliberately out of the cab, sticking one hand toward the parting of his coat as if to brace herself, but Somerton's long arms snatched and steadied her before her feet touched the ground. She looked up at his face, inches away. The lurid glare of the cab's single lamp made him look like an apparition.

"You have gained my trust, Mr. Markham," he said in a low voice, almost a snarl. "See that you don't squander it."

FIVE

Inside the Earl of Somerton's town house, the lights had all been turned down, though it was only half past nine o'clock. A blank-faced footman answered the door, dressed in an elegant gray livery; the butler appeared an instant later.

"Is her ladyship at home?" asked Somerton, perfectly neutral.

"She is upstairs in the nursery at present, sir. May I take your coat and hat?"

"No. Order the carriage at once. I am going out." Somerton made a gesture in Luisa's direction. "Have Mrs. Plum see to that scratch on Mr. Markham's neck directly."

The butler's gaze turned to Luisa for the first time and flicked downward to her collar. His eyes made the faintest movement, as if to widen. "Of course, sir."

Luisa squared her jaw. "That won't be necessary, Mr. Johnson. I am quite capable of attending myself. Has the garden door been bolted yet?"

"No, Mr. Markham."

"I shall need to see to Quincy's convenience at once. Please ensure that nobody bolts the door until we return."

Somerton turned to her. "Quincy? Who the devil is Quincy?"

"My dog, sir."

"Your *what?*"

"My dog. A corgi, well trained. We are inseparable." She looked back at him with her haughtiest gaze.

He looked as if a hurricane might break out at any instant around his head, from the sheer force of atmospheric energy being generated within. "I do not recall giving permission for a dog to be installed in this house, Mr. Markham."

"I find, your lordship, one achieves more by asking for forgiveness, rather than permission."

The butler made a faint choking sound. The rest of the house remained as silent as a tomb. Not even the clock perched atop the hallway fireplace dared to tick.

Bit by bit, the earl's narrowed black eyes returned to their usual state. His shoulders relaxed a telling quarter inch. "I see, Mr. Markham, you're going to cause me a great deal of trouble in the course of your employ. Let us both hope you prove yourself worth the disruption."

"Of that, I have no doubt, sir." She bowed her head.

Somerton adjusted his gloves. The dimness of the hallway gave his cheekbones additional heft, made his keen eyes especially black. "I don't want to see this dog of yours, Mr. Markham. I don't want to smell him. I most particularly don't want to hear him. Is that understood?"

"Quite, sir."

"That will be all, Markham."

The dismissal in his voice was irrevocable. Luisa turned and marched to the soaring marble stairs without another word. Behind her, the door crashed shut, and Somerton disappeared back into the night.

With the state ring of Holstein-Schweinwald-Huhnhof still tucked securely in his waistcoat pocket.

A dark-haired woman stood on the landing when Luisa reached the top of the stairs. One hand gripped the railing, and the other was hidden in the folds of her dressing gown.

Luisa stopped and bowed. "Lady Somerton, I presume."

The woman stepped into the light from the single sconce burning in the hallway. Luisa had to bite back a gasp; her beauty was so striking, so immaculate, she seemed to belong to another world. The air around her smelled of roses. "Good evening. You are his lordship's new secretary, I believe?"

"I am. My name is Lewis Markham."

The countess's gaze fell to his collar. "You're hurt!"

"A trifle." Luisa shrugged. The simple action made her abused head ring and her shoulders creak.

Lady Somerton sighed. "You're no better than my five-year-old son. Come along. It must be seen to at once." She turned and began to ascend the stairs to the upper floors.

"But I can't . . ."

"It's not a request, Mr. Markham."

Something about her air of quiet authority reminded Luisa of Miss Dingleby. She watched the young countess climb upward—float, really, as if she had wings rather than feet—without so much as glancing behind her. The delicate nape of her neck caught the glow from the sconce on the landing.

She shrugged again, a terrible mistake, and raised her foot to the steps.

"Where are we going?" she asked civilly, when the next landing passed by without a pause.

"To the nursery," said Lady Somerton. "I keep salves and plasters there. My son, I'm afraid, stands in constant need of patching up."

"Haven't you a nurse for such things?"

"Some do." Lady Somerton turned at the half landing and glanced at Luisa. "Are you quite all right? You seem rather stiff."

"Quite all right."

She resumed her upward march. "I suppose he's had you out on one of his little expeditions. Were you obliged to kill anyone?"

"I . . . no." Luisa paused. "Though it all might have gone vastly better if I had."

"There's the spirit. I'm sure you'll prove a tremendous success. You might even last until Candlemas, if you're especially fortunate. Here we are." The countess slipped a set of keys from her pocket and opened the door. She turned to Luisa and held her finger to her lips. "I've just got him to sleep," she whispered. "Don't spoil it."

Luisa tiptoed through the darkened room behind the graceful swaying shadow of the Countess of Somerton. To her left stood a cluster of furniture: table, chairs, desk. Evidently this was the day nursery; a door stood ajar on the opposite wall, fully black within, where young Lord Kildrake no doubt lay sleeping.

Lady Somerton led her in the opposite direction, to the nursery bathroom. She closed the door and switched on the light. Luisa blinked furiously at the sudden brightness of the gaslight in the white-tiled room.

"Good gracious. What a dreadful amount of blood." Lady Somerton clucked her tongue and opened a white-painted cabinet. "You'll want to soak that in cold water immediately."

Luisa watched her ladyship in astonishment as she burrowed matter-of-factly about the jars and tubes. Not even the harsh glare of the bathroom light could erase her beauty; her creamy skin remained smooth and flawless, a little pink perhaps in the apples of her cheeks, and her eyelashes swooped to sinful lengths beyond her brow. The delicate symmetry of her profile was almost mesmerizing.

Lord Somerton's wife. Who was she? What was she like? Did she love him?

Did he love her?

Well, obviously they didn't love each other. Luisa's own bedroom was proof of that. But how could even a beast like Somerton fail to adore such a lovely rose-scented creature, with her perfect profile and her extravagant eyelashes? One who shunned the endless social amusement of London to tuck her son in bed, instead of ordering a nurse to do it? One who drew a lowly clerk upstairs to tend his wound herself, instead of ordering a maid to do it?

For an instant, Luisa imagined that saturnine face lowering to press a kiss on Lady Somerton's rosy lips. His body pressed against Lady Somerton's porcelain skin. Kissing her. Touching her.

The image stung with unexpected sharpness. She pushed it away. Revulsion, no doubt. Somerton was an unpleasant beast, the sort of man she had always taken care to avoid.

She glanced again at the countess, who was now biting the corner of her lower lip as she hunted among her shelves.

Probably she wasn't sophisticated enough for Somerton's taste. Perhaps she was simply a pretty face, with nothing inside to interest him.

Not that Luisa gave the slightest damn about the state of the Somertons' marriage.

"Here we are," her ladyship said, in that melodious voice of hers. "If you'll be so kind as to unfasten your collar, Mr. Markham. I shall dampen this washcloth with a bit of soap and hot water."

"I am perfectly capable . . ."

"A young man of your age knows nothing about how easily even the most superficial of wounds can become infected with germs, Mr. Markham." Lady Somerton returned, brandishing the white washcloth like a weapon of war. "I daresay you would go to bed without even washing."

"That's not true," Luisa said indignantly, and then "Owww!" as the countess dabbed at her neck.

"Be still. I haven't even touched it yet. My goodness, your skin is sensitive. I . . ."

Luisa pushed her hand away. "That's enough."

"But I haven't . . ."

Luisa snatched the washcloth and turned to the mirror. "I'll wash, if you please." Her heart beat hard against her chest. What had she been thinking, to let the countess examine her tender feminine skin? It had felt so natural, the way she and Emilie would braid each other's hair at night, trading secrets.

But Lady Somerton was not her sister.

Suddenly, the ache in her head and shoulders seemed to penetrate to her bones.

"At least you're thorough," said the voice behind her, and Luisa glanced at the corner of the mirror to see Lady Somerton's face pointed attentively toward her.

Too attentively.

She let the washcloth drop into the basin. "There. Now the salve. Your ladyship," she remembered to add, with a touch of humility.

"You're a self-assured young man, I'll give you that," said the countess. She handed Luisa the jar.

"What's this?"

"A concoction of honey, among other things. Marvelous for

preventing putrefaction. Just a dab, Mr. Markham, and then the gauze."

Luisa dabbed carefully at the nick on her throat. For a wound that had produced such a prolific amount of blood, it was rather disappointingly small, a triangle of no more than a centimeter's length. A thin trickle of blood rolled downward, where the cleaning had disturbed the clot.

"Would you like me to wrap the gauze for you, Mr. Markham? A few turns about the neck should be sufficient." A little note of amusement had crept its way into Lady Somerton's voice.

"Thank you, no. I shall manage it." Luisa snatched the gauze and wrapped the thin strip about her neck twice, tying it securely with the ends. She stared sternly at her reflection. No beauty, she. Her features were too strong, her nose too large, her chin too uncompromising. On the other hand, such things served a princess well, when she was going about as a young man.

She turned to face Lady Somerton, who ought to be regarding her with a mixture of disgust and annoyance. Lowly secretaries did not address countesses in such brusque and casual terms, after all. But her ladyship seemed to have taken it all in good humor. She had crossed her arms across her chest, and a little smile turned up the corners of her pretty mouth. Her eyes were large and quite blue, and something about them, some fleeting trick of expression, some trace of sadness at the corners, seemed years older than the rest of her.

"Thank you, your ladyship," Luisa said sincerely. "Forgive my abruptness, I beg you. It has been rather a trying evening."

Lady Somerton nodded. The hint of smile faded from her lips. "Of course it has. I quite understand, believe me."

Luisa refastened her collar and tightened her necktie to its proper position. "I won't trouble you any longer, then."

"I'll see you out." Lady Somerton moved quickly, turning down the light before opening the door. Again they padded softly through the day nursery; again the countess opened the door and closed it again, turning the lock with the key from her pocket.

"Why do you lock him in? Aren't you afraid of some accident?" The question slipped out before Luisa could consider the propriety of asking it.

"No. I sleep in the room adjoining, which has its own door into the nursery." She smiled benignly and held out her hand. "Good night, Mr. Markham."

Luisa took the hand and shook it briefly. "Good night, your ladyship."

L uisa awoke, sometime later, to the muffled crash of glass against a wall.

She startled upward against the pillows; a book fell away from her chest. She hadn't meant to fall asleep at all. After taking Quincy for his walk, she had tried both the knob on Somerton's bedroom door and their shared connecting door. She'd found them both securely locked, foiling her plan to hide under the earl's bed until he came home and went to sleep . . . without, she hoped, first taking the time to examine his new ring more closely.

Next, she'd planned to wait until he returned, and then create some sort of distraction—a loud choking fit, or perhaps a small controlled explosion—that would send him crashing into her room. In the resulting confusion, she could find some excuse—a needed glass of water, a stealthy bash over the earl's head with that sturdy-looking vase on the mantel—to slip into his room and locate her ring before morning.

Fortune favored the bold, as her father always said.

And now here she was, startling awake in the middle of the night like a schoolboy caught out in his studies, while the connecting door remained shut and the Holstein state ring remained in the possession of the Earl of Somerton.

She simply wasn't cut out for this kind of work, was she?

Luisa stretched out her legs beneath the covers and craned her ears for further signs of Somerton's return, but the room remained quiet after that signal crash of glass. Perhaps she'd imagined it, after all.

A floorboard creaked faintly, and then a sound that might have been a grunt.

At the bottom of the bed, Quincy lifted his ears and swiveled his head in the direction of the connecting door. "Shh," Luisa whispered, reaching for his head. She scratched between his silky ears. "He's not at all amused by dogs."

Quincy broke free and jumped off the bed. His claws scrabbled on the wooden floorboards and came to a stop in front of the connecting door, where a thin line of yellow light rimmed the bottom. Quincy strained forward and let out a tiny whine.

"Shh! Come back!"

Another whine.

Luisa jumped out of bed, a task made far more straightforward by her masculine blue-striped pajamas: the one item of clothing she genuinely preferred to her old feminine wardrobe. Quincy reached out a paw and scratched furiously at the crack of light.

"Stop that!" Luisa whispered. "You'll have us both thrown out!" She bent over and scooped up the dog.

Quincy let out a furious series of barks.

"Quiet, Quincy!" She tried to cover his mouth with her hand, but he tossed his head and squirmed his lithe body in her grasp. His short legs wriggled furiously, as if he were swimming in a race, and his little heartbeat rattled against her hand.

From the other side of the door came the sound of determined footsteps.

Quincy yipped twice and leaped from her arms, just as the connecting door wrenched open and the Earl of Somerton, wearing only a pair of crimson drawstring pajama trousers and a thunderous expression, planted his feet on the floor before her.

SIX

W hat the devil . . ." began Somerton.

Quincy darted between his legs and scampered through the door.

"Quincy!" Luisa dodged past the earl's thick shoulders and into his bedchamber. She took two running steps and staggered to a halt.

The room might have been a monk's cell. There was no plush Oriental rug, no profusion of dark wood furniture, no wealthy display of handsome gilt-edged paintings on the white plaster walls. The fireplace was surrounded by ornate carved marble, but the mantel held only a square brass clock of the sort used by military officers on campaign, ticking away with loud and ruthless precision. A bookshelf along one wall contained an immense number of close-packed books, each spine turned outward and arranged in exact vertical order. There were two wooden chairs, a washstand, a wardrobe, entirely without decoration of any kind.

And a bed, of course. Straight, narrow, dressed in crisp white linen, and home at the moment to a fluffy golden corgi wearing an expression of immense self-satisfaction.

"Quincy!" Luisa swallowed her astonishment and rushed across the room to snatch the dog from the center of the Earl of Somerton's Spartan bed. He let out a yip of disappointment and wriggled his body, attempting escape, but this time Luisa held firm. "Naughty dog. Very naughty dog," she said in his ear, which he swiveled dismissively away.

Slowly Luisa rotated back around to meet the full force of Somerton's rage. As crimson, no doubt, as his silken pajamas.

He stood silently, with one hand gripping the other arm, and his formerly immaculate black hair dipping into his forehead. She tried not to look at his chest, which bore—she couldn't help noticing, in the lower periphery of her vision—not an ounce of unnecessary padding. It just went on and on, acres of olive skin covering endless peaks and valleys, a vast topography of male muscularity. Utterly impregnable.

"This is a trifle awkward," she said, into the silence.

"It is, I believe, the most extraordinary first day's employment in the history of personal secretaries," Somerton drawled.

"I apologize for Quincy. He heard a noise and became alarmed . . ."

"And he makes that sort of racket whenever he's alarmed?"

"I was on the point of silencing him when you opened the door," she said. "You only set him off again by venturing in to cast down your thunderbolts of justice."

He frowned. "Thunderbolts of justice?"

"Yes. If you hadn't taken it into your head to interfere . . ."

The frown smoothed away into the hard angles of his face. He let out a sigh and turned to walk across the room to the door on the opposite wall. "You misapprehend, Mr. Markham. That wasn't the reason I opened the door."

Luisa swallowed again. His back was nearly as impressive as his front, thick and powerful, held in place by shoulder blades the size of dinner plates. She refused to look any lower. It simply wasn't seemly to . . . another man when . . . Peter lay . . . dear Lord. Taut, round buttocks, covered in crimson silk.

She closed her eyes. "It wasn't?"

"I regret to say that I have met with a small accident, and require your assistance."

"An accident?" She opened her eyes again. He was walking toward her, holding a white cloth in his right hand, which was firmly attached to his left forearm. "Good heavens! What happened?"

"I was pouring a drink. The glass slipped. If you would be so good as to hold the dressing in place, while I wrap the bandage around it." It was not a request.

She stared at the white dressing on his wrist. A few specks of red had already soaked through the cloth.

"Sir!"

"You may set down the dog, for now."

Luisa loosened her arms, and Quincy leapt to the floor. He rushed straight to Somerton's bare feet and set down his hindquarters on the polished wooden floor, staring up the sweeping length of bone, muscle, and crimson pajama with anxious eyes.

"What the devil is he doing?" asked Somerton.

"Possibly he likes you." Luisa placed her fingers on the edges of the dressing and smothered a smile. "I can't imagine why."

"Impudent beast."

Luisa wasn't sure whether he meant her or Quincy, and she hardly dared ask. She stared instead at the red-speckled dressing and the muscled forearm beneath, while Somerton's large hand whipped the gauze expertly around in overlapping strips. His breath reeked of whiskey. For some reason, the scent was not unpleasant.

"You seem to know what you're doing," she said.

"I have lived forty years upon this earth, Mr. Markham, and have incurred the odd scratch from time to time. If you will move your right forefinger out of the way."

"How did the glass slip?"

"An accident."

"An odd sort of accident, to create such a wound."

"There we are. May I ask you to knot the ends, Mr. Markham?"

"Of course." Luisa took the ends of the gauze and tied them securely together. "I performed the same service for myself, only a few hours ago."

"I recall I had asked the housekeeper to tend you."

"In the end, Lady Somerton came to my aid."

The whiskey breath stopped. "Did she?"

"Yes. She was very kind."

Somerton pulled away and walked briskly to the tray of drinks. A pile of shards glittered on the floor next to the wall, ten feet away, as if someone had thrown a glass against it. "She can be very kind, to those she likes."

Quincy rose to his feet, and Luisa leaned down to pick him back up. "Stay here, love. You'll splinter your paws."

"Did she bandage your wound for you?"

"No, I did it myself. I dislike fuss."

"Good man. Drink?"

"No, thank you." Luisa shifted her weight. As she watched, Somerton poured a generous glass and lifted it to his lips. "I should be getting back to bed."

"What's this?" Somerton turned and leaned against the table, drink in hand, facing her. "You have no questions? Why, for example, does my dear wife sleep upstairs in the nursery, instead of in the room you yourself inhabit? Why do I not keep such a tempting creature busy in my own bed at every opportunity? You cannot deny, Mr. Markham, that my wife is an astonishingly beautiful woman."

The blood climbed in Luisa's cheeks. "She is lovely, of course. But that is your own affair."

"Affair. Yes." Somerton laughed and finished off the glass. "An excellent choice of words, though in fact the affair is not, strictly speaking, mine. But go to bed, go to bed." He waved the empty glass at the connecting door. "Take your upright self back to your room and into innocent slumber, my dear Mr. Markham. The deep sleep of an untroubled conscience. Enjoy it while you can."

Something about his words, about the dangerous edge of his voice, the cold recklessness of his expression, made Luisa turn instead to the bed and place Quincy back on the pristine white linen. She walked by Somerton's laconic figure without a glance and bent to pick up the shards from the floor by the wall.

"What are you doing?" he demanded.

"You'll cut yourself. Again." She placed each one, piece by piece, on her open palm, and when she had found all the large ones, she dropped them into the washbasin, for lack of a nearby dustbin.

"Unnecessary. My valet will see to it in the morning."

He was quite drunk. She could hear it now, the determined precision of his words, the negligent spilling of personal details. The hint of self-defense.

She picked up the washcloth and returned to the floor,

where she began to wipe up as many of the tiny slivers as she could find.

A hand appeared on her wrist. "Stop that," he growled. "You are not paid to perform menial labor."

"Better this than be forced to stitch up your foot in the middle of the night."

"I can stitch it up myself."

His shoulder pressed against hers, his warm breath suffused the air between them. He was so hot and large, so electric with unpredictable power. Luisa was afraid he could hear the thumping beat of her quickened heart, could feel the thrust of her pulse beneath her skin.

She tried to think of Peter, to raise his poor image in her head. She was a widow; she had lost her husband not two months ago. And now here she was, standing next to a half-naked married man while her heart pounded beneath the bands of linen that flattened her bosom, while her skin tingled and her thoughts blurred.

This tingle of blood under her skin: arousal, or shame?

How could she tell? She'd never felt this way before. Peter, sweet Peter, had been her friend, a mere dear acquaintance, cheerful and distracted. Of his dutifully intimate fumblings under the covers at night, she remembered little. In the morning, the two of them had always pretended those necessary intimacies did not exist. It was all too embarrassing otherwise.

But still. She owed something to his memory, didn't she? She owed him at least the respect due to a deceased husband, that she would not fall prey to base sexual attraction within weeks of his death.

Luisa jerked her arm away and stood. "Very well, then," she said, handing him the cloth. "Clean it up yourself. It's your mess, after . . ."

She stopped in mid-sentence, for she had just spotted an object on the rim of the washstand. A small, round, glittering object.

The state ring of Holstein-Schweinwald-Huhnhof.

"After . . . ?"

She shifted her gaze back to the earl. "All. After all. It's your own mess, after all." A novel sentiment, coming from her. Until that fateful October day, she had relied on servants to wipe clean every spill and stain in her life.

"You shame me."

Luisa edged closer to the washstand. "I doubt anyone has the capacity to shame you, Lord Somerton. Least of all me."

"You're mistaken. I find I value your good opinion, for some unknown reason."

"Likely the effect of the whiskey you've been drinking." She nodded at the tray.

To her disappointment, he didn't follow her glance. "Perhaps. But there's something about you, Markham. I ought to have sacked you a dozen times already, and I haven't. In fact, the offenses for which I ought to have sacked you, I find myself admiring instead."

Keep him talking.

"Offenses? How have I offended you?" She stole another step.

Somerton lifted his hand and counted on his fingers. "Your insolence, your signal lack of respect, your disobedience of my direct orders . . ."

"I am not insolent."

"Your dog."

Quincy lifted his head at the word *dog*.

"My dog offends you?"

She caught sight of the ring again, from the corner of her eye, alluring as a magnetic center. How could he fail to wonder at it? Tomorrow morning, when he was sober, and the sunlight streamed through the window and banished this strange melancholy of his, he would pick up that ring and his eyes would narrow. He would turn it about in his fingers. He would see the inscription and read it. His sharp mind would link the pieces of the puzzle.

Luisa angled her foot idly. Two more steps, perhaps three.

Somerton twisted the glass in his palm. "He does. He reminds me of you, utterly lacking in respect for his betters."

"That's because he has no betters. He is a dog of impeccable moral standards."

"And that, you see . . ." Somerton wavered, making another gesture with his empty glass. Luisa took another step, and another, as his gaze left her and traveled around the room.

"And that?" she pressed.

"And that is why I forgive you, I suppose," he said quietly. "Because an honest, straightforward, loyal chap is the very devil to find in this world. A . . . a needle . . ."

She had reached the washstand. She placed her hands casually on the edge. The ring lay so close, eighteen inches at most. So easy to slip into her pocket. Just a little movement of her hand, when his face turned away . . .

"What are you doing?"

Luisa jumped. Somerton's gaze had refocused on her, keen and black once more.

"Nothing. Merely waiting for you to continue. You're vastly entertaining when drunk."

His eyebrows came down in two forbidding lines. "Whelp. Off you go, then."

"No, no. Pray go on." She clutched at the edge of the washstand. Her fingers yearned around the bowl. She could almost picture them curling around the hard gold band, the bumps and ridges of the familiar gemstones . . .

Somerton stepped away from the table. His face was old and hard, all broad planes and unforgiving angles. "I said *go*, Markham," he barked.

She held up her hands. "Very well. I . . ."

Without warning, Quincy leapt down from the bed and trotted to Somerton's feet.

Somerton looked down. "What the devil are you doing, you half-witted mongrel?"

Quincy's tongue lolled happily from his mouth, as if Somerton had just pledged his undying loyalty. He struck out one paw and stroked the earl's bare left foot.

Like a seasoned thief, Luisa snaked her hand along the washstand and swept the ring away, into her pocket.

She could have sworn that Quincy winked.

"I'll be off, then," she said cheerfully. "Good night, pleasant dreams and all that. Come along, Quincy."

She turned to leave. Behind her, Quincy's claws scrabbled on the polished surface of the wood.

"Wait a moment."

The silkiness of the earl's voice made her foot arrest in midair. She took a deep breath, placed it back down, and forced a smile to her lips.

"Yes, sir?" she asked, turning back.

"Perhaps, Mr. Markham, you would like a moment to reconsider."

The ring weighed heavily in her pajama pocket. She was afraid to look down and see what a lump it made, sticking out from her hip like a piece of coal.

"Reconsider what, sir?" She lifted her hand to smother a yawn. "I'm awfully tired. Quite done in."

"Reconsider taking the ring from my washstand."

At her feet, Quincy let out a whine and thumped his tail against the floor. A roaring sound rose up in Luisa's ears, an ocean of fear.

"Sir, I don't . . . I . . ."

"Mr. Markham. Do me the favor, if you will, of not playing the fool." Somerton's voice was sharp enough to cut steel. His face had gone blank, blank and hard-edged, a plaster mask of unknown intent. "I have faced down far more clever deceit than yours, believe me."

She anchored her gaze on his nose, which was large and slightly Roman, an ancient gold coin of a nose. So must a butterfly feel, with the pin stuck firmly in her thorax.

"The ring is not yours," she said.

"You think so? But neither is it yours."

How it burned through the flannel of her pajamas. She stuck out her chin. "You are quite wrong. It is mine."

"Yours?" He laughed brutally. "My dear fellow. Yours?"

"Mine."

"A ring of such value, belonging to a common young clerk? Of such singular appearance? I can picture it now, a most unusual arrangement of stones."

"It is a family heirloom. My only legacy from my father." She kept her voice steady, her gaze trained on his, communicating truth.

"Ah. A family heirloom."

"Yes. For generations."

The brass clock ticked its slow military tick. Quincy huddled against her ankles, hangdog. Somerton stood rock-still before her, half clothed and magnificent, a cunning beast whose every sense seemed to reach out and penetrate her skin. A single muscle flexed at his chest, and then relaxed.

"This family heirloom. This legacy from your father. It simply dropped from your person during the attack?" he asked.

"The thief took it from my waistcoat pocket, right before you arrived."

"Hmm."

She waited for him to speak. To tell her she was a liar, to ask for the ring back. To ask her to show it to him.

"Why didn't you claim the ring back immediately, in that case?" he asked, in that same inscrutable low tone.

"I didn't think you'd believe me. As you say, a lowly clerk, with a ring so valuable. I thought you might think it suspicious."

"It *is* suspicious, Markham. Damned suspicious." He walked up to her with deliberate strides and stopped just shy of her body, a foot too close. She had to tilt her head upward to meet his black gaze, exposing her vulnerable gauze-wrapped neck.

"Then I suppose you don't believe me." She slipped her hand into her pocket and clutched the ring into her palm.

Somerton's breath was thick with brandy and tobacco, tingling her skin. He raised his hand and touched her face. One finger dragged lazily along her bruised cheekbone, around the tense corner of her mouth, down to her chin. He captured the tip lightly between index finger and thumb.

"On the contrary, Mr. Markham," he said softly. "I believe anything you choose to tell me."

For an instant, she didn't quite understand him. The words revolved in her head like some sort of drunken parlor game, attempting to find their correct order.

I believe anything you choose to tell me. Had he really said that?

Her chest seemed to glow and expand, as if a crushing weight had been lifted away.

Luisa drew in a massive breath and stepped back. "Thank you for your trust, your lordship. Good night."

She was about to close the door behind her, when Somerton's stern voice cut the air a final time.

"Until proven otherwise, Mr. Markham."

SEVEN

London
February 1890

The front room of Mrs. Duke's house in Battersea smelled like a barnyard.

"My deepest apologies," said the duke, scratching delicately under his wig. "My neighbor to the left appears to have introduced a large and incontinent sow into the premises during the late cold spell. We are considering legal remedy."

"Not at all." Luisa removed her hat and set it on the hall stand. Quincy leapt from the crook of her left arm and pattered across the worn Oriental rug to the tips of Mrs. Duke's leather half boots. One ear cocked hopefully.

"Oh, very well," said Olympia. He reached for the tea tray and broke off a piece of ham sandwich. "With compliments."

Quincy caught the sandwich in midair and swallowed it whole.

"You really shouldn't. The servants in Chester Square spoil him shamelessly, to say nothing of Somerton's boy." Luisa eased herself carefully onto the faded velvet sofa next to the fireplace. Experience had made her cautious.

"Consider it my revenge against the sow," said Olympia. "Warm yourself, warm yourself. The cold is intolerable today."

"I don't mind. Winters in Holstein were far worse. We used to be snowed in for days." She reached for the teapot. "May I?"

"Go on, go on. I've swallowed three cups of coffee this morning in an effort to thaw myself. Where is that damned slatternly maid? *Dingleby!*" He lifted his voice to a friendly roar.

"Bugger yourself," came the friendly reply, floating through the parlor door.

"Good servants are so difficult to find these days," said Olympia.

Luisa bent her head over the cup and warmed her face in the fragrant steam. "Indeed. Have you made any progress this week? Is there any news from my sisters?"

"I find," Olympia said, selecting a ham sandwich with less-than-feminine grace, "that one usually asks questions about others when one wishes to distract from oneself."

"Bugger yourself."

"Tut-tut. Such language from a princess of Germany."

"I have absorbed myself into my role, as you suggested. And now I should like to know how my sisters are doing. You haven't mentioned them in weeks."

Olympia chewed, swallowed, dabbed a napkin to his mouth. "As it happens, there is news. I daresay you'll see it in the papers shortly. Our dear Emilie's employer has discovered her true identity."

Luisa's cup clattered into the saucer. She jumped to her feet. "*What?* Is she safe? Is she . . . is she . . . ?"

"Whole and unmolested? I very much doubt it. But the man in question is an honorable chap. He'll make her happy enough, I daresay, if she allows him to."

Luisa worked her mouth, which had gone rather dry. "She's . . . she's getting married?"

"She may not realize it yet. But yes. If all goes well, she'll be the Duchess of Ashland by Lady Day." He coughed slightly into his napkin. "If not sooner."

She placed her hands on her hips. "*If all goes well.* What the devil do you mean by that?"

"Dear me. All this talk of buggery and devils. Perhaps I ought not to have packed you off to Somerton's lair after all."

"Uncle." She deepened her voice to a warning growl. "Is my sister safe?"

"She is under the strictest protection, at my own house in Park Lane, guarded assiduously by the duke himself."

"That's not the same thing as safe."

"My dear Luisa," he said kindly, "none of you are safe. Not one person on this good earth is safe. You might be struck by an omnibus leaving this house. A scrape on your elbow might go septic. Typhoid, consumption, war, lawsuit . . ."

"Now you're trying to distract *me*."

"What I mean to say is this: Nothing in life is accomplished without risk. Fortune favors the bold. There is a tide in the affairs of men, which if taken at the flood . . ."

Luisa dropped to her knees before the chair on which Olympia sat, in a pool of striped cornflower blue silk. "What have you done, Uncle?" she whispered.

He took her hands on his lap. "Listen to me, my dear. We have not been idle, these past few months, Miss Dingleby and I. We have discovered that there is indeed a group of agents in England this minute, tracking down the three of you. We have discovered, moreover, that they are getting their information from a person with some knowledge of your situation. We believe we can turn this . . . this disruption of Emilie's disguise to our advantage." He patted her hands, as if to console her.

Quincy, who was sniffing the tea tray for further traces of ham, turned his head in Olympia's direction and let out an inquisitive growl.

"Use her as bait, you mean." Luisa could hardly move her lips.

Miss Dingleby's voice interrupted the barnyard air of the parlor. "We have made our plans with the utmost care. We will hold an engagement ball, with great fanfare and public bally-hoo, in Olympia's house. Dozens of our agents will be placed there, in every room. The Duke of Ashland will guard her personally . . ."

Luisa turned to Miss Dingleby, who stood at the parlor door, lean and angular in her gray maid's uniform and incongruous white cap. "Oh, indeed! What on earth could possibly go wrong?"

"My dear, we've done these sorts of things endless times. Our agents are highly trained."

"And Emilie will be right there in the middle of it all, with a target painted on her forehead . . ."

"She will not be touched, Luisa. I promise it."

Luisa leaned forward and grabbed her uncle by his blue silk shoulders. "I will not lose her, do you understand me? I've lost my mother, my stepmothers, my father, my own husband! I will *not* lose my sisters as well!"

"There, now." Olympia took her arms gently in his broad hands. "I quite understand."

"They are all I have left."

"Nonsense," said Dingleby. "You have . . ."

"I quite understand," said Olympia. "And I would sooner send a bullet through my own head than cause the slightest harm to you or your sisters."

Luisa laid her head on his cheap silk knees and closed her eyes, so she wouldn't see Miss Dingleby's incredulous and somewhat disapproving face staring down at them. A long, warm tongue licked at her ankles, wetting right through her black wool stockings to her tender skin.

"Dear me," said Olympia.

She didn't cry. She wouldn't cry; crying had long since been banished from her repertory of emotional display, such as it was. But she felt a certain brimming heaviness around her eyes and her heart. It had, after all, been a trying week. A trying winter, to be perfectly honest. She had never known anything like the atmosphere of the Earl of Somerton's household, with its lines of battle etched out invisibly on the floorboards and its inhabitants tiptoeing about the heavy silence as if the life had been frozen out of them. As if they had all fallen into a trance of some kind, a nether-existence that was not living at all. Though Holstein Castle had been run along strictly formal protocols, and her father had treated her with brusque professionalism, and her stepmothers had died in childbed, her home nonetheless managed—perhaps even because of these struggles—to seethe with life and laughter and sisterly love.

She thought of Emilie now, golden-haired and quiet behind her spectacles, and tried to imagine her falling in love with a duke. Experiencing that great transformative joy—so the novels claimed, not that Luisa had read many novels—in which her family now played no part. No Luisa or Stefanie to share her happiness and sorrow, the unexpected moments of ecstatic connection and the all-too-frequent crushing disappointment of loss and uncertainty and . . .

Not that Luisa knew what that was like. Not at all.

"My dear Luisa." Olympia patted her hair awkwardly. "Is there something you wish to tell me?"

She lifted her head and pulled away. "No, nothing. Good heavens. Nothing at all. Only a trifle worn today. A long evening of rather tedious work, followed by a disturbed sleep, remembering all the things I'd forgotten to sort out . . ."

"Any news to report? Unusual activities? Notes, letters, visitors?"

"No."

"His wife, perhaps?"

"Lady Somerton is much as she's always been. Very lovely, very kind, and unfailingly distant to everyone except her son."

"*Their* son."

"Yes, their son. He's a dear little fellow, actually. She's an excellent mother. But she keeps him away from the earl as much as she can. I think he'd like to be a better father, but he doesn't know how. If she'd give him the chance to get to know the boy . . ."

"Yes, all very fascinating, this . . . this familial . . . whatever." Olympia made a little movement of his hand and looked out the window at the smudged gray February beyond. "Is it too early for sherry?"

"Decidedly too early."

Miss Dingleby jumped from the doorway. "Never too early for that, in a London winter. The sun's halfway down already."

"Such as it is," said Luisa. "I much prefer England in summer."

"Off you go, then, Dingleby. Fetch the sherry from whatever cupboard you've hidden it." He waited until her footfalls faded down the hall, and the crash of cupboard doors echoed through the wood and plaster. "Now, Luisa. Listen to me carefully. This has nothing to do with you and your sisters, I'm afraid, but the time has ripened for another plan I've had in contemplation for some time . . ."

"Oh no. No, no, no." Luisa backed away and found the sofa with her black-trousered calves. She sank downward. Quincy jumped into her lap the instant it appeared and settled in with a sigh of canine contentment.

"It's too late for that, my dear. You're already involved." He cast a quick glance to the parlor door. "I'll be quick. Lord Somerton, as you know, has long harbored suspicions about his wife . . ."

"Ridiculous. She may not love him, but she's faithful, I'll give her that."

"They are true."

"True!" Luisa's eyes widened. "But that's impossible! She positively lives for that boy of hers. She only goes out for church and a bit of shopping and visits to her sister."

"She has been in love with my grandson Penhallow for the past seven years."

"Lord Roland? My cousin?"

"Yes."

"How do you know this?"

"It's not important. They were nearly engaged once, and I . . . that is, Lord Somerton stepped in with a better offer when Roland was . . . well, elsewhere." He cleared his throat.

"But that doesn't mean she's . . . she's . . ." Luisa searched for the right word.

"Have you ever wondered, my dear, why Lady Somerton betrays not the slightest hint of love toward her husband?"

"I don't see why she should. He's brutal and overbearing and secretive, and he can't be bothered to offer more than an occasional word of affection or even approbation, and while he's rather superbly masculine, particularly when dressed in his formal suit, if you're the sort of female whose head is turned by a mere set of broad shoulders and a face that might have been taken from a Roman coin . . ."

"My dear girl. Remember yourself."

Luisa closed her mouth and reached for her tea. "In any case, there's no reason she should love him. Not at all."

"I don't disagree. However . . ."

The rattle of glassware in the hallway caused Olympia to turn his brilliant red-wigged head. "Ah! There we are. Just the thing to banish the odor of pigsty from the old senses, what? Have these glasses been washed, Dingleby?"

Miss Dingleby set down the tray with a little more force

than strictly necessary. "I often wonder whether we need to maintain these disguises behind closed doors, Mrs. Duke."

"Nonsense. What if one of the neighbors were to twitch her lace curtains, catch a glimpse through the window, and find things out of order?" Olympia rose to his full magnificent height and made for the table in a voluminous rustle of skirt and petticoat. "There we are, my beauty. That will be all, Dingleby."

"Bugger yourself," she said, and turned for the hall.

"You may close that door behind you, if it's not too much trouble."

"Hmph. Your wig is askew, by the way. All that unwholesome scratching, no doubt." The door slammed dangerously in its moldings.

"I believe she resents this particular disguise. I can't imagine why. Sherry?" Olympia turned to her with glass outstretched.

Luisa hesitated, and then held out her hand.

"Good man. Er, so to speak. In any case . . . dear me, where was I? This damned female costume makes my wits go feeble. I daresay yours, on the other hand, have sharpened out of all recognition." He winked.

She scowled. "You had a plan."

"A plan. Yes. Now, I don't mean to shock you, and I beg you to remember that this information is to be held in the strictest confidence, but . . ."

"Lord Somerton is a government spymaster?" Luisa sipped her sherry.

Olympia's mouth, on the verge of its first eager sip, formed a round rouge-edged hole.

"I'm not a fool, Uncle. I guessed it from the beginning, more or less, and your interest in him only confirmed the fact. Do go on. That vacant expression rather alarms me."

"Yes. Quite." He downed his glass in a single hearty swallow and reached for the decanter. "In any case, you need not know any more about it, other than this: We like to play a few games with each other, his department and mine, and the time has come for me to . . . how shall I put this? Volley the ball in his corner."

Luisa's fingers tightened around her glass. She took a sip and threaded her other hand through Quincy's fur. He raised his head and looked up at her, inquisitive. "Do you mean to hurt him?" she asked, as casually as she could.

"Hurt him? Dear me, no. I rely on him to keep you safe, after all."

"Do you mean *me* to hurt him?"

"No, no, no. Not at all. You quite misunderstand me." He fiddled with his sherry glass. "As I promised in the beginning, your role shall be strictly one of observation. I only ask you to be prepared for any events, as they may arise."

"Events? What sort of events?"

He drank his sherry and tapped his vermillion lips. "Ask no questions, my dear."

Luisa finished the sherry, set Quincy carefully to the floor, and rose to her feet. She handed her empty glass to Olympia. "I will not betray him, Uncle. I cannot play both sides."

"You won't have to. Everything will turn out for the best, Luisa."

She shook her head and crossed the room to open the parlor door. She half expected Miss Dingleby to be lingering in the hallway, listening through the keyhole, but her onetime governess was nowhere to be seen.

She plucked her hat from the hall stand and bent down to scoop Quincy into her arms. "Thank you for the sherry, Mrs. Duke. I'm glad to see you're well. Keep me apprised of your gamble with Emilie's life, if it's not too much trouble."

Olympia folded his arms against his false bosom. His eyes shone a bright blue in the light from the gas sconce affixed to the cheap burgundy fleur-de-lis wallpaper. "I do rather wish you would bend that spine of yours an inch or two and trust me."

"Good day, Mrs. Duke. I'll see myself out." She turned and unbolted the door.

"Mr. Markham."

She stared at her hand on the knob. "Yes, Mrs. Duke?"

"I suspect your employer may wish to have a word with you, on your return."

EIGHT

"Johnson, tell Mr. Markham I wish to have a word with him," said the Earl of Somerton, without looking up from the papers arranged before him.

The butler crossed his arms behind his back. "I regret to say that Mr. Markham is currently enjoying the liberty of his weekly half day, sir," he said triumphantly, as if to inform his employer that he had caught young Mr. Markham stealing bread from the local orphanage.

Somerton raised his head. "Half day? Half day, did you say? Who authorized this . . . this *half day* of his?"

"You did, sir."

"*I* did?"

"He has been taking them regularly since his arrival." Johnson left *the lazy young bastard* to dangle unspoken in the chill air of his lordship's study.

"Has he? For God's sake, why?"

"I believe it is a customary condition of British employment, sir. In some cases, the working man is entitled to a half day on Saturday, as well as the entirety of his Sunday, quite at leisure." Johnson's voice was dark with disapproval.

Somerton frowned. "Particularly distasteful in a nation

that prides itself on its habit of sober industry. One expects these sorts of ramshackle customs on the Continent."

"There are also the bank holidays, sir." As he might say *the lands of Sodom and Gomorrah*.

"Mark my words, Mr. Johnson. These so-called *week-ends* and *bank holidays* will lead inevitably to the decline of the British nation. We shall end up no better than the Spaniards. Next thing, it will be afternoon siestas, paid for by your honest beleaguered factory owner."

The butler shuddered. "Or sick leave."

"God forbid. Where will it end, if we pay workers to be sick? Weeklong holidays by the seaside every year, I suppose, with full compensation of wages."

Johnson's throat worked, as if he were struggling to contain tears.

"There, there, my good fellow," Somerton said soothingly. "It won't come to that, not if I still maintain my seat in the Lords. Though I expect the damned socialists will be after that, too, before long."

Johnson removed his handkerchief from his pocket and dabbed at the corner of his eye. "Quite right, sir. As to Mr. Markham, sir. Shall I tell him to join you in the study when he returns?"

"I see no other recourse, I'm afraid."

An hour later, Mr. Markham strolled through the door, with his dog trotting confidently at his heels. Mr. Markham never knocked before entering a room. He scarcely even paused. For a chap who scraped along the bottom rungs of the social ladder, Mr. Markham carried about a remarkable air of owning every chamber he occupied.

"How was your *half day*, Mr. Markham?" Somerton said, when the secretary had settled himself in his chair and picked up his pen.

"Why, very well indeed, thank you. I was visiting my dear old aunt in Battersea."

A soft weight settled on Somerton's left foot. He gave his ankle a little jerk, but the little beast simply dug himself in more firmly. "I hope you have enjoyed yourself in Battersea, Mr. Markham, while the rest of us toiled the afternoon away."

"I did indeed. My aunt's maid makes a superb cup of tea.

Quincy thoroughly enjoyed the ham sandwiches. Didn't you, my dear?" He aimed an indulgent smile at the damned furry ball covering Somerton's feet and waggled his fingers.

Somerton filled his lungs with air, causing the buttons of his jacket to strain in a most satisfactory manner. He looked down his long beak at Markham's face—that delicate young face, those quiet brown eyes, why did they affect him so?— and used his most earth-rattling voice.

"Perhaps, in future, Mr. Markham, you would be so kind as to inform me of your plans when you elect, in the manner of a lady of leisure, to treat yourself to an afternoon entirely devoid of productive labor. As it happened, I had several urgent tasks awaiting your immediate attention."

"Had you? I confess, after all these months, I'm rather dashed you haven't noticed that I visit my aunt each Sunday afternoon, without fail." He looked down to the surface of his desk and heaved his thin shoulders. "My only remaining family."

"You have no need of family," Somerton said harshly. "You have a job."

"How unfortunate, since I vastly prefer her company to yours."

"The quality of the company is irrelevant. Your loyalty is to me, and to this household, above all else. I believe I have paid generously for the privilege."

"Loyalty is not a commodity to be purchased, Lord Somerton."

Somerton roused his throat into a laugh. "What a naive chap you are, Mr. Markham. So full of fine ideals. But I assure you, a man's loyalty can be bought. I have done so many times."

"Forgive me, sir, but that's not precisely true. You rule by bribery and fear. This loyalty you crave, this loyalty you think you've purchased, it's not to you personally. It's to your money, or to your subject's own desire for self-preservation."

Somerton clenched his fingers around his pen. He said icily, "What does it matter, as long as the result is the same?"

"Because, should you find yourself stripped of your money and your capacity for intimidation, I daresay you would find yourself betrayed in an instant."

The mongrel's wet tongue began to lick his exposed ankle in a quiet rhythm. He wanted to kick it away, to send an unmistakable signal that he, the Earl of Somerton, needed neither man nor beast to demonstrate a single iota of affection toward him. But his feet remained still under the patient licking, the soft nestling of Quincy's body against his.

"Then let us hope, Mr. Markham," he said, rather softly, because he was afraid his voice might crack if he spoke at full volume, "I am never deprived of either one."

Markham picked up his pen, dipped it in the inkwell, and turned his attention to the paper before him. "I suppose that was insolent of me."

Somerton cleared his throat of its absurd dryness. "I choose to ignore your insolence, Markham, because at the moment I require your services for a task of great delicacy."

"And what is that, your lordship?" Markham did not raise his head.

"I require you to search my wife's bedroom for evidence of her association with Lord Roland Penhallow."

Markham startled upward. "What's that?"

"The details remain personal. My suspicions are of long standing, however, and have recently been further revived by a chance piece of knowledge that came my way this morning." He reached down and fingered the scrap of paper in his pocket.

"You're mad. Lady Somerton is innocent."

At the word *innocent*, Somerton tore his fist out of his pocket and crashed it against the solid mahogany surface of his desk. The paper was still tucked inside. "She is not innocent."

"I would stake my word on it."

"You would lose."

Markham laid down his pen. The winter night had already fallen, and the heavy green damask curtains had been drawn snug by an efficient housemaid hours ago. A coal fire hissed steadily in the grate, though it was not enough to banish the February cold entirely, and the tip of Markham's nose was nipped with red. His eyes, however, were large and warm and compassionate. "Sir, this unreasonable jealousy of yours, this madness . . ."

"It is not unreasonable!"

". . . will destroy what remains of your happiness, and hers. Why don't you simply talk to her? Some . . . some loving gesture . . ."

He banged his fist again. "You forget yourself, Markham."

"Because it pains me to see you so unhappy."

The room went hollow. There was no air, nothing for him to take in and breathe out, nothing to nourish him at all. He wanted to yank away his necktie, to gasp, to find some cursed, all-damned oxygen. Would someone just give him some bloody *air* to breathe?

He bolted to his feet and set his hands against the edge of the desk. Quincy jumped aside with an astonished yip. He opened his mouth and expanded his chest, and to his vast relief, his lungs obeyed him at last. "We have strayed far from the point, Markham. This is what comes of allowing you such extraordinary liberties."

"I cannot sit back and watch you . . ."

"You can, Markham. Your duty, for which I pay you handsomely, is to execute my orders without question. My order at the moment is to search the countess's bedroom and recover evidence of her association with Lord Roland Penhallow, brother of the Duke of Wallingford, grandson of the Duke of Olympia, God rot every last man of them. Your personal reservations are to be kept to yourself. Do you understand me?"

Markham stood and met Somerton's gaze with an expression of fiery defiance. "Sir, I cannot countenance such an outrageous violation of . . ."

"Or I shall sack you at once, Markham. *At once.* I will turn you out on the street without pay or reference this instant." He said the words forcefully, stabbing the air as he spoke, but he didn't shout. He congratulated himself for that. Self-control was the bedrock of leadership.

"Sir." Markham looked a little dazed.

"I do hope this dear old Battersea aunt of yours has a spare room, Mr. Markham." A nice touch, that. Back to his old hard, invulnerable self.

Markham frowned at the mention of his aunt. The gaslight hit his face from an odd angle, making him look a trifle too thin, a trifle gaunt. His narrow shoulders looked as if they might be swallowed whole by his black wool coat. His fingers pressed into the desk so forcefully, the tips had gone quite white.

Somerton noted these telling details with pride.

"Well, Mr. Markham? The choice is yours. Never say I forced you to it."

Had Markham looked pale before? He was now positively white-faced. "I will do it, your lordship," he said softly, "but only to prove that you're wrong. To clear her ladyship's name. I want your promise that if I find nothing, the entire matter will be closed forever."

Somerton walked around the side of his desk, toward Markham. The young fellow stood nobly, chin tilted, arms now crossed behind his back. Somerton admired the way his white neck held firm, the way his shoulders braced. He raised one massive leg and settled himself on the edge of the desk.

"My dear Mr. Markham, I couldn't ask for more."

Luisa waited until half past nine o'clock in the morning, when the door had shut firmly behind Lady Somerton and her son.

She paused at the top of the stairs and glanced out the window to confirm their departure, heading hand in swinging hand across the street to the barren square gardens, as they did every morning. Lord Kildrake's nurse trailed behind, looking more like an unwanted chaperone than a proper British nursery nurse. The poor woman spent most of her time reading novels in her tiny room, drinking gin quietly by the measured capful. (This from Tess, the housemaid with whom Luisa had struck up a tentative friendship over the past few months.)

When at last the three figures had passed through the black wrought-iron gate, had slipped in amongst the skeletal trees and disappeared from view, Luisa turned away to face the nursery door.

The small metal key in her pocket sagged downward with an unnatural weight. She had felt like a criminal, asking Mrs. Plum to take it off her ring. *An important errand on his lordship's behalf,* she'd said, avoiding the housekeeper's gaze, the slow hostility with which the woman had unhooked the loop, sorted through the various keys, and lifted one away. *Thank you,* she'd said, and instead of replying with the usual cheerful *You're quite welcome, Mr. Markham,* Mrs. Plum had merely muttered something about returning it promptly and turned away.

Well, she couldn't blame Mrs. Plum. The entire staff adored Lady Somerton. Even Johnson the butler harbored a certain softness for the countess, though the affection clearly taxed his divided conscience.

Luisa stiffened her shoulders, pulled the key from her pocket, and unlocked the door.

The windows in the day nursery faced south, and the room was bright and still, each toy put away in its cupboard, each cushion set back in its chair. In the center of the rug stood the desk on which young Philip wrote his letters and worked his sums; he was a precocious boy, already reading well, entranced by soldiers and horses, with that early reader's endearing habit of mispronouncing words and speaking in oddly formal constructions. The family had spent December and most of January at the earl's estate in Northamptonshire, and Philip had gone out riding regularly with a particularly sympathetic yellow-haired groom named Dick, while Lord Somerton had followed the hounds with the local hunt until Boxing Day signaled the end of the season. Luisa hadn't joined them. For one thing, she felt exposed riding astride, with her all-too-feminine legs encased in boots and snug breeches.

For another thing, she hadn't been asked.

Luisa turned away from his lordship's schoolboy desk and walked to the door on the right. In earlier days, it might have served as a nanny's room, but it was now given over to the countess's use, an entirely unsuitable location that everybody pretended was quite ordinary and matter-of-course for the wife of the Earl of Somerton.

Luisa hadn't ever glimpsed the interior. During the very few times she'd passed through the nursery, Lady Somerton's door had remained closed, giving off the unmistakable whiff of the sacrosanct. A kind of altar, on which her ladyship's youth and beauty were made sacrifice. The nunnery upstairs.

The door was not, however, locked.

When Luisa turned the knob, expecting resistance, she found it opened so easily she staggered inward, off-kilter. The gentle scent of roses drifted into her head, making her pulse jump, as if Lady Somerton herself had sprung out of the wardrobe and stabbed an accusing finger.

Except that Lady Somerton would never do that, would

she? She would simply stand there in all her quiet perfection, casting out her look of grieved accusation.

Luisa straightened herself and looked around. The curtains were drawn, shading the watery February sunlight, but she could easily make out the shapes of a well-furnished room, done in blues and creams, surprisingly large for a room on the nursery floor. Perhaps they had taken out a wall. A white-painted iron bed stood in the center, neatly made. A pair of fine old walnut wardrobes filled the shorter wall, opposite the window, clearly brought up from downstairs; in another corner, a washstand and dresser formed a nook of convenience. Bookshelves had been built into the walls flanking the window, and a seat below it; this was piled with blue and cream cushions, an invitation to read. A closed bureau sat opposite the foot of the bed, topped by a glass vase filled with dried hydrangeas.

Where on earth could she begin? Any one of those books might conceal a cache of love letters. The bureau—undoubtedly locked—might be stuffed with illicit correspondence and *objets d'amour*, or it might be stuffed with bills and household lists. Should she open that first? Miss Dingleby had taught her how to pick a simple lock with a hairpin, during one of her Battersea afternoons, but she would rather not if she could avoid it.

On the other hand, a locked bureau was the obvious place to start searching for evidence of a love affair.

Luisa dragged herself across the floorboards—hygienic, if rather ascetic—and placed her hand on the smooth-polished lid of the bureau. Sure enough, the key had been removed from the lock. She reached into her pocket for the hairpin. Oh, the grubbiness of it all, the low sneaking vulgarity. Looking inside a countess's private papers, and for what? To feed the mad jealousy of a scorned husband.

She should stand firm. She shouldn't do this. She wasn't a spy, like her uncle. Like Somerton himself. Even if she were, there was a world of difference between gathering intelligence for the greater good of one's country—ransacking the papers of traitors and state enemies, or worse!—and fingering through the personal effects of a private and exceedingly virtuous citizen.

But what if she returned empty-handed?

She would be sacked, turned out, left without protection. Her uncle's schemes interrupted, her own identity perhaps exposed, her beloved people left under the rule of revolutionary despots. The effects of failure went far beyond the injured privacy of Lady Somerton.

A head of state must sometimes do the unthinkable on behalf of his country. She could hear her father's voice as if he were in the room, speaking in her ear. *It is the greatest burden of leadership.*

She fingered the hairpin, took a deep breath, and stuck it in the lock.

The burled wood brushed her knuckles, sleek with polish. An elegant, well-made desk: It reminded her of her own bureau, back in Holstein Castle, left locked just like this one. Had some member of the Revolutionary Brigade of the Free Blood picked her lock? Read her private papers? Opened her drawers and found the acorns Stefanie had given her as a present, fifteen autumns ago? The little infant's cap she had begun knitting for her stepmother's expected baby, which had never required finishing? That first halting and endearingly awkward note from Peter, after their engagement?

Who the devil *was* she, anymore? What had she become?

Luisa slid the hairpin back out of the lock and straightened her spine.

"What are you doing?"

Luisa jumped and turned, all in the same motion. "Wh-what?"

Young Philip stood by the window, watching her with his dark and solemn eyes. How long had he been there? For God's sake, a moment ago he'd been walking in the square gardens. She'd seen him dash through the gate with her own eyes. "I said, what are you doing in my mother's room?"

"I . . . No . . . I . . ." Luisa ran a frantic hand over her hair and eyed the distance to the doorway. "Shouldn't you be with your mother?"

"Mama's downstairs. I forgot my marbles. Have you lost something, too?" His innocent young voice lifted inquisitively.

Luisa's thoughts dashed in circles. She forced them to slow down, forced herself to breathe. He was just a five-year-old boy, after all. A stranger to logic. "No! That is . . ."—an idea flashed—"that is, yes. Yes, I have. I'm looking for something. Your father asked me to fetch something of your mother's, but he forgot to tell me where it was. Isn't that silly?"

He smiled. "That's silly. What is it?"

"It's a . . . it's a . . . it's a grown-up . . . a grown-up thing, Philip."

"Oh." Disappointment.

"So I'm trying to think where it might be. Where she might keep it. It's something very special, something she loves very much and likes to keep safe. So of course it's tucked away somewhere. I was just wondering where."

"Oh." He jiggled something in his hand. The marbles, no doubt. "Just wait here and I can ask her." He turned to the door.

"No! No, let's not trouble her. It's supposed to be a surprise."

Philip nodded sympathetically. "I like surprises."

"Yes. So I'll just run down to ask your father, and . . ."

"Father won't know. He never comes up here."

"I'm sure that's not true, Philip."

"Yes, it is. He never comes up here."

Luisa turned the hairpin over and over in her palm. "I expect he comes up at night, after you're asleep."

Philip tilted his head, considering.

"Off with you, now. You . . . well, you'll keep our secret, won't you?"

"I can keep a secret." He paused in doubt. "Unless Mama asks me."

"Yes, of course. If she asks you outright, you must tell her the truth, Philip." Luisa slipped the hairpin back into her pocket. For some reason, her eyes stung with tears.

"I've got to be a man of my word, after all. That's what Mama says."

"Yes, you do. She's right, that's the most important thing in the world. Now go enjoy your games in the park."

"All right. You'll let me know when you're going to surprise her, won't you?" He smashed his cap back on his head and wiggled it into a position of comfort.

"Oh, of course."

He grinned and turned to the door. "I'll bet she puts it in her treasure box."

"Her what?"

He was already trotting out the door, marbles rattling. "Her treasure box in the wardrobe! She lets me play pirates with it as long as I put all the jewelry back when . . ." The rest of his words were lost in the hallway.

Luisa stood without moving, right in the center of the countess's austere blue and cream bedroom.

Oh, damn. Now why on earth did the little chap have to go and say that?

NINE

Lord Somerton and his companion prowled between the tables of the Sportsmen's Club dining room, spreading silence like a virulent miasma in their wake.

His lordship was not unaware of the effect. He knew his fellow members cordially disliked him, that he had only been accepted inside the hallowed walls because the relevant committee members had feared for their lives otherwise. He knew they would in fact draw such a collective sigh of relief as to rattle the trophies in their cases, should he be so good as to tender his resignation. He had long since ceased giving a damn.

Damned scoundrel, someone muttered behind him, a trifle too loudly.

"You'll find the wine is excellent, the food mediocre, and the company mewling," he said, as the waiter led forth to the snug table in the back corner, "but a London club, however ossified its membership, is nonetheless vastly preferable to a mere public dining room."

Though Somerton was normally quite capable of lowering his voice to a discreet hum, indecipherable from more than a foot away, he didn't bother lowering it now.

"I quite agree," said his companion, lowering himself into

the proffered chair. "Though I have never been so fortunate as to have been offered membership."

"I am hardly surprised. The sons of privilege are never more close ranked than when confronted with a man with the balls to make his own fortune." He took pleasure in putting a slight emphasis on the *balls*, so that the word projected halfway across the room and bounced about like a rubber quoit off the horrified faces of the assembled diners.

Mr. Nathaniel Wright, founder and chairman of that colossus of British finance, Wright Holdings, Ltd., was unperturbed. "Or to have been born to parents so careless as to have neglected to marry each other."

"Ah, but the old earl who sired you had no choice, had he? Divorce is such a distasteful affair, and he could hardly commit bigamy." Somerton smiled, to make sure Wright caught the humor in his words. So many people unaccountably missed it.

"Certainly not in order to perform the entirely unnecessary duty of marrying the daughter of a tea shop owner, who merely happened to be carrying his child." Wright's face contained all the warmth and expression of a plaster of Paris mask.

Somerton rather liked that in a man.

When the plates had been cleared and the wine finished off, and the waiters had brought out the cigars and brandy and retired to a respectful distance, Somerton reduced his voice to a confidential drawl.

"I am so glad, Mr. Wright, that I was able to supply my little mite of assistance in that affair of yours," he said.

Wright took a slow draw of his cigar. "Indeed. I'm grateful."

"Have you reached a satisfactory conclusion?"

"I suppose that remains to be seen. The immediate object, however, has been achieved. The young man in question is about to find himself in a very tight spot indeed. He's an ingenious fellow, however, and I'm not at all certain he won't find a way to wiggle out of it." Wright tapped a thoughtful crumb of ash into the tray and waved aside a lingering curl of smoke. "Do you know, I rather hope he does. Wiggle out of it, I mean. Either way, I shall be fascinated to observe the performance."

"Good, good." Somerton tried to summon up a measure of sympathy for the beleaguered young Lord Hatherfield—God knew, he himself had some experience with tight spots and overbearing fathers—and failed. In professional matters, he had long since acquired a hardened detachment to the fates of his subjects. Work was work, after all. Someone had to do the dirty tasks in a civilized society. Someone had to blacken his fingers.

"And you, Somerton?" Wright rolled the brandy lazily in its snifter and observed Somerton's face with his patient gray eyes. "Is there anything I can do to return the favor?"

"How good of you to ask, Mr. Wright. In fact, as it happens, I do have a matter of my own that might better be handled outside the influence of official channels."

"Indeed."

"You impress me, Mr. Wright, as a man of both discretion and initiative. A man on whom—and I never render this judgment lightly—a man on whom I can rely."

Wright lifted his left eyebrow an inquisitive quarter inch, and nodded cordially.

Somerton took this as an indication of acquiescence. "You have some influence in shipping matters, I believe."

"I run a mere humble countinghouse, Lord Somerton, not a shipping empire."

Somerton regarded Wright's sleek dark hair, his rigid and blinding shirtfront, his fine wool dinner jacket stretched over his broad shoulders, blackest black, identical to Somerton's own. The scent of hushed expense that wafted from his substantial figure. "But shipping empires, to use your words, come to you for capital, do they not? Capital to buy more ships, capital to finance cargoes."

"From time to time, they do."

"So if, for example, and speaking hypothetically . . ."

"Hypothetically, of course." Wright took a drink of his brandy and picked up his cigar.

"Hypothetically, if one wished to arrange a berth for a certain passenger and his luggage, quite at the last minute and without any questions asked as to the content of said luggage, you might find yourself in a position to effect this removal?"

"Discreetly, I presume."

"Discreetly, of course."

Another drink of brandy. "To which continent, sir?"

"Let us say, for the sake of argument, to South America." Somerton made an expansive gesture with his hand, drawing a thin blue curl of cigar smoke in the air.

"And when would this voyage take place?"

"*If* it were to take place, it would be soon. Perhaps before the end of the week."

Wright let out a low gentlemanly whistle.

"Too soon?" Somerton asked.

"Not necessarily. Hypothetically, I suppose I might be able to pull a string or two. Call in the odd favor."

"My dear fellow, I am vastly pleased to hear it."

"I would have one condition, however, were such a proposal to be made. A concern to be laid at rest, as a point of honor."

"Name it."

"I will not, under any circumstances, commit an action that would in any way, or to any degree, prove to the detriment of Great Britain, Lord Somerton." Wright set down his empty brandy snifter precisely in the center of the table and fixed Somerton with the kind of gaze that might melt the walls of an iron safe. The rich scent of cigar smoke teemed between them.

Somerton smiled. "I assure you, Mr. Wright, I am most fervently of the same mind."

"Very good." Wright stubbed out his cigar, rose to his feet, and tilted his body in the most perfunctory of bows. "Thank you for the excellent dinner, your lordship. I look forward to hearing from you when your plans are more definite."

When he had gone, Somerton reached inside his waistcoat pocket for the note that had arrived yesterday with the morning post.

One hears that Lord R. P. may be planning a voyage of indefinite length in the coming weeks, and he will not be traveling alone.

He placed the note in the ashtray next to Wright's cigar stub and held his own over the paper until a tiny trail of smoke wisped upward from the top right corner. A flash of orange flared and spread quickly across the message, leaving only a small pile of dust to merge with the remains of the cigars.

Three or four months ago, Somerton might have finished off such a satisfactory meeting with an hour or two in a whore's bed, or perhaps a prearranged engagement with someone's restless wife, followed by a few more hours of drinking and gambling at some den of suitable iniquity.

Three or four months ago, in fact, he had. It was October, and the night had smelled of frost when he emerged up the area stairs of the Duke of Southam's town house in Cadogan Square, dogged with a dissatisfaction that had little to do with Her Grace's disappointing performance in bed. Like most famous beauties, the duchess proved the old saw that the hunt was more interesting than the kill, and since the duchess was a long-practiced adulteress, even the hunt had been brief and lackluster at best. As a rule, Somerton preferred to seduce wives who had never strayed before: so much more challenging, such a frisson of danger and betrayal, such an explosion of untapped passion. The more virtuous the lady, the more headlong her capitulation. In that first slick entry between a pair of forbidden legs, he felt, at least for a fleeting moment, that his world had righted itself.

But the dissatisfaction had always returned, and this time more than ever. The duke was an old self-important fool who deserved to be cuckolded, his wife was even worse, and yet Somerton couldn't shake the sensation that he had done something wrong. That his soul had gone so far off its kilter, it might never recover. And as he had walked down Cadogan Gardens in the chill October air, and the brown leaves had swirled around him in the London midnight, and a pair of drunken gentlemen staggered past, Somerton had felt colder and colder in his fine wool coat, and sicker and sicker, and he had found a sewer drain and retched up brandy and bile until his stomach seemed to have turned inside out.

Afterward, instead of proceeding in the direction he had intended, where a table and a bottle awaited him, along with a pack of cards and a pack of identically dark-souled men, he turned around and staggered down Sloane Street in the direction of his own house.

He couldn't approach his wife like this, only minutes out of another woman's bed, green-faced and defeated. But perhaps in the morning, fortified by coffee, he might head upstairs to the nursery and begin a conversation of some sort. A few words, to bridge this years-wide chasm between them. To rest one knee at the altar of her virtue, and ask for God's blessing from her.

When he turned the corner of Chester Square, his steps had quickened. He felt warmer already, and a kind of peace had invaded that region of his belly that had heaved itself almost into oblivion a short while ago.

Then Somerton saw him.

A tall figure, wearing a dark hat, lingering outside the area gate of Somerton's own mansion, the way Somerton had lingered briefly at the area gate of the Duke of Southam. Just like Somerton, the man had pulled his hat farther down his forehead, turned, cast a last glance upward at the magisterial windows above, and walked briskly away.

Somerton's feet had screwed themselves into the ground. Had he wanted passionately to move them, he could not. He could only stand there helpless as the figure approached, as the head ducked away at the last instant, and the Adonis features of Lord Roland Penhallow burned once more into the tissue of his brain.

The next morning, instead of climbing the stairs to the nursery, he had sent a message around the usual channels to Mr. Norton.

He had not, however, returned to his old nocturnal habits. Whenever he contemplated another seduction, or another businesslike transaction with a well-trained whore, the taste of vomit had risen most inconveniently in the back of his throat. The sensation of sickness and decay was so great, he sometimes had to sit and put his head between his knees, to draw in several slow breaths of air, until the wave of nausea passed at last.

Now, on this frigid February night, he emerged from the Sportsmen's Club to find the piles of gray slush freezing in place on the pavement, and the streets unaccountably devoid of hackneys. It was hardly yet eleven o'clock, yet he knew better than to consider a visit to Cousin Hannah, or to the faithful old Black Seal in St. Katharine Docks.

Instead, he turned his steps to Piccadilly and a cold trudge homeward, huddled in his overcoat, knife and pistol tucked securely in the inner pockets, and when at last he arrived in his study, his mind was calm enough to take in the sight of the jewel box in the center of the leather blotter without any inconvenient physical symptoms.

He stood a moment, without moving, as if to memorize the details. In reality, the carvings, the gilt design, the letters stamped on the lid—EHM, her maiden initials—drifted through his eyeballs without making any permanent impression inside.

He sent a glance around the room, to see if Mr. Markham were sitting in one of the chairs by the fireplace, or the window seat at the opposite wall, but no slim, brown-suited secretary rose up to greet him. Above him, the members of his household slept quietly on their various floors. He was quite alone.

So he walked carefully around the side of the desk and sat down in his comfortable leather chair, and without any weakwilled hesitation he opened the lid of the box.

He recognized a few of the pieces. He had given them to her himself. Throughout the course of their marriage, he had never shirked that essential duty of an aristocratic husband; at every birthday, every Christmas, he had presented her with a bauble appropriate to her station, always more expensive than the one he gave to his current mistress, if he had one. Now he picked through the glittering mess of familiar diamond bracelets and pendant sapphires, the rings and brooches, until he found the false bottom and lifted the tray upward to reveal the object that lay beneath.

He lifted it up into the light.

The miniature was a fair likeness, he acknowledged, though it failed to capture the mischievous glint in Penhallow's hazel eyes, the charming, idiotic flop of golden brown hair that invariably made its way onto his brow. Moreover, you couldn't see those muscular shoulders that had powered

Oxford to victory in the 1882 Boat Race, nor the negligent posture he assumed as he leaned against some fluted Grecian column in a London ballroom, expecting worship the way other men expected breakfast.

Still, the beauty was all there, the perfect features, the damned happy smile. Why shouldn't he smile? He'd been sitting at the bottom of the jewel box of the most beautiful woman in London, the wife of one of its most powerful aristocrats. Why the devil shouldn't he be as happy as a clam, as the cat who stole the cream.

Damn you, Markham. He mouthed the words rather than said them.

Markham didn't answer. Markham had simply deposited this box and left the room, so that Somerton might examine its contents alone.

Perhaps that was for the best, after all.

And yet. He felt the strangest surge of yearning in his belly for the secretary's straightforward, thin shoulders, his quiet posture, his guiltless face and patient brown eyes. The warmth and promise of his clean young limbs.

He picked up the jewel box and flung it against the wall. It struck with a thud rather than a crash, and rolled unharmed into the Oriental rug, surrounded by its sparkling contents. For a moment he stood, not breathing, and then he walked over and picked up each piece, one by one, and put them all back where they belonged.

A warm, wet tongue lapped Luisa's nose and cheeks, drawing her upward out of a deep and dream-clogged sleep.

"Quincy!" She flung her arm around the dog. "What the devil? Is it morning?"

The room was dark; not the slightest hint of light emerged from the cracks of the heavy velvet drapes. Quincy went on licking her ear with businesslike strokes, until she was gasping with unwilling laughter.

"Stop it. Stop it, I say!" She struggled to her elbows and blinked to recall herself. For a moment, she was surprised to see the room around her. She had been dreaming of home, of the colorful autumn Schweinwald set against the violet mountains,

except that the man galloping at her side was built on a different
scale than lanky Peter, and his hair was velvet black . . .

She bowed her head into the sheets. She wasn't Princess
Luisa; she was Markham. This wasn't her light-filled chamber
facing the grand panorama of Holstein province; this was a
dark and stately room in a London town house, and she was
wearing blue-striped flannel pajamas and a thick linen bandage around her breasts, because the Earl of Somerton slept
on the other side of the wall, in all his masculine majesty.

Quincy licked her hand. She looked down, where his furry
shape made a dark smudge against the bedspread. She reached
out and felt for her pocket watch on the bedside table, but it
was too dark to see the face.

Quincy yipped urgently, bumping her hand with his head.

"What's the matter, love?" she whispered. "Go back to
sleep."

The dog turned and leapt off the bed and ran to the hallway
door. She couldn't see him in the blackness, but she could hear
his paws click on the wooden floorboards as he turned in
impatient circles below the knob.

Luisa smothered a yawn. "Quincy, for God's sake. Can't
you wait until morning?"

Clickety-clickety-click. Quincy landed back on the bed in
an explosion of furry urgency. He butted his head against her
chest, he raised himself up and smothered her face with
sweeping licks of his long tongue.

"All right, all right!" she whispered fiercely. She set him
aside and swung her legs off the bed. Her robe lay on the armchair next to the wardrobe; she shrugged herself into it, shoved
her feet into her slippers, and trudged to the door, where
Quincy was lifting himself into the air in ecstatic pirouettes.
She turned the knob, and Quincy squeezed out the crack and
shot down the hallway toward the stairs like a greyhound.

The lights had been put out long ago, but enough glow
remained from the streets outside to guide her down the grand
staircase to the entrance hall. Quincy stood waiting at attention on the marble tiles, head tilted to one side, wondering at
the vastness of her lethargy.

"I shall have to find the key to the garden door," Luisa
began, but Quincy was already darting off, not in the direction

of the garden, but down the hall to the earl's private study. "Quincy! What on earth?"

He turned around, whined, and scampered the rest of the way to the study door, from which, Luisa could now see, a dim bar of light glowed at the bottom.

"Oh, Quincy," she whispered.

He danced and whined, staring back at her plaintively.

Luisa's heart tripped. She hurried after the dog, inhaling the cold air of the hallway in anxious gasps. He would have found the jewel box by now. What had he done?

"Is something wrong, Quincy? Is he all right? Has he hurt himself?"

Oh, please God. Not that.

She grasped the handle, and in her haste and panic, it was not until she had actually begun the motion of flinging open the door that she heard the delicate strains of the cello within.

For a moment, she didn't see him. He wasn't sitting at the desk, his usual posture. The fire was nearly out, the room chilly, filled only with a music of gaping loneliness, of abandonment. A pungent spiciness note saturated the air, the scent of Scotch whiskey.

The notes were coming from the corner near the window. She turned slowly. Quincy settled at her feet with a relieved sigh.

He played with his eyes closed and his jaw set, at an angle away from her. He must have known she was in the room, but he showed no sign of it: not a flinch, not the slightest curious movement in her direction. His arm plied the bow, and the sensitive wood called out in sorrow.

Luisa could not have said how long she stood there. When the last low note dissolved into the whiskey-scented air, she hardly dared to breathe. Somerton sat without moving, head lowered, resting the tip of his bow on the edge of the red-patterned Oriental rug, as if listening to the dying echoes of the music, and then he picked up the glass on a nearby shelf and drained it.

"What were you playing?" she whispered.

He didn't answer. He lifted his bow and loosened the hair, and then he plucked a cloth from the open case beside him and wiped first the bow and then the strings of the cello itself. He propped the instrument against the chair and walked, with a kind of studied steadiness, to the tray of drinks, where he refilled his glass.

"Something to drink, Markham?"

"No, thank you." She tightened the belt of her robe and slid her hands into the pockets.

He made his way to the desk and sat down in his accustomed place, from which he controlled his immense wealth, his vast networks of spies, his intricate schemes, his web of power. He set down the drink and put his head in his hands and stared at the jewel box before him.

"My lord," Luisa said, in a low voice.

"She never loved me," he said.

Luisa bowed her head.

"Her heart is closed to me. It always was." He picked up the drink and swirled the liquid in a gentle circle about the sides. "I remember the day we married, the way she looked at my damned beak of a nose, my plain face, as if she were looking at a corpse. As if she were attending her own funeral."

"Sir . . ."

"I was madly in love with her. I saw her at a garden party, and I knew I had to have her. I had to make her mine. And do you know what she did?"

"No, sir."

"She went off with Penhallow. Before I could secure an introduction, he had taken her off in the shrubbery. I never stood a chance, did I? A handsome chap like him, a smooth-skinned, lyric-tongued Adonis." He took a drink. "But I got him out of the way, didn't I? I gave her parents a hundred thousand pounds for her. An offer no one could refuse."

"Oh my God." Luisa's throat closed; she had to swallow, twice, to allow herself to breathe.

"I did my best. I swear I did. I was never any good at wooing women, but I know how to give them pleasure in bed, and by God I gave her pleasure. And even that didn't work. It made her hate me more. She thought, you see, that if she endured me like the martyr she was, if she felt nothing, she could still be true to him. But I made her want me, and she hated me for it."

"She doesn't hate you," Luisa whispered.

He looked up at that, and the bleakness of his smile made

her ribs ache. "My dear Markham. I assure you, she does. When she got with child, I retired from her bed. I couldn't stand the way she looked at me afterward, as if I'd betrayed her by making her spend. She never said *no* to me. That was a point of pride with her. Oh no, she never said *no*; what a good, obedient wife. So I was the one who walked away. I never visited her bed again, from that day to this."

He rose from the desk in a lithe movement. How extraordinary, that a man built on such burly lines could move with such animal grace. Luisa watched him cross the room, tossing down the rest of his whiskey as he went, and when he couldn't go any farther he hurled the glass into the fireplace and pounded his two hands against the mantel.

"She never loved me. She never loved me at all."

Luisa stood near the door, brimming over. Quincy's wet nose nudged her ankle. In her mind, she heard the cello vibrate with agony, that searing phrase at the end, over and over.

She took one hesitant step, and another. Her feet were cold in her slippers, as if all the blood had gathered near her heart. When he did not object, or bark at her to go away and leave him in peace, she came closer, and closer, until she could feel his warmth tingle the tiny hairs on her skin.

She laid her palm against his white linen shirt.

A sound came from his chest, like the low howl of an animal, but she kept her hand in place on his back, counting the strikes of his magnificent heart, the slight contractions of muscle that told her he was sobbing.

"My son," he said. "I don't even know my son."

"Oh, my lord."

Somerton drew in a long breath and straightened. The glass case of the mantel clock reflected a portion of his face, his cheekbone and a single bleak eye.

"Go to bed, Markham. We will both endeavor to forget this hour."

"Sir, I can't . . ."

"Go to bed."

Luisa let her hand slide away, down the granite curve of muscle. She curled her fingers into a fist and stuck them back in her pocket, and then she walked slowly to the door, Quincy trotting at her heels.

At the last instant, with her hand on the knob, she stopped and turned her head. "You should sleep, sir."

He hadn't moved from his position at the fireplace, braced in place against the mantel. His dry and humorless laugh hurt her ears.

"Ah, Markham. I shall sleep in my grave."

TEN

The newspaper headline was thick and crisp: LOST PRIN-
CESS FINDS LOVE IN ENGLAND; SET TO WED
DUKE OF ASHLAND IN STORYBOOK ROMANCE;
ROYAL BALL TONIGHT IN PARK LANE TO CELE-
BRATE ENGAGEMENT; PRINCE AND PRINCESS OF
WALES EXPECTED TO ATTEND.

Below it, her sister Emilie's blurry face peeked out, empty
of her usual spectacles, from between the heavy charcoal-clad
shoulders of two giant men. One was the Duke of Olympia,
gray hair wisping from beneath the brim of his black top hat,
and the other was in the act of lifting his hat to reveal . . .

The paper flashed away from her hands.

"It's that thrilling," sighed out Annabelle, the new housemaid, holding the folded sheets above her porridge. "The most
romantic thing I ever heard. Imagine, a princess like that,
walking about London. Imagine if we was to bump shoulders
on the pavement, her and me."

"Imagine," said Luisa. She fought back the anxious jump
of her pulse and returned her attention to her breakfast, which
she now took below stairs, since that was where one discovered anything of interest about the household. Besides, the
flow of chatter, the companionable clink of chinaware and

cutlery gave her the comforting sensation of fellowship. Of belonging to a place and a set of people: not quite a family, but a well-meaning substitute for it.

Strange, really, how a simple shared half hour made one feel capable of almost anything. This morning, weighed down by thoughts of the countess's jewel box, by the deadly silence in the room next to hers, she had needed the reassurance of ordinary human contact more than ever.

And then the newspaper had appeared next to her plate, emblazoned with her sister's unsettling tidings.

"I think she's pretty. Don't you think she's pretty?" Annabelle tilted the paper helpfully.

Luisa smiled. "Oh, very pretty. Very lovely indeed."

"But that duke what she's marrying! Isn't he a sight! With that . . . that mask to one side of his face, like a pirate. And that white hair!"

"He might be blond."

Annabelle peered closely, nearly brushing the paper with her long nose. "No. No, I'm sure it's white. What a frightening cove he looks. I think she could do much better, and her a princess."

"I'm quite sure she could."

"He's fearfully rich, however. That's what Mrs. Plum says. I suppose that makes a difference, if you ha'n't got a proper fortune anymore, like her. Though he looks such a pirate, p'raps she means him to go back to her own country and fight the anarchists for her."

Luisa's fork froze at her lips.

"He'd settle their hash, wouldn't he, a great big fellow like him. He looks as if he might as well kill you as look at you."

"Yes," Luisa whispered. She lowered her fork back to her plate and stared at the remains of her breakfast.

Good Lord. Why hadn't she thought of it before?

If she could win Somerton over. Confide in him, convince him to take her side. He'd take action faster than Olympia, that was certain. None of this waiting about, fiddling with spies and intelligence, waiting for the so-called right moment, as if such a thing existed when one's country was controlled by despot revolutionaries.

He'd settle their hash, wouldn't he?

If the upright and honorable Duke of Ashland could make anarchists cower in his path, what might an all-powerful and entirely unscrupulous Earl of Somerton achieve?

But would he help her at all? Could she trust him with her secret? What promises would he ask in return? What could she offer him, other than herself? What might he take for himself, if he rousted out the Brigade by his own hand?

"But the thing I wonder is," said Annabelle, oblivious to the racing thoughts in Luisa's head, "where has the other princesses got to?"

"What's that?" Luisa forced her hand in the direction of her teacup.

"The other princesses. This one's turned up, but where are the others?"

"I . . ." Luisa drank a sip of tea. "I can't imagine."

"I daresay they're hiding out somewhere, in some poor cottage in the moors," said Annabelle.

Polly piped up from the other side of the table. "I think they're in some crumbly old castle by the sea, huddling around a single peat fire and attended by a loyal old servant and a . . ."

Annabelle clucked her tongue. "You're reading too many of them novels, Polly Green, that's what. What do you think, Mr. Markham?"

Luisa swallowed the rest of her tea, dabbed her mouth with her napkin, and rose to her feet. "I think I'm likely wanted upstairs by now. If you'll excuse me."

The Earl of Somerton, as she suspected, was already dressed and sitting in the chair before his desk when she strode through the doorway five minutes later. The gilded jewel box still sat to one side, next to the leather blotter, gleaming in the morning sunshine. He looked up with his characteristic expression of glowering disapproval, as if—as he had suggested—last night's meeting had been banished from his mind.

"Mr. Markham. How good of you to join me." He cast a pointed gaze at the clock above the mantel.

She followed it. "It's only a quarter past eight, sir. I'm not expected until eight thirty."

"Having left such a parcel for me to discover last night," he said, nodding at the box, "did you not then consider the necessity of arriving early this morning, in order to deal with the consequences?"

"I did not, sir, as I cannot directly read minds, despite my multitude of other talents."

"Insolence, as usual, primary among them. No, don't sit. I have an errand for you."

"I am at your service, of course."

Somerton returned his attention to the paper before him. The scratch of pen filled the vast stillness of the study, in a percussive duet with the ticking clock. "You will this evening, at half past seven o'clock, attend her ladyship, who I presume will be found in the nursery at this hour, reading to our son. You will present my compliments, and inform her that I require the honor of her company here in the study on a matter of great urgency."

Luisa cast an agonized glance at the jewel box and swallowed back the bitterness at the back of her throat. "Sir, I . . ."

"Did you not imagine that some account must be made of the contents? Or did you not trouble to inspect them?"

"I found the portrait, of course, but it doesn't necessarily mean . . ."

Somerton looked up. "I beg your pardon. Did I ask for your opinion on the meaning of another man's portrait in my wife's jewel box?"

"No, sir, but . . ."

He folded up the paper with brusque strokes of his fingers and reached for a stick of black sealing wax. He held it next to the blue flame of the gas lamp. "Then have the goodness to communicate this simple message to Lady Somerton at the appointed hour. In the meantime, you will take this note to Mr. Nathaniel Wright, of Wright Holdings, Limited, in London Wall." He pounded the seal into the melted wax and held out the note to her.

She held it between her fingers and examined the seal. "Rather archaic, isn't this?"

"A convenient way of ensuring that one's messages are read only by the intended recipient."

"Your lordship, I don't know what it is you're planning, but I must forcefully advise you—"

"Advise me? My own secretary, *advise* me?"

"—that revenge of this kind, for an offense of this kind, invariably hurts the man who inflicts it. Can you not contemplate—"

"What I cannot contemplate, Mr. Markham, is why you have the effrontery to imagine that I either care or heed what you have to say."

"Because I want you to be *happy*, sir!" The words exploded from her mouth and disappeared into the wood-paneled walls of the study. "I want you to be good," she finished in a whisper.

Somerton's face did not betray the slightest flicker of reaction. "How kind of you, Mr. Markham, to take such an interest. And since you demonstrate such a ravenous appetite for afternoons of leisure, you may take the rest of the day off once you've delivered Mr. Wright's note, so long as you return in time to deliver the message to her ladyship."

"That's not necessary. I . . ."

"I shall see you here this evening at half past seven o'clock, Mr. Markham."

The voice of finality.

Luisa tucked the note into her inside jacket pocket. Her mouth had gone dry. "Will there be anything else?"

Somerton smiled his mirthless smile, baring his even white teeth. "I think that's sufficient for one morning, don't you?"

The Duke of Olympia held the paper above the steaming teakettle with a pair of efficient steel tongs.

"This does not sit well with my conscience," said Luisa.

"You'll find that sort of squeamishness dries away soon, my dear. You've done the right thing, bringing this to me."

She watched him tilt the note to a precise near-vertical angle. His hands were perfectly steady. "Only because I'm afraid of what he might be planning. What it will do to him—to all of us—if he succeeds."

"Yes, he is a rather unscrupulous chap, isn't he? But not beyond reform, I believe." Olympia lifted the paper away from the teakettle and popped away the seal with the tip of his knife.

"You're quite certain you know what you're doing? Won't this Mr. Wright know that the seal's been opened?" Luisa peered anxiously over his brown-tweed shoulder. She had found him out riding in Hyde Park, as he usually did at ten o'clock in the morning, in case she had any message to communicate too urgent to wait for Sunday afternoon.

Not that she had accosted him directly, of course. She had made the agreed-upon signal and proceeded to the agreed-upon pub on a street near Piccadilly, where a secretary on his business about town might reasonably be expected to wet his thirst on a pint of good English ale. This was the first time she had visited this agreed-upon back room behind the agreed-upon wood panel, and she was suitably impressed by the efficient array of professional tools laid about the cabinets and walls. Including, it seemed, a teakettle and a humble gas hob.

"Quite certain," said Olympia. He read quickly, refolded the note, and opened a small drawer filled with neat rows of sealing wax in various colors.

Luisa made a noise of outrage. "You're not going to let me see it?"

"Of course not. It has nothing to do with your situation, my dear."

"Then what *has* it got to do with?"

"Matters that do not concern you."

She put her hands to her hips. "Uncle, I am a head of state, if you'll remember. Besides, I'm quite sure it has something to do with poor Cousin Roland."

"You're quite right about that. But there's nothing to fear. Lord Somerton is only doing exactly what I hoped, and exactly when I hoped it. It's all going quite according to plan." Olympia was rummaging through a cardboard box filled with seals, examining each one. "With any luck, Penhallow will be safely out of the country within a fortnight, and—"

"With Lady Somerton?"

"Questions, questions. Ah! Here we are." Olympia held up a seal triumphantly and set the box aside. With his other hand, he held the wax stick next to the hob, until it gleamed a rich tar black.

"Well, is he?"

"I suppose that remains to be seen, doesn't it? In any case, none of these activities has to do with your own case. Another matter entirely, and one of the highest possible secrecy." He stamped the seal into the wax and held out the note to her. "Now, off you go, and never fear."

"But you've already involved me. I need to know—"

Olympia shrugged his overcoat back over his shoulders and replaced his hat on his gleaming gray head. "My dear, you have it all wrong. The less you know, the safer for everybody concerned. Most especially your own valuable self." He took her hand, kissed it, and winked. "Trust your old uncle, eh?"

The rest of the afternoon off.

Luisa sank into her chair and removed her gloves. Her hands, so cold in the bitter February air outside, now prickled with perspiration in the typically overheated atmosphere of another of the ubiquitous ABC tea shops.

What had Somerton meant by that? Nothing good, of course. He must be planning something particularly dastardly, if he wanted her away from the premises, unable to interfere.

She should interfere. She should go back right now and . . . what?

She looked down at the cup of tea before her, the anemic watercress sandwich. Actually, she detested watercress. She wasn't quite sure how she had come to order it; she had been moving along like an automaton ever since leaving Olympia's secret Mayfair bolt-hole at noon. She hardly remembered delivering Somerton's note. If someone had asked her to describe the offices of Wright Holdings, Limited, or indeed Mr. Wright himself, she would have answered, with difficulty, that both the offices and the man were discreetly magnificent.

He had given her a sharp and searching look. That had nearly jolted her out of herself, awakening her protective instincts with a start. Gray eyes, very keen, the only vivid memory she had of the entire errand.

No doubt he'd been curious because she had insisted on delivering the note in person, had had him pulled from some sort of meeting that was no doubt essential to the delicate nerves of Britain's financial markets. "From Lord Somerton," she had said, thrusting the note toward him.

He had broken the seal, read the note, and looked back at her in that examining way.

"Will there be any reply?" she said, eager to be done with the whole sordid task.

"Does his lordship expect one?"

"I am not privileged to know that, sir."

"My compliments to his lordship, then," Mr. Wright had said, or something like that, and he had turned without another glance and walked back to his meeting, without even the courtesy of offering her refreshment.

They were all alike, weren't they? Somerton and his friends. Not a worthy bone in their bodies.

She'd been a fool, really. Allowing herself, over the past few months, to develop a sort of sympathy for him, mired in his loveless marriage, his proud loneliness. Yes, she could admit it now. It was perfectly natural, after all. She'd lost her sisters, her husband, the extraordinary privilege of her life in Holstein Castle. Her commanding father, to whom she had always looked in hushed admiration, desperate for a crumb of approval or affection. She'd been cast into constant intimacy with the Earl of Somerton, who despite the errors of his character was a man who radiated power and a kind of dark charisma, whose shoulders were broad and thick and whose austere face she'd caught herself studying far too often. Whose soul seemed to contain an aching hole of which she had been allowed only the briefest and most tantalizing of glimpses.

Compelling. He was compelling.

Only natural, then, that she—a healthy young woman of childbearing age, deprived of her own near male relatives—should find herself . . .

Attracted to him.

There. She admitted it.

She curled her hands around her teacup. Her stomach rumbled, though not quite insistently enough to make the watercress sandwich the least bit tempting. She hadn't finished her breakfast, she remembered. She really should eat something.

She picked up the sandwich and nibbled at the edge. The taste of butter and tired watercress rested on the tip of her tongue, not quite so unpleasant as she'd feared. She took another bite and swallowed.

She had to find another situation. That much was clear. She would come back this evening, collect Quincy and her things, and be gone by morning. She could go to the house in Battersea and wait there for Olympia or Miss Dingleby. She would demand, in any case, that they allow her inside their plans.

She would be an active participant in her own rescue, from now on.

Another bite of sandwich, and another. The bread was really quite good. Almost enough to counterbalance the watercress, which had not been sprinkled plentifully anyway.

A small black fly landed on the edge of her saucer and crawled a cautious quarter inch down the slope, before dashing away.

The rest of the afternoon off.

Well, Luisa? She drummed her fingers on her teacup. *What are you going to do with the hours allotted to you? Sit and stew in an Aerated Bread Company tea shop?*

Or do something?

In a brisk motion, she stuffed the rest of her sandwich in her mouth, bolted the rest of the tea, and wiped her mouth.

"Thank you," she said to the approaching waitress, and she tossed a shilling on the table and walked out of the shop.

ELEVEN

The Duke of Olympia's London house occupied a prime slice of Park Lane, a hundred or so yards to the north of Wellington's noble posture. Luisa leaned against the rough bark of a tree in the park opposite, London *Baedeker's* in hand, and studied the stately ducal windows over the crisp edges of her guidebook.

Her heart beat smartly in her chest. She could almost taste its energy at the back of her throat. Somewhere behind one of those heavy-draped windows sat her sister Emilie, perhaps reading a book, perhaps pacing the elegant floorboards of her allotted room. Perhaps sitting with her duke, the one with the strange mask and the white hair. Perhaps peering out the window and wondering who stood outside.

Despite the cold February air, the unfashionable time of year, the house was bustling. A stream of people eddied around the entrance steps, laden with flowers and parcels and musical instruments. Several vehicles lay alongside the curb, horses' necks all lowered at the same resigned angle. Just outside the massive front entrance, a man in livery directed the flow of traffic, stopping each man, delivering instructions. All this activity must be preparation for the ball tonight, for Emilie's engagement ball. No doubt the mews entrance at the rear was even busier.

If Luisa knew where Emilie was—if all London's trades-men apparently knew what was taking place at the Duke of Olympia's town house tonight—then so did the conspirators. Those agents of the Revolutionary Brigade, who were sup-posed to be in England this instant, hunting the princesses down—where were they now? Were they among the alarming swarm of men entering and leaving that grand marble portal? Were they among the drivers hunched atop the delivery vans just outside, any one of which might contain enough ordnance to blow up the Houses of Parliament?

Or that portly fellow walking up the path, looking occa-sionally to the right, for example. Was he glancing with a tour-ist's curiosity at the magnificent houses bordering Hyde Park? At the extraordinary activity along Park Lane? Or did his gaze have a more sinister purpose?

Olympia claimed that Emilie was safe and well guarded in his house, but if that was the case, why hadn't he kept the three of them here from the beginning? How could Emilie possibly remain safe in the middle of all that anonymous and business-like humanity?

The man walked by, continuing toward Marble Arch without a pause. Luisa watched his wide woolen backside diminish inno-cently between the trees. At the last instant, just before her head and her attention turned back to the house across the street, she caught a glimpse of movement from the edge of her vision.

Slowly, idly, so as not to draw any particular attention, she adjusted her posture against the tree and returned her gaze to the section of path to her left.

Trees, a few hurried walkers. A woman in a smart black coat and cap, pushing an infant's high-wheeled perambulator.

Perhaps she'd imagined it. Or perhaps it was just another walker, someone lingering for a second or two to light a ciga-rette or . . .

A man stepped out from behind a tree, gazed across the street, and tugged his ear.

Luisa reached up and settled her hat farther down on her forehead. A little gust of wind made the bare winter branches creak and scrape above her. She turned her head back to her *Baedeker's*, feigning study, and discovered that she was hold-ing the book upside down.

From the corner of her eye, she saw the man tug his ear again and lean back against a tree, one foot propped against the trunk.

Luisa pulled her watch out of her pocket, glanced at the face without seeing, and strolled to a nearby bench. A man sat at the other end, head turned back, snoring softly. She eased herself downward and crossed one trousered leg over the other. Over the top of the guidebook—now right side up—she observed the house on Park Lane.

The bustle went on. One fellow dropped a flat of orchids—a bit excessive, orchids in February, but a princess didn't get engaged every day—and the resulting fuss occupied the entire considerable breadth of the entrance steps. A bottleneck formed in the efficient flow of men and goods from pavement to house. Someone swore, so fluently and loudly that the words carried right through the cold winter wind, between the delivery vans and a half-empty omnibus, to land squarely in Luisa's ears.

Next to her, the sleeping man startled upward, clutching his dislodged cap with woolen fingers, and glanced across the street.

Luisa turned a page in her guidebook. A pair of bicycles rattled by, obstructing her view for a second or two, and when Olympia's house reappeared, a tall, broad figure had emerged from the doorway and was skirting around the orchid-scented pandemonium on the steps to dodge casually around the traffic on Park Lane.

His hat, like hers, was pulled low on his forehead, and she couldn't quite glimpse his face. But the ears, large and protrudent as the wings of a giant butterfly, she knew well. Likewise the chin, which she had stroked a hundred times, fiddling curiously with the stubble, trying to nudge that wide mouth into a smile.

Usually, she had succeeded. Hans was like another father to her, a warmer and more forgiving one, who kept sweets in his pockets and who, after dressing Prince Rudolf in his magnificent dress uniform, frogged in gold and shouldered by epaulettes the size of dinner plates, would invariably bring Luisa and her sisters around the minstrels' gallery to watch the colorful splendor of a state ball. Hans had acted as her father's valet since the day Prince Rudolf turned eighteen. He had trimmed his every whisker, had straightened his every necktie. He had dressed him for the last time, before laying the prince in his satin-lined coffin with his own strong hands.

He had guarded the princesses along that cold midnight journey to England. She and her sisters had walked through the shelter of the Duke of Olympia's door at three o'clock in the morning with Miss Dingleby leading the way and Hans standing watchfully at their backs.

Now he swung over the low park railing with one swipe of his long legs and joined the man at the tree, side by side, hands shoved in pockets, comrades in arms.

The man on the bench sat up, stretched his arms, and rose to his feet.

Luisa couldn't breathe. The muscles of her chest had frozen in fear and shock. She tilted her head away, so that she could scarcely see them in the outermost corner of her vision, and concentrated on her heartbeat, on drawing a single shallow breath into her lungs. She dropped her gaze to the pages before her and tried to read the words.

Hans. Surely not. Surely he was meeting with Olympia's men, surely they were all preparing for tonight's ball, readying themselves to trap the conspirators.

That was it.

Except that Hans couldn't speak more than a few words of English.

Well, no doubt he had picked up more since arriving here. He would have had to, wouldn't he? And Hans was clever enough. He could carry on a conversation by now, if he had applied himself diligently to the study of English.

The words blurred before her, the ink ran together. The snoring man was now ambling toward Hans and the other man, among the trees.

A bicycle went by, and another. The two riders shouted to each other.

Luisa rose to her feet and made as if she were trying to find her way to Marble Arch, looking up at the street and down again to her guidebook. The pages shook a little between her hands. She rolled her weight about on her feet, steadying herself.

Calm down, she thought sternly. This is Hans.

With an air of decision, she turned and walked north, staying on the graveled path, so she would pass behind the backs of the three men. She drifted close to the edge, as close as she could, and the low murmured voices rumbled in her ears.

Step, step, step. The voices grew louder, but their tone remained unintelligible, kept just below the range of ordinary conversation. As if deliberately hushed. English, or German? She couldn't be certain. The sounds were thick, a bit glottal, but wasn't English sometimes less than crisp, when spoken by bulky men in hushed voices? Wouldn't Hans's English—if he now spoke English—carry a heavy German accent?

Step, step. She was almost directly behind them now, as close as she would get. She strained her ears above the sound of her own shoes, crunch, crunch, crunching on the fine gravel.

Please, God. Let it be English.

The single word *Musiker* rose above the rumble, and passed into memory.

It took Luisa some time to locate the mews entrance to Olympia's town house. In the first place, the alley was naturally dark and narrow, made more so by the fading winter afternoon, clogged with London soot and smoke.

In the second place, she'd never seen it. She didn't even know the number. What use had she ever had for house numbers and mews entrances, when visiting her uncle before? A driver had navigated her to the house, a footman had ushered her in the front door with all the ceremony due her royal status. Except when she had arrived in October, of course, and even then she'd had Hans and Miss Dingleby to lead the way.

She paced down the rough-cobbled alleyway, counting the wide carriage doors, until she thought she had the right one. It was painted a sleeker shade of black than the others, and the familiar ducal crest decorated the area where the brass knocker would be, if carriage doors sported brass knockers. A large delivery wagon stood by, and as she approached, the entrance sprang open to admit a pair of men, laughing, carrying an empty crate between them.

"Excuse me," she said, "do you work for the Duke of Olympia?"

One of them swiveled his head in her direction. "Sorry, mate. Fruitmonger. But you can go on in, if you likes, and tell the big cove guarding the way that Sam Apples sent you." He winked.

"Thank you," she said.

"You can thank me later, if you like, lad," he muttered in her astonished ear, as she sidled past.

"Not bloody likely," she muttered back.

Inside, the stable area was dark and smelled of horseflesh and leather. A few white-flecked equine faces stared curiously at her from the stalls, as if trying to place her. As Sam Apples had suggested, a large man blocked the door at the back that led through the garden to the main house; she prayed he wasn't someone who might recognize her.

She strode up and spoke in her lowest voice. "Good afternoon. I have a message for Miss Dingleby."

"What's that?" He looked startled.

"A message for Miss Dingleby. She's a . . . an attendant of Her Highness." Luisa watched the man carefully: Did he recognize the name? Had she guessed correctly that Dingleby would be staying here in the same house as Emilie?

He paused and knitted his brows together. "What's your name, lad?"

"My name is Markham. I'm a friend. Could you tell her that I'm here to see her, with an important message?"

He bent down slightly—he really was an enormous beast, three or four inches above six feet—and peered at her face. "Markham, you said?"

"Yes. Mr. Markham. I'm the Earl of Somerton's private secretary."

He straightened and turned to the door. "Jack, the lad here says he needs to speak to that Dingleby woman, urgent-like."

The reply was unintelligible to Luisa, but the guard nodded and turned back to her.

"Wait here," he said, nodding at a stool between two stalls.

Luisa ignored the stool and reached for a horse instead. He was one of the duke's famous matched blacks, a big, sleek fellow designed to pull a crested landau in the company of three more identical animals. He nudged eagerly at her chest. "I haven't got anything for you," she said softly. "I suppose you've been cooped up all day, poor fellow."

She bent her face to his and absorbed the comfort of his breath, the raw power of him, now still and contained beneath her touch. For some reason, Somerton's image rose in her head. Black and sleek and magnificent, just like the horse, and filled with strength to be used for good or ill. Cooped up in his civilized cage for far too long.

"Mr. Markham."

Miss Dingleby's sharp voice shattered the dusty idyll.

Luisa released the horse and spun to meet her. "Miss Dingleby," she said. "Thank you for coming."

The governess's arms were like two iron bands across her chest. Her face, even in the semidarkness of the stable, was stern enough to scatter gravel. "What the devil are you doing here, Mr. Markham? This is no place for you. Today of all days, when I specifically instructed . . ."

"I've a message. An important one. I've . . ." Luisa cast a quick glance at the doorway, and lowered her voice. "I've discovered something rather important."

"What is it?"

Luisa reached out and took Miss Dingleby's sleeve. Evidently her old governess had yet to dress for the ball; the material was a serviceable blue wool, the sleeves long and businesslike. Luisa pulled her into the shelter of the horse's long black neck.

"The traitor," she whispered. "I've discovered the traitor."

The muscles of Miss Dingleby's face made a strange movement, a contortion. In the wavering light from the safety lantern hanging from the low mews ceiling, her expression looked almost demonic, all heightened eyebrows and narrowed eyes. "What's that? You've what?"

"The traitor." Luisa's voice nearly broke. "It's Hans."

Miss Dingleby dropped her arm away from Luisa's grip and set her hand on the edge of the stall door. The horse nudged her shoulder. "Are you certain of this?"

"I think so. Yes, quite certain. I was in Hyde Park, watching the house . . ."

"You did *what*?"

"I had to. I had to see for myself, to see that Emilie was safe."

"Stupid, stupid girl. You might have ruined everything. You were told . . ."

"I don't give a damn what I was told. I . . ."

"Lower your voice, for God's sake."

Luisa swallowed and continued, more calmly. "She is my responsibility. My own people are my responsibility. I can no longer sit back and allow you and Olympia to control the matter without my advice and consent. Yes, I came to Hyde Park, I watched the house. And I saw two men signaling the house from the park, and a man come out to join them. It was Hans, and they were speaking in German. Something about musicians."

Miss Dingleby muttered something under her breath. She turned to the horse and stroked his neck with her long-fingered hands, slow and thorough strokes, from cheek to withers. "Did any of them see you?" she asked at last.

"No. I'm quite sure they didn't."

"If they had, you wouldn't have known." She sighed and turned to Luisa. "Listen to me. Thank you for the information. I shall discuss this at once with Olympia and decide how to proceed."

"Very good. Lead the way."

Miss Dingleby held up her hand. "No. Not you. We haven't the time; we've got to adjust all our plans now, to—"

"To find Hans and force him to reveal who his fellow conspirators are—"

"Exactly."

"Because he has betrayed us, Dingleby, betrayed us all in the vilest manner. He was Father's valet, he was like a father to us." Luisa fought the tears back. "Let me in. I must talk to Olympia."

"No, my dear." Miss Dingleby's voice turned gentle. "You don't understand. You haven't the training, you don't know how these things work. We shall have to spend valuable resources in protecting you, and then where will we be? How will we explain your presence? Everything has been planned to the very last degree."

"What?" Luisa shook her head. "Do you mean to say you're still going through with it? Now that you know who the traitor is?"

"Of course we are. The point is to rid ourselves of the conspirators, and the ball will attract them all here, instead of having to go out and hunt them down. That was the point from the beginning. Hans's involvement, however distasteful, doesn't affect the scheme in the slightest, except perhaps to ready ourselves for the corner from which the attack might come."

"I don't understand. Why risk Emilie's life, when we know where to look for these men?"

"Of course you don't understand." Miss Dingleby laid her hand on Luisa's shoulder. "Your uncle will quite agree with me. Listen to me, my dear. Go back to your earl. Pack your things. Be ready for our signal. It's not impossible we will set out for Germany at dawn."

"At dawn!"

"If all goes well. If we can catch them all tonight. But we can't do that, Luisa, if we're not prepared. So return to Chester Square and wait, won't you? It's for the best. You're the Crown Princess, after all. We can't risk you, above all."

"But Emilie—"

Miss Dingleby smiled in the feeble light. "Emilie has the best protection in the world, I assure you. And so do you, if you'd trouble yourself to return to it."

At her words, Somerton's face appeared before Luisa again, the way it had looked in the gaslight all those weeks ago, when he'd just dispatched the footpad who had attacked her. Something gave way inside her, taking her breath. She would no longer have his protection again. No longer work quietly by his side, sharing space, existing together in the tolerant understanding of two people with much to hide. No longer take comfort in the nearness of his big body, his strength and loyalty interposed between her and the unknown threat outside the door.

She would slink away before daylight. She would return to Germany and regain her birthright, and Somerton would never know what had happened to his personal secretary.

She would not even have the chance to say a proper good-bye.

Luisa lifted her chin and ducked around the gelding's gleaming neck. The other horses, startled, turned their heads back in her direction.

"Very well, then, Dingleby," she said. "I shall expect your message by dawn tomorrow. And for God's sake, don't fail me."

Despite the Earl of Somerton's repeated protests, the damned dog insisted on occupying his lap.

"You've got no discernment, have you?" he growled at the beast. Quincy lifted his large ears and examined Somerton's expression the way a doctor might examine a patient. "I killed a man just last week, did you know that? A rather execrable scrap of humanity, to be sure, a filthy traitor and a liar to boot. But I killed him with my bare hands, and felt only a trace of remorse afterward."

Quincy licked his hand, which had unaccountably moved closer to the dog's small wet nose.

"No doubt you smelled it on me afterward. Murder must have its own particular smell, quite out of range of human sensation. Though I could have sworn I smelled it on him, that man, just before he struck. He was about to kill me, you know. Nearly did, the bastard."

Quincy heaved a thoughtful sigh and laid his nose on his paws, which were perched at the edge of Somerton's thighs.

"I've been distracted, you see. But it's all come to a head now, hasn't it? That damned Penhallow might have escaped by the skin of his neck the other week, but when the Bureau discovers that their chap at the Russian Embassy has departed for South America, and Penhallow's fingerprints all over it, why . . ." He glanced up at the clock above the mantel and frowned. "He's late, damn him. Markham is never late."

But just as the word *late* escaped his mouth, the door handle jerked abruptly downward.

Without an instant's pause, Somerton picked up the dog and dropped him on the floor next to the chair.

"Quincy!" exclaimed Markham, crouching on the floor and holding out his arms. His overcoat sparkled with rain. The corgi galloped across the rug and made one of those acrobatic little-dog leaps into his master's arms.

Somerton set his teeth against the warm surge of feeling in his chest, quite out of order.

"You're late," he said gruffly.

Markham rose slowly, Quincy clutched in his wet woolen arms. "I am not late. I am giving notice, effective immediately. I shall pack up my things and . . ."

The warm feeling in Somerton's chest smothered instantly, as if dashed with cold water.

"The devil you say," he snapped. "Where have you been all this time?"

"You gave me the afternoon off."

"The *afternoon* off. It's nearly eight o'clock."

"I had business." The young man lifted his chin to a haughty angle. "I was visiting my aunt in Battersea."

"Damn your Battersea aunt, and damn your business. You are still under my roof, and in my employ. You will take off that bloody wet coat and warm yourself, and you will march upstairs and inform her ladyship—"

"I will not!"

Somerton took two long strides and placed himself, scintillating, a foot away from Markham's defiant young body. Quincy looked up inquisitively between them. "You will," he whispered.

"You can't force me to do it."

There was something so brave and afraid about him, some new quality of desperation that seemed to have penetrated Mr. Markham's skin like the cold rain that gleamed on the tip of his nose. God, that bare and elegant face, so strong and delicate all at once. Why didn't he grow a set of whiskers, to hide all that beautiful vulnerability?

"Is something the matter, Markham?" he heard himself ask quietly.

Markham took a step backward. "Nothing."

"Nonsense. Something's happened. Was it your aunt?"

The young man hesitated. "Yes. Yes, she's not well, that's all."

"Is the condition dangerous?"

"I . . . I don't know. It's too early to tell. I ought to go back, I *need* to go back, I—"

"Can she afford a doctor?" The words came out a little more gruffly than Somerton intended.

Markham's eyes widened. "Yes, she can. She has . . . she has resources. I'm simply concerned, that's all. And wet."

"I shall send a message to my own physician to attend her at once. In the meantime, you will go upstairs and summon Lady Somerton, as you were instructed to do this morning." He kept his place, right there on the rug, glowering down at Markham. If he could just win the man over somehow. Make him understand, through sheer force of will; make him realize what Somerton himself could not articulate.

"I won't. I can't. I can't be a party to . . . to whatever it is between you. Find another servant to do your dirty work." He turned away, set Quincy to the floor, and slung off his coat. "One that's still employed by you."

"No, it must be you."

"Nonsense. Why me?" Markham tossed the coat over the door of the wardrobe and went to the fire, which had been built up not a quarter hour earlier by Somerton's own hand, not that he was prepared to reveal that humbling piece of information. Quincy trotted anxiously at his heels.

Somerton folded his arms and said, through his teeth, "Because you're my right hand. You are mine."

"What a thing to say. I am not *yours*, Lord Somerton. I am my own man. I thought I had made that clear from the beginning."

Somerton forced his anger back, forced his brain to calmness. Markham stood with his hands stretched out, his auburn head bowed, unconscious of his own appeal.

"Mr. Markham," he said, "I quite understand your notions of integrity. I assure you, I mean no harm to her ladyship."

Markham laughed. "Oh, quite. Just a harmless little chat in your study, of the sort you conduct daily."

"She has betrayed me. She has betrayed me from the first."

"You haven't precisely been the most admirable of husbands, you know."

Somerton tightened his hands about his arms. "I quite agree. The two of us are not suited for marriage together. I therefore intend to offer her . . ." *Say it. Make it true.* "A divorce. I have already drawn up . . ."

Markham whipped around. "A divorce!"

"Yes." He barked the word, to drown out the terror in his heart, the queasy feeling of finality. Everything going into motion at last. No turning back now. *Divorce.* God, what an unwholesome word. A word of failure. An admission of culpable sin. "So you see," he went on, more calmly, "this will, no doubt, be welcome news to her ladyship. You are summoning her to her own deliverance."

Markham's eyebrow lifted slightly, as if detecting the note of irony in Somerton's voice and wondering what it meant.

"Do you really mean this?" he whispered. "Divorce her? What about your son?"

"We will make arrangements, of course. He'll hardly notice my absence. He's been her child from the beginning, hasn't he?"

The fire hissed quietly. The room had grown too hot, too quickly. He shouldn't have laid on so much coal. Like a mother, worrying over an infant.

Markham took a small step forward. "I wish you would—"

"What, Markham?"

"You're so bitter."

Somerton gathered himself. This had gone on far enough, like a bloodletting he had grown too weak and sick to stop. "I am not bitter. I am filled with resolve, Mr. Markham, and all will shortly be arranged to everyone's satisfaction. Now go upstairs and do your duty."

Markham stood in the red glow of the coal fire. His brown eyes were huge and rimmed with gold, a trick of the light. His skin looked almost translucent.

"Mr. Markham?" Somerton prodded, to break the silence.

Markham's thin shoulders moved up and down. "Very well. I'll go to her. But merely as the act of a friend, and not your secretary."

"I beg your pardon?" The floor seemed to be sinking away beneath his feet.

"As I said, I am leaving your employ and your house. Tonight, possibly, or tomorrow morning at the latest." Quincy whined at his feet, and he leaned down to give the dog's head a reassuring pat.

"You can't be serious."

"I am."

Somerton gave himself a moment to answer, so as not to alarm either Markham or himself with the initial response, violent with panic. "If your aunt's health is so precarious, Markham," he said in a drawl, "she is quite welcome to stay in Chester Square until you can bear to part with her."

"I am afraid it won't do, sir. If you will allow me, sir." He bowed and made a motion with his arm, shooing Somerton away from his path to the door.

Leave. Markham was leaving.

Naturally, that was to be expected. A cold and ruthless beast like himself, a corrupt and unpleasant soul such as his: Why would someone so pure and upright as Markham wish to pollute himself further?

There was no need for this visceral reaction, this blood roaring in the ears. Markham was only a secretary, after all. Somerton could find another, just by snapping his fingers. Just by holding out a fistful of money. Someone as old and cold as himself, this time: someone in whom he would never think of confiding.

It was better that way, after all.

He stepped to one side.

"I shall be waiting in my study, Mr. Markham."

TWELVE

Luisa climbed the stairs with heavy feet. With every step, the burden of guilt weighed down in greater mass: She had done this, she had found the jewel box, she had driven the last fatal stake through the marriage of Lord and Lady Somerton. And having driven it, she would whisk herself away, and leave them both to the consequences.

She pressed her eyes shut for an instant, and recollected the bolt of anger that had struck her chest at the sight of that portrait lying among the jewels. Her own cousin Roland, Olympia's golden grandson, laughing and handsome as ever: How could Lady Somerton possibly have done this? Her husband had never stood a chance, had he? She had clung and clung and hadn't let go . . .

No.

Luisa pushed herself up the final flight. Her head was aching, her body empty of vital force. She had to put this out of her mind. The marriage had broken down irretrievably years ago; it had perhaps never really existed to begin with, not with damned Roland in the picture. In any case, it was none of her concern anymore. One last summons, one last inevitable errand, and she would be done. She had larger concerns. She had her throne to regain, conspirators to root out and punish. A constitution, perhaps, to put into place, to ensure that such a thing would never occur again in Holstein-Schweinwald-Huhnhof.

The routine breakdown of a typical aristocratic English marriage was neither here nor there, in the grand scheme of her life.

The nursery door was ajar. Luisa knocked briefly and pushed it open, without waiting for Lady Somerton's gentle words of permission.

The day nursery sat empty and dark, the toys put away. A wedge of light pushed open the door to the night nursery, Philip's bedroom, and the murmured cadence of a mother's voice followed. Luisa's heart ached at the sound.

But she didn't pause. No, that would be fatal. She reached for the knob and turned it, and Philip's head and Lady Somerton's head turned toward her at the same exact angle of surprise. The light from the lamp cast soft shadows across their faces.

"Why, Mr. Markham," said Philip. "What are you doing here? Are you back to—"

Luisa cleared her throat. "Madam, his lordship presents his compliments and asks you to join him in his study at once."

Lady Somerton, betraying not an ounce of anxiety, laid her finger along the glossy illustrated page from which she was reading and closed the book around it. "At once?"

"If you're finished with the story, of course." She couldn't look at Philip's curious face, at his black eyes so precisely the same shade as his father's.

"*Father* wants you?" he asked, incredulous.

"It appears so." She laid the book on the bedside table and turned down the lamp until it went out in a wink. She bent over Philip's bed to kiss him, and Luisa looked away.

"I guess you'd better go, then," Philip said, in the darkness. "I hope he's not cross."

The silken rustle of skirts. "I hope so, too, darling. Good night."

Luisa walked from the room, and the Countess of Somerton trailed sedately behind her, saying not a word, all the way down to the study, from which the dimmest of lights crept beneath the door.

Luisa knocked smartly on the wooden panel.

There was no answer.

She turned the handle and opened the door. "He'll be downstairs shortly, no doubt," she said, as Lady Somerton swept by in a dignified swish of dark blue silk.

"No doubt," replied her ladyship.

Luisa watched in a kind of professional admiration as Lady Somerton proceeded to the armchair before her husband's massive desk and took her seat gracefully, like a schoolgirl called in by the headmistress. Her spine stretched to the ceiling in a perfect plumb line, and her shining dark head could have held a dictionary level. She was, in that moment, more a princess than Luisa herself.

"Good evening, your ladyship," Luisa said respectfully.

Lady Somerton did not turn her head. "Good evening, Mr. Markham."

Luisa cast a last glance around the Earl of Somerton's study, where she had spent so many long hours in quiet and oddly companionable industry. The simple furniture, the shelves of books, the marble fireplace she had so often stacked with coal, the great desk where Somerton had sat, scribbling drafts and issuing orders: how forbidding it had looked once, and how familiar now. Somerton's image floated past, his profile sharp against the blurriness of the opposite wall, as hard and distant as Caesar.

Luisa backed out of the room and closed the heavy door. For a moment, she hovered outside, leaning against the knob, the same way she had all those weeks ago when she had first arrived.

And now she was leaving.

Luisa pushed herself off the door and down the hall. As she paused in the entrance hall, seized with an uneasy reluctance to return quietly to her room, a footman called her name.

She turned. "Yes? What is it?"

"A message for you, sir. Brought around the area entrance ten minutes ago." It was John, the newest footman, a cousin of Annabelle's, a large fellow with plain brown hair and a blank face. After three weeks, Luisa still couldn't decide if he were irredeemably stupid or extraordinarily cunning. He held out a small square of paper.

"Thank you." She tried not to snatch it away too eagerly.

John went on standing there, arms hanging loosely at his sides, expression hanging loosely from his face, while she unfolded the paper. She looked up and glared at him. "Are you waiting for a reply?" she asked sharply.

"No."

She tilted the paper away from his view and read the quick scribble: *Meet me at Wellington Arch make haste. D.*

A tiny dark drop marred the lower left-hand corner of the note, just below the D.

"Markham?"

The Earl of Somerton's bark made her jump. She folded the paper together with shaking fingers, along all the wrong creases, and turned toward the stairs. "Yes, sir?"

He stood with one hand on the newel post and one foot still poised on the stairs. He had taken off his coat, and his waistcoat strained to contain the powerful breadth of his chest and shoulders beneath the white shirt. In the darkness of the hall, his face seemed even more rugged and Caesar-like than usual, weighed down with an expression of extreme displeasure that she, Luisa, recognized as grief.

"Is something the matter?" he asked.

"No, sir. A message from my aunt."

"Is she in danger?"

Luisa opened her mouth to deny it, but changed her mind at the last instant. "I'm afraid so, sir. My presence is requested without delay."

He waved his hand. "Off you go, then. John, hail a hackney at once for Mr. Markham and ensure the fare is paid in advance. Would you like John to accompany you, Mr. Markham?"

He said the words with brusque efficiency, but in Luisa's shocked state, paralyzed by fear and dread, exhausted by interrupted sleep, the unlooked-for kindness nearly brought her to her knees. She had to swallow first, in order to speak. "That won't be necessary. Thank you, sir."

"Don't thank me." He resumed his journey in the direction of the study, like a beast on the prowl. "I haven't the time to deal with a visit from the constable, that's all."

On a bleak evening in unfashionable February, Hyde Park Corner should have been deserted, except for the occasional desultory hackney or businessman returning late to his family in

Kensington. Instead, it swarmed with horses and vehicles and imperious members of the London constabulary, a panicked melee that continued up Park Lane as far as Luisa could see.

"Something's up, looks like," said the driver, with the thoroughly unimpressed air of an experienced London cabman, as he brought the hackney to a rocking halt on the corner of Green Park.

Luisa smacked her hand on the doors. "Let me out!"

"All right, mate, all right," the driver grumbled, and the doors sprang open. He called out, "I'll be waiting here on the corner!" but Luisa was already ignoring her aching head and the weight of malaise to dodge between a policeman, a lamppost, and a clutch of drunken young gentlemen to round the corner of the railing and hurry up to the base of the arch.

A woman's figure emerged from the shadows. "There you are!" exclaimed Miss Dingleby, holding out her arms.

She was dressed in a silk ball gown that gleamed in the gaslight between the buttons of her plain wool coat, which she had left unbuttoned in apparent haste. Her hair was pulled back in an immaculate chignon, not a strand loose, and her gloved hands gripped Luisa's arms with fanatical strength.

"What's happened?" Luisa gasped.

"I don't know. It's a shambles. We've been betrayed—"

"Was it Hans?" Luisa took Miss Dingleby by the shoulders.

Miss Dingleby closed her eyes.

"What's happened? Is Emilie safe?"

Miss Dingleby shook her head. "They've taken her."

Luisa fell to her knees. "No. Oh, God. No. You said . . . you said she would be safe—"

"Stefanie . . . they've got her, too—"

"Stefanie? But how?"

"I don't know. No one knew her location except Olympia and me." Miss Dingleby spoke in hard, swift words, absent of feeling. "Listen to me, Luisa. Compose yourself. You're our only hope. You must come with me at once, before they discover you, too."

"But my sisters! We've got to find my sisters!"

"We haven't time. We've got to move quickly."

Luisa staggered to her feet and placed her hand against the cold stone of the arch's base. Above her, the Corinthian columns soared upward, dwarfing her feeble human frame. The horror of it all churned in her gut; her head began to throb. "They'll kill them! We've got to . . . got to—"

"No, they won't. They're too valuable. They'll simply use them to get you, my dear. The real prize, the crown jewel. As long as they don't have you, they'll keep your sisters alive." She grasped Luisa's hand and tugged. "Now come along. I have a safe location for you, a place to hide."

Luisa ripped her hand away. "No. I've got to think."

"Luisa, my dear, you must."

"No. I've had enough of your schemes. I'm going to return to Chester Square and summon the earl, and by God, he'll find my sisters . . ."

Without warning, Miss Dingleby's hand flashed out and struck her cheek. Luisa spun sideways into the arch, striking her forehead against hard stone.

"I'm sorry," said Miss Dingleby composedly. She laid her hands on Luisa's shoulders. "But you must come to your senses, my dear. My hackney is right here. Off we go."

Luisa's head was ringing with pain and shock. She wanted to object, to shrug off those managing hands and run down the pavement to her own waiting hackney, her experienced London cabman who would take her back to Chester Square and Lord Somerton. Somerton would help her sort this out. Somerton would rise up like an avenging devil and . . . and . . .

Her limbs were heavy. She couldn't seem to work up the necessary energy to cast off Miss Dingleby.

"Come along." The governess's voice was soothing in her ears. "You need to rest, my dear. You've had so many shocks. You've been so terribly strong through all of this. Come along with me, somewhere safe."

Luisa wanted to refuse. Some inner voice rose to a shout inside her, saying, *No, no! Keep fighting!* But the voice couldn't get out, and her head was ringing, and her limbs were heavy.

Miss Dingleby's arms closed around her. "There we are. Right this way."

Luisa woke sometime later, in the middle of a dream of bouncing carriages and the smell of a stable, and her sister Emilie's voice calling out in German.

She was lying on a pallet of some sort. Her head still hurt. She was going to be sick.

She rose up on her hands and vomited, just missing the edge of the straw mattress on which she lay. There wasn't much; she hadn't eaten in more hours than she could count. Still she heaved on, and the bile burned the back of her throat, and her eyes watered with the force of her heaving.

When at last the contractions stopped, she collapsed back on the pallet.

A distant shot rang out, making the wooden floor vibrate for an instant.

With enormous effort, Luisa raised her head. "Emilie?" she whispered.

Had she dreamt it, or had she really heard Emilie's voice, shouting out in German? But Emilie was dead.

No. Emilie was captured, Miss Dingleby said.

"Emilie," she whispered. But she hardly heard the word herself.

The nausea returned, but she was too weak this time, and her head hurt. It was easier to fall asleep.

The second time she woke up, two strong arms were burrowing beneath her body and lifting her upward into the stable-scented darkness.

"There we are, my good fellow," said a low voice, rough-edged and familiar.

Her dry lips moved. "Somerton?"

"What a mess, Markham. A damned awful mess."

The arms were like bands of iron beneath her body. She relaxed against them and turned her face into the warmth of a fine woolen waistcoat. The sense of motion overtook her. She was swinging into the unknown.

A vulgar curse passed above her aching head.

"I shall take the cost of the waistcoat out of your wages, Markham," said the voice, and Luisa closed her eyes in profound relief.

THIRTEEN

A woman sat next to her bed.

Luisa blinked her heavy eyelids to dispel the unfamiliar silhouette, but it persisted, unmoving, a dark-colored feminine blur against a darker background.

"Go away," Luisa croaked. Her tongue was sticky and tasted sour.

The woman moved, and Luisa realized she was looking at her bowed head, topped by a tiny white cap.

"Oh! You're awake," the woman said.

"Yes, I am bloody well awake," Luisa said, though the words didn't quite sound the way she expected. They were low and raspy and slurred together, as if coming from a drunkard.

"Now, now," the woman said. "Don't try to speak."

"Who are you?"

"I'm Pamela, his lordship's maid. He'll be that happy you're waking up at last." The woman rose and placed her hand on Luisa's forehead. She was wearing a plain dove gray uniform under a white apron, crisply ironed. The edge of her starched cuff brushed Luisa's cheek. "The fever broke yesterday, thank the Lord."

Something warm and wet was touching her hand. She

moved her head and saw Quincy, licking her skin, his large ears pointing hopefully toward her.

Pamela gasped and waved her hands at the dog. "Oh! Shoo, now. Down you go. Haven't I told you?"

"No, let him stay," Luisa tried to say, but Quincy, apparently familiar with this particular interaction, had already jumped from the bed and retired somewhere in the room. His claws rattled on the floor nearby, and he heaved a canine sigh of some deep emotion, either relief or resignation.

"I'm thirsty," she whispered.

"Of course you are, poor lamb." The woman stretched her arm outside the boundary of Luisa's vision. When it appeared again, she held a glass of water, which she pressed to Luisa's lips. "Try this."

Luisa sipped. The sweet taste made her want to cry with relief. She pushed forward desperately, until the liquid sloshed over her mouth and chin and dripped onto her chest.

"There, now."

The glass of water disappeared and a linen cloth pressed against her skin. Anxiety replaced the momentary relief of the water, anxiety and confusion: Where was she? Who was she? What was she doing, what had happened?

She was Luisa. There was . . . something bad. Her sisters.

"My sisters." She tried to raise her head, but her neck couldn't take the strain.

"I don't know anything about your sisters, dearie," said Pamela. "His lordship might be able to tell you."

"His lordship."

"Lord Somerton."

At the word *Somerton*, a dam cracked in Luisa's brain. The study. The jewel box. Her disguise.

Olympia, Dingleby. Her sisters. Peter and her father.

Good God. Her *disguise*.

"Now you just lie there and rest," Pamela said, rising from her seat, "and I'll send word to his lordship that you've awakened at last."

"No! No, I—"

The door opened, allowing a painful beam of daylight into the room. Luisa turned her head to the wall and its thick drapery.

"He'll be right pleased, he will," said Pamela. "He's sat by
your bed enough himself, watching you fight it off, delirium
and all."

"F-fight? Fight what?"

"Why, the typhoid, miss. A terrible case. We thought you
was done for, all excepting his lordship."

The door closed with a gentle click.

As a solitary boy—his sister and brother had both suc-
cumbed at early ages to the usual host of childhood
diseases—the Earl of Somerton had learned every hill and
stream of the family's ancient Northamptonshire seat, every
grove and pathway, every cottage and commons. In the
meadow by the millpond he had run down his first fox (or
rather, the hounds had) and been duly blooded by the master
in the gory aftermath; in that fragrant hayrick in the shelter of
Jacobs Hill he had carried on all summer with Bess, the young
wife of Billy Sikes, who had farmed the Jacobs Hill land for
forty years and who was as pleased as Punch with the strapping son born under his roof the following April. Somerton
had been seventeen years old, and stunned to view the squall-
ing black-haired consequence of his dalliance. *Isn't he a fine
strong lad?* Billy said proudly. *He'll be taking on the farm
after me, your lordship, you'll see.*

The hayrick was empty now, and the apple tree next to the
door was just beginning to blossom. Somerton nudged his
horse into a canter, as if he could outrun the memory. Little
Billy had indeed taken over the farm on his eighteenth birthday, and his pink new wife was already expecting a baby of
her own. Bess Sikes had written a letter to tell him the news;
it had arrived two weeks before his fortieth birthday, when a
man ought to be surrounded by his loving wife and children
and a pair of slobbering hounds. Somerton had dictated a reply
to Markham and told him to enclose a fifty-pound note as a
present for the expectant parents. Markham had raised his
eyebrows and done as he was told.

Her eyebrows. As *she* was told.

The rush of blood began, as it always did when Markham
returned to the forefront of his thoughts. He urged the horse

faster, until the chimney peaks of Somerton Hall appeared over the rise of Jacobs Hill, and the old red bricks glowed like fire in the brash April sunshine. In the southeastern corner, the windows of Markham's room flashed back the morning light. He would speak to the housekeeper and make certain the curtains were shut tight. The light hurt her eyes. They would open the windows for a bit in the late afternoon, when the sun had dropped on the other side of the house, so the air in the room could be freshened. He hated the smell of sickrooms, that scent of death and decay. Outside, the spring air was laden with new grass and clean rain, with life. That was what Markham needed.

He focused on these orderly details, as he had every day since he had brought her here over a month ago, shivering and burning with fever, muttering in delirium. He had left London because he couldn't stay a moment longer, and Markham had paid the price: on the rattling train, on the rattling carriage, growing worse and worse every hour. He had carried her into her room himself, and called out for a doctor, and undressed her with his own hands . . .

Somerton's hands clenched the reins, making the horse throw his head in annoyance. The remembered sight of her body still jolted his gut, the horror and wonder of her white breasts and the delicate flare of her hips, the snug drawstring of her plain linen drawers limp against her flat belly. The rage and pity at her deception, the beautiful and elegant mystery of her.

The stable yard lay to the left. He was off Byron's back almost before the chestnut had stopped, and tossed the reins to the waiting groom. "Cool him down properly, mind you," he said over his shoulder, and he strode to the broad white marble steps of Somerton Hall as fast as another man might run.

Would the fever return? It was often reduced in the morning, raising his hopes, only to rush back again at noon in an uncontrolled tide of shivering and delirium that no amount of heightened fire and added blankets could abate. Once, when no one else was nearby, he had climbed into the bed and held her hot body against his, until she stopped shaking and the only movement in the bed came from her chattering lips, the string of nonsensical words that streamed from her stricken brain.

But no. The fever had been gone for two days, and the doctor had assured him that Miss Markham had turned the corner, had passed the crisis. That she would be waking soon, that the period of convalescence had now begun. Somerton had stared at her motionless body, cradled by white sheets, her shaved head fragile against the pillow, and could not believe it. Could not quite trust that the corruption would not return to claim her again. Could not quite trust that this precious and necessary scrap of life had somehow prevailed.

His boots crashed against the step. He flung the door open before the footman could reach it first and hurried across the old stones to the grand staircase, taking the steps two at a time.

"Your lordship! Sir!" Pamela's voice, high with animation.

Panic rushed through his veins. He stopped and spun around. "What is it?" he barked. "Is the fever returned?"

But Pamela was smiling at him, her plain face stretched to its utmost expression of delight. "No, sir! She's awake! Just a moment ago, and I was off to find you—"

He was already bounding down the hallway, already crashing to a halt outside the familiar six-paneled door. His hand reached for the knob, cold and smooth beneath his skin. He closed his eyes and collected himself.

This would not do. This high pitch of emotion, he had to quell it.

He focused his mind on the size of the metal knob in his hand, on the unsatisfactory beat of his heart, far too quick. He gathered into himself the recollection of her deception, months long, and the games she had played with him. The various possibilities—Who had sent her? What was her purpose? How much harm had she done him?—all of which had served, in the many moments of stark fear that had overcome him in the past five weeks, to turn back the tide. To return him to reason. To place the cold hand of caution on his thumping heart.

He had felt this way before, he remembered. And he had married her.

This is your weakness. This is your peculiar susceptibility.

When he was sober once more, he pushed open the door. His hand tingled only a little.

Ah, then. He was not sober enough, apparently, to quell the surge of disappointment that engulfed his throat.

Pamela was wrong. Markham lay asleep, her exhausted head forming a deep hollow in the center of the pillow, at such an angle that he could see her pulse flicker in her neck. Her quick breath moved the sheets up and down, up and down. The room was still dark, still smelling of sickness.

He stepped closer, and the floorboard creaked beneath his heavy booted foot.

Markham's eyelids fluttered, those impossibly thick eyelashes. How had he not seen through her disguise? He, of all people. He watched those eyes open, large and brown in her emaciated face, and he could not imagine her as a man.

He had been a fool, a fool, a fool.

"Sir?" she whispered.

The single word set off an instant chemical reaction inside him: joy and confusion and profound relief. It was true. She was alive.

She had deceived him.

She had redeemed him.

She was full of wiles. She was full of grace.

Who was she?

He rolled his thumb along the knob of his riding crop, which he still held in his right hand. "Well, well, Markham. It seems you have escaped death with your usual nimbleness. What have you to say for yourself?"

She wet her lips and considered him. "Where am I?"

"At Somerton Hall, of course."

"You brought me here?"

"I did not have you sent in a box by parcel post," he said. "It is now the beginning of April, Markham. You have, in the manner of the woodland beasts, slept right through the end of winter."

She turned her head to the ceiling and squeezed her eyelids shut. A tiny dot of a tear tracked down the corner of her jaw, narrowly missing her ear. "I have failed," she said, so softly he wasn't quite certain he'd heard her properly.

He laid his crop atop the soft rolled arms of the chair in the corner, the chair in which he'd nodded asleep more than once in the past month. "You can thank me later, of course, for having saved your life and nursed you back to health, entirely at my own trouble and expense."

"Thank you."

"Ah, that's better. Brimming over with the usual Markham gratefulness. Which reminds me." He held up a finger, as if an idea had just occurred to him. "What the devil am I to call you now? *Mister* Markham being so singularly unsuited to your present state."

"My present state?"

"My dear girl," he said dryly, "I undressed you with my own hands."

She rolled her head to look at him, and he could have sworn that she was blushing, had she any additional blood to spare for those pale cheeks. Her mouth formed a silent O of horror.

"I am devastated to perceive that you don't remember," he said. "Never mind. You were, I'm afraid, hardly in an aspect to inspire admiration."

"Be quiet, for God's sake," she snapped, and turned away. Her hair was only half an inch long, a slightly darker auburn than it had been before, or perhaps it was only the dimness of the room these past five weeks.

"Ah! That's the old Markham spirit. I'm glad to see it's returned so quickly. Do you mind if I crack open the curtains a trifle? I find the sickroom air a bit oppressive." He moved to the window, unable to bear the pathetic sight of her.

"Louisa," she said. "My name is Louisa."

He paused with one hand on the green damask drapery. "Louisa," he repeated.

Louisa. Her name. A common enough name. He had said it a thousand times before, never knowing it was hers. That she was the one true Louisa, the woman for whom the word was created.

He pushed back the curtain and looped the tasseled cord around it. The window was shut tight, with traces of condensation at the corners of the panes. He turned the latch with his thumb and thrust the bottom sash upward a few inches. A gust of fresh spring breeze invaded the room. A yip reached his ears; he looked down and saw Markham's corgi at his feet, ears cocked, eyeing him with a certain air of smugness. "Have you a surname, Louisa?" he asked.

"No."

"I see." He turned. "When you have regained a little of

your strength, perhaps you might relate to me a little of how you came to arrive in my employ over five months ago, disguised so convincingly as a young man, and why you chose to commit such an extraordinary act." He began to walk toward the bed, around the solid carved post at the bottom, until he arrived at her side, looming over her. His voice turned caressing. "And then, when you are quite yourself, perhaps we might discuss how your debt to me might best be repaid."

In the daylight spilling from the window, she looked even paler than before. But she was most definitely blushing.

"I see," she said.

"You have put me to a great deal of trouble, my dear girl, and I never allow myself to be put to trouble without some expectation of reward."

She went on staring straight back at him, with her brave dark eyes, as if she could see right through his hard expression to the tumult within.

Alive. She was alive. She would live. The spark of life, he could see it right there, animating her features, dimmed but present. He wanted to fall on his knees and thank whatever God still listened to the prayers of a man like him.

"I see we understand each other," he said.

"Your lordship." She wet her lips again. "May I trouble you for a drink of water? The glass is on the table beside me."

He picked up the glass and held it to her lips, and when her neck seemed to fail her, he slipped his hand beneath her head and supported it while the muscles of her throat slid up and down beneath her tissue-thin skin.

"Thank you." She turned her head away and closed her eyes.

He set the half-empty glass on the table, picked up his riding crop, and went to the door.

"You're welcome," he said.

FOURTEEN

The telegram was unsigned, but few of the Earl of Somerton's regular correspondents were prepared to claim ownership of the messages they sent him. He studied the crisp
black typescript with his hands steepled protectively at his
temples:

CONTINUED NO SIGN OR RECORD OF SUBJECTS AT CHANNEL
PORTS OR RAILWAY STATIONS STOP ADVISE FURTHER ACTION

No sign of them. Not of his wife and son, not of Roland
Penhallow, all disappeared from England on the same day.
The day after he had confronted Elizabeth.

As if Europe had swallowed them up.

It was now approaching the middle of April, and his wife
and son had been gone for over six weeks. No one at the London clubs, no one in the circuit of English gossip had heard of
any planned destination. Somerton's sources at Her Majesty's
Bureau of Trade and Maritime Information—where Penhallow plied his own spycraft with singular skill, rot him—had
all returned blank.

Somerton rose from his chair and strode to the map that
hung on the study wall. He had always had a great fondness
for this room, which could only be reached by a door at the
end of the great Somerton Hall library, nearly invisible in the

old walnut paneling. A man could hide here, with his brandy
and his cello and his private business. A comfortable chair, a
soft leather Chesterfield, an occasional smoke. Were it not for
the need for nourishment and exercise, he could exist here
forever.

The map spread across six feet of wall, depicting Europe
in all its detailed variety at the center, and America and Asia
at the peripheries. Africa existed in the lower half of the map,
overlapped on the wainscoting, but he thought he could disregard that beleaguered continent for the time being: Elizabeth
would never take the boy to a land in which yellow fever and
creatures with tusks lurked about untamed. Atop the little
shelf that crowned the wainscoting, he kept a small jar full of
pins: blue-tipped ones to indicate where his operatives had
searched, and red-tipped ones to indicate where the countess
(or some member of her party) had been detected.

A field of blue-tipped pins decorated the ports and capital
cities of Europe, without a single dash of red to interrupt them.

Somerton glanced at the telegram. His hand hovered over
the jar of pins, and then fell away. There was no news, really.
No progress to mark.

He lifted up the jar of pins and hurled it against the wall,
just as a sharp knock rattled the old panels of the door.

"Come in," he barked.

The door opened to reveal a bristle-headed figure engulfed
in an old dressing gown of dark green brocade, the sleeves of
which had been rolled several times in a gallant attempt to
free the hands. From the bottom, which dragged a few inches
on the floor, a small golden brown head emerged, followed by
the remainder of a corgi body.

"Markham," he said.

"My lord."

The sight of her, standing in his study, apparently on her own
power, dressed in his own discarded dressing gown, stunned
him into momentary dumbness. He hadn't visited her room in a
week, not since she had first awoken from her illness. She
needed her rest, the doctor had said. She would be bedridden for
days, perhaps weeks. (The doctor had given him a pointed look
at the word *bedridden*.) Somerton had latched onto this excuse
gratefully. Of course, it was quite improper that he should visit

her now, awake and unmarried and undressed as she was. He, who never regarded propriety as anything more than a rule to be enjoyed in the breaking, nearly convinced himself that his better nature had prevailed. That he was not afraid of her power at all.

He was simply observing the proprieties.

"You should not be here," he said at last. "You are supposed to be bedridden."

"I am quite capable of walking short distances. I have been moving about my room for three days now. You might, however, offer me a chair."

He walked to the yellow armchair and braced his hands on the back. "Here you are, my dear."

She walked slowly, rather stiffly, as if her bones were made of lead pipes and not quite under her full control. Quincy walked patiently by her side. Somerton had to dig his fingers into the upholstery to stop himself from going to her, to carry her physically into the chair, notwithstanding the stubborn tilt of her chin.

"Thank you," she said, with a touch of irony, reaching down to pat the dog's faithful head.

He moved to the desk and propped himself on the edge, one booted foot resting on the floor, one swinging negligently in the air. "To what do I owe the honor of this visit?"

Her gaze was fixed to the wall. "That map was not here at Christmas."

"Ah. Dispensing with the formalities, I see. No, you're quite right. It was not."

"What is its purpose?"

He swung his foot a few times before replying. "The morning after we arrived here in February, when you were just beginning the course of your illness, I received word that my wife and son had left the house in London. They have not been seen since."

"And you are trying to recover them?" Her eyes shifted from the map to him.

"Yes. Or rather, I'm trying to recover my son. My wife can go to the devil." *And Penhallow must pay, by God.*

"You can't mean to separate them."

"I can't mean to live apart from my son, without so much as

knowing his whereabouts. For one thing, he is heir to all this."
He waved his hand at the comfortable study around them.

"She won't let him go."

Her voice was strangely dull; her entire demeanor, in fact,
lacked that certain zing he had always associated with the old
Markham, even when the secretary was obediently copying
letters and taking dictation. This Louisa bore no resemblance
to that fellow. She was the skeleton version of Markham,
stripped of flesh and hair and spirit, her bones poking through
every inch of exposed skin.

"You should be in bed, you know," he said quietly.

"If I stayed in my room, I should never have the opportunity to speak to you."

"Very well. What did you wish to discuss?"

She lifted her shoulders back an inch or two. "I wish to
discuss my future here with you."

Somerton's heart froze. To disguise the paralysis, which
traveled all the way up his neck to his vocal cords, he ran his
hand along the slope of his quadriceps and examined the
smoothness of the fine pin-striped charcoal wool. "At the
moment, my dear Markham—you don't mind if I call you
Markham, do you? I find it difficult to imagine you otherwise."

She inclined her head.

"At the moment," he continued, "I am rather more interested in your past than your future."

"I'm surprised you haven't deduced that already, you and
your network of spies. Your calculating brain."

He shrugged. "I've been distracted. In any case, my men
are too valuable and highly trained to waste on a dull and
uninspiring case of petty identification."

The corner of her mouth turned upward a quarter inch.
"I see."

"Particularly when the solution to the problem is sitting
right in front of me. Tell me, Markham. Louisa, as you call
yourself. In clear, straightforward language. Who are you, and
why did you enter my employ, disguised as a man?"

There, the words were out. He held his breath, waiting for
her response. Afraid of her response.

She shook her head. "It doesn't matter anymore."

"I beg your pardon?"

"My lord, how did you know where to find me, the night we left London?"

He rose and walked to the window. "I had my footman follow you, of course, since the streets of London are hardly benign at such an hour, even in February. He saw you engage in an altercation with a woman at Wellington Arch, who then bundled you into a hackney and took you to a mews behind Eaton Square."

"Eaton Square!"

He glanced back at her. "You didn't know?"

"I didn't." She swallowed hard and looked at her lap. "And what did you find there?"

"It was quite late by the time I arrived. Perhaps two in the morning. I had been otherwise engaged, you see, when John arrived home with his information." He turned back to the window and gripped the curtain, to dispel the memory of what he had been doing that night. What he had done, the last desperate act of his marriage.

"Was anyone else there?" she asked, in a whisper.

"No. Quite deserted. There were signs of some sort of activity about, but not a soul in the building, except for the horses."

"Has there been any note for me since? Any message?"

"None at all." He turned back to her and crossed his arms. Markham—Louisa—sat with her hands in her lap, staring at her fingers. The windows faced east, and the sun had already climbed above the angle of direct light. The diffuse glow surrounded her too-thin body, emphasizing the fragility of her bones, the paleness of her skin. Only her hair showed any life, glimmering with reddish fire. The wholeness of her grief shocked him.

"Is something the matter, Markham?" he asked, as gently as he could.

"It doesn't matter," she said. "It doesn't matter anymore."

You matter. His brain screamed the words. *You matter.*

He thought of her stricken body on the floor, her hair matted with vomit, her helplessness. The pulsing panic in his limbs when he had emerged in despair from his bedroom at two o'clock in the morning and found John waiting patiently near the door—*I didn't want to disturb you, sir, not with the countess inside*—with the news that Markham had been taken, Markham was in danger, all while he had been in bed with his wife—oh, always compliant, because a good wife never refused her husband's carnal appetites—in a vain and despairing attempt to salvage the last fragile tie that might possibly have held them together, before he uttered those fatal words: *I intend to offer you a divorce.*

Actually, he had planned to say them straight out. He had planned to end the whole sham right there. But as she sat before him, cool and composed, beautiful and remote, he had thought of Philip, of what might have been, and a feeling of desperation had overtaken him. His final chance. Once the word *divorce* was spoken, he couldn't take it back. The family, the unfulfilled promise of the three of them, would be irretrievably broken. So, sitting there on the other side of the desk, with the guilty jewel box between them, he'd challenged her instead to prove the fidelity she claimed, to prove that she was innocent. To return to their marriage, before it was lost forever.

She had taken his offered hand and gone upstairs with him, like the pretty martyr she was. And he had given her pleasure; he was sure of it. By God, he had made sure of it. He had tried everything in his power to bring her back to him, to bring back the hope that had once filled his heart, such as it was. And she had found pleasure, because they were both made of flesh and subject to fleshly desire; and still she had looked at him afterward with a kind of grieved loathing. The old look, the one she had cast him on their wedding night.

Because nothing had changed, had it? Nothing ever would.

An urge now seized him, a primal urge to run through the door, into the vast natural cathedral outside, and roar with frustration, with anger and longing. He had been in bed with his wife who despised him beneath her obedient facade; had been engaged in a fruitless act that brought him little physical pleasure and far greater heartsickness, while Markham needed him. He hadn't understood the emotion that had gripped him then, when John had told him Markham was in danger; he understood it better now, but it didn't help. The understanding only deepened his frustration: He was trapped, tricked once more into investing his craving for human connection into an impossible object: one that did not, and would not, ever crave him in return.

God hated him.

"Well, then, Markham." He launched himself away from the window and strode to the desk. "I suppose we must first find you a set of clothes appropriate to your station. I'm afraid I've had the contents of her ladyship's wardrobe given away to a home for fallen women, so—"

Markham straightened in her chair. "That won't be necessary. It's what I meant to discuss with you. I no longer have a home to return to, nor a family who needs me. I should prefer to resume my . . . my masculine disguise and return to work as your secretary. Until other arrangements can be made, of course."

"Rubbish. Impossible."

"It's not impossible. Only the household here knows my true sex, and loyalty, as you yourself observed, can be easily purchased."

His knuckles ground into the wood. "You will not dress as a man. You are a woman."

"I was a woman before. I have need of gainful employment."

"You will not labor for a living, Markham!" The words exploded from his throat.

"And why not?" she said calmly. "Labor is the lot of mankind."

"It is not yours."

"Then what do you propose?" She pushed up the sleeves of the dressing gown, which had fallen down over her hands. "I must do something, and I detest sewing. I haven't the patience to be a governess. I suppose I might apply for work as a waitress in a London tea shop, though I daresay I should mix up all the orders and find myself sacked within a week for my insufferable cheek."

He said, between his teeth, "Don't talk nonsense. You are under my protection, Markham. You need have no further concern for your well-being."

She folded her hands back in her lap, and the sleeves fell back down to cover them. How straight she held her spine, though the balls of her shoulders curled forward in exhaustion! And her chin, still so proud, and the stubborn symmetry of her bony face, and the way her brown eyes regarded him in that unflinching way, smudged with shadows beneath. The bravery of her.

"How kind of you, Lord Somerton," she said, "but I prefer to earn my bread honestly. Even in my reduced state."

He shot to his feet. "Damn it all, Markham, I did not mean—"

His words fell away, because that straight spine before him had begun to waver. Her eyes lost focus, and then recovered, and then wandered again.

"Markham!"

Quincy let out a piercing whine.

She braced her hands on the arms of the chair. "I'm quite all right. Just a . . . a momentary . . ."

Somerton vaulted around the corner of the desk and caught her just as she slumped forward.

"Damn you, Markham. You shouldn't be up." He laid her head against his shoulder and lifted her in his arms. "You damned little fool."

She was so frighteningly light, almost buoyant, like a child, like a hollow-boned bird. What had he been thinking, letting her stay downstairs in her proud posture?

Her breath warmed his shoulder. He turned the doorknob and stuck out his foot to open the door.

"I'm all right," she muttered.

"You're a damned little fool, and you're going back to bed."

"I had to speak to you—"

"In the future, you will kindly send a message through Pamela, and I will trouble myself to attend you at my earliest convenience." With Quincy trotting at his heels, he strode down the length of the library and into the great corridor that ran along the eastern end of the house, past a pair of astonished housemaids dusting the cabinetry. A staircase stood at the end of the hall, the one the family used to access the apartments above.

The family, such as it was.

"I'm sorry." The words were soft, muttered into his shirt, either weakly or reluctantly.

"So you should be, Markham. Very sorry indeed." He had reached the stairs, he was climbing them, he was cradling her against his chest. She smelled of some sort of feminine soap, floral, quite unlike her, but pleasant nonetheless. "You are a very great deal of trouble to me, you know. You always have been."

She sighed, and the warmth of her breath penetrated his skin and soothed his chest. "I have always . . . endeavored . . . to give satisfaction."

"You are not required to give satisfaction, Markham." There was her door, white and quiet at the end of the hall. The northeast corner, overlooking the lake and the sunrise. It had been his own room, after he left the nursery upstairs, before his father had died. "You are only required to recover your strength without doing yourself further injury. Is that so very much to ask?"

"No. It is just so . . . bloody *boring*."

God, she would kill him. He reached the door and kicked it open. Pamela started and made a little scream, holding up a white linen sheet as if to shield against evil.

"What the devil are you doing?" he asked.

"Ch-changing Miss Markham's sheets, my lord!"

"Finish your task at once, if you will. Miss Markham is in need of rest."

Pamela's mouth went as round as her eyes. She whipped the sheets into place with the speed of a well-oiled machine, and spread the blankets over. Somerton stood, legs planted into the rug, while the beat of Markham's heart made its way through her dressing gown and between his ribs. She lay so absolutely still in his arms, he thought she might have gone to sleep, except that her hand had crept upward and was now curling around the edge of his waistcoat.

Pamela plumped up a final pillow and pulled down the covers. "There we are! Fresh and clean."

"Move aside, please." He stepped forward, laid Markham in the middle of the bed, and raised the covers around her body in its green brocade dressing gown. *His* brocade dressing gown, which had once covered his own skin, and now sheltered hers. "I will return at three o'clock this afternoon to take you outside for an hour of fresh air. Pamela, see that Miss Markham is well rested and dressed warmly."

"Yes, sir. But the doctor said . . ."

"Damn the doctor."

"Yes, sir."

Markham's eyes closed. He turned to the door. His arms ached with emptiness.

"Thank you, Pamela," he said, and walked back into the hall, closing the door firmly behind him.

Downstairs in his study, he stared at the map on the wall. If he wanted, he could scribble a telegram right now and have it sent to the post office in the village, which had been wired for the telegraph five years ago on his own orders, and at his own expense. He could order one or another of his minions to investigate the ownership of the mews in which he had found Markham, to track down the references in his letters, to find out who she really was. An afternoon's work, really. The clues surely abounded, waiting to be followed.

He picked up his pen and twirled it between his fingers. A rapid clicking sound drifted through the door, louder and louder, until Quincy's inquisitive face peered around the edge of the door, which Somerton hadn't closed.

"I could ask *you*, couldn't I?" Somerton growled. "I daresay you know everything."

Quincy trotted across the study floor and came to rest at his feet, looking upward with an air of expectancy.

Somerton laid down the pen and turned back to stare at the map. "But that's the thing, you see. It seems I'm afraid to know."

FIFTEEN

The warmth of the June sunshine soaked agreeably through Luisa's jacket of summer-weight brown tweed. By afternoon, she judged, the rays would grow too hot for outdoor tramping, and she would shed her jacket in favor of her waistcoat and shirtsleeves in the shade of Somerton's study while she toiled at her little desk under the dark weight of his disapproval.

But now, in this moment, the sun was perfect.

She had learned to hold such moments close. When you had been stripped of everything, when all hope had gone and the chamber of your ambition had to be refurnished from the bare walls, you started with small things. June sunshine, and the scent of ripening roses. A glass of sweet-tart lemonade, squeezed from the lemons in Somerton's well-tended greenhouses. The healing silence in the study, as she and Somerton worked side by side, Quincy nestled between them in the quietude of shared understanding.

The growing strength of her legs as she strode through the meadow toward the millpond, while Quincy trotted along gamely at her heels.

At first, she had rebelled against that growing strength, as if her body were betraying her by thriving, when everything else had been flattened. But her limbs persisted. They twitched with returned energy, they yearned for the outdoors and the greening meadows. They wanted to live. So she had followed them, and had taken a reluctant pleasure in the return of pleasure. A virtuous circle in which she hadn't wished to participate.

At the edge of the millpond, a massive oak tree waited for her. For weeks now, she had sat in its shade and stared out at the rippling water, as the spring breezes chased themselves across the surface. On the other side, where the stream entered the pond, the mill wheel turned tranquilly, making a gentle continuous splash into the country stillness.

Another small pleasure, the comforting wash of the water mill.

How long would it last, this healing routine of sleep and work and sunshine? Not long, around Somerton. The earl was not made for resting. He would be back into action again, back into his schemes. Telegrams arrived almost hourly from the village, some of which she was privileged to read and answer, and others that he dealt with on his own. "Any word on her ladyship?" Luisa would ask, eyebrows up, and he would shake his head, scribble a reply, call for the footman, and burn the original with a few quick strikes of a safety match (the fireplace had remained unlit, coals stacked expectantly, since early May).

Why hadn't he returned to London yet? Why hadn't he found Lady Somerton?

Why hadn't he discovered Luisa's own identity? It couldn't be hard.

If he actually tried.

She reached the edge of the shade, removed her jacket, and spread it out on the damp morning grass. A month ago, this walk would have exhausted her, and she would lie down and watch the chasing clouds until the strength returned to her body, while Quincy curled confidingly into her waist.

Now, she merely settled herself on her jacket, drew her knees to her chest, and—

"My dear Luisa."

Luisa shot to her feet, stumbled, recovered. "What the devil?" she called out.

A branch rustled, somewhere inside the canopy of shade. Up flew a startled bird, in a flurry of feathers and leaves.

Quincy barked twice and made a rattling growl, ears cocked forward at an almost impossible pitch.

"I can't tell you how glad I am to see you looking well," said a familiar voice.

Luisa breathed out slowly. "Good God," she whispered.

A shape emerged from behind the thick trunk of the oak tree. It was tall, and commanding, and it wore a magnificent straw hat.

"M-Mrs. *Duke?*" said Luisa.

The woman who stood before the Earl of Somerton looked vaguely familiar, though he could not quite place her face. Her shape, however, was unmistakable: rounded with a pregnancy of perhaps seven months' gestation, in Somerton's expert estimation.

"I beg your pardon," he said. "I don't believe I know your name."

"It's Yarrow, your lordship." She bobbed an awkward curtsy. "Mrs. Yarrow. Lord Kildrake's nurse."

Outside, a cloud slipped past the sun, and the windows flooded with a rush of light, illuminating the drowsy motes of dust in the air between them.

Somerton rose slowly to his feet. "What did you say?"

"Lord Kildrake's nurse, sir." Her eyes filled with tears. "I'm sorry to disturb you, sir, but I've nowhere left to turn. Her ladyship, she turned me away in Milan when she found me increasing, and then John . . ."

"Milan!" Somerton's gaze shot to the map on the wall.

"Yes, sir. And I stayed there until there was no more money, because she told me you would have me beaten if I returned in this state, but I have nowhere left to go, sir, no one at all, and John insists it isn't his . . ."

"John the footman? *John* put you in this condition?"

"Yes, sir."

Somerton's brain was reeling, sending off sparks of conjecture. Where was Markham? He needed Markham.

Mrs. Yarrow was wavering on her feet. He came around the edge of the desk and led her to the chair. A faint scent of wet wool drifted from her clothes, the sourness of neglect.

"Milan, you say. Did you travel there by train?"

"By steamship, my lord, through the Bay of Biscay and the Strait of Messina into the Mediterranean. A worse voyage I've never had." She fished a damp handkerchief from her pocket and dabbed her eyes.

Somerton walked to the bell cord and gave it a single tug. "Did her ladyship say where she was headed after Milan?"

"No, she didn't, sir. But I heard her tell Miss Harewood to buy tickets for Florence."

Miss Harewood. That would be Elizabeth's cousin Abigail. If young Miss Harewood had traveled with Elizabeth, so must her guardian, Elizabeth's other cousin, the beautiful widow Lady Morley. A managing sort, Lady Morley, and singularly cunning. She had probably arranged everything herself, the entire disappearance. No wonder he hadn't been able to trace them.

"Florence." He paced across the room to the map and drew out a single red pin from the jar. His heart jumped so hard, it jolted his hand as he hovered above the crown of Italy's boot. "Did she perhaps have any gentlemen traveling with her? Other than my son, of course."

"Why, no, sir."

Never mind. Penhallow was undoubtedly waiting for her, at whatever little Continental nest they'd arranged for themselves. Wherever Elizabeth was, he would find Penhallow.

Of that, he was certain.

A knock on the door.

"Come in," he said.

A footman walked in. "You rang, sir?"

"I did, Thomas. Bring in a tray of tea for Mrs. Yarrow, with plenty of food." With a triumphant strike of his hand, Somerton jabbed the red pin into the dot marked FIRENZE. He turned and folded his arms. "And tell Mr. Markham I want him in my study at once."

My dear niece," drawled the Duke of Olympia, "you look confounded. Do sit, I implore you. I understand you have been ill."

"I am quite recovered now," Luisa said stupidly, unable to

think of anything else. Was that a genuine stuffed sparrow in the duke's hat, or merely a lifelike imitation? "Where the devil have you been?"

"Tut-tut." Olympia walked toward her and held out his hands. Quincy, at her feet, let out a disapproving growl. "Such language. And still in your male costume. I'm surprised his lordship didn't plumb your disguise during your illness. Give me a kiss, now."

Luisa took his hands in a daze and kissed each powdered cheek. "What are you doing here? Where have you been? I thought you were dead."

"Thought I was dead? Good God. Where did you come by such a notion?"

"From Miss Dingleby. She said . . . I don't remember exactly . . ." Luisa rubbed her forehead, and all at once, the wonder of it burst over her like a firework. She flung her arms around his tall, silk-shouldered figure. "You're alive. My God, you're alive!"

"Yes, yes. Quite alive. Mind the lace."

"But my sisters." She drew away. "What's happened? All this time . . . my God . . . I thought she'd caught us all, that everyone was dead, that I would be dead if it hadn't been for Somerton . . ."

"Who caught us all?"

"Miss Dingleby! The night of the ball!"

"Ah." He disengaged gingerly from her embrace and set her down in the grass, lowering himself with only a faint creak of his long limbs. A light scent of sandalwood drifted from his clothes, not at all feminine. Luisa wanted to take him by the shoulders and shake him.

"Uncle, what's happened? Where is everyone? Emilie and Stefanie. Are they . . . ?" She couldn't say the word. Her hands were shaking, her heart had been captured between the wings of a butterfly.

"Your sisters are safe," he said gently.

At the word *safe*, Luisa buried her face between her knees and burst into tears.

"There, now." His hand rested on her back. "Poor lamb. Did you really think, all this time . . . ? Ah, poor lamb."

She couldn't speak. She couldn't say, *I thought I was alone,*

I thought everyone was dead, I wanted to die. She turned instead into her uncle's chest and gripped the material around his magnificent false bosom.

"Now, now. Mind the lace, I said."

"Where are they?" she whispered. "Where are they?"

"They're . . . well, they're safe. You needn't worry."

"But Miss Dingleby . . ."

The chest beneath her face heaved with a sigh. "Miss Dingleby. What an immense disappointment."

Luisa looked up. "She betrayed us, didn't she?"

"I'm afraid so."

"But what's happened? Where is she?"

"I don't know, my dear. I've spent the last two months trying to discover the answer to that question."

"Two months? But . . . but the ball was in February."

"Like you, my dear, I was stricken with an unfortunate episode of typhoid fever, shortly after that tumultuous evening." He held up his hand at her exclamation of dismay. "I had it as a child, so my case was not so severe as yours. I had my valet convey me to a rather remote house in the country, quite unknown to even my most trusted friends, so no one would suspect my condition. When the fever abated and my senses had returned, I had my agents investigate. Miss Dingleby had disappeared, but in the kitchen in Battersea, inside one of the cupboards, my men found a laboratory culture that, when tested, was found to contain the causative organism for typhoid fever."

Luisa put her hand to her mouth.

"Which, as you may be aware," Olympia went on calmly, "is a disease communicated primarily by oral transmission of infected matter. Those engaged in the preparation of food are particularly effective at spreading the agent."

Luisa's stomach made a little heave. "The tea."

"Or the cake. Let us hope, for dear little Quincy's sake, that it was not the ham sandwiches."

Luisa couldn't speak. She shook her head, blinking, trying to quell the nausea in her belly.

"In any case, Dingleby appears to have left the country shortly after the events of that evening, and hasn't been seen since. The agents of the Revolutionary Brigade appear to have departed England as well, according to my sources, or at the very least they have not made the slightest stir."

"And you're trying to find them?"

The duke fingered the brim of his hat and stared toward the waterwheel on the other side of the millpond. "My most recent intelligence suggests that she has returned to Holstein-Schweinwald-Huhnhof. To the conspirators there, who are trying to quell popular unrest on your behalf."

Luisa straightened her posture. "Quell? What do you mean by quell? What are they doing?"

Olympia waved his hand. "Summary arrests and interrogations by the secret police. Random midnight raids of suspected royalists. Terrorizing of women and children. That sort of thing."

She jumped to her feet. "How dare they! By God, they'll pay for that!"

"Calm down, my dear. We shall take care of the matter, never fear. Besides, all this works to our favor. The people shall be clamoring for your return. In any case, I'm off to the Continent tomorrow—I have other business there, so it's all quite convenient—and I shall investigate the state of things personally."

Luisa lifted one eyebrow and razed him, from the top of his extravagant hat to the tips of his enormous heeled shoes, constructed of pink kid leather. "I daresay you shall slip in quite unnoticed."

Olympia picked at his dress and sighed. "Yes, that's the trouble, rather. Dingleby is intimately familiar with my methods and disguises, blast her."

Luisa put her hands on her hips. "Intimately, Uncle?"

Another wave of the ducal hand. "But I shall confound her, never fear. I've already had a pair of lederhosen constructed for me by an authentic Tyrolean tailor. The effect is exactly what one might wish."

Luisa shook her head. "Let me do it."

"What's that, my dear? I don't believe I heard you correctly. These old ears."

She sank to her knees and looked at him earnestly. "Let me do it."

"You do it? Ha-ha. My dear, how you amuse."

"I'm quite serious. Dingleby will smoke you out in an instant, but I . . ."

"Have been raised and educated by her since childhood." He took her hand gently. "It won't do, my dear. We both know it."

"But it's my duty . . ."

"Listen to me, Luisa. I came here not to acquaint you with all this, because I assure you I have it all well in hand, and will shortly be presenting you with your little kingdom . . ."

"Principality."

"Principality. Yes. On a silver platter, tied with a bow, everything neat and tidy, and only a husband missing. Though I believe enough time has passed, I can confide to you that I was never quite satisfied with your father's choice of such a . . ."

"Don't say a word against poor Peter."

"There you have it, in a nutshell. *Poor* Peter. Hardly the epithet of an admiring wife."

She bowed her head.

Olympia continued, "He was not unworthy, of course. But a princess needs a consort with a little more vim. A man strong enough to support her by day, to get fine, healthy sons on her by night. The sort of chap who will confound her enemies and do her dirty work, behind the scenes, so she may appear as an unsullied angel to her subjects." He coughed. "Where will such a man be found, I wonder?"

Luisa rose to her feet. "How subtle of you. I fear the man in question, however, is already married."

"Not for long." Olympia opened up the bodice of his gown and rummaged inside. "There we have it. A copy of a certain legal document, which will shortly mean the liberation of both Lord Somerton and his long-suffering wife." He held a folded paper aloft.

Luisa snatched it. "What's this?"

"A decree nisi for the dissolution of the marriage between the Earl and Countess of Somerton, et cetera, et cetera, following a suit for divorce initiated by the wife this spring for various matrimonial causes, including adultery and brutality. Not yet issued, mind you, so keep your knowledge sub rosa. In any case, the marriage is not officially ended until the decree absolute is issued after the probationary period . . ."

"Good God." The blood thudded in Luisa's temples as she

read the intricate lines of legal black ink. "Where did you get this?"

"Oh, the old school tie." He shrugged and rose to his own feet in an astonishingly agile movement for a man of sixty-five years and seventy-five inches, clothed in a silk dress and crinoline. "If you must know, the judge was my fag at Eton."

"How convenient for you."

"In any case, I have come to ask a favor of you. Or rather, to renew a favor already granted."

Luisa sighed, folded up the paper, and handed it back to him. "You want me to spy for you again."

"*Spy* is such a vulgar word."

"I will not carry tales to you. He saved my life."

"For which I am forever grateful."

"Except that you mean to use him for your own purposes."

Olympia shook his head, and his lined face lost all trace of levity beneath its rouge and powder. "I mean to right a certain wrong I committed nearly seven years ago, which has imparted such irreparable grief to the parties concerned."

Quincy lifted his head, shook his ears, and rose to his paw tips. He looked up at Olympia with an anxious whine.

Luisa bent and caressed his head, without moving her gaze an inch from Olympia's face. "Uncle, what have you done?" she whispered.

"My dear . . ." His expression changed, lifting into jollity before her eyes. He said, in a carrying falsetto, "I am delighted, delighted to see you so well. The country air! How it heals. I was saying to my old chum Martha, I said . . ."

"Mr. Markham!"

Luisa turned her bewildered face in the direction of the voice that carried across the meadow grass. A footman was pacing toward her, every swing of his arms communicating profound irritation.

"Mr. Markham! What the devil are you doing down here?"

"Thomas. Good morning. Have you met my dear aunt, Mrs. Duke of Battersea?"

Thomas pounded to a stop a few feet away and nodded at Olympia with a granite face, as if the duke's sparrow-topped hat and rose silk skirts were the most commonplace sight in Northamptonshire. "Madam," he said acidly.

"Charmed," said Mrs. Duke.

Thomas turned to Luisa. "The master wants you in his study on the double, Mr. Markham." He placed a slight sneering emphasis on the *Mister*, because while Somerton's gold could buy discretion among his servants, it could not buy forgiveness for a woman masquerading as a man for no good reason.

Olympia raised a mild eyebrow, missing nothing. "You had better get on, then, my dear nephew." He took Luisa by the shoulders and gave her a smacking kiss on each cheek. "There you are! Run back to your earl, there's a good fellow. Punctuality is godly. I'm off on my holiday. Do look out for a postcard or two, for I shall be sure to write." He turned to Thomas's sour gaze and waggled his fingers. "Good-bye, Mr. Thomas. Mind you take good care of my favorite nephew, or I shall be quite, quite angry with you." A step forward, a hint of menace. "*Quite* angry, Mr. Thomas." A step backward, all bright and cheery once more. "Off you go! Good-bye!"

Thomas turned and walked back across the grass.

"Follow him, my dear," said Olympia quietly. He slipped something into her hand. "If you need to reach me."

"Uncle . . ."

But the Duke of Olympia was already putting up his frilly pink parasol and straightening his skirts. "Until we meet again!" he called out, waving his hand.

SIXTEEN

The Earl of Somerton was scribbling furiously at his desk when Luisa entered the study ten minutes later. He looked up and threw down his pen. "There you are! Damn it all, Markham, where the devil have you been? I sent for you ages ago."

"Walking outside." The room was hot under the full glare of the morning sun. Luisa removed her coat and tossed it on the armchair. "What's the matter?"

"I've found them."

Quincy leapt up onto her jacket, turned twice, and settled himself in the center of the brown tweed with an exhausted sigh. He placed his nose on his paws and stared up at her with reproachful eyes.

She turned slowly. "Found them?"

Somerton was folding up a paper with hard strokes. "They're in Italy. Philip's nursemaid was given the boot in Milan for being with child. No doubt her ladyship believes it to be mine." His mouth curved into a sneer.

"My lord."

"We'll depart for London at once, and prepare for our journey from there."

"Our journey?" Luisa swallowed heavily.

He looked up. "To Italy, Markham. They were last seen in Florence."

"I . . . I'm going with you?"

Somerton's urgent face stiffened into its familiar mask, the one he wore when assailed by emotion. "What the devil does that mean? Of course you're going with me, Markham."

Luisa shook her head, quite slowly, giving herself time to choose her words. "Sir, I cannot be a party to this expedition. I must beg to be excused."

Somerton's hands, which were raised to fold the paper, dropped back to the desk. "That is quite impossible, Markham. You're coming with me."

"I can't, sir."

He pounded the desk. "You will! You must."

"You can't ask this of me, sir." She straightened her spine, straightened her courage. Her brain, still reeling from the information imparted by Olympia, tried to make sense of this new development. Lady Somerton was in Italy. She couldn't go to Italy. What might Somerton have planned? She dreaded to know. And there was everything else, the desperate hope now revived in her heart: How could she go to Italy, when her people needed her?

"Why the devil not? You're my secretary. I need you." Somerton's voice cracked slightly on the last words. Quincy's head lifted from his front paws at the sound.

Luisa whispered, "What do you mean to do to her?"

"To her? I don't mean to do anything to her, except to find out where she lives, to ensure my son is safe. It's Penhallow I want, by God."

Penhallow. Her cousin Roland.

Luisa curled her hands behind her back. "Don't do it, sir. In the end, revenge harms most the one who perpetrates it."

Somerton barked out a laugh. His eyes were so dark and hard, Luisa felt their despair in her bones. "As it happens, I don't give a damn. I don't care if I bleed for it. Penhallow must pay. By God, why do you think I've gone to all this trouble, all this time? For *her*?" His voice was scathing.

He stood behind his desk, large and brutal and snarling, the way a wounded beast might snarl to protect himself. Luisa watched his face, the proud bones of him, the broad planes and dark hollows. No, he wasn't handsome. He was something beyond that, something ancient and austere, carved by a pagan hand.

I need you.

Her heart beat in hard, slow thuds that numbed her ears. She licked her dry lips. "For whom, then?" she said softly.

He held her gaze without moving, except for the steady rise and fall of his massive chest, a little too rapid. His black eyes watched and watched, taking the measure of her. "Whom do you think?" he said at last.

"For yourself. For the revenge you think your honor requires."

With deliberate steps, he walked around the corner of the desk and crossed the rug toward her. The sunlight flashed across his face as he passed through the beams from the window, and then he stopped, in shadow, a foot or so away from her. So close, she could reach up and lay her palm against the sleek weave of his charcoal gray waistcoat, shielding the muscles of his chest. So close, she could see that his eyes were not quite black after all, but a dark rich brown, like the deepest molasses. Her breath left her body. She could not look away.

"Haven't you guessed by now, Markham? I have no honor."

The heat of his body touched her skin. "Yes, you do."

"Then possibly, Markham, you understand nothing about me."

She lifted her chin. "Yes, I do. I understand you better than you understand yourself. If you had no honor, you would have ruined me by now, knowing I was a woman. Instead you've let me continue on as before. You've ordered your servants to go along with my disguise. You've protected me, without even inquiring why."

"Ah. You raise an interesting point, Markham." Without breaking the charged gaze between them, Somerton lifted his hand and played with the folds of her necktie. "I've spent a great deal of time, far more than I should, wondering why you persist in this charade of yours, when we both know what lies beneath the costume."

He was steering her deftly away from her question, and she knew it, but she was powerless to return. She was too conscious of his hand on her necktie, his warm gaze fixed on her. "Because, as a woman, I cannot remain under your protection."

"That is not precisely true, Markham."

"I *will* not remain under your protection as a woman, then."

His nimble fingers were loosening her necktie, brushing the skin of her throat. He was inches away now, and his voice dropped even further, almost a whisper, stirring the thin atmosphere between them. "Markham. Did you really think you could hide from this forever? Live with me, by my side, without the two of us coming together?" His thumb pressed into the hollow of her throat. "Did you think this necktie of yours, this jacket and waistcoat, would protect you from the inevitable?"

Luisa tried to take a step backward, but his other arm slipped behind her waist and held her in place, like an iron bar.

"You want this, too, Luisa. You want me. You wouldn't have stayed with me if you didn't. But you're afraid, aren't you? You're afraid of giving in, afraid of losing yourself in my bed. You go on wearing your neckties and think it's enough to keep me at bay. As if that could make me want you less."

"That's not true."

"Don't be afraid, Markham. Luisa. Don't be afraid of this. Have you never lain with a man before? I'll be gentle, I swear it. I'll worship you. Let me serve you." The necktie fell apart. His large hand slid around the side of her throat. "Use me. Use my strength. God knows, I can give you that, at least. Whoever you're hiding from, he's no match for me. I will kill with my bare hands the man who threatens you."

His words made her blood boil over with primitive heat. "I'm not afraid," she said.

"No?" He seized the back of her head and kissed her.

The suddenness of his kiss froze her chest, froze her arms and her thoughts. As if she had been picked up without warning by an ocean wave and carried along its crest, with no idea where she might land.

His mouth was hard and hot and desperate. It hurt her lips, even as her belly ground against his, as the tips of her fingers tingled, as her flesh loosened, as her tongue reached out to find him.

"Christ," he muttered. "Markham. Sweet Christ." His lips softened into a caress, allowing the kiss to deepen and slow, allowing his tongue to slide luxuriously around her, his breath to mingle with her breath. Luisa had never felt anything so sensual, so deliriously intimate as the velvet stroke of Somerton's tongue against hers.

Want. The word screamed in her brain. She wanted *this*, she wanted more, she wanted *him*. Had wanted him for months, had craved him since she first walked into his study in Chester Square. Her breasts, crushed beneath their linen bandage, constricted by layers of shirt and waistcoat and self-control, felt as if they might burst from the pressure of her yearning.

A man to get fine, healthy sons on her by night.

Oh, God. She was lost. Her hips moved into his; her right knee lifted all by itself, sliding upward against his massive thigh. She was kissing him, kissing Somerton, and her insides were liquid, and she was opening, opening . . .

Oh, God. She was lost. She shouldn't feel this, she shouldn't want this. She was a widow, she had shared a bed with another man, with her husband, not nine full months ago, a good, clean, virtuous married bed. This was a different embrace, a different universe of sensation. This was sinful, this was dark and delicious and . . .

Oh, God. Lost to all shame. *Peter.*

Poor Peter, eclipsed by the black sun of Somerton.

Somerton's lips left her mouth and traveled to her ear. "You want me. Say it." His hands cradled her head, his legs had planted themselves on either side of hers, like Roman pillars. Trapping her, protecting her. "Say it. Say it, and I'm yours to command. Your lover, to pleasure you in bed, to give you every possible luxury. Your right hand, to smite your enemies."

She whispered, "You don't know what you're promising. You don't know who I am."

"Do you think it matters? The only thing that matters is that you're mine, Markham. I protect what's mine, whatever the cost. If it kills me."

She was drowning in sensation, drowning in the dark heat of him. Her hands were traveling up his muscular back, sliding beneath his waistcoat. His lips came down on hers again, and she groaned into his mouth.

"Markham." He pulled her face away. His voice was low and rough. "Stay with me. Come with me to Italy. I can't do this without you."

"Do what?"

"Finish it off. Slice this . . . this rotten limb from my body, once and for all. Rid myself of the corruption. Once he's dead, the wound will close, and you . . . with your pure heart . . . by my side . . . in my bed . . ." His hands were stroking her bristling hair, as if to flatten it to her head. He kissed her again, with aching gentleness. He whispered, almost impossible to hear: "Help me, Markham."

Your pure heart.

She yanked back from his embrace. The coldness of his absence shocked her; the look of sudden pain on his desire-flushed face made her throat hurt. "No! No, I can't."

His chest was heaving, as if he'd run for miles. "Why the devil not, by God? Your loyalty is to me." He reached for her again and growled, "You're mine, Markham. We both know it. At my side, in my bed."

She held up her hands, palms outward. "I'm his cousin!"

Cousin.

Cousin.

Cousin.

The word seemed to echo about the room. No turning back now.

Somerton flinched. "His *what?*"

"His cousin. I'm Roland's cousin." She took a step backward and straightened her waistcoat. Her heart was still beating madly, in desire and fear and the imminence of her exposure before him. The weight about to fall at last.

Somerton's eyes were narrowing, his body already tensing, as if anticipating the blow to come. His arms crossed against his chest, and his voice was cold and deadly.

"Explain yourself, Markham."

Say it.

She lifted herself up in defiance. "My last name isn't Markham. I haven't got a proper last name at all, because I don't need one. I'm Her Royal Highness Luisa, Princess of Holstein-Schweinwald-Huhnhof, and Lord Roland Penhallow is my second cousin."

"By God," whispered Somerton.

His hands dropped to his sides. He stood stock-still, his face now drained of blood, his eyes stark and open with shock.

Behind her, Quincy made some movement, rustling against the upholstery of the chair.

"It's not true," said Somerton.

"You know it is."

"You haven't the slightest accent."

"My mother was English, and so was my governess. English is my first language."

He shook his head. "No. By God. Not the damned German princesses. It's not possible. When was it?"

"October."

He swore.

"October, when my father was murdered, and my governess brought us to England," said Luisa. "To my uncle's house."

"Your uncle." His hand slapped his thigh. "You're Olympia's niece. He planted you here."

She hesitated. "Yes."

His eyes. Oh, God, his eyes. His expression, so soft with desire a moment ago, had hardened with calculation, each angle sharp, lips thin and tight. But it was his eyes that hurt her.

"Your dear old aunt in Battersea," he said.

"Yes."

"All this time."

"I never betrayed you. I never told him a single secret. He never asked for that." Her conscience pricked her. "Except once. Your letter to Mr. Wright. Because of Roland, you see. I know he was vile, he was deceiving you with your wife, but . . . he's my cousin, and I couldn't just stand by . . ."

Without warning, Somerton whirled around and slammed his fist into the wainscoting. An inhuman roar split his lungs apart.

"Please believe me. I never did you harm. I never would have done you harm. You must believe that."

Another roar, not quite so loud. As of despair, instead of anger.

His hands slid up the wainscoting to rest on either side of his head, fingers spread, palms against the plaster wall. The sunshine tumbled unheeding through the window to his right, turning his hair a rich dark brown on one side, an inky black on the other.

A soft whine trembled from Quincy's throat.

"A damned corgi," said Somerton. "I should have known."

"You must have known. How could you not? The clues were everywhere. My photograph was everywhere. My sisters wore whiskers, but they were too itchy for me, I couldn't bear them . . ."

"Princess Luisa." He still faced the wall. His voice was bitter. "Hiding from her enemies. How very clever of our friend the duke. I'm flattered he chose my humble establishment to shelter you."

"He knew you would protect me."

"Did he? Or was the old devil using us both for his own mysterious ends? No matter." Somerton turned, and the face he presented to Luisa made her blood chill in her veins. "I could have saved him a great deal of trouble if he'd presented his bargain to me in a more straightforward and rational manner."

"His bargain?"

"Indeed. A clever fellow like Olympia understands the art of the deal, the delicate balance of favor for favor." He walked right past her to ring the bell for the footman.

She swiveled to follow his movements. "What are you doing?"

"Why, calling for Thomas, of course. We have a certain amount of packing to do, if we're going to catch the last train for London."

"I'm not going to London." A shadow of foreboding stole across her brain.

"Aren't you?" Somerton walked to his desk, without sparing her a glance. "But you can't back out now, Mark . . . Dear me. I suppose *Markham* is hardly the proper protocol. Still, we had best call you by your accustomed name for the meantime, until your end of the bargain is fulfilled."

"I haven't made any bargain with you. I don't know what you're talking about."

Somerton was sifting through the papers on his desk. He looked up in feigned surprise. "Why, yes, you did. A favor for a favor. I understand Olympia wishes me to assist him in restoring you to your throne?"

"No! He never said that."

"Of course he didn't say it, my dear. A man of Olympia's

caliber would never be so crass. But we understand each other, he and I. I know exactly what he meant. A kind of calling card, in the manner of honor among thieves. He sent his most valuable prize, the queen of the entire chessboard, to me, because he knows I'm the only man in Europe with the necessary resources to set you atop your rightful throne, scepter in hand, once more. You do want to resume your throne, don't you, my dear princess?" His smile was sneering.

"Of course. I want justice for my people. I want . . ."

"Very good. You give me Penhallow, I give you Holstein-Schweinwald-Huhnhof. A fine trade, don't you think?"

The door opened. Thomas stepped inside, before Luisa's horrified eyes, and made his bow. "Yes, sir?"

"Ah. Thomas." The earl's eyes did not leave Luisa. "Kindly tell Graves that Markham and I will be departing on the evening train to London. Our things are to be packed up at once."

"Yes, sir," said Thomas.

Luisa stepped forward. "But I . . ."

"Tut-tut, Mr. Markham." Somerton raised his finger. "We have our bargain, and I assure you, I don't intend to let you shirk your end of it. Thank you, Thomas. That will be all."

The footman bowed and left the room. Quincy jumped off his chair and scampered past Thomas's feet, to disappear around the corner of the library.

"I never agreed . . ." Luisa began.

Somerton walked up to her. The door was still open to the library, exposing them to the eyes of any passing servant, but he didn't seem to notice. He ran his finger along the edge of her jaw. "Think of it, Markham. Your kingdom restored to you, your enemies vanquished. Your father and husband—I believe you had a husband, too, did you not, the poor chap?— yes, your beloved husband revenged. Justice for your people. You have only to assist me in a single trifling matter."

"It is not a trifle."

"Compared to the fate of an entire people? I think, when you reflect on the matter, during our long and rattling journey to London, you will reconcile yourself to your duty. A princess must always put the needs of her people before her own personal inclinations, mustn't she?" His thumb brushed her bottom lip. "Her own desires."

She slapped his hand away.

Somerton laughed. He tilted his head slightly, watching her. "Poor Markham," he said. "What an undignified arrangement you've endured, these past several months. Entirely unsuited to your station. I shall endeavor to make it up to you at every opportunity."

"You really are a beast, aren't you?"

He laughed again and returned to his desk.

"My dear Markham. That's exactly why your uncle gave you to me."

SEVENTEEN

Florence, Italy
Midsummer 1890

The Florentine sun lay hot on Luisa's shoulders as she emerged from the shelter of Santa Maria Novella station, and the air was thick with manure and unwashed male bodies. She settled the brim of her hat another half inch lower on her damp forehead and turned to Somerton's broad figure beside her. "There should be . . ."

"Signore!" called a voice, across the swarm of carriages and men in the Piazza della Stazione.

"There's our man," Somerton said calmly. He lifted one hand and stepped forward.

A moment later, a closed carriage maneuvered through the lines of waiting vehicles outside the station and a man jumped from the driver's seat, swearing in theatrical Italian. "*Buon giorno*, my lord," he said, with a sweeping bow, as if Somerton were a returning Medici prince.

"*Buon giorno*," Somerton said dryly. "To the Grand, if you please. As quickly as possible. Our luggage will follow."

The driver sprang back into his seat, leaving Somerton to climb into the carriage first. He held out his hand to Luisa, which she ignored, casting a sympathetic glance back to the valet with his four large valises. She had never paid much attention to luggage before; in her previous life, it simply arrived

politely where it was supposed to, without any visible effort.
Now she knew the challenge of making arrangements for one's
personal effects, in the heat of a European summer, and in the
crawling confusion of a terminus taxi queue. Somerton had
insisted they leave these arrangements to his valet, but Luisa
had felt a pang of conscience for the poor man every time.

For one thing, it was hot. Damned midsummer hot.

She sank into her seat and lifted off her hat to fan herself.
"This damned heat," she said.

Somerton shrugged. "What one expects in Florence, at this
time of year." He didn't appear to be affected by the weather
at all, despite his size and his neat layers of correct English
clothing. He sat tranquilly in the rear-facing seat—he always
ceded the forward-facing seat to her, as her right—and gazed
out the window as the carriage lurched through the midday
traffic. Only a faint sheen of dew gleamed on his temples,
beneath the straw weave of his hat.

"Have you visited Italy often?" Luisa ventured.

"I suppose so. Not recently, however."

A movement caught her attention: the drumming of Somerton's fingers on his knee. She had never seen him do that
before.

She cleared her throat. "Have you stayed at the Grand
Hotel before?"

"I have." He turned his head to face her, and his mouth was
curled with a faint amusement. "Have you?"

"No. My father always preferred the coast of France."

"Too many Englishmen, I've always thought."

She wanted to scream at the polite tone of the conversation,
the brittle surface that persisted between them, keeping everything else unsaid. In the past fortnight, filled with travel
arrangements and telegrams, the intricate piecing together of
Somerton's plot to entrap Lord Roland Penhallow, he had
treated her with an efficiency even more cordially brusque
than he had done in the winter, as if the desire he'd felt for her
in Northamptonshire had been utterly smothered by the reve-
lation of her true identity.

Except, sometimes, in the evening, when he had had a glass
or two of brandy, and he would approach her with his innuen-
dos and his double entendres, standing too close, letting her

know that he *could*, if he wanted. That she was detained at *his* pleasure, not her own.

That the power was his.

But he never went further than that. At the last instant, he turned away, and told her to go to bed. To get some sleep. So she would lie in her bed and fall asleep to the melancholy strains of the cello in the adjoining room. Which was, of course, for the best. Once he'd helped her regain her throne, she could have no further use for him. A princess without heirs did not take lovers. She chose a suitable husband from the panoply of royal European prospects and did her duty. She maintained her public virtue. She set a proper example for her subjects.

She did not dream about a pair of muscular shoulders rising above her in the dark of night, about a pair of velvet lips capturing her mouth, about a pair of powerful hips driving against hers . . .

"Mr. Markham."

Luisa blinked in the shaft of sunlight that bolted suddenly through the window. The Earl of Somerton's face came into focus before her, still smiling that faintly amused smile. "Sir?"

"We've arrived."

The carriage had stopped moving. Luisa turned to the window just as the door was flung open and the stately facade of the Grand Hotel appeared in the rectangle of exposed daylight. A rush of hot air flooded the stuffiness of the carriage, scented with rotting damp from the river.

"After you, my dear," said the Earl of Somerton.

By the time he returned from the villa he'd leased upstream on the opposite bank of the Arno, having installed his valet and Mrs. Yarrow to his satisfaction and ensured that everything lay in perfect wait for tomorrow's games, the red sun lay dying on the horizon and an elderly man in a tasseled sky blue uniform was igniting the arc lamps outside the Grand Hotel, one by one.

Somerton took in a long breath of the cooling air and paused on the pavement near the hotel entrance. To his left, the Ponte Vecchio sat athwart the river, its old stones turned a volcanic red orange in the sunset. The busy tide of traffic had fallen away, and the tourists now wandered in relative peace, guidebooks in hand, waiting to catch that coveted glimpse of the twilight Arno, *a sight essential to the Continental tour of every discerning traveler,* or something to that effect. He tossed his reins to the waiting groom. "See that I have a sturdy horse, saddled and ready, at an hour before midnight," he said, and drew a golden English guinea from his pocket.

The groom's eyes lit with wonder. "*Sì*, signore."

Perhaps, in another life, Somerton might have walked across the lobby of the hotel with some recognition, if not outright appreciation, of its fine frescoes, its elegant columns and plasterwork, its magnificent stained glass ceiling. But the present man merely reached the front desk, asked for his key, and inquired for the manager, a man by the name of Sartoli.

"He is not here at the present moment, signore," said the desk clerk, with a neutral expression.

Somerton drew another guinea from his pocket and slid it across the polished wood.

The clerk looked up. "Wait here a moment, signore."

A quarter hour later, Somerton ascended the stairs to the second-floor suite that he—or, in actual fact, Markham—had booked for their use. What a remarkable thing, to have a princess regnant booking his hotel rooms, but there it was. She was still his private secretary, until the successful conclusion of tomorrow's affair. That was the bargain, that was the favor she had reluctantly granted him, in exchange for the recovery of her throne.

And then . . . what?

Somerton removed the key from his inside jacket pocket and opened the heavy door.

There was no sound inside, nor any light from under the bedroom door. He had expected her to be still at her desk, or enclosed in an armchair, reading, but there was no sign she existed within these walls at all. Just a roomful of dark, cool air, scented with lavender, a cave of unexpected tranquility.

He switched on a light—the interior of the hotel had recently been wired for electricity—and looked about. The luggage had all been sent on to the Palazzo Angelini, except for a few necessary articles, and the sitting room showed no evidence of a paying inhabitant. An extravagant bouquet of lavender sat on the round gilded table in the center of the room, the source of the perfume.

"Markham?" he called out softly.

There was no answer. No matter. She wouldn't have left.

Somerton removed his jacket and tossed it on an armchair. The bathroom lay to the right. He opened the door and turned on the taps in the tub. Added a dash of oil. Settled in with a long sigh. The water was good and hot, melting away the grime of travel, the accumulated layers of effort and worry. He allowed himself a luxurious five minutes before reaching for the soap, and then he went to work with purpose, cleaning and shaving, toweling himself dry, wrapping his hard and graceless body, his hair-sprinkled chest and his brutal too-thick limbs, in a dressing gown lined in Turkish toweling.

For an instant, he paused with his hand on the bedroom door. Perhaps he should knock.

He pushed open the door and strode inside.

Markham lay on the bed, fully clothed, her head turned to the window and a book tumbled at her side with the pages splayed upward. Had probably been reading by daylight, and fallen asleep with the setting sun. He leaned against the wall and studied her in the gloaming, admired the elegant curve of her cheekbone as it gathered the dusky glow of gaslight from the window. He breathed in the dampness rising up from the river, the scent of sun-warmed pavement and cigarettes. The window must be open.

So Markham had sent a telegram to the Duke of Olympia while he was gone. Sartoli had not made a copy of the contents, alas, but Somerton could guess. Well, it was no more than he expected, anyway. That Olympia was already in Milan surprised him even less. Penhallow had never lacked for allies, had he? Like a jack-in-the-box, he had always sprung up again, merry as ever, handsome and effervescent, no matter how often Somerton tried to stuff him back into the darkness.

He levered himself away from the wall and came to sit at the edge of the bed. Her hair had grown out a little more, wine dark and gleaming against the whiteness of the pillow. He longed to see it down around her shoulders, spread across her breasts in the flushed aftermath of love. He lifted his hand and brushed the line of her regal cheekbone, the curve of her noble lip.

Her eyes came open. She sat up with a little cry.

"I beg your pardon," he said. "I didn't mean to startle you."

"Yes, you did." Her shoulders eased a quarter inch. She took in his dressing gown, his damp hair, with her sleep-blurred eyes. Caught unawares, without her usual haughty aspect, she looked as innocent as a child, a girl dressed in her brother's Eton suit. "Have you finished your business?"

"Indeed. All stands ready for tomorrow."

"If all goes according to your plan."

"It will." He played with her collar, glowing blue white in the faded light. "You sent a telegram this afternoon."

Her eyes widened. "Yes."

"I wondered whether you would. How much did you tell him?"

"I had to do it. I had to warn someone."

He shrugged. "Did you think I would be angry? Of course not, little one. I expected nothing less, than you would defend your dear cousin with all your strength, against all evil. Betray me at every turn."

"Then why did you bring me along? Enlist my help?"

"Because I can't leave you to your own devices, Markham. God only knows what harm you might do, out of my sight." He stroked the round edge of her collarbone with his thumb. "And perhaps I have a different sort of revenge in mind for you, when this is finished."

She remained still under his caress. "I haven't betrayed you, my lord," she said quietly. "And I don't think you're as evil as that."

"But not so good as that nonpareil Penhallow, eh? The *parfit gentil* knight, adored by all women, admired by all men."

"I don't adore him. I hardly even know him. The last time I saw him was . . . God, it must have been eight or nine years ago. One summer in England. I was a child." She caught his hand at her collar, and her eyes caught the light, gleaming with tears to which she would never admit. "You're the one in greater danger. If you commit this act, what will it do to you?"

"I have killed men before, Markham, and polished off my breakfast without qualm the next morning."

"My lord, don't do this. Revenge has nothing to do with honor or duty. Let them be. Stay here in Florence."

He spread his fingers around the slender base of her throat. Her pulse ticked against his skin, rapid as a cat's, giving the lie to her steady demeanor. "Stay here, in this room. With you, Markham?"

Her lips parted slightly, and then closed without replying. But she did not say *no*. She did not turn away.

"What's this? You'll even whore yourself for his sake?" He leaned forward. "I don't need to bargain with you. I could take you right now, if I wanted you, right on this bed. That's what scoundrels do, don't they?"

"Don't. You're better than this."

He laughed. "My dear princess. I'm not better than this." He rose from the bed and went to the wardrobe in the corner. "Penhallow wants to take my wife for himself, to take my son for himself. You cannot think I'd allow him to usurp me, without a reckoning."

"You can make arrangements. You can divorce her, and have Philip stay with you from time to time. You can still be a father to him, you can still know him . . ."

Somerton let the dressing gown drop to the floor. A startled gasp came from behind him, and a flurry of movement. Burying her dignified face in the pillow, no doubt.

He slid on his undershirt and drawers, without the slightest concern. "But so much easier, if he has no other father to poison his ears against me."

"Roland wouldn't do that." Her voice was muffled.

"Wouldn't he? He had no scruples when it came to running off with my wife and son in the first place."

She didn't answer. Somerton went on buttoning his shirt, drawing on his riding breeches, fastening his waistcoat. He drew his jacket from its hanger and slipped it over his shoulders.

"My boots, Markham." He turned. "Since my valet is elsewhere."

She was sitting upright in the armchair, watching him. God knew how long. "This sickness inside you," she said quietly. "This is not the cure."

"You're quite right. There is no cure for me. But justice is a dirty business, my dear, as you'll soon learn when you're attempting to rule a country by your shining upright principles. My boots?" He held them out to her.

She made no move, only sat there in her chair with her calm dark eyes, Princess Luisa on her throne, regarding a subject whose fate she had to determine.

He sat on the edge of the bed. "Very well. I suppose I can manage myself."

Markham rose from the chair and took the boot from his hand. "My lord."

She held the boot firmly while he inserted his foot, kneeling before him while her gaze stayed fixed on his knee. The top of her head shone ginger in the light from the electric lamp next to the bed. The supple leather slid up his calf, a perfect fit, and Markham nudged his ankle into place with an expert twist of her long-fingered hands.

When she had fitted him into the other boot, she dropped her palms to her thighs and looked up at him. "After this is over, whatever the outcome, what do you intend to do?"

"I intend to accompany you to Germany and roust out these regicidal rascals, which have given my good friend Olympia such a great deal of trouble."

"And after that? If we succeed." Her gaze was direct, straight between his eyes.

Somerton's heart made an unexpected lurch in his chest. Perhaps it was that extraordinary word *we*, dropped so carelessly into a short and commonplace sentence.

He stood abruptly and stared down at her, on her knees in the carpet before him.

"Then our association, Markham, must necessarily come to an end. Did your governess never tell you?" He reached for her hand, drew her up hard to her feet, and leaned in close to her lips. "Princesses can have nothing to do with scoundrels."

EIGHTEEN

The sun was high overhead when Lady Somerton's pale figure finally appeared through the crowds of people crossing the Ponte Vecchio, a rose among the wilted ragweed. She was riding a horse, and looked as if she were ready to drop from her saddle.

For a few seconds, Luisa only stared at her, fighting back a tide of unreasonable anger that swamped her without warning at the sight of all that breathtaking beauty. Anger, or jealousy? The countess had known the dark magic of Somerton's body on hers, had conceived a child with him. Had been married to him for six long years, and had never once appreciated the gift she had been given. Had not known what to do with a man like Somerton.

And then her ladyship's eyes turned in Luisa's direction, and Luisa saw the panic in them, the agony of a mother who has lost her child, and her anger dissolved.

He really was a scoundrel, after all.

She stepped forward. "Your ladyship! Lady Somerton!"

The countess's face jerked to attention. "Markham!"

Luisa grabbed hold of the horse's headstall. The animal was dark with sweat, the saddle leather foaming at the edges against his gray coat. Lady Somerton slid from the saddle and grabbed the lapels of Luisa's jacket.

"Where is he?" she demanded hoarsely. "Where's Philip?"

"He's safe. I promise you. He's safe, he's well." Luisa drew the folded note from her pocket and held it before Lady Somerton's dusty face. The countess snatched it away and opened it with shaking fingers. "Whatever else he might do," she said quietly, "his lordship would never harm his son."

Lady Somerton scowled over the edge of the paper. "You will forgive me, Mr. Markham, if your words are little comfort to me."

A hot reply rose to Luisa's lips, adultery and abduction and faithlessness. She bit it back. The countess's grief was too genuine.

Already Lady Somerton was folding up the note with sharp strokes of her fingers. "Are you to accompany me to this villa of his?"

"Yes." Luisa nodded to the hackney waiting by the curb.

Lady Somerton held out the reins. "Is there somewhere nearby I can stable my horse?"

A quarter hour later, they were crossing the Arno in the hackney, enjoying—if that was the word—the relief of the draught that rushed against their faces. The sky was hot and blue, and the air laden with spiciness by the dark green cypress trees lining the dusty road toward the villa. "He should not have taken Philip," Lady Somerton said suddenly. "He should leave the boy out of it."

"You took him away! Without leaving word, without saying where you'd gone. Philip is Lord Somerton's son, too. He doesn't belong to you exclusively."

"He's never shown an interest in him before."

"Because you never let him. You've guarded the door to Philip's heart since the moment he was born."

The countess knotted her hands in her lap. "Because I know what my husband is like. You don't know what a brute he is. How easily he could hurt Philip, or turn him into another version of himself."

Luisa hesitated. "Yes, he can be brutal. But he has also the capacity for great devotion. And you never knew. You never gave him a chance, did you? You never opened your heart to him."

Lady Somerton turned away and watched the cypress slide by.

The Palazzo Angelini stood alone between the road and the river, at the top of a hill that sloped down gradually to the brown green width of the summer Arno. Luisa had sat up waiting in the drawing room the night before, Quincy at her feet, until Somerton arrived in a carriage shortly before sunrise, carrying the sleeping Philip in his arms. She had led them both to Philip's room on the third floor and woken Mrs. Yarrow to care for the boy, and then she had followed Somerton to his own magnificent bedroom, the master's room. His eyes were rimmed with exhaustion. "He went right to sleep in the carriage," he said, and there was an odd sort of joy in his face, amid the heavy lines. "He's a good lad."

The valet entered the room at that point, shrugging on his jacket as he went. "Get some rest," Luisa had replied, and she had taken Somerton's carriage back to the Grand Hotel, leaving Quincy behind to curl on Philip's bed until the boy woke. As she looked back, the pinkness of dawn turned the brick chimneys bright red.

Now, under the white midday sun, the old stones of the villa blazed in pale Palladian splendor at the end of the graveled drive. The fountain rustled calmly in the center of the outer courtyard. Luisa leapt out of the hackney first and held out her hand for Lady Somerton.

"Thank you," the countess said coldly. She looked up at the white portico. "Where is my son?"

Luisa glanced at the third-floor windows and down again. "He's well. Lord Somerton would like to see you first."

"Naturally." Lady Somerton's voice was bitter.

She followed Luisa into the villa and up the curving marble staircase to the room Somerton had set aside for the purpose, furnished with a pair of chairs and an escritoire. When the countess had settled into her chair, Luisa went to Somerton's chamber and knocked on the door.

"Come in."

He was standing before the window in his trousers and shirtsleeves and an immaculate waistcoat of gray houndstooth, drinking a cup of coffee from a small blue and white cup of nearly translucent delicacy. His black hair was brushed, his cheeks faintly pink from a recent shaving. "How is she?" he asked, without turning.

"Exhausted. Upset. But in good health, considering the circumstances."

He drained the coffee and set the cup aside in its saucer with a distant clink. "Then we had better get to it, hadn't we?"

"You can still put an end to this," she said. "You can still bring about a sensible resolution. You have allowed her divorce petition to proceed without protest."

He turned. His necktie was folded in precise creases that echoed, somehow, the strict austerity of his features. His eyebrows lifted slightly. "And how did you come by this information? Olympia, I suppose?"

"Does it matter?"

"Not really. But you must know that the decree is only preliminary."

"You can't possibly intend to reconcile."

Somerton drew a charcoal tweed jacket from a nearby chair and shrugged his arms inside. "Of course not. But it remains a chip with which to bargain, does it not?"

Luisa shook her head. "Can you not simply forgive each other and part as friends? Must you destroy her?"

Somerton adjusted his cuffs and walked to the tray of liquors next to the armchair. He poured himself a glass of brandy and drank it in a single smooth gulp, and then he walked with great calmness to the door. Just before he reached it, he lifted his hand and covered Luisa's cheek with his broad palm.

"My dear, you look tired. When all this is finished, you must endeavor to rest."

She couldn't stand it. Her heart felt as if two strong hands had grasped each side, and were rending it down the middle. "Don't hurt her," she said.

His hand dropped away. He opened the door and paused, staring into the open hallway. "It is not Lady Somerton I intend to hurt," he said.

Twenty minutes later, the click of boots on marble startled Luisa out of a reverie, as she stared through the French doors at the back of the entrance hall, all the way down the length of the precisely trimmed garden to the high green hedges of the maze at its rear.

She turned. The Earl of Somerton stepped toward her, every hair still in place, every fold of his necktie still precisely laid, except that his face had drained of blood. "It's done," he said. He held out a folded paper. "She wrote the note. Now take my carriage, and make haste. He may already have arrived at the hotel."

Luisa took the note and slipped it into her jacket pocket. "Yes, my lord."

She had dreaded this meeting, ever since Somerton had first outlined his plan to her, on the overnight train to Milan from Paris. As the carriage bore her back into town, she dreaded it even more. True, she hadn't seen Roland in a decade, not since she was an awkward carrot-haired girl on the brink of adolescence and he was a young man at Eton, golden and glamorous. He hadn't noticed her then, and he would hardly be searching out the features of that unremarkable second cousin Luisa in the face of the young personal secretary to his archenemy, the Earl of Somerton.

But she would know him. His charm, his good looks, his magnetism. Above all, his status as the beloved grandson of her own uncle, the Duke of Olympia.

How could she remain indifferent?

If he hasn't already arrived, Somerton had instructed her, *wait for him in the bedroom.*

Luisa had wondered how Roland would know which rooms were theirs, and how he would gain entry.

Somerton had laughed at her. *My dear girl, he'll be up in a trice, never fear.*

As Somerton had told her, she had the carriage pull up to the rear entrance. Sartoli was waiting for her there, his collar glowing white in the shadowed vestibule. "Has the English lord arrived yet?" she asked breathlessly.

"No, signore," he said. He handed her the room key.

"Very good. When he does, you're to tell him that Lord Somerton checked out of the suite an hour ago, alone." She handed him a guinea.

He made a slight bow. "The service stairs lie to your right, signore," he said.

"Thank you." Luisa wrapped her fingers around the cold metal key and hurried up the stairs to the second floor, until she came to the suite of rooms she and Somerton had occupied the day before. The space was empty now, of course. What few personal articles she and the earl had brought yesterday had gone with Luisa to the Palazzo Angelini, soon after Somerton had departed for the Tuscan castle to which his wife and Lord Roland Penhallow had been traced. The gilded furniture, the heavy drapes might have belonged to any luxury hotel in Europe. Luisa closed the curtains in the sitting room and crossed to the bedroom, where she performed a similar act, enclosing the room in a murky dimness.

Just in case.

After all, the less Roland saw of her face, the better.

The clock on the desk chimed the hour in two delicate pings. Luisa settled herself into the armchair while her eyes accustomed themselves to the darkness.

The Earl of Somerton paced across the length of his bedroom in measured strides, brandy in hand. A small bowl of roses had been placed inexplicably on his bedside table—the bedside table of a bed he had never slept in—at some point during his absence, and the scent reminded him of Northamptonshire, and Markham standing in his study, about to be kissed.

He came to a stop in the center of the floor and stared at the empty glass in his hand. His fingers curled around it, as if to splinter the crystal into his calloused palm.

Now came the reckoning. He had sent Markham off to fetch Roland, had trusted her with the blind and reckless faith of a man hopelessly in love.

Would she return?

The afternoon sun coursed through the windows of the room, which faced west, toward the river breezes and the red-tiled rooftops of Florence, away from the road and the courtyard. Upstairs, his wife played with their son within a well-appointed room, locked from the outside. If he stood quite still and strained his ears, he could hear the rapid click of claws on the polished wooden floorboards, as Markham's damned dog chased a ball for Philip's amusement. That was something, anyway. Some piece of Markham left behind.

The clock on the mantel chimed two thirty. He took out his watch from his pocket to be certain. Yes, two thirty. Markham and Penhallow should have arrived by now, unless there had been some delay. Unless she had decided not to return after all, that her throne wasn't worth her cousin's life. Or that the talents of her uncle the duke—and Somerton had to give Olympia his due, the cunning old puppet master—were sufficient to secure her birthright from the anarchist assassins who had overthrown her.

He set the brandy glass down on the tray with a crash. By God, he would wring the necks of every last one of those damned bloodthirsty revolutionaries, once his business here in Italy had concluded. Whether or not Markham asked him to.

And then his head bowed.

If she asked him to.

What would he do if she didn't?

He should have made love to her in the Northamptonshire study while he could. Or any one of a dozen opportunities between then and now: the sleeper train compartment, the house in London, the hotel in Paris. The dulcet early evening in the Grand Hotel, before he had left to spirit his son away. Now the chance had fled. Markham had fled, and he might never have the chance again. Might never know the feel of her skin against his, the kiss of her, the life of her.

As it should be, his conscience whispered.

A roar rose up in his throat. He forced it down and lifted the brandy decanter.

But as he drew the stopper from its neck, another sound drifted faintly through the half-open door.

Footsteps. Voices.

He set the stopper back and placed the decanter on the tray once more, right next to the dark ruby port.

Beneath the layers of his clothing, his heart was beating too fast. He stared at the tray of liquors and concentrated on calming his emotions, the old tricks he had learned from childhood: slow the breathing, relax the fingers, unclench the belly. The very act of concentration freed his mind, as it always did, and the familiar clarity settled upon him. Each sound, each sight, each sensation of touch and taste reached his brain with separate acuity.

He was ready.

He glanced at the chest of drawers next to the window, upon which his knife and his revolver lay, ready for use.

No. This fight would be man-to-man, skin to skin, primitive and honorable.

He straightened his cuffs and walked out of the room to the stairs.

NINETEEN

As beautiful as the Palazzo Angelini was, white-faced and elegant along the winding road into Florence, its true worth lay in the surrounding grounds. The terraced lawns, the symmetrical beds planted with rare and beautiful flowers, the hawthorn maze protecting the house from the river traffic below: All these had been laid out centuries ago, and still looked as fresh as yesterday morning.

The Earl of Somerton appreciated none of this. He emerged from the maze at a dead run, panting and perspiring, with the sun in his face. He lifted his arm to shield his eyes and cast about the sloping meadow to the dull brown ribbon of the Arno below.

Where had she gone?

Where had she taken his son?

He would never forget the shock of walking into her room and finding it empty, the window open, a rope from one of Philip's pull toys stretching down from the balcony to the trees below. All his plans, thrown instantly into disaster. Who knew that Elizabeth harbored such intrepid determination—worthy of one of his finest agents—behind her ladylike facade?

Or that she hated him so much.

Perhaps they'd had it all planned out, she and Penhallow.

Perhaps he'd gotten a message to her somehow, to meet him down by the river. And this time, they would escape for good. They would find some remote corner of the world, and he would never see Philip again.

He was not a good father. He knew that. How was a good father supposed to behave? He'd never known. His father had largely ignored him, until that fatal fifteenth birthday jaunt to the brothel. And now he had four children of his own, by four different mothers, and he was at a loss, helpless to fill the holes in his heart that each one had created, helpless to find the ways into theirs.

If he failed now. If he failed with this boy, with this son, he might never have another chance.

God grant him another chance.

A movement caught his eye, near the trees at the riverside. A voice carried upward from the water.

"Father?"

He heard a woman's voice, smothering the child's, but the single word was enough.

He bolted down the slope at a dead run, legs pumping, arms swinging. The two figures came into view, Elizabeth and Philip, the little boy holding out his arms and the mother crushing him to her chest, the way Penhallow had held Markham a short while ago.

Out from his lungs came a furious noise, a snarl of rage.

Elizabeth turned and tried to run, tugging Philip along with her, but the boy struggled out of her grasp and ran toward him.

Toward *him*.

He staggered to a halt, several yards away. The words jumbled in his head. *A father should be stern yet kind. A father should command his household. A father should. A father should.* "Young man . . ." he began.

"Father, where's the doggie? I want the doggie," said Philip. His face was pleading.

The *dog*? He wanted the damned *dog*?

"That's Mr. Markham's dog, Philip. Now come with me." He held out his hand.

"No, Philip!" Elizabeth snatched the boy's other hand. "Come along."

Philip looked at him apologetically. "Mama says I should come with her, sir."

Elizabeth began to pull Philip down the river path, and something snapped inside of Somerton's heart.

He would never have Philip, because his wife would never let him. She stood like a knight in front of Philip's young heart, refusing entry, refusing even to let him try. To try to be a father, to try to learn, somehow, what it was that fathers were supposed to do.

A growl started in his ribs and parted his lips. He bent down and swooped up Philip in his arms, and by God, the boy laughed. He laughed with glee, and the growl choked in Somerton's throat, strangled by the joy of holding his own son, his own warm-bodied, eager-limbed son in his arms.

"Stop it! Put him down!" screamed Elizabeth. "You'll hurt him!"

Enough was enough. He swung the delighted Philip under one arm and grabbed Elizabeth by the other hand and hauled them both across the grass, up the slope toward the maze. "Into the house, by God. We're going to settle this, we're going to . . ."

"No! You can't have him, do you hear me? You brute, you lecherous madman . . ."

"Not in front of the boy, Elizabeth. For God's sake." He brought his arm around her shoulders and went on striding up the hill, dragging her along with the force of his determined momentum. "We'll discuss this inside. I am not giving him up."

"You can't take him! I'm his mother, I . . ."

The words died away. Elizabeth twisted her body and looked up the hillside. "Oh, look!" she cried out. "Roland's here!"

Somerton looked up.

He had forgotten entirely about Penhallow. The thoughts of revenge that had consumed his hours had somehow dissolved into the warm skin of the little boy now tucked under his left arm. But Penhallow himself had not dissolved. He stood poised at the entrance of the maze, bathed in afternoon sunshine, like a god returned to earth. He sent them a cheerful wave and called something down.

In the instant of surprise, Somerton loosened his grip on his wife's shoulders. She whirled around and drove her fist into his back.

The shock of it nearly sent him to his knees. Philip scrambled out of his other arm.

"Run, Philip!" Elizabeth screamed. "Run for the maze!"

The boy pelted happily up the hill. "Uncle Roland!" he called out. "There you are!"

Uncle Roland.

Like a nightmare, the scene unfolded before him. Philip, his boy, his dark-haired son, ran away through the trim green grass, his little calves pumping with effort. And Penhallow, golden Penhallow, Fortune's favorite child, grinning like a lunatic, dropped to one and stretched out his arms.

Philip ran straight into Penhallow's embrace, to be enfolded by those long arms, to be kissed on the top of his dark head by those smiling lips.

When Somerton was not much older than Philip—eight, perhaps, at the most—he had wandered into the music room one afternoon and found his mother lying on the chaise longue by the window with a strange man on top of her. His mother's clothes were rumpled, her breasts bare, her skirts up around her waist. The man had his clothes on, except for his bottom, which was bare and white. He had his mouth on her mouth. He was braced on his elbows, grunting and pumping his bottom on top of her, and his mother was crying out softly.

Somerton had thought that the man was trying to hurt her. He had grabbed the poker iron and dragged it across the room and, in the strength of panic, had lifted it up and bashed the man on the back. "Get off my mother!" he'd screamed.

The man had gotten off his mother, all right, and he'd boxed Somerton's ears so hard they rang for a week. But it was his mother's words that hurt the most. *You stupid boy, look what you've done. You stupid, ugly boy, oh, my poor Rupert, my sweet darling, did he hurt you?* She had turned away from Somerton and embraced her lover tenderly, kissing him all over, begging his forgiveness.

Whenever the memory of this particular event pushed above the surface of his mind, Somerton smashed it back down again. But he couldn't forget the pain. It still echoed across his ribs. He couldn't forget the way his heart had felt, as if someone had ripped open his chest and taken it out to see if it was still beating.

The way Lord Roland Penhallow had ripped out his heart just now.

"You see!" Elizabeth's voice hissed in his ear. "You see how he is with him! He loves him!"

She hurried forward to join them, but Somerton reached out his arm and snared her effortlessly. "Vicious little thing, aren't you?" he said.

"Let me go! Can't you see it's hopeless? Can't you see you won't win?"

He turned his mouth to her ear. "He shan't have you. By God, he shan't."

"Then kill me! Kill us all! What the devil do you mean by all this? Do you think to save your pride with revenge?" She was panting with emotion. "It won't work. It never works. Revenge is hollow; don't you know that, by now?"

Markham's voiced rattled in his head. *Revenge harms most the one who perpetrates it.*

Wise old Markham.

"That's it, isn't it?" whispered Elizabeth. "You haven't a clue what to do with us. You can't bring yourself to let us go, but you can't bring yourself to end it all. You're a coward, Somerton. A bully and a coward."

She was right, wasn't she? *Stupid, ugly boy.* A bully and coward.

He lifted his hand to rake it through his hair, and a movement snagged his attention, near the river. A flash of subtle color in the brush.

He straightened his back and freed Elizabeth's arm from his hand. He was dimly aware of Penhallow approaching, saying her name tenderly, urging her back to the maze with Philip. Safely away from her brutal husband.

There it was. A figure emerged from the brush, tall and gray-haired, dressed in immaculate tweed. His hat was under his arm, and a walking stick kept a stately pace by his side. He stepped onto the flagstones of the river terrace, dabbed his forehead with a handkerchief, and looked upward to the maze and gardens of the Palazzo Angelini.

The Duke of Olympia.

Luisa pressed her fingers into the papery bark of the tree and watched her uncle advance to the terrace.

The damp smell of the river filled her nose, mingling with the rampant green vegetation by the water's edge. Her chest was still heaving. She'd run downstairs from Philip's empty room, out the door and up the road, where she'd met Olympia in the agreed-upon place, the summer pavilion of the neighboring villa.

"You've got to come now," she'd said, holding a pillar for support. "Lady Somerton and Philip have escaped, and Penhallow's after them, and God knows what Somerton will do when he finds them."

The duke had risen and picked up his walking stick from the bench beside him. "Calm yourself, my dear." He patted his pocket. "This unsavory drama was, I'm afraid, necessary for all parties. The only way to bare the truth. But I've the solution to it all right here."

Her gaze had fallen to the wide patch pockets of his tweed jacket. "The divorce papers?"

"The same. Lead on."

She had led on, and Olympia had followed her swiftly along the river path, betraying a little more urgency than his calm words had suggested.

When they reached the open lawn of the Palazzo Angelini, he'd placed a warning hand against her chest. "Stay back, my dear. These things never quite go according to plan. My man Mr. Beadle is waiting by the bridge, if help is needed."

Mr. Beadle, another of Olympia's network of agents, crisscrossing Europe. Luisa leaned her head against the tree trunk and concentrated on bringing her breathing under control, bringing her heart back to a more reasonable pace.

She tilted her head around the tree to gather the scene. Somerton, Penhallow, and Lady Somerton stood on the grass, near the base of the slope, staring at the river terrace where Olympia stood. Of Philip, there was no sign.

"What the devil are you doing here, Olympia?" Somerton called out. His hands were on his hips. Penhallow was holding Lady Somerton, whispering something in her ear, and she nodded and turned up the slope, hurrying toward the maze, where a small figure—Luisa craned her neck—could now be seen, sitting in the grass at the top of the hill.

Philip. Thank God.

Olympia's voice rang out in reply, but he was facing away from her, toward the figures on the grass, and Luisa couldn't hear them.

Olympia advanced toward them, like a policeman brought in to sort out a brawl. Luisa leaned her head against the tree and forced her limbs to remain still. Not to go. Not to run to Somerton's side and defend him. He could defend himself; he had to. The four of them had to bring everything, every secret and lie and subterfuge, into the open together, in this complicated and heartbreaking affair in which she, Luisa, had no part.

They had to do it, for the sake of Philip.

And he would do it. In the end, Somerton would do what was best; she was sure of that. When the markers were all on the table, he would give up his fury and his revenge, and he would do the honorable thing.

He *would*.

The fury was still there. She could see it in his face, in his stance, as he argued there with Olympia and Penhallow. But there was something else, some subtle slope in his shoulders, that told her something else. The presence of pain, or perhaps defeat.

What had happened, there on the lawn, before she arrived? She looked back up at Lady Somerton, who was holding Philip close, watching the scene below as anxiously as Luisa was. Her faultless beauty glowed in the sun, even from this distance. She and Penhallow, they were a glorious pair.

"Damn you for that!" Somerton's voice carried across the grass.

Olympia was pounding his gold-knobbed walking stick in a theatrical manner. Penhallow had his fists balled by his sides. Luisa stood uncertainly. Should she run down to the bridge and find Beadle?

A burst of faint laughter reached her ears. She turned to the river, where a tourist boat was making its way downstream, filled with frilly pastel dresses and parasols, with men in rumpled linen suits. The lighthearted chatter rattled against her nerves.

Luisa looked back to the lawn. Olympia was beckoning to Lady Somerton, reaching inside his pocket.

The divorce papers. The decree nisi, the preliminary decree of divorce.

What would Somerton say? But he knew the decree existed. He'd told Luisa he wasn't going to contest the petition; after all, he'd originally planned to offer Lady Somerton a divorce himself. That was back in Northamptonshire, however. What if today's events had changed his mind? What if, out of pure venom, he ripped the papers up now, demanded Philip, demanded Penhallow's blood? A decree nisi wasn't a final judgment, after all. If there were new evidence, evidence of adultery, for example . . .

He wouldn't do that.

Lady Somerton was holding the papers in her hand. She was looking up at Somerton in amazement. He made a little bow.

Luisa's body sagged with relief. It was all right, then. They would divorce, and they would work out something reasonable for Philip, who would one day, after all, be the next Earl of Somerton.

But something wasn't quite right. They were still arguing. She could hear their voices rising, even here.

Lady Somerton's hand flashed out and struck her husband's cheek. He hadn't been expecting the blow; he staggered sideways. Luisa took a step forward and forced herself to stop. Her fingers bit into the bark of the tree.

Somerton wiped the corner of his mouth and smiled. Oh, God. What was he planning?

Penhallow interposed himself between Somerton and the countess, who placed her hand on her belly in a protective gesture, and then moved it hastily away.

Her belly.

Luisa's breath caught in her throat.

She knew that gesture. She'd had two stepmothers. She'd watched them progress through pregnancy after pregnancy.

Luisa stared at the countess's waist. She was perhaps a

hundred yards away, and the sun shone fiercely on her clothing, obscuring the details. But that jacket was certainly more
rounded than its trim outline last winter.

A baby. Whose?

Her gaze shifted to Somerton, and at once she saw that he
had realized it, too. Had realized that his wife was harboring
a precious secret beneath her heart. His gaze was raking her,
from top to bottom, and his stance was straightening, growing
rigid, ready to explode.

Then everything went into motion. Olympia put out his
walking stick and pushed Somerton back. Penhallow turned
Lady Somerton about and urged her up the hill.

"Is it mine?" Somerton shouted. His booming voice carried
across the grass, echoed against the opposite bank of the Arno.
"Is it mine, by God?"

Lady Somerton whipped around and said something back,
fierce and low. Luisa strained forward, but she couldn't hear
the words. She pounded her fist against the tree. It was time to
go. Time to go find Beadle. This had all gone out of control.
Something was going to happen, something awful. Olympia
was holding Somerton back with both hands on his walking
stick, wielding it like a baton, but with all his height and
strength he was no match for Somerton, in the prime of his
life, massive and furious as a young bull.

The countess turned to head back up the hill, and Somerton
broke free.

Penhallow reached into his pocket and whipped out his
knife.

Luisa started forward. There was no time for Beadle, no
time for anything but to get that knife out of Penhallow's hand.
Olympia lay sprawled on the grass, picking himself up.

Somerton came to a halt, just outside Penhallow's reach,
circling about. He said something in a taunting voice. Penhallow straightened and tossed the knife away, into the lawn.

Thank God. Luisa checked herself and looked back and
forth between Olympia and Penhallow.

Somerton burst into motion. He leaned down, picked up
the knife, and charged up the hill after his wife. In the next
instant, Penhallow dashed after him, two yards behind him,
one yard . . .

He launched himself at Somerton's back, just short of the countess's horrified gaze.

They rolled in the grass together: tawny hair and dark, clean limbs and thick. The knife flashed in the sun, and disappeared into the tangle of struggling arms and kicking legs. The slope of the hill pulled them inexorably downward, toward Luisa, toward the boating terrace and the river beyond it. She couldn't tell who had the advantage; they were both fighting for their lives, fighting with a deadly mixture of skill and treachery and brute male intent, Somerton's strength matched against Penhallow's lightning quickness.

Luisa stood frozen and helpless, hands cupped at the sides of her mouth, wanting to shout something, anything, to make them stop.

But no words came.

In a sudden graceful movement, Penhallow broke free and sprang to his feet. He balanced the knife in his hand and backed away, step-by-step, downstream, to the opposite side of the terrace from Luisa. Leading Somerton away from the countess and Philip.

Luisa turned to Lady Somerton, standing near the top of the hill with a shocked Philip standing behind her, as helpless as Luisa.

"Go!" she screamed. "Go! Take the boy!"

The countess looked at her in amazement.

"Go!" she screamed again, but Lady Somerton wavered, unable to act while her husband and lover fought below.

But Philip. Philip had started into motion, running down the hill.

"Watch him! Watch him!" she yelled at the countess, pointing to Philip.

But Lady Somerton had turned the wrong way and missed him as he pelted past her, running in a panic toward his father and his Uncle Roland. Too late, she spun around again and saw the boy.

Luisa darted forward, but Philip had the momentum, he was closer. Penhallow seemed to hear him and turned in the boy's direction, and Somerton, not realizing what was happening, lunged for his opponent's unguarded middle.

"No!" Philip shouted, and he ran into his father's back, arms outstretched.

Somerton staggered to the side, caught off balance, and put his hand out to the crumbling stone balustrade of the terrace. It gave way beneath his weight, tumbling into the river, and for an instant Somerton stood poised above the river's edge in a queer sort of arc, his immense arms stretching out as if to embrace a lover.

And then he fell into the water, ten feet below.

Luisa stood stunned for a second or two, not quite able to believe what she had just witnessed. Penhallow moved first, running to the low terrace wall and peering over the edge. He whirled around and sat down. "My boots!" he said.

Luisa ran forward and grasped the heel of his right boot and tugged with all her might. Her hands were shaking with fear. She moved to the next boot, yanked it off, and Penhallow rose up and dove into the water.

She staggered upward on her unsteady feet. Lady Somerton rushed beside her and looked over the edge, and Luisa turned to join her.

His body—good God, his limp and lifeless body!—was floating downstream, facedown, yards away already. Penhallow stroked swiftly toward him, his white shirt flashing in the muddy water. He grasped him by the shoulders and turned him over.

A rush of red blood ran down Somerton's forehead, past his closed eyes and his proud Roman nose and into his mouth. His head lolled uselessly against Penhallow's shoulder.

Beside her, Lady Somerton gasped.

Luisa forced her legs into action, off the terrace to the path by the river, where Penhallow was dragging Somerton's unresisting body to the bank. "Is he alive?" she shouted.

Penhallow couldn't answer. He stroked hard with his legs, on his back, while Somerton lay propped on his chest, above the water.

Luisa scrambled to the bank and plunged in the water, without stopping to take off her boots. She waded to her knees while Penhallow approached, dragging Somerton through the murky water, until his feet found the bottom and he stood. The blood was still pulsing down Somerton's white face.

"Is he breathing? Is he alive?" she demanded.

"There's a heartbeat. Help me get him on the shore. He's built of bloody stone."

Penhallow slipped his arms under Somerton's shoulders. Luisa splashed around and grabbed his feet, with the preternatural strength of panic, and together they wrestled Somerton's immense body to the riverbank.

"Bloody hell. I don't think he's breathing. Get that wound on his head, if you can, and let's roll him over."

Luisa whipped out her handkerchief and blotted the streaming blood, while Penhallow struggled to get him into position. His face was so white, so still. The lips hung slack, the head lolled to one side, against Penhallow's arm. Already her handkerchief was soaked with blood.

"Breathe, damn you! It's me, it's Markham. You've got to breathe!" She looked at Penhallow. "For God's sake, do something!"

"Help me turn him over. A few good thwacks on the back."

She grabbed Somerton's shoulder and yelled in his ear, "Breathe, you idiot! I *order* you to breathe!"

Without warning, the earl's chest made a single powerful heave, sending her sprawling into the muddy riverbank.

"Turn him over! Now!"

She scrambled up and braced one shoulder while Penhallow flipped that burly body and held him up while he heaved and heaved, water and vomit pouring from his mouth, mingling with the blood from his forehead, with the deep groan from the bottom of his chest.

Alive.

She was covered in blood and vomit and muddy river water. She didn't care. He was alive, he was breathing. They could fix everything else. She could survive everything else, but she could not survive his death.

She loosened his jacket and collar. A clean handkerchief appeared before her hands. She looked up and saw her uncle's face, creased with concern.

"He lives," she whispered. "He lives."

"So he does." Olympia shook his head. "The lucky devil."

TWENTY

The thin cracks of sunlight at the edges of the curtain made his head throb.

He closed his eyes again. Much better.

"Would somebody please shut the bloody curtains," he said, to no one in particular. The air was still and cool around him, smelling of roses. The bowl by his bedside, he remembered. He could picture the flowers quite clearly: yellows touched with pink at the tips, as if they'd been dipped in . . . dipped in . . . something pink. Or red. Something . . .

A hand touched his forehead. "They're already shut," said a gentle voice. Markham's voice, only softer and kinder than usual.

"They are not shut. There are . . . cracks. Blistering cracks."

"I can't do anything about that, I'm afraid. You've had a nasty blow to the head, and the light will hurt your eyes for a few days yet."

A blow to the head. He remembered now. The riverbank. Elizabeth, Penhallow, his son. Olympia.

A sense of crashing loss came down upon him. He was drowning in it. He couldn't breathe.

Markham.

"Where am I?" he whispered.

"We're still at the Villa Angelini, until you're well enough to travel."

Of course. He knew that. His aching head, the vague feeling of nausea and vertigo. Someone waking him, giving him a sip of water, letting him sleep. Then waking him again, far too soon.

A concussion. That was what the doctors called it. His brain had been bruised.

He moved his hand against the sheets. A few slender fingers curled around it.

"How long have you been here?" he said.

"I haven't left," she said.

Some untold time later, he opened his eyes again, and this time the cracks of light didn't pierce his skull with quite the same white-hot fury. His thoughts fell obediently into line, or most of them. He was at the Villa Angelini. He had lost the fight. His brain was bruised. There were roses next to his bed. Markham was here.

He closed his eyes again.

"Markham," he said.

"Sir."

There was a rustle of clothing, and her hand touched his. He wrapped his fingers around her, testing their strength.

"You should call me Luisa now," she said.

"You'll always be Markham to me."

She said nothing. He opened his eyes. In the dusky light, he could make out her outline, quite close, soft and blurred. A gentle glow of light shone on her cheekbone.

"Well, Markham . . ."

"Luisa."

"Luisa. Am I going to recover my senses?"

"I believe so. I hope so. In another week we should be able to move you out of here."

A week. He'd be damned if he lay in this bed for another week. "Where is my son?" he asked. At the word *son*, the black weight fell down upon him again, the thick, oily substance of his grief. Failure, and loss, and the knowledge of his sins.

"Philip is with his mother and Lord Roland, not far away. I believe they're waiting for the decree absolute to be issued by the judge in London, so they can marry."

"She is with child."

A slight hesitation. "So I understand."

"It's his, of course. I suppose that's a relief, though I thought, for an instant . . . there was a small chance . . ." He turned his head away from her. "I behaved badly, I think. When I saw that she was expecting, when she told me it was Penhallow's child . . . I wouldn't have hurt her, never that, I just wanted to . . . take that knife and *run* somewhere . . . killed myself, probably . . ."

"You have a habit of behaving badly, my lord. But I hope this matter is now behind you."

He closed his eyes again. "Yes. She can have whatever she wants. Only let me see him, from time to time. My son. To see how he's doing."

A glass nudged at his lips. He drank the water obediently and went back to sleep.

A small hand lay inside his own.

It was the first detail he noticed, when he opened his eyes. He turned his aching head and looked down at his son's anxious black eyes, and for an instant he thought he was looking in his own childhood mirror.

"Philip."

"Are you awake, Father?"

"Yes. Why are you here?"

A rustle of silk, a woman's voice. "I brought him, my lord. He wanted to see you."

Somerton rolled back and closed his eyes. "Elizabeth."

"Father, I'm so sorry. I didn't mean to hurt you." Philip's voice began to crack. "I didn't mean to push you in. I only wanted you to drop the knife, before you hurt Uncle Roland."

Somerton whispered, "You did the right thing, Philip. Brave boy."

"Does your head hurt very much, Father?"

His head was going to split apart. "Not at all, son. I'm just resting, that's all."

God, a pair of small, damp lips. Right there on the knuckle of his thumb. He opened his eyes again and looked down at his son's bowed head.

"I'm sorry, Father."

"Don't be sorry, Philip." He lifted his hand and touched Philip's soft hair.

Elizabeth spoke softly. "Philip, my dear. May I speak to your father for a moment?"

"Yes, Mama."

Philip kissed his thumb again and disappeared, and an instant later Elizabeth's body appeared in his place, on the chair next to the bed, rounded with her lover's child, the face above her white collar blooming with health and love and happiness.

"You're looking well," he said.

"Thank you. You look a little better than last I saw you."

"I'll heal. I suppose you want my blessing," he said. "To assure yourself of my compliance."

She hesitated. "I *am* sorry about what's happened. You must believe that. I was wrong to run away, but you . . . but we . . ."

"We were never suited."

"No." She looked at her hands.

He turned his face back to the canopy above his bed and brought his hand, the one Philip had kissed, across his chest. "I behaved badly, Markham says."

"He's quite right. But I was not without fault, either. We have both made the most dreadful mistakes, and I hope . . . I hope . . ." Her voice groped and fell away.

"I apologize," Somerton said stiffly. "If you want my blessing, take it. Marry him. I have no doubt he'll make you happy at last."

"I hope you'll be happy, too, one day."

Something stung the backs of his eyes. He gathered himself. "Take care of my son. Both of you."

"We shall." She pressed her cool fingers on his forehead, for the briefest instant, and rose to her feet. "For what it's worth, Somerton, he never heard a word against you. Either from me, or from Roland. And he never will. But the rest is up to you."

Somerton pressed his thumb against his heart. "If I can be of any assistance in the future, madam, you have only to ask."

She didn't reply. He heard her murmuring to Philip, rustling her ladylike silks again.

"Good-bye, Father!" his son called cheerfully from the door.

"Good-bye, Philip."

When the door closed, he turned his head and studied the painted wood, the dark shadows cast there from the meager light, until he fell back asleep.

W hen you said *move you out of here*, Markham, what precisely the devil did you mean?"

It was the next day, or possibly the one after; he had lost track of sunrise and sunset in this dark cave of a bloody bedroom. He was now sitting up in bed, unable to read, unable to stand up without wavering, unable to do anything interesting, and his temper had begun to fray.

"It's Luisa, my lord. Have a little broth."

"I am not an invalid! Luisa." He mumbled the last word.

"I beg your pardon, sir, but you are. You are unable to stand unassisted, and your temper is very much of the invalid sort." She sighed and set the broth aside. "Not that I expected anything else from you."

"You stray from the point, Luisa. I have a number of affairs requiring my attention. Misdeeds, you understand, which only I can execute properly."

"My lord, I have a proposition for you." She knotted her fingers in her lap.

He peered at her. The room was still dark, though a little more sunlight had been allowed in today, and she appeared to him in grays and browns, not quite precise. He could see that she no longer pomaded her hair, so its scanty inches fell about her face; she was wearing a loose white shirt and no waistcoat. She wanted him to call her Luisa.

These were all clues, he knew.

"What is this proposition?" he asked suspiciously.

She took in a little breath and straightened her shoulders.

"I have been giving our respective circumstances a great deal of thought for the past few days."

"No doubt you have, Markham."

"The decree absolute will be formally issued in London court in three or four weeks, ending your marriage to her ladyship."

"Yes."

"Would it then be possible . . . would you be willing to consider . . ."

"Markham . . ."

She met his gaze with her haughtiest Markham eyes. "Marrying me."

The Earl of Somerton was a man accustomed to shocks. They had occurred with regularity in the ordinary course of his life; they arrived even more frequently in the course of his chosen profession. He had once arrived for a hazardous rendezvous in Copenhagen with his most trusted associate, the one man above all he had thought incorruptible, and found himself in the center of an ambush at the end of a blind alley, surrounded by enemy agents. He had barely escaped with his life.

His associate, on the other hand, had not. Of that, he had made certain.

He was accustomed to shocks. He prided himself on his ability to take in the new information, to make the necessary adjustments, to act.

Now, as the words *marrying me* revolved lazily in his bruised brain, bounding and rebounding off the tender walls of his skull, he found he had only one thing to say.

"Marry you? Are you mad?"

"You needn't look so appalled," she said, a little indignant. "Marriages of state are a matter of business, a . . . a thing of convenience."

"Convenience?"

"For the advantages conferred."

"Advantages?"

She leaned forward. "Listen to me. It isn't just a matter of defeating these damned anarchists who have taken over my government. I had only just ascended the throne when I left; they had never had a female ruler before. My father had to change the articles of succession to allow it. My support among the populace was hardly strong, which I suppose is why the Revolutionary Brigade picked that moment to act."

He nodded, scowling.

"Alone as I am, having been away from my country for nine months, I stand little chance of rallying people to my cause. I understand that. I remember the looks on their faces, that last day in Holstein Cathedral, at my father's funeral. They were not going to accept me, a female, as their ruler."

"If any one of them dares to say a word against you . . ."

"But if I return with a consort, a man of strength and resolve, an English nobleman . . ." She drew in another deep breath, and her cheeks seemed to take on a touch of color in the dimness. "If I return already increasing with a young prince . . ."

Somerton felt a little dizzy.

". . . I may just be able to sway their hearts."

"I beg your pardon, Markham. Did you say *already increasing*?"

She looked at her lap. "Peter and I . . . we tried faithfully, every week, but I was never so fortunate as to conceive. You, on the other hand, are an expert. You are a proven sire of a strong and healthy son . . ."

She had to be stopped. Now.

"In fact, I have three," he said.

Luisa's head shot up. "What's that?"

"Three sons, that I know of. Philip, you have seen. I got a child on a tenant's wife when I was seventeen—I rather believe she was using me for the purpose—and another from a mistress of mine at Oxford, a careless mistake. She was several years older than I, and had some ambitious notion that she could manipulate my young will into making her the Countess of Somerton for her trouble. She left for America shortly after the birth; I haven't seen them since."

"Good God."

"I have also a daughter," he said softly. The words hurt his throat as he said them. "I entered into an adulterous affair with an officer's wife, while he was stationed in India. He returned hopelessly disfigured, and she . . . she threatened to get rid of the child if I didn't leave with her for the Continent. So I did as she asked. A great mistake. She was not the sort of woman . . ." He caught his breath. How to describe the Duchess of Ashland, God rest her troubled soul, now dead these two or three years? When Luisa's own sister had since married the widowed duke. A rather awkward detail, to be sure, and one he lacked the energy to deal with, at the moment. "In any case, I left her eventually, though not without insisting that she place the girl in London with a relative, instead of exposing her to the damned dissipated existence she was then living in Rome. I sent money. I didn't try to see the girl; I thought it was better for all concerned if I didn't. But she exists. Four children, at least that I'm aware of. I have, since then, exercised a great deal more caution in my private affairs."

"I see," she whispered.

"I have never told another soul about all this," he said.

"I don't doubt it. Such a shameful history is hardly a matter of pride, though at least it leaves your ability to sire children without doubt."

"You should be appalled."

"Appalled? My own father was notorious for siring bastards right and left. If you had mentioned the notion of exercising caution, he would have looked at you in amazement. He considered himself the father of his people in a very literal sense."

For a moment, Somerton stared at her.

Then he threw back his head and laughed. The action made his head hurt, but he went on anyway, because it felt so good to laugh like this, from his belly upward into his heart. "But you loved him anyway," he said at last, wiping his eyes.

"I loved him anyway." She was smiling, too, watching him with indulgent eyes. "The trouble, of course, was that he couldn't get any children on his wives, after we three girls were born. Each time one of my stepmothers became with child, she would miscarry, often quite late in her confinement."

"How many stepmothers did you have?"

"Two. When the last one died, my father gave up. He altered the old rules of succession so that a firstborn daughter could inherit the throne, and I was married to poor Peter shortly after. Having a husband and—we hoped—a thriving heir would rally the people behind the idea of a female ruler."

Somerton frowned. "I see."

A silence stretched between them, raw and tender in the aftermath of these unexpected revelations, this new intimacy of mutual knowledge. Somerton wanted to pull the blankets up his chest, to hide himself again. But it was too late.

Perhaps, with Markham, it had always been too late.

Luisa gathered herself. "Will you consider it, then? I realize it's a great deal to ask, but you did promise to assist me in regaining my throne. Your strength and cunning would prove the utmost help, I'm sure, and the entire project a welcome distraction for you, given your recent reverses."

"How kind. And what makes you think I have any desire to experience the bonds of matrimony again?"

She cleared her throat. "The position is not without its compensations . . ."

"Indeed." He let his gaze wander downward to the buttons of her shirt.

She rose from her chair and walked to the window. "You needn't answer now, of course. I've sprung it all suddenly, because there isn't much time. You may take a few days to decide. But I really must know by the end of the week, so I can begin to plan."

"Plan?"

"Olympia hopes to strike by the end of August." She lifted the curtain a few inches to the side and looked down at the garden.

The end of August.

"You're a fool," he said. "You know what I am."

"I do. That's exactly why I want you for the job," she said coldly. "Besides, I haven't any time to interview other candidates."

He watched her where she stood, at the opposite wall, her back turned to him. She was wearing her tweed trousers, the ones that cupped her bottom in a manner altogether too distracting for a man confined to his bed with a bruised brain, and the shaft of afternoon sunlight turned her white shirt nearly transparent.

Damn it all. His prick was rising, right there beneath the sheet, just when he needed to think rationally.

Had he even heard her correctly? Marry her. Become the consort to a princess, protect her from all threats. Get her with child as a matter of sacred duty, a child who would one day rule a minor German principality under principles of absolute power.

His thoughts reeled. Good God, he wasn't even properly divorced yet.

On other hand, had he ever really been married, except as a legal formality? Certainly his wife, his former wife, would lose no time in marrying his rival.

Marriage. Marriage to Markham, to an extraordinary woman with no other man in her heart. What might that be like? At the very least, he would have her in his bed at last, willing and open, warm and soft skinned, perhaps even passionate. Yes. He would have, at the very least, the blessed oblivion of sexual congress, as often as he needed it. With her, with Markham. *His* Markham, his own Markham, offering now to bind herself to him for life.

By his side. In his bed. Never to leave him.

His prick surged against the linen, eager to complete the formalities of consummation.

The sick despair inside him, the sense of black loss, receded by a fraction of an inch.

He was accustomed to shocks, he reminded himself. And the faster a man adjusted himself to his new circumstances, the greater his chance of survival.

"Your Highness?"

She turned from the window in a startled jump.

"I shall take the matter under the gravest consideration. Now close that damned curtain before my eyeballs combust."

TWENTY-ONE

They were married on a Thursday, in a small medieval church in Fiesole, by an Anglican minister brought up the hillside from Florence by the Duke of Olympia atop a bad-tempered gray mule. It was the last day of July, and the air smelled of ripening fruit.

"Is it quite legal, however?" Somerton said to Olympia, when they had emerged, blinking, from the shaded recesses of the chapel to the Tuscan sunshine outside. Luisa, dressed in a pale yellow gown of almost peasantlike simplicity, clutching a small bouquet of pink-tipped yellow roses from the Palazzo Angelini gardens, was speaking in fluent Italian to the wife of the sacristan a few yards away.

Olympia removed his hat, blotted his forehead with a white handkerchief, and peered at the sun. "Oh, you're married, right enough. No getting out of it now. I'm not up to shepherding any more divorces through Chancery; I should simply kill you this time, quick and efficient, and save myself a world of trouble."

Somerton glanced at the ethereal figure of his bride, next to the chapel door. The early afternoon turned her shorn auburn head to flame. She seemed to be studiously avoiding any contact with him; even before the altar, she hadn't even met his eyes when they repeated their vows. Strictly speaking, she had actually plighted her troth to the minister.

"I mean as regards her status as the ruler of Holstein-Schweinwald-Huhnhof. Can she marry a divorced man?"

Olympia shrugged. "There's no law against it. Chiefly, I suppose, because the matter has never before arisen. Mind you, the laws have generally been written by the rulers themselves. You will enjoy the state of government immensely, Somerton: no messy parliaments, no pesky constitutional safeguards. Just a sort of bond of primeval trust between ruler and ruled."

"Now why on earth would any sane subject wish to change such an efficient arrangement?" Somerton shook his head.

"My sentiments exactly." Olympia squared his hat back on his head and turned to his niece. "My dears, I must be off. Missions to accomplish and all that. Enjoy your honeymoon. I shall send for you when the time comes."

"But Uncle! You're not going to stay?"

"Stay? For what purpose?" He looked back and forth between them. "I should be very much in the way, I assure you. I make it my general policy to avoid newlyweds at every opportunity."

"A fine policy," said Somerton. "I follow it myself."

"Except in this case, of course." Olympia coughed.

Somerton looked at Luisa. She looked away.

"Yes, well." Olympia took his niece by the shoulders and kissed each cheek. "Best of luck, my dear. He's a blustering sort, and cunning, and occasionally vicious . . ."

"Rather like a certain uncle of my acquaintance."

"But I do believe he'll make you a fine husband nonetheless. And you, sir." He turned to Somerton. "How very satisfying to have buried the hatchet at last, as the Americans say. A brand-new nevvy! Splendid!" He held out his hand.

"My very dear uncle." Somerton saturated his voice with irony.

Olympia's large hand gripped his and pulled him in close for a confidential whisper. "Just remember what I said about death and divorces, my boy. Accidents are so common, and can so easily be arranged." A friendly clap on the shoulder, a return to his jovial voice. "Treat her well!"

Somerton clapped a friendly one in return, nearly knocking Olympia to the paving stones. "Safe travels, my dear fellow."

Luisa ranged up by Somerton's side as Olympia climbed nimbly into his carriage and waved cheerfully from the window. "What did he say to you?"

"What's that?"

"When you were shaking hands."

"Oh, the usual wedding-day rubbish, ball and chain sort of thing." He turned to her and held out his hand. "Off we go."

She gave him a shy smile, not a Markham sort of smile at all, and placed her hand in his. The sight of that smile, the soft feel of her hand, caused a little shiver in his humors. He frowned it away. This was marriage, a civilized arrangement for mutual benefit and the procreation of the next generation of Holstein despots, not a damned country dance.

If only the fabric of her pale yellow gown would not cling to his new wife's breasts in such an innocently alluring manner.

Luisa's smile faded. "The sacristan's wife said she would take us to the cottage."

"Lead on, then."

It had been Olympia's idea to give up the prominent Palazzo Angelini, with its domestic staff and its position on a primary road into Florence, and take refuge in a discreet cottage near Fiesole until the time was ripe to act against the conspirators. Somerton, still plagued with headaches, his body still weakened from its fortnight of inactivity, had agreed that an Italian palazzo had its disadvantages for a princess in hiding, particularly one who was giving up her male disguise in order to marry an English nobleman. He wasn't yet at full strength; he couldn't take any chance of ambush.

"A sort of honeymoon," Olympia had said, over sherry the night before, having reappeared with his usual abruptness just in time for the wedding.

"It is not a honeymoon," Somerton said. "This is a marriage of convenience."

Olympia had looked him over with his too-sharp blue eyes. "And yet, it is still a marriage."

It is still a marriage.

Somerton glanced sideways at his bride, as they followed

Signora Scotto along the dusty little path out of town, passing cypress and vineyards, villas and cottages, the undulating golden hills of a Tuscan summer. His bruised head ached dully in the sun. Luisa, on the other hand, looked fresh and bright, holding up her skirts an inch above the path, staring straight ahead with her chin tilted high. Her cheekbones were faintly flushed from the heat and the exercise. She had let his hand drop away from hers as soon as they were out of the churchyard.

What else had Olympia said to him last night, just before retiring? He rubbed his forehead. Something to do with being a husband.

You can be a husband to her, or not. The choice is yours.

"*Qui siamo,*" said the sacristan's wife, turning with a swish of her bright blue skirts at the doorway of a small building of creamy stucco, nestled in the shade of a group of cypress. The tiled roof glowed red against the depthless blue of the late July sky.

Somerton frowned. "It's rather small."

"It will do very well," said Luisa. She took the woman's hand and asked, in Italian, whether there was any food for dinner.

Somerton pushed open the door and stood in shock at the entrance.

"Bloody Olympia," he said.

There was only one room. A fireplace interrupted the middle of one wall, surrounded by cooking implements, fronted by a serviceable table with two rush-seated chairs. From the opposite wall stretched a bed, not particularly wide, covered by a cheerful blue bedspread and two plump pillows.

That was all.

Well, not quite all. On the table rested a bottle of wine and a pair of clean glasses. A note lay trapped beneath the wineglass. Somerton stepped over and tugged it free.

With compliments to the happy couple. Olympia.

Bastard.

H er new husband was in a black mood.

Well, she could hardly blame him, could she? Between her and Olympia, they hadn't given him much choice.

Now here he was, not five days freed from a disastrous marriage, finding himself yoked to an entirely different wife, an entirely different life.

He picked up his glass of wine and finished it, without looking at her. Between them sat the crumbs of the dinner they'd shared, cheese and apples and bread from the well-stocked cupboards. Outside the cheerful red curtains, the sky was turning pale in preparation for sunset. The austere lines of Somerton's face looked as if they might break under the weight of his scowl.

Evidently, he was not looking forward to the coming of night.

Luisa finished her wine and gathered her courage. "I feel I should make a few things clear, before we . . . before we proceed."

He looked at her at last. His brow was so fierce, it might have cast its own separate shadow on the smooth wooden table below. "Yes, my dear?"

"I understand, of course, that this marriage is hardly one of your own choosing."

"I agreed to it, however."

"And we are not in love, in the manner of ordinary couples who stand before ministers and vow eternal fidelity. Moreover, I gather that you are a man of strong carnal appetites, requiring both abundance and variety to satisfy them."

He raised one dark eyebrow and reached for a peach from the platter of fruit.

"So naturally I would not expect that you keep exclusively to our marriage bed. I do ask two things, however. One, that you conduct any affairs of that sort in a discreet manner, so as not to embarrass the court. Secondly, that when we are . . ."

Damn it all, there was a blush, warming her throat and rising up to her cheeks. And she had practiced this speech twice before the mirror this morning, just to avoid any display of unsettling emotion. Not that Somerton appeared to notice; he was slicing his peach with great concentration, hardly regarding her at all.

"Yes, my dear? And secondly?"

She went on stoutly. "During those times when we are seeking to conceive children, that you do me the honor of restraining yourself to our bed alone, until a . . . until the happy news is confirmed."

Somerton had finished slicing the peach. He took one section in his mouth and watched her while he ate, considering his words. "How very reasonable. And you, my dear? Will you follow these rules you've laid out in such exactitude?"

"I have no need of them. I shall not take any men to my bed, other than you."

"Are you quite certain of that? The winter nights are long and often dull. You may meet a gentleman whose charms you cannot resist. Peach?" He offered her a slice.

But I already have, she thought, without warning. Her heart gave a little pang. She took the slice from his fingers and ate it swiftly.

"I suppose that's possible," she said. "But while the act of union is not unpleasant, it's hardly worth putting my crown in peril. A prince may take all the lovers he wishes, but a princess must remain virtuous, or face dissatisfaction from her people. And these sorts of liaisons are almost impossible to keep secret."

"Ah, of course. I never thought of that. Naturally, a princess must always put public duty before private longings. My sympathies, my dear. It seems we're doomed to an unequal arrangement."

His voice was so low and rich, it sent shivers along her spine that gathered between her legs. She rose to her feet, a little unsteady, and placed her fingers on the edge of the table. "Do we understand each other, then?"

"It seems so." He drew himself lazily upward, up and up, until his big body towered above her, unnaturally massive. The muscles of his throat slid beneath his skin as he swallowed the last of the peach. "I believe I shall take myself outdoors for a cigar, if you don't mind. I expect you'll want a moment or two of privacy."

Her breath lost itself somewhere in her chest. "Yes, thank you."

He made a courtly little bow and disappeared into the evening dusk, ducking slightly as he passed under the lintel. Luisa stood for a moment, listening to her heart smack against her ribs.

Her husband—*husband!*—would return in a few minutes, perhaps a quarter hour. He would return and take her to bed.

God help her. The moment had come. What should she do? What would he expect of her? He must have taken a hundred women to bed, women of all sorts, women of skill and experience. She tried to remember her wedding night, and all she could recall were confused images of embarrassment and awkwardness and clothes shifting about and a somewhat painful jabbing about between her legs. By the end, she hadn't even been sure they'd actually done what they were supposed to do. Peter had seemed equally perplexed. ("Did I . . . did I get it in you?" he'd asked afterward, breathing hard, and the truth was that she wasn't fully sure if he had.)

Somerton, she felt certain, would have a different approach. Her skin prickled beneath her clothes.

A quarter hour later she lay in the bed, washed and dressed in her nightgown, with the covers pulled up to her chin. She'd debated lighting the candle, but a few dregs of light still made their way between the cracks in the curtains, which she'd drawn tightly shut. She stared at the rough plaster ceiling and counted the whorls in the wooden beam right above the bed.

. . . twelve . . . thirteen . . .

The door burst open.

"Markham?" he barked.

"It's Luisa, my lord," she called softly. "I . . . I'm here. In the bed."

The daylight had faded faster than she realized. Somerton was a blurry outline as he stomped toward the bed, yanking off his necktie, peering into the dimness as if he couldn't make her out. The outdoor air swirled inside with him. He came to a stop a few feet away, too large for words.

"So you are," he said.

She watched him from the corner of her eye. He appeared to be unbuttoning his shirt.

"And what the devil are you doing there?" he said. "Auditioning for the queen in a wooden chess set?"

"Waiting for you. Obviously." She paused and licked her lips.

"This is how you wait for your husband's visits to your bed?" He sounded amazed.

"Yes, of course."

He placed his hands on the edge of the bed and leaned over her. His unbuttoned shirt fell apart, exposing the vast pale expanse of his muscled chest. His voice had gone smooth and quite, quite low. "Luisa. My dear bride. Are you still wearing your nightgown?"

"Of course I'm wearing my nightgown," she said indignantly.

He was smiling. She could see his face now, shadowed and far too close, eyelids heavy and lips curving darkly in a way that made her prickling skin vibrate with sensation. "Let me guess. Does this nightgown button all the way up to the neck?"

"Yes, it does. Naturally. What sort of nightgown doesn't have proper buttons?"

"Show me."

Well, he *was* her husband. She lowered the covers a half inch.

"More," he said.

She sighed and obliged by another inch. Which was really quite generous of . . .

He took the covers in his hand and drew them slowly to the baseboard, as if he were unwrapping a gift at Christmas.

"Oh!" Luisa sat up and crossed her arms over her chest.

Somerton stared at her, mouth still curved in that ironic smile, black hair askew and smelling of cigars. "My dear. My hat is off to the gallant Peter. How the devil did he ever manage to find you beneath all that linen?"

Luisa jumped from the bed and ran.

Well. There was nowhere to run, as she belatedly realized, except out the door and into the settling Tuscan twilight. She went to the window instead, thrust aside the curtain, and forced open the pane. The air outside was still heavy with warmth, but that was nothing compared to the heat in her cheeks.

He was coming up behind her. She could feel his body drawing closer. She closed her eyes.

"Markham." His hand touched her waist. "Luisa. Don't run away."

"You needn't humiliate me like that."

His body was no more than an inch away from hers. His shirt brushed against her back, disturbing the abundant fall of linen from her shoulders. His voice was so soft, she hardly recognized it. "I'm sorry. I didn't realize. What a beast I am. I'm sorry, love."

I'm sorry. Had he actually said that?

She whispered, "I don't know what you expect of a woman. I don't know what you want of me."

His hand crept up around her waist, reaching the bottom of her ribs. "My dear Luisa. It's very simple. As it happens, I have denied myself the pleasures of a woman's body for some time, so I believe my end of the business will require little encouragement. Strictly speaking, we don't even need a bed."

His fingers continued upward. His breath stirred her short hair, smelling of wine and cigars. She couldn't move; she could hardly breathe. "We don't?" she whispered.

"Shall I show you, love? Right here?"

"It's not . . . it's not decent . . ."

"You're my wife now, Luisa. You can forget everything you've ever imagined about decency."

Very gently, he brought his hips against her, and the hard thickness of his member pressed into the small of her back, just above her bottom. Her breath caught in her throat.

"But how . . ."

"Let me worry about *how*, Luisa." His hand plucked at the ties of her nightgown. "But first, I'm going to need to rid you of this encumbrance of yours."

"No, don't!"

But he was already untying the ribbons, already sliding the loosened neckline over her shoulders. She cried out as her breasts sprang into view, unguarded, and tried to cover them with her hands.

"No," he said. He kissed her neck and took her hands. The nightgown, with nothing to hold it up, pooled around her waist. Somerton made a movement of his hips, releasing her for an instant, and the linen dropped to the floor. "My God." His hands left hers to curl around her breasts. "My God. Luisa. Have you really been hiding these from me so long?"

She couldn't help herself. She looked down and saw his tanned hands caressing her smooth skin, his broad brown thumbs brushing against the tips of her nipples. The sight made her gasp, made sensation shoot through her nerves, made her legs wobble beneath her.

"Steady," he whispered in her ear. "I've got you."

And he did. His muscled thighs pressed against hers, supporting her; his stomach was like a cradle, holding her in place. She leaned tentatively back, and that beautiful wide chest met her like a rock, unyielding, the dependable platform on which she could stretch herself as far as she was able.

"That's it. Lean on me, Markham. Let me touch you. Let me see how beautiful you are."

His voice murmured in her ear. His fingers caressed her breasts, melting her skin, melting everything inside.

"Look how the sunset touches your skin, love." He drew one hand down the valley between her breasts. "Do you know how much I want you? How long I've wanted you? I think I wanted you that first night, when you came into my room with your dressing gown and your brave eyes and your damned dog. I came so close to kissing you."

His hand went lower, describing lazy circles on her ribs, on her belly, while his other hand took the tip of her breast between thumb and forefinger and tugged in gentle strokes.

"But you thought I was a man!"

"You were still *you*. You were Luisa underneath. I want you whatever you're wearing, whoever you are. I want you in the morning, I want you at midnight. I want you over my desk and in my armchair and my train compartment. Whenever you're in the room, I'm thinking about putting my prick inside you." He bent his head and ran his tongue along the line of her shoulder, making her cry out. At her belly, his hand drew lower still, lower, until his finger was toying with the curls below. "And now you're right here, ready for me. I can smell you, Luisa. I can tell you're ready, and it drives me mad with wanting you, like no other woman I've ever known. If I slip my finger lower . . . like this . . ."

His hand wound a slow path over the crest of her mound, dangerously close now, not close enough. She gasped and squirmed against him, but his other arm slipped beneath her breasts and held her firm. His hard male flesh prodded fiercely against the skin of her back. "Shh, my love. All in good time. Lie back, now. Let me touch you. Let me into you."

He was crooning in her ear, the wicked Earl of Somerton, crooning to her as if she were an infant. "That's it. My lovely

Markham. Always so strong. Let me be your strength now. Let me carry your burdens. Let me take care of you. That's what you want, isn't it? That's what you need. That's it, love."

His finger slid with exquisite slowness between the lips of her most tender flesh.

"Ahhh," she breathed out. She should be ashamed, she should be bolting away from that powerful finger, but God! It felt so good. So hard and gentle, gathering heat, gathering molten energy until she felt she might burst if she didn't have more.

"You're so wet," he crooned, "so wet and soft. Ah, God. You want me. Tell me."

"I want you."

His finger moved delicately, the lightest teasing dance outside her passage, brushing against a place of such sublime sensitivity she called out his name like a benediction.

"Ah, there it is." He kissed her neck. "Beautiful." His finger moved away.

"No! Please!"

"*Please* what, my dear?"

"Please . . . keep . . ." Her brain fumbled with the words.

"Keep touching you there? With all the willingness in the world."

He found the spot again, a small nub of hard flesh, and she arched her body with the joy of it, the fragrant whorl of undreamt-of pleasure.

"Look at you, love," he said. "Haven't you ever touched yourself? Don't you know yourself?"

"My nurse said it was wicked," she whispered. "She said it would give me a disease."

He took her earlobe between his teeth. "And a lovely disease it is, too. But now you have a wicked husband, a scoundrel without conscience, and I'll be touching you in this depraved fashion every night."

"Oh!" She couldn't say more, because the tension was too immense and too perfect, rising from her flesh like an outside force, like the sun.

Just when she thought she might fly away entirely, his finger slipped downward. Her cry of disappointment caught in her throat and turned into a growl.

"Patience, my love. The longer we wait, the richer the reward."

She was almost weeping with need. She shoved her hips hard against his finger, begging, but he only laughed and drew a slow circle around her entrance, deeper and deeper, until with a hissing indrawn breath he slid the finger inside her.

"Somerton!" she gasped.

"Ah, so snug and wet. Tighten yourself on me. Can you do that?"

She clenched herself around his thick finger, grasping eagerly at the rough-smooth sensation of his skin and knuckles sliding against her.

"Oh, my dear girl. My very, very dear girl. Passionate Markham. Ah yes. That's it."

She hardly noticed when his other hand released her waist to fumble in the space between them. Her entire being was focused on his finger inside her, sliding up and down, teasing her without mercy.

"Love, I can't wait any longer." His voice was no longer smooth, but rough and tortured. "I've got to have you, I've got to be inside you."

The finger disappeared. His hands gripped her waist, hoisting her off the floor, and something much larger than a finger pressed against her. The world shifted, her weight shifted; he was moving behind her, bracing his hard thighs beneath her, holding her in place with his strong hands.

"Open your legs, love." A raspy whisper. "Open for me. I've got you."

She spread her legs apart, and his velvet tip pressed inside her.

"Christ," he muttered.

For a moment, they stood there together, perfectly balanced, with the head of his organ lodged in her entrance, teetering atop a fixed point of pure marvelous anticipation, of potential about to be realized in full. In that instant of joining, she could read his thoughts, she could feel him gathering the shreds of his self-control, pushing back an imminent climax, holding himself in check.

For her.

"Somerton," she whispered.

He splayed his left hand snugly across her ribs, and pressed his right against the wall, next to the window.

He was damp with sweat, and so was she. They were stuck together, panting, delirious. She reached out and covered his hand on the wall.

A low growl filled her ears. The pressure at her entrance built, and then he was sliding inside her, all the way up, stealing her breath. She cried out at the immense fullness of him, the strength of him flooding her, touching her deep.

"Don't move," he said.

His thighs were hard and flexed beneath hers, still covered in his light wool trousers. The thick muscles of his arms held her still.

His hips shifted, and he glided slowly outward, paused, and glided back in.

"More, Luisa?" he whispered.

"Oh, God. More."

He made another of his animal noises, and began to thrust in earnest, a hard and steady rhythm, up her and down her, over and over, lifting her up on a rising tower of tension. She was weightless, suspended in granite muscle, in humid skin and the smell of cigars and wine, in the slick force of her husband's organ cramming inside her from behind.

His voice came urgent in her ear. "Only you. Do you understand me? Only *this*, and *this*, and *this*. No other goddamned silly women. Me inside you, until I die of it."

"Yes," she gasped.

"Say it. *Only you.*"

"Only me. By God. *Only me.*"

He answered her with a mighty thrust, a cry of need. "Markham. Time to finish. Spend for me. Now." The tempo came faster, faster, demanding hot flesh shoving and shoving, and his fingers reached down and touched the engorged wet peak of her, and all at once she burst free in a release of extraordinary ferocity, throbbing down her legs and arms, showering her brain.

She sagged backward into the lion's roar of his climax, into the grip of his hands as he spent his seed into her womb.

TWENTY-TWO

In the fog of aftermath, Somerton knew only the body in his arms. Her limbs were slack, her sweet flesh still pulsed gently around his cock. She smelled of sun-warmed cypress; she was Luisa; she was his wife.

Markham was now his wife. Markham was his, in the eyes of God and man.

His wrist was stiff against the wall, supporting the force of their passionate act, but he hardly felt it. He bent his head and nuzzled her neck. The climax still roiled about his groin, tingling his balls. Possibly he would feel it forever.

Other sensations began to nudge at his brain. The final ray of sunset, disappearing below the hills to the west. The sound of her breathing, slow and replete. The knowledge of the little room around them, impossibly rustic and cramped a few hours ago, now perfect in every detail.

Luisa stirred, as if waking up from a dream. Her head moved against his shoulder. "There you are," he said. "I told you it could be done without a bed."

She pulled forward an inch, separating herself from his hot skin. "Am I too heavy?"

"Not at present."

The words were intruding again, destroying the intimacy.

Why couldn't he find the right words? They had come to his lips so easily in the throes of congress, coaxing her into taking him inside that heavenly secret recess of hers. Now, as the air cooled between them, they froze in his brain.

She put her hand out and braced herself against the wall. His cock slid out of her, still engorged, gleaming with his spending and hers. She turned toward him and looked down, and her body tensed with shock.

"Oh!" she said, as if she'd never seen a man's prick, never seen the essence it produced. She ducked under his arm and ran for the bed.

"What the devil are you doing?" he asked in astonishment.

Luisa sprang atop the bedspread and propped her feet against the wall above the headboard.

"Good God," he said. "Are you actually . . ."

"Damn it all," she said. "I think it's come out."

Somerton lifted himself away from the wall and stalked to the bed. "Are you quite sane?"

She turned her head. Her eyes were large and pleading. "You don't understand. If we miss this chance . . ."

Somerton stared at her a moment. The laugh was rising in his chest, threatening to explode him. He turned away quickly, before she could see him smile—so sensitive to ridicule, Luisa— and went to the cupboard. He selected a fine amaretto, opened the bottle, and poured a generous splash for each of them.

By the time he returned to the bed, he had the threatened laughter quite under control. Luisa was still lying there with her legs propped upward, crossed at the ankles. She turned a worried glance in his direction. "I'm afraid we may have to do it again."

He took a deep breath and offered her the glass. "Sit up, my dear."

"But I . . ."

"Sit up and have a drink."

Reluctantly she let her legs drop and swung herself upward. She accepted the glass and took a mournful sip. "I'm sorry. I should have been more careful. Though it was you who insisted on performing the act standing up, a foolish idea . . ."

He put his hand over her mouth. "Stop. Please. I can't stand it."

Her eyes widened.

"Luisa, I'm flattered . . ." Christ, how could he say this? "I'm flattered that you treasure the . . . er, the substance of my loins so closely. But I assure you . . ." Another deep breath. "I assure you, not only does a significant measure of this . . . substance . . . still remain inside you . . ."

"Somerton, I *felt* it come out . . ."

He sighed manfully. Why argue against his own interests, after all? "Then we shall simply have to do it all over again, won't we?"

She looked down into her glass. "I'm sorry. I don't mean to tax you. Will you be enough recovered by tomorrow night? Or would it be safer to wait until Saturday?"

She couldn't be serious. Was she secretly smiling, as she gazed into her amaretto?

"My dear, for the good of the people of Holstein-Schweinwald-Huhnhof, I am prepared to make any sacrifice. I might even be persuaded to repeat the conjugal act tonight."

Her head shot up. "Tonight?"

He nodded solemnly. "This very hour, in fact."

"But that's impossible!" She paused. "Isn't it? That is to say, the male body must . . . must manufacture more . . . more of the . . . the . . . well, surely you know the technical word . . ."

"Ah yes. The sperm, do you mean?" He took a measured sip of amaretto. "In fact, I believe a significant amount of the procreative fluid remains in reserve after the initial ejaculation, for just such an emergency as this."

"Really?" She brightened. "Because Peter said . . . that is . . . after he consulted a book of medical reference . . . the ill effects of engaging more than once weekly, twice at the most, sapping one's vital strength and so on . . ."

Somerton felt a surge of unexpected pity for poor Peter, who evidently might have benefitted from a candid conversation with a trusted male relative.

He reached out and took her glass, together with his own, and set them on the shelf next to the bed. "Luisa, my dear. Our marriage may have been made in a certain amount of haste, and owing itself to a certain degree of expedience, but I assure you I take my duties as your royal consort with the utmost seriousness."

She was gazing up at him, naked and flushed and delectable, the rosy tips of her breasts hardened into luscious nubbins. As he watched, the tip of her tongue flicked out across her lips, in that maddening nervous habit of hers.

"You do?" she said.

His trousers were still unfastened, his shirt unbuttoned. He tossed the linen from his shoulders and let it fall to the floor. "I do," he said. He hooked his thumbs around the waist of his trousers and tugged. "I shall not rest in my efforts, my dear, until the next prince of Holstein-Schweinwald-Huhnhof grows apace in your belly. It's the least I can do, for the sake of an enslaved and beleaguered people." He kicked the trousers aside and pulled down his drawers.

Her eyes went round at the sight of his prick, springing from his hips with renewed excitement.

"Look at my face, Luisa."

Reluctantly, she drew her gaze upward.

"I promise you, I shall miss no opportunity." He took her hands by the wrists and urged her backward against the mattress. "Night and day, I'll summon the strength to make love to you, Luisa. I'll take my pleasure inside you, spend my seed inside you time and again, until you beg for a moment's peace of me." He lowered himself to kiss her. "Even if it saps my vital strength beyond recovery."

"Oh," she said. "I must say . . ."

He kissed his way down her throat to her bosom, and captured her nipple at last between his lips.

She gasped.

". . . I certainly hope it doesn't."

He suckled deep and long, one nipple and then the other, until she was panting and squirming beneath him, and then he stretched her arms high above her head and slid his happy cock to the root inside her.

"Like this, Luisa?" he said. He ground his hips in a circular motion, until she opened her eyes wide and gasped again with astonished pleasure. He bored his gaze into hers, daring her to close her eyes, daring her to look away. "My prick thrusting into you, my hands on you, my mouth." He kissed her hard, slicking her with his tongue, while his hips began to pound her below, in a slow and relentless beat.

God, she was perfect. Markham was perfect, perfect, perfect. She found the rhythm effortlessly, she lifted herself to meet his every thrust, she devoured his searching mouth as if he were made of nectar. Perfect perfect perfect. Those little sounds she made in her throat, the way her back arched, the way her breasts curved. The feel of her sweet walls around him, juicy and swollen from their mutual pleasure before. He drove the tempo faster, unable to hold back. *Perfectperfectperfect*. She felt so good, so damned impossibly *good*, he wanted to live inside her.

His climax boiled impatiently in his balls, waiting for the signal, waiting for the short, hard thrusts that would set it free. "Say yes, Luisa. Tell me this is what you want."

"Yes," she gasped, against his lips. "Yes. I want it. I want it. Give it to me."

He gave it to her, hard and fast, until she was crying out with the joy of her release, and then he crashed into her a final time and spilled himself in swift ecstatic contractions, body stretched, head thrown back, savoring every last spurt of his seed inside her.

He collapsed on her chest, pinning her with his weight, still gripping her hands high against the pillows so she wouldn't leave, wouldn't turn aside, wouldn't escape him.

She brought her legs around his and pressed her heels into the backs of his thighs.

"Stay inside me," she said. "Just to be sure."

He smiled into her short hair and fell asleep.

A humming sound danced in the Earl of Somerton's ears. He cracked open his eyelids. For a moment, he was disoriented. A rough plaster wall coalesced before him. He was lying on his stomach—his stomach! He never slept on his stomach—with a pillow clutched under his left arm. The right one splayed across a white sheet, feeling rather . . .

Empty.

Luisa. He lifted his head in the direction of the humming.

She was standing in front of the fireplace, doing something with a teakettle. A thin white shift covered her body, but the glow of the fire outlined her curves in such a way that

Somerton's mouth watered, that his prick came to instant attention. What was she humming? Some aria or another, he couldn't quite place it. Her hips swayed as she hooked the teakettle in place, and the entire panoply of the previous evening played across Somerton's brain. Consummating marriage against the wall, in a climax of brain-numbing intensity. Making love again in the bed, his wife's lithe body urging him at every stroke; pouring himself wantonly into her womb, the white wash of ecstasy. And then oblivion, dark and thick, a velvet sleep such as he had never known since childhood.

He shook his head. The ache was gone, he realized. His bruised brain had healed.

Silently he rose from the bed and walked in her direction. She went on humming, poking at the fire, ethereal in her delicate shift. His heart tumbled to the floor.

At the last instant, sensing his approach, she straightened. He didn't know how to touch her, how to greet her. How did you greet your wife in the morning, after a night of unrestrained passion? He had no idea. He had always left Elizabeth's bed immediately, so as not to inconvenience her further, or to accidentally encounter her expression of grieved disgust.

But Elizabeth seemed very far away now, a confused blur from a different life.

His new wife remained still before his eyes. Waiting. Humming. A delicate gift wrapped in linen.

He lifted his hand. Hesitated. Wrapped it tentatively around her middle.

She let out a gentle sigh and leaned against his chest.

He closed his eyes and pressed his lips into her hair, and they stayed that way, fitted together, separated only by the whisper-thin linen of Luisa's shift, until the teakettle began a soft, high whistle.

Somerton leaned forward and raised the kettle off the hook. "Come to bed," he said.

"The tea . . ."

He set the teakettle on the table and lifted his wife into his arms. "The tea can wait."

TWENTY-THREE

The hot August sun was melting the back of Luisa's dress to her skin, and it was only ten o'clock in the morning. She clipped another rose and laid it in her basket, and moved on to the herbs in their boxes, which were presently enjoying the shade of the cypress trees.

She had never been terribly interested in gardens back in Germany. Gardens were places to be enjoyed, to pass through, to provide flowers and food for an abundant table, to be tended by a small army of laborers who dissolved into the landscape as she approached. She was far too busy with affairs of state to interest herself in the art and science of growing things.

Now, of course, she had all the time in the world.

She clipped a few leaves of basil, a few sheaves of rosemary. She was just reaching for the parsley when a hand closed around her shoulder.

She jumped and turned, nearly sticking her husband with the gardening shears. "Good Lord! You've got to stop sneaking up on me like that."

An injured air. "I prefer the word *stealth*, madam. *Sneak* has such a vulgar cast to it."

"It's your natural style, I suppose. You can't help sneaking about, after all those years of hunting down traitors and assassins." She waved the shears for emphasis.

"Among others. Put those down, for God's sake. You make my blood run cold."

But though his voice was its usual acerbic self, the Earl of Somerton's blood seemed anything but cold. In fact, he looked decidedly warm. His skin had taken on a golden tan, his hair shone sleek and black in the sun. His shoulders looked as if they could hold up the world. Luisa turned back to her herbs just in time to hide her smile.

He was thriving. He was alive.

"Are you gathering herbs again? I hope you're not planning to make another ill-fated assault on the kitchen, my dear."

"God forbid." She shuddered. "I like the scent of them in the house, that's all. I'm going to put them in jars on the shelves and lie there on the bed and just smell them."

"How imaginative. I pant with anticipation." He reached for the basket, plucked out a stalk of rosemary, and sniffed it.

"Have you been out walking?" she asked.

"Up the hill and back." By *hill* he meant *mountain*, and by *mountain* he meant the one three miles away by the beaten path, which he climbed daily. He had, as usual, left directly after breakfast, wearing his white shirt and breeches and a white cloth hat; the hat was now gone, and his shirt was sticking transparently to his skin, revealing every hill and hollow of his burly chest.

She cleared her throat and turned away. "And a bathe in the lake afterward, apparently."

"I had no wish to offend my bride." He brushed the rosemary against the back of her neck.

She rested the shears against the edge of the planter. "You could take me with you."

For an instant, the rosemary stilled against her skin, and then resumed its slow circle at her nape. "You were sleeping so soundly, madam. I hadn't the heart to disturb you."

I missed you. The words filled her mouth, but she could not quite bring her lips to open and release them. Absurd. They had spent the last fortnight and more making love with abandon, with unchecked depravity, at every opportunity, in every possible location, in every possible position, by the lakeshore and against a cypress tree, and on her belly over the table with her hands curled around the opposite edge and Somerton on his feet behind her, gripping her hips, thrusting into her like a stallion servicing a mare, while she screamed with the raw, unending intensity of the pleasure. They slept side by side every night, in a tangle of possessive arms and sultry breath, as if they could not get close enough, could not get enough of each other's skin.

Why, then, should the simple admission that she missed him, when he left her bed at dawn and went out walking for hours in the Tuscan countryside, seem to violate the unspoken pact they held between them?

Somerton's large body pressed against her back, humid from exercise and the clean lake water. Already her flesh was responding to him, already the familiar warmth of desire pooled in her belly and between her legs. She couldn't stop her hand, when it snaked up to enclose his silky dark head; she couldn't stop the gasp that escaped her lips when his fingers found her breast.

She turned in his arms and took his face between her palms. But instead of kissing him, as she usually did, stopping any chance of conversation with the wordless communication of sexual union, she said, "Are you happy here?"

Somerton's eyes, heavy lidded with desire, opened warily. An instant's telltale hesitation, and then: "Of course, my dear." He removed one of her hands from his face and kissed it. "Are you?"

"Yes." *Speak. Say something. Break the stalemate.* "I don't want to leave," she said in a rush.

The tension about his eyes softened briefly, and then his eyebrows rose in that self-contained way of his. "I beg your pardon."

"I was thinking, just this morning, when I woke up. What if Olympia doesn't come? What if . . . what if the situation can't be recovered?"

"Then we shall march over to Germany ourselves, I suppose." He was still holding her hand, and gave it a little squeeze. "I gave you my promise, after all."

She whispered, "What if I don't want you to keep it?"

His expression didn't change. Above them, a flock of sparrows took flight from the cypress, in a gigantic flurry of wings and disputed positions.

"What do you mean?" he said at last.

"Listen to me. All my life, I've been groomed for my position. My education, my upbringing, all of it was designed to fit me into my place. The place God intended for me, my father said. My life, my choice of husband, my duties, they were supposed to be a fair exchange for all that luxury and privilege. For which I'm grateful, but . . ."

"I think I understand you." He removed her other hand and held them both between his, next to his chest. "You've had a taste of freedom, haven't you? The simple life, a bit of passion to stir the humors. You don't want to back to your castle now. You're perhaps even a little afraid of going back."

"No."

Somerton glanced up at the sun and back again. His expression remained inscrutable; she couldn't imagine what he was thinking. Her pulse beat madly in her neck. Did he welcome this admission? Was he flattered by it? Did he agree? *A bit of passion.* Was that all this was to him, these weeks of undreamt-of pleasure and intimacy?

Did he even understand what she was really trying to say?

"You know it's not possible," he said at last, not unkindly. "The trappings of your life, you can't escape them. You are who you are."

She was falling, falling from a great height, and there was nothing below to catch her.

"Yes, of course. I was only trying to say . . ."

"Olympia will arrive, I'm afraid. You will be obliged to act once more. God willing, we shall restore you to your throne. Life will go on, one dutiful step after another. In the end, I suspect you wouldn't really be happy otherwise. Purpose, after all, is what keeps the human condition from becoming unbearable."

"I suppose you're right," she said numbly.

"And this, of course. This makes it bearable." He released her hands and took her in his arms and kissed her, long and slow, with strokes of his tongue she might have called loving, if they came from another man. A man who loved her. She gave herself up to the kiss. She gave herself up to the hands that caressed her. She unbuttoned his shirt with eager fingers and sighed at the familiar expanse of masculine chest before her, the evidence of his great strength, of his heart buried somewhere beneath. If she laid her ear on it, she could hear it beating.

"You are so beautiful," she said. "Beautiful and brutal. You're like an ancient Roman coin. Like Caesar himself is taking me to bed."

Somerton picked her up and set her on the stone bench. It was warm from the sun, adding to the heat in her loins. He lifted her skirts around her waist and dropped to his knees between her bare legs, and her body thrilled with anticipation of what he would do to her.

His mouth was hot and knowing on her delicate flesh, exploring her expertly, teasing the core with tender flicks of his tongue. Oh, he knew how she liked it best. His hands wrapped around her thighs, holding her steady while she moaned her approval, while her hands dug into his black hair in animal delight for the connection between them.

They had *this*, at least. They had this powerful surge of desire that ran between them, like a massive electrical current. When her flesh contracted against his lips in a shimmering climax, she knew he was relishing her response, relishing the scent of her desire and the sight of her arousal. He was enjoying *her*. And when he lifted her up, sat on the bench, and settled her astride him, she knew the thick rod that pressed into her folds would be as hard as stone, would fill her to bursting, would surge in and out of her with the energy of a beast mating in the wild.

So she rode him with joy, because this was the joy that had been allotted to her. She threw back her head and called out his name when a second marvelous climax throbbed through her body from the hard male organ buried inside her. She took his shout of release into her skin, absorbing his ecstasy within her own, and when she sank on his neck and shoulders, sweat soaked and replete, she listened to the slowing thud of his pulse and knew that his silence, like hers, was meant to be shared.

It was their silence, together.

She didn't want to move, though the sun was hot, though her husband's body was even hotter. The air was so thick and pregnant with heat, it lay around them like a cloak. Perhaps they should go down to the lake together and bathe. The cypress trees rustled with birds, still agitated.

"Somerton."

"Yes, Markham?"

She smiled. He still called her that when his guard slipped, when he was as close to happy as his nature allowed. His most affectionate endearment.

"It . . . *that* . . . It's late." The words, which had been rattling in her head for three or four days now, were easier to say than she had imagined.

"What's late?" He sounded drowsy.

"*That*. I mean me. I'm late."

He made a noise in his throat. "Late for luncheon?"

"Late for . . . well, for not being with child." A peculiar feeling rose and swelled inside her, as she shared this intimate detail with him. She couldn't quite put a name to it.

"I see." No longer drowsy.

She lifted her head. "Are you happy?"

He looked at her with grave eyes. "Are you quite sure?"

"Of course I'm not sure. It's only a few days. But I thought . . . well, it's never happened before, I've always been exact to the day, and . . . I wanted to tell you." Now she was blushing. Curse Somerton and his searching gaze.

He straightened himself and lifted her away in a seamless motion of his powerful arms. "Very good. Excellent news." He set her carefully on the bench, handed her a handkerchief, and rose to his feet, fastening his trousers as he went. His face was dark. "How gratifying to discover I've already executed my duty in such a satisfactory manner. Naturally, I am at your service in the future, when further children are required to fill out the royal nursery."

She jumped up from the bench. "What the devil does that mean?"

"Have I mentioned, my dear, how relieved I am that your language hasn't gone missish since you resumed wearing dresses," he said.

"Don't be a beast. I didn't want to tell you yet. It's so early, and nothing's certain. It might be something else, or maybe I've miscounted, and . . . and anything could go wrong. But I thought you would be happy at the possibility, at least. I thought you wanted a child with me."

He stood stock-still, looking down at her with his blackest scowl. "I am happy."

"You look as if I've just passed you a sentence of death."

"Naturally I'm happy. This was the entire point of our heroic efforts this past fortnight or so, wasn't it? Our rabbitlike devotion to the business of copulation. To populate your royal womb with . . ."

A sound interrupted the motionless garden air.

A human sound.

A careful yet masculine cough.

With horror, Luisa listened to the delicate crunch of gravel on the garden path behind her. She looked desperately into Somerton's face for some clue, some indication of the identity of the man behind her. That it was not whom she feared.

But the expression on her husband's face was exactly as she dreaded: a glowering and decidedly hostile resignation.

He laid a hand on her shoulder and turned her gently around.

"Your Grace," he said. "What an extraordinary coincidence. We were just speaking about you, not half an hour ago."

A fine abode," said the Duke of Olympia, waving his wineglass to the white walls around him. "A trifle small, of course, but newlyweds only need a single room for their purposes, eh?"

Luisa made to leap from her chair and attend the fire, except that the fire hadn't been lit for days, since this present wave of heat began. But Somerton settled his arm around her shoulders, preventing her cowardly departure. Olympia was *her* bloody uncle, after all.

"We have been more than satisfied with the accommodation," he said.

Olympia smiled benignly. "So I perceive."

Beside him, Luisa shimmered. If he looked at her, he knew

her cheeks would be deeply flushed. She moved again against his arm, but he kept it there, like a bar of loving iron. She needed to remain by his side, united against her uncle. There was no other way to keep the crafty devil from overreaching himself.

So I perceive. Just how long had Olympia been standing there, in the garden shadows? Somerton remembered the startled flight of the birds, just before he had picked up his wife and buried his greedy face between her legs. He didn't remember the outside world after that. He never did, when he was making love to Markham. The satisfaction of release still buzzed along his nerves. And then the animal leap of blood in his veins at the words *late for not being with child*, the tantalizing image of Markham's belly ripening with his seed under the Italian sun.

The cold fear that had chased that initial surge of joy.

I don't want to leave, she had said. Christ, what did that mean? Stay here with *him?* Had passion addled her wits so thoroughly? Or was it sunstroke?

He tightened his arm around her.

Luisa reached for her glass and downed the cool white wine in a series of eager gulps.

Olympia watched her, eyebrows raised. "In any case, I have news," he said.

"You had better have news, by God. Sneaking up on a man and his wife like that."

"*Sneak* is such a vulgar term."

Somerton fixed his eyes on Olympia's innocent face. "A vulgar term for a vulgar practice, and one that was more than the lives of most men are worth to me."

Olympia waved that away. "I assure you, my eyes were quite averted. In any case, I really have been most frightfully busy, while the two of you have lolled about these Elysian hills, billing and cooing in the usual manner of bride and bridegroom. Various affairs here in Italy, and then I've been keeping a careful watch on a certain murder trial taking place in London."

"A murder trial?" asked Luisa sharply. "Shouldn't you be keeping a careful watch on the affairs of my country instead?"

"So I have. This particular murder trial involves the affianced husband of your own sister, Princess Stefanie."

"Stefanie! *Stefanie's* engaged?"

"I presume the chap is a relative of the deceased?" said Somerton, watching Olympia's face with the utmost attention.

"Indeed. He is also, I'm afraid, the accused, and I have had a telegram this morning that he has just been found guilty of the crime in question, and will be sentenced tomorrow, likely to hang."

Beneath his arm, Luisa went rigid with instant tension.

Somerton gripped her shoulder with his hand. "I beg your pardon. Did you say *hang*?"

"I'm afraid so."

Luisa leaned forward. "But what are you doing about it? What can be done?"

"Nothing, I'm afraid." Olympia spread his hands.

She leapt to her feet, shrugging off Somerton's arm. "But you're the Duke of Olympia! You've got to do something! You've got to . . . to . . ."

"What, my dear? Spirit him away from the Old Bailey in the dark of night?" He shook his head. "It's quite unexpected, of course. The prosecution's case was circumstantial at best. Had I anticipated such an extraordinary outcome, I might have been able to act . . ."

"You can still act!" She turned wildly to Somerton. "You can act! The two of you, you command every secret channel in London!"

"For what purpose?" said Olympia. "So that the two of them will live as fugitives all their lives? That a princess of Holstein-Schweinwald-Huhnhof should bear the children of a convicted murderer?"

Somerton kept his gaze on Olympia, though he could feel Luisa's desperation next to him, thrumming like a live wire. "Who is this fellow? What sort of man is he?"

"I believe you know him, by reputation if nothing else." Olympia smoothed the wood with one hand. "He is the Marquess of Hatherfield, heir to the Duke of Southam."

"Hatherfield! Good God. On trial for the Duchess of Southam's murder?"

"The very same."

Somerton shook his head. "And my wife's sister has been living with him, all this time?"

"Not with him, no. She is a clerk for the defense."

Luisa dropped to her chair and wrapped her hand around his forearm. "Somerton. You can do something, can't you? What about Stefanie? Please, can't we bring her here with us, can't we . . ."

He steeled his voice against her plea. "Well, Olympia? What's to be done?"

"Luisa's sister will be taken care of, of course, but I'm afraid our own business lies elsewhere." He steepled his fingers together and looked back and forth between the two of them. "I also had word a fortnight or so ago that Dingleby has embarked from the port of Hamburg in a packet steamer, bound for England, accompanied by several associates. I've been unable to account for her since, but she—and, more importantly, the apparent leader of the conspiracy in Holstein—have not been seen in Germany since."

The sun had shifted, and the light now streamed through the glass panes of the window to bathe the three of them in suffocating heat. The perspiration had already begun to trickle beneath Somerton's shirt. He rose to his feet and stepped to the window—the same one by which he had consummated his new marriage—and closed the curtains before it. The action seemed strangely final.

How many times had they come together since then? Eighteen days since the vows were spoken. Let us say twice a day on average, though perhaps it was more. Let us say thirty-six acts of union. Thirty-six times he had made love to Luisa, and if he tried, he knew he could remember each one, the place and time and position, the way she had looked and felt and smelled, the sounds she had made. The specific quality of the climax: long and rolling, intense and explosive, some brain-altering combination of the two. Then the aftermath. God, the aftermath. Each time, he lost himself so thoroughly inside her that the return of consciousness, the return of reason, the return of *himself* came as a blistering and unwelcome shock.

And now, the most unwelcome shock of all: that it was over.

He resumed his seat next to the mute Luisa and said, "I see.

And what, exactly, does this signify, in that scheming brain of yours?"

The Duke of Olympia smiled patiently.

"It means, my dears, that the months of exile are over at last. The time has come to act."

TWENTY-FOUR

Sometime in the night, Luisa woke. The train had stopped.
She rose to a sitting position, nearly bumping her head
on the roof of the compartment. "Somerton?" she said softly.

On the floor next to the berths, Quincy raised his moonlit
head and let out a soft whine.

Luisa slid carefully down to the floor and glanced at
Somerton's berth below hers, though she knew it was empty.
She had known his absence as she knew her own presence.
She bent down and stroked Quincy's head. "Where is he, love?
Why have we stopped?"

Why did trains ever stop? No one ever knew; the stops and
starts of overnight trains were inscrutable to mortal knowledge. A faulty switch, perhaps.

Or some sort of disturbance.

But that couldn't be it. Somerton would wake her if there
were a disturbance, or a danger of any kind; even if he didn't,
Olympia would, from the compartment next to theirs.

She gave Quincy a last pat, found her dressing gown at the
bottom of the berth, and slipped out of the compartment.

She found Somerton outside, on the balcony at the end of
the wagon-lit, gazing out the side over an empty moonlit field.

He was smoking a cigar, nearly finished. She hesitated and touched his shoulder.

He didn't flinch. Of course he had perceived her approach.

"You should sleep," she said.

"You know better than that."

"You slept well enough in Italy."

He ground out his cigar and tossed the end on the stones of the railbed. "We're not in Italy any longer."

There wasn't much space on the rail next to him, but she forced herself in anyway, moving aside his steely arm. With a long-suffering sigh, he lifted his hand and placed it down on her other side, enclosed her in the shelter of his shoulder. She breathed in the warm night air, the scent of his skin. The cigar, fading away in the breeze from the mountains. His arm was solid around her, a reassuring weight.

"Do you know why we're stopped?"

"To let another train pass, I believe. Go back to bed, my dear. God knows, we may have little rest tomorrow."

"Why," she said, "do you always call me *my dear* when you're being formal, and *Markham* when you're feeling some sort of passing affection for me? It seems backward somehow."

He didn't reply.

"All right, then. Where are we?"

Somerton nodded across the purple night sky. "We've just come out of the mountains in Austria. You can see the peaks to the south. I daresay we're about two hours away from Huhnhof Baden, once we start up again."

"And Olympia's men will meet us there."

"Yes. The revolutionary police are apparently weakest in the western province, where support for you remains strong. Or so claims Olympia's intelligence, which I have no reason to doubt."

"And then we shall simply storm the palace?"

"According to your uncle's plan, yes."

"What about *your* plan? What do you think?"

The shoulder behind her head moved slightly, the flex of a single muscle.

"Well?" she said. "Surely you've thought about all this at great length, in that scheming mind of yours. Tell me your thoughts. If nothing else, we've always been able to understand each other."

"This child . . ." He checked himself.

"If there is one."

"If there is one." Somerton's hands tightened around the railing. "As you no doubt comprehend, I'm far better suited for siring children than raising them. Elizabeth and Penhallow, thank God, have made sure I have as little opportunity as possible to contaminate young Philip's childhood."

"That's not true. They've promised to arrange visits." She stopped, because the words sounded so hollow and empty. And *she* was the one who had asked him to start a new life, a new family. Inevitably, Philip, raised in a different home, would become little more than a distant acquaintance. He would look to Penhallow as his father.

A distant whistle sounded from the north. The other train, perhaps. The one they were waiting to let pass.

When Somerton spoke, his voice was flat. "I want to make things perfectly clear, so there is no question of disappointment and recrimination later. I am not suited to fatherhood. I shall take as limited a role as possible in the rearing of this child, once it's born."

"I . . . I don't understand you."

"In my profession, I assign men to the tasks for which they're best inclined. I would be a fool, for example, to send a man skilled at forgery to perform a delicate assassination."

"Are you really comparing fatherhood to assassination?" She tried to laugh, but her chest was too hollow.

"Merely an analogy. You will undoubtedly want more children, of course, and I have no objection to continued conjugal intercourse, once you're safely delivered and the child properly weaned . . ."

"Are you quite mad?"

"I shall not stray to another bed in the meantime, if that's what concerns you. I have learned the value of self-control in these matters."

"How lucky for me."

"But I cannot allow myself to repeat the mistakes that led to such a disastrous conclusion seven weeks ago."

She tried to pull away, but his arm caged her in. How could he speak so coldly, and yet require her continued physical closeness? "On the contrary, it seems to me you're doing exactly that. A semi-detached marriage, a semi-detached child."

"It's not the same at all," he said. "You and I have a remarkable partnership, or so I flatter myself. Mutual respect, a satisfactory sexual connection."

"Satisfactory!"

"All in all, the foundation of a happy marriage."

"You don't sound happy at all."

"Happiness, my dear, was never in my nature. Let us say, a marriage that serves its purpose well, and does as little as possible to cause grief to either party."

"How very alluring."

"My dear, I cannot give you what I don't own."

"Perhaps you don't know what you really own. Perhaps you simply have no idea how to drag it out of the attics of your soul."

He was quiet. The rails began to sing. A faint rumble came down through the air, a rushing of the atmosphere.

"You have chosen rather ill, you know." His voice was still flat, still devoid of any particular emotion.

"Chosen *what* ill?"

"Me."

She could have borne it if he said the word morosely, the result of a passing mood, of the melancholy effect of moonlight on a mountain peak. But he was so frighteningly matter-of-fact, as if he'd thought the matter through carefully and come to a cold and logical conclusion.

"Do you know, just before I joined you here, I was lying in my berth thinking exactly the opposite," she said. "I have one of the most cunning intelligence masterminds in Europe as my consort, a ruthless and relentless man, skilled and inexhaustible in bed, and he has already perhaps given me an heir. I have seen with my own eyes to what lengths he will go, in order to protect me. My throne and my people's future assured, all in one efficient stroke."

"You're mistaken. I'm a failed husband and an inept father,

and my last grand intelligence scheme ended in near-fatal disaster." He opened up his palms. "God knows what I shall do to you, in the hours ahead. In the years ahead, if we make it that far. My star, I believe, has passed. Yours is still rising."

"What bloody melancholy rubbish. It must have been the wine in the dining car. Absolutely contemptible stuff. I shall write to the company myself."

He went on staring at his hands, his massive palms, criss-crossed with deep lines and patched with calluses.

She covered them with hers. "I trust these hands. I trust you."

He drew his hands away from her grip and placed them back on the railing. "In any case, it's too late to turn back. The die is apparently cast."

The rumbling grew louder, a cacophony of machine and steam and grinding steel. The train began to shiver. Luisa braced her hands on the rail. Just before the impact, she moved her head a quarter turn into Somerton's protective shoulder.

The opposite train thundered rhythmically by, whooshing and rattling, coach after coach. Luisa's left ear filled with palpable noise, while her right burrowed into the soft linen of Somerton's shirt, the reassuring tension of his shoulder.

Then, as suddenly as it arrived, the train was gone. The air sighed, the rails shrieked softly.

Peace crept over Luisa's heart, as the noise receded. A strange sensation. She thought of the gentle touch of Somerton's lips in her hair the morning after they were married. The tender way he had carried her upstairs, when she was ill in Northamptonshire.

How could that man possibly be the same one who held her now? Who had just spoken those cold words?

Which one did she believe? Which one had she married?

"We should be moving soon," said Somerton.

Luisa filled her lungs with clean, silvery air. With hope. "Yes. Onward to Huhnhof. And then it will all be behind us at last. We storm the palace, we secure the throne once more, we . . ."

"I beg your pardon. We?"

"You and me and Olympia. And any loyal supports who will join us."

"My dear, you're quite mistaken." He removed his hand from the rail and laid it upon her shoulder. "Olympia and I shall storm the palace, as you put it. You shall remain where you're hidden."

"I have no intention of . . ."

"This is not your particular area of expertise, my dear . . ."

"Don't call me that."

"Whoever the devil you are. You are of immense value to the people of your country, and you will stay in a place of safety until these damned revolutionaries have been cleared out, every last one of them."

Clean, silvery air, indeed. Hope, indeed.

"I see." She ducked beneath his arm and turned to the door. "I suppose that's that, then. Protect the queen at all costs."

"My dear . . ."

She flung open the door.

"Markham. My dear Markham." He was still facing the field. His proud Roman nose was tilted upward, as if he were testing the breeze. "You are also of immense value to *me*."

She stood with her hand on the door handle, watching the glint of moonlight on his dark hair.

Damn him to hell. How did he do that?

"I'm glad to hear it," she said softly, "because I rather believe I couldn't live without you."

She walked inside the coach and let the door fall shut behind her, just as the whistle sounded a long and keening cry, and the coach lurched forward at last.

S omerton found his bride in his berth, curled up against the wall. Her striped pajamas peeked out above the top of his blanket, and Quincy lay in a contented ball at her feet.

"Stubborn little fool," he muttered. He tightened the belt of his dressing gown and left the compartment.

Next door, Olympia was fast asleep. His contented snores made the satisfaction all the greater when Somerton pounded on the window of his compartment and interrupted them.

"Kicked you out, has she?" the duke said, by way of greeting.

"On the contrary. She's sleeping soundly in my berth this instant." Which was not a lie, after all.

Olympia lifted his gray eyebrows and gestured. "Won't you come in, Your Highness?"

The words jolted Somerton, though he maintained his habitual grim expression. The air inside the compartment was stuffy and smelled of sleep. He went to the window and cracked it open. The instant rush of air cooled his nerves.

"Make it quick, then, for God's sake. An old man needs his rest."

"Your plans. You're quite sure of them?"

"As certain as these things are. The people are dissatisfied with the quasi-cabal of anarchists ruling them from the comfort of Holstein Castle. They begin to realize that the early promises have not been delivered, nor will they be, and that the wealth of the country is very probably being milked for the purposes of the Revolutionary Brigade itself. They particularly dislike this secret police now in place."

"The leader of which is now missing."

"Yes. I believe him to be traveling in Miss Dingleby's party, for England."

"Their purpose?"

"Why, to capture Stefanie, of course. She's the one princess Dingleby knows where to find, at present. Given the late unrest in the provinces, the near-revolt in Huhnhof, the cabal has apparently realized a figurehead of some kind is necessary, a relic of the old days, to pacify the people."

Somerton turned from the window. Olympia was leaning against the berth, arms crossed, face lined with weariness. But the eyes were still bright and blue, still catching every detail of the man and the scene before him.

"You know this for certain?"

"So claims my source."

"And what precautions have you taken on Princess Stefanie's behalf? My wife harbors a great deal of affection for her sisters."

Olympia smiled. "Yes, she does. I have sent telegrams. Stefanie will be protected. The judicial proceedings of her lover, it seems, have taken an unexpected turn for the better, and I expect they shall shortly be married. The sooner the better, by the way, from the point of view of a legitimate succession."

"And the house where Luisa will stay, until we have the situation at the castle under control. Its owners are beyond suspicion?"

Olympia levered himself away from the berth and stretched his arms upward with a barely suppressed yawn. Between his height and the low ceiling, he didn't get very far. "Oh, no one is above suspicion, my dear fellow. You should know that."

"And yet you've trusted me, of all people, with your most priceless jewel."

"Did I make a mistake, Lord Somerton?"

He folded his arms across his chest. The silk dressing robe slipped against the skin of his hands. "Her Highness may be with child," he said.

Another elegant elevation of the ducal eyebrows. "Indeed? Excellent work. Short work, but excellent."

"Save your congratulations. It's quite early yet, but we have reason to hope. Her safety, therefore, is paramount in this endeavor. I need your assurance that she will be placed in no danger whatsoever."

"You, of all people, know I can't give you that assurance."

"What safeguards are available? Damn it all, man. She's your niece!"

Olympia's hand came to rest on the berth beside him. His expression gentled into compassion. "My dear fellow. Nothing in this world is certain. Don't you know that? We must simply do our best, we must strive for the ideal, in hopes that we will do some little good in this world and find our ultimate justice in the Hereafter."

Somerton parted his lips to reply, but his throat was too stiff.

Olympia stepped forward and laid his hand on the earl's shoulder. "Go back to your berth and make love to your wife, if you can manage it on this damned rattling contraption. Fall asleep in her arms. Be thankful for the gift God has given you."

The weight of Olympia's grip bore into his shoulder. Somerton lifted his hand and picked the ducal fingers delicately from his dressing gown.

"Thank you for the advice, my dear uncle," he said, and started for the door.

"Bloody idiot," said Olympia.

The train rolled into Huhnhof Baden just before sunrise. A gentle hand shook Luisa awake at twelve minutes to six. "Markham, it's time," said her husband.

He was dressed and shaved, his cheeks still damp. He helped her out of her pajamas and into her shirt and trousers, wrapping the linen bandage around her breasts without a word, without a single untoward brush of his fingers.

A sharp knock hit the compartment door. "Huhnhof Baden!" called the steward.

The valise was already packed. Somerton lifted it in one hand and opened the door with the other. "After you, my dear."

Luisa blinked her eyes as they stepped onto the familiar platform, on which she had alighted so many times before, to waiting bouquets from the mayor's daughters and an enthusiastic oompah from the local Huhnhof philharmonic. This morning, however, the platform was deserted, except for the conductor and a pair of passengers alighting at the other end of the train. A thin line of orange on the exposed eastern horizon suggested the coming sunrise. "This way," Olympia said brusquely, and they hurried after him down the platform and through the station to the stone steps outside, where a modest carriage waited by the curb, pulled by a single brown horse with sloping ears.

Her triumphant return to Holstein-Schweinwald-Huhnhof.

The ride was short, four or five miles at most. The sun hadn't fully risen by the time they pulled off the road and into a well-kept farmyard. The white daub walls of the house and stables were luminescent in the watery early morning light. A woman appeared in the doorway, removing her apron, patting her hair.

"Your Highness?" she breathed, as Luisa sprang from the carriage in her immaculate tweed jacket and trousers.

"Tut-tut. None of this, if you please." Olympia hurried

forward and took the woman's hand before she could sink into an imminent curtsy. He spoke in perfect German.

"My most grateful thanks for your hospitality, Frau Schubert," said Luisa.

The woman shook her head and gestured to the door. Her eyes were shining. "Come inside, come inside."

"I'm afraid we cannot stay," said Olympia, when the bread and coffee had been passed around. "We must reach Holstein by nightfall, and we cannot risk the train."

"So soon?" Luisa looked up from her steaming cup. She glanced at her husband's hard face. He was watching Frau Schubert the way a magistrate studies a criminal brought before the dock.

"Yes." Olympia finished his coffee and stood. "Somerton?"

The earl rose to his feet. "A moment with my wife, before we depart."

"Of course. I'll wait in the carriage. Frau Schubert? I have a few trifling matters to lay before you, if you don't mind." He held out his hand.

When the door shut behind the two of them, Somerton turned to Luisa. His face had lost none of its hardness, and his black eyes held hers intently.

"What is it?" she asked.

"I have a confession. That morning, two days ago, in Fiesole, before Olympia arrived. I hadn't walked up the mountain and back, as usual. I walked to Florence."

She'd been expecting something else. Some formal goodbye, some admonition to keep herself safe, the ordinary pieties. "Florence? Why?"

He slipped one hand into his pocket. "It occurred to me that I hadn't offered you any sort of bauble to mark the occasion of our marriage, as a husband ought to do for his wife, whatever the circumstances of the wedding. I found a jeweler to mend the oversight." He held out a flat rectangular box.

She gazed at the box, and then back to his face. Her throat went dry. "Why didn't you tell me before?"

"Because you have a way, Markham, of sapping the courage from a man, just when he needs it most. Take it, if you will. I must be off, and would rather not carry a fortune in jewels around with me, given the company I shall shortly be keeping."

Luisa took the box and lifted the lid. Inside lay a necklace, just long enough to fit around her collarbone. It was made of rubies, each one surrounded by a circle of tiny diamonds. The one in the center was larger than the others, a clear wine red pool, priceless.

He cleared his throat. "I was reminded of the verse in Proverbs. *For her price is far above rubies*, or whatever it is. The proper sentiment for the occasion, I suppose."

"It's beautiful."

"No doubt you have piles of jewels already, locked away in the royal treasury."

She looked at his face, which was deeply shadowed by the light from the window, and masked by its usual expression of granite indifference. "None that actually belong to me."

"Hide it somewhere secure, then. I daresay the sheepfold is probably the safest place. You should hear from us within a week, if all goes well."

If all goes well.

"Somerton . . ." She swallowed. "Leopold." His Christian name tasted foreign on her tongue, and daringly intimate.

His face stretched in surprise.

"Please be careful. These men are treacherous, horrible people. I can't . . ."

"I assure you, my dear, I'm not inclined to approach with frivolity the perpetrators of my wife's attempted assassination."

"Naturally not. I don't believe you approach anything with frivolity. But I shall worry just the same, so for God's sake, have a care for yourself."

He made a slight bow.

"And thank you for the necklace. I shall treasure it." She closed the box and took a hesitant step toward him. His hands were knotted behind his back.

"Another thing, before I leave." He glowered down at her. "You're to take the strictest care of yourself, do you understand? Don't show yourself to visitors. Don't stray outside the farmyard. Eat wholesome foods, get plenty of rest, and above all . . ."

"You might just kiss me good-bye, you know," she said. "You might just take me in your arms and say, *Farewell, my darling wife, my helpmeet, my treasure. I shall remain true to*

*you in thought and deed. I shall think of you every moment, I
shall dream of you in bed, I shall kiss your photograph every
night.*"

"As it happens, I don't have a photograph of you."

She turned away and clutched the box to her chest. "You're
a beastly . . . *beast.*"

His hands slid over her shoulders. He said, quietly, into her
hair, "I have my own men posted nearby. If anything goes
wrong, the slightest suspicion, go to the grange hall in the next
hamlet and tell them my name. Failing that, make your way to
Huhnhof Baden and send a wire to Mr. Nathaniel Wright in
London Wall."

"To Nathaniel Wright?"

"I have left instructions with him. He can be trusted."
Something soft pressed against the crown of her head. He
whispered, "Farewell, darling wife."

She spun around in amazement, but Lord Somerton was
already striding out the door, cramming his hat on his head.
He did not look back.

At Frau Schubert's urging, she retired to her room and
bathed in an old tin hip bath, with hot water brought up in
canisters by the woman herself. She felt vaguely unwell, but
that was only natural, after such an exhausting twenty-four
hours.

It was not until she was dressing herself afterward that she
noticed the smear of blood on her underthings, and not until
nightfall that she had given up hope at last.

TWENTY-FIVE

One week later

A pair of muscular male arms came down and trapped her within the pillows. His lips covered hers, tender and demanding, tasting of brandy. His naked chest brushed against the tingling tips of her breasts, and his hips descended on hers, inexorable, inevitable, until her desire-swollen flesh gave way and a surge of pleasure filled her middle and radiated outward to her fingertips. She cried out with joy, but his mouth muffled her voice. His kiss grew deeper and deeper, smothering her senses, until she couldn't breathe, she was suffocating under his lips and body, his relentless burly strength.

"Come for me," he said.

Or was it *Come to me*?

With all her strength, she heaved herself against the enormous weight that covered her. Her body flew forward, her fingers grasped wildly into . . .

Nothing. Empty air.

She looked down at her arms, clutching the white pillow. On the table beside her bed ticked her gold pocket watch; she reached out her arm and held the glass up against the faint light from the open window.

Twenty-four minutes past five o'clock in the morning.

She lay back down among the pillows—Frau Schubert had

denuded every bed in the house for her sake—and stared at
the shadows above. Every atom of her body ached with disappointment. The dream had been so real this time. She had *felt*
him, his hot skin and his demanding brandy mouth. She had
been back inside the little house near Fiesole, making love to
Somerton under the warm Italian night, in the soft comfort of
their bed. The solid weight of her husband's body had replaced
everything in the world.

And now he was gone, and the world had returned. It was
now eight days since he and Olympia had left in the modest
black carriage, and she hadn't heard a word from either of
them since. They had disappeared without a trace into the ripening German summer.

She turned her head to the window.

Eight days. Somerton had said she would hear from them
within a week, if all went well.

If all went well.

Her body still tingled from the dream, but the sickening
sense of dread was already chasing it away. One of them
should have sent word by now, whether the news was good or
bad. Which meant the news had to be very bad indeed.

Or not. She stared fiercely at the crack in the curtains, at
the imminent dawn of the eighth day, trying to find a reason
why her husband wouldn't find a way to reassure her. Careless-
ness, or constant industry, or the inability to find a trusted
messenger.

Luisa threw the covers from her body and swung her feet
to the floor.

Impossible. If the Earl of Somerton had promised to send
word, he would find a way to do so. If he could do so. Which
meant that he couldn't, that something had happened.

And it was up to her to find out what it was.

She reached for her trousers and shirt, for the linen binding
for her chest. She splashed water on her face and buttoned her
waistcoat and her jacket.

Outside, the sun was beginning to lighten the sky above the
foothills to the east. Luisa settled her hat on her head and
closed the door softly behind her.

"Your Highness!"

Luisa jumped and turned. Frau Schubert was walking

across the farmyard from the barn, dangling two pails of milk from her sturdy hands. Her white apron glowed like a ghost through the predawn air.

"Good morning, Frau Schubert."

"What are you doing up so early? His Highness left strict instructions for your rest." She hurried up to Luisa and set down the milk pails. "You must go back to bed. I'll fetch you a bit of breakfast."

"Please don't trouble yourself. I couldn't sleep; I'm off to take a walk, that's all."

"But His Highness said . . ."

"His Highness has been away for over a week, Frau Schubert, with no word at all." She hesitated, but surely the woman could be trusted. She'd guarded Luisa faithfully, seeing to her every need as if she were honored to do the service. "My husband told me to seek out men in Hohengruben if I had any reason for concern."

"But that's three kilometers away, Your Highness!" Frau Schubert was scandalized.

Luisa smiled. "I assure you, I'm up to the challenge."

"You mustn't. What if you're seen? My sister's son arrives today, on his way back home to Holstein. He'll see to it." Frau Schubert put her hands together and leaned forward in her distress. "His Highness wouldn't want you to put yourself in danger, madam."

"I'm afraid it can't be helped. Every moment is of the essence."

"Oh, do let my Gunther go instead! He can be trusted, madam. He's one of them leading the opposition in Holstein. Why, I do expect you know him. He is the late mayor's son."

"The mayor? The mayor of Holsteinton?"

"The same. Gunther Hassendorf is his name, madam, and I trust him with my life. He stops here to hear my news, when I have it. Things that might be useful to the cause." She lifted her chin. "A good boy, our Gunther. A true royalist."

An image flashed through Luisa's mind: her sister Stefanie, dancing with the mayor's son at the harvest ball one year, flirting with him openly. Luisa had spoken to her about it afterward. *I don't care*, the eighteen-year-old Stefanie had said, eyes flashing. *I love him, and he loves me, and he's going to marry me next spring.* A tall, sturdy fellow, young Gunther. Entirely unsuitable, of course, and while he had indeed married the next spring, it was to a daughter of a wealthy burgher, and at the urging of his practical-minded father. Herr Hassendorf had wisely seen no benefit and a very real danger in allowing his son to elope with the beloved youngest daughter of Prince Rudolf.

"Gunther! Your nephew is Gunther Hassendorf? *Stefanie's* Gunther?"

Frau Schubert's eyebrows drew inward. "I beg your pardon, madam?"

"Never mind. I believe he can be trusted." She bent down and picked up one of the pails of milk. "Let me carry this for you, Frau Schubert, and help you with breakfast. No, I insist." She brushed away the widow's protests with a manful sweep of her tweed-covered arm.

"But it isn't at all proper!" twittered Frau Schubert. "A princess carrying the milk!"

"I assure you, I've carried far worse these past many months." She opened the door for Frau Schubert and followed her in. "And let it be a hearty breakfast, my good woman. I'm off to Holstein with your nephew Gunther, as soon as he arrives."

T his is most distressing." Gunther shook his blond head and spoke in a low voice, though the last occupants had emptied the third-class compartment when the train reached Schweinwald Central, leaving them alone at last. "You say they left a week ago?"

"Eight days. They went by road, so as not to attract attention, and should have arrived in Holstein last Wednesday." She looked at her hands. She hadn't taken off her wedding band, though it was a most unusual object for a man to wear. The gold shone subtly in the dim lights of the railway carriage.

"Do you know who they were meeting with?"

"No. My uncle had gathered together a band of committed loyalists."

He shook his head again. Since his youth, he'd grown into a man of substantial proportions: His head nearly brushed the luggage rack above, and his clothes strained to cover the width of his chest and shoulders. He reminded her of Somerton, at least in his build. "What stupid luck that I was called away from town. I would have known, at least, where to begin the search, and with whom. But never mind. There are a few obvious choices. You still command the hearts of many men in Holstein."

"And I thank you for yours, Herr Hassendorf. I have seen enough betrayal these past months. My father's valet Hans turned out to be among the conspirators, and my own governess Dingleby, too, who raised me and my sisters herself after my mother died." She paused delicately.

"Your sisters," said Gunther. "How are they?"

"I have heard very little, but I understand them to be well. I hope they may soon be safe to return to this country, and you can see for yourself."

"The Princess Stefanie. You have had no word of her recently? In the past few days?"

Luisa hesitated. "Not in the past several days. Not since I came to Germany. But I believe she has faced her own difficulties in England."

"I shall take great pleasure in exacting revenge with my own bare hands," he said fiercely, punching one hand into the opposite fist.

"I know you cared for her, once."

For a moment, he didn't answer. "I had hopes . . . But of course, a mayor's son could never dream of marrying a princess. My father made that abundantly clear. Ideas above my station, he said." His voice turned bitter.

She cleared her throat. "I hope that revenge won't be necessary. I hope to avoid bloodshed as much as possible. I only want to rescue my people, to restore a just and rightful rule to our beloved country." Tears pricked at her eyes. "To find my husband, who I know will do so much good for Holstein-Schweinwald-Huhnhof, if only he has the chance."

Gunther patted her hand. "We'll find him, never fear. Trust me, Your Highness."

By the time they rattled into Holstein Terminus, the hour was growing late and Luisa's belly rumbled with hunger. Gunther bought her a sausage roll from one of the vendors and led her discreetly out the side entrance of the station. "We'll go to my own house for tonight," he said. "You'll be safe there, while I go out and make inquiries."

"I presume your wife and servants are discreet?"

His expression became blank. "My wife died last year of typhoid, two days after our son."

"Oh! I'm so sorry."

"It was God's will."

Luisa let the conversation die. What could she possibly say, after that?

Gunther Hassendorf occupied his father's old house, in the shadow of Holstein Castle itself. The streets nearby were strangely deserted, the few citizens walking swiftly, hunched into their jackets, hats pulled low. Luisa risked a glance up the hill at the familiar gray walls of her home, overlooking the town in benign solitude. The tips of the towers were touched with pink in the dying sun. A single golden light shone in the window that had once been her father's chamber. She couldn't breathe. She ducked her head again and followed Gunther around another corner, while the warm evening air returned to her lungs.

Gunther's house stood a little apart from the others, an imposing white square building, trimmed in blue. He rapped smartly on the door with his walking stick, an action strange in itself, since Holstein had always been the sort of town in which citizens might confidently leave their houses unlocked and their virgins unguarded. The door was opened by a young woman in a black dress and a starched white bib apron. "Good evening, Herr Hassendorf," she said, and took his hat and walking stick.

He turned and motioned Luisa inside. "Frieda, this is Herr Markham, an English gentleman of my acquaintance. You will please make him comfortable in the blue bedroom. He will be staying the night."

The maid curtsied. "Yes, Herr Hassendorf."

The house was furnished sumptuously in bright jewel colors and gilded trim work. As Luisa followed the maid up a sweeping main staircase, she caught glimpses of fine Louis Quatorze furniture, of magnificent paintings in ornate frames. They turned down the corridor on the third floor, where the blue bedroom turned out to be an enormous chamber swathed in sapphire velvet and blue chinoiserie wallpaper. She touched the crested peak of a gilded headboard and thought that it could not have been less German.

"Would you like a refreshment, Herr Markham?" asked the maid.

Luisa turned. "A simple tray of supper, perhaps, if it does not inconvenience the staff at this hour."

The maid started and stared at her. "Yes, sir," she whispered, bobbing a curtsy, and backed out of the room.

Luisa swore softly and tossed her hat across the floor.

Gunther arrived a quarter hour later with his own hat under his arm and his walking stick in his hand. He nodded at the tray of meats and cheese on the elegant tripod table near the window. "I see you have been made comfortable. Is there anything else you need?"

"I need my husband," she said. "Let me go with you, please. I want to be doing something right now, not just sit here in your lovely bedroom and pace paths into your rug."

Gunther cast an alarmed glance at the rug, a thick Persian masterpiece of cream and sapphire blue. "It's far too dangerous. And you would be recognized, of course, even in your male costume."

Luisa made a frustrated noise and turned to the window, which gazed up at the walls of Holstein Castle itself, now shrouded in a deep violet twilight. "Hurry back, then. And with good news, if you please."

He made a little bow. "I will do my best, Your Highness. One small matter, however." He reached into his pocket.

"What's that?"

"Your room. It locks from the outside, and I fear—for your protection, of course—it ought to be secured while I'm gone. Do you object?"

She stared at the small brass key in his hand, an ornate affair of curlicues and polish, eminently suited to its station. A frisson of uneasiness passed across her heart. "Are you quite sure it's necessary?"

"Your Highness, I regret the necessity deeply, but I cannot answer for the state of the town. Neighbor is set against neighbor, servant against master." He shook his bright head mournfully. "I should not forgive myself if any harm came to you under my roof."

Luisa remembered the startled reaction of the maid, the shifty glances of the townspeople as they walked along the streets. She gazed into Gunther's serious face. His mouth was tightened into a downward arc of embarrassed contrition.

She tried to smile. "Then lock the door, my friend. I will endure my captivity with fortitude."

He grinned back in deep relief. "You are, as ever, the soul of grace, Your Highness."

He bowed and left the room, and the click of the lock echoed softly after him.

A fter he had gone, Luisa tried to rest. She took off her jacket and lay on the grand sapphire bed, staring at the plasterwork above, but her mind would not quiet. Over and over she pictured not Somerton and Olympia, but Prince Rudolf and poor Peter, with their hands crossed over their chests, nestled in white satin while the Gothic arches of Holstein Cathedral soared above them.

She could not go through that again.

They must be alive. They must.

If only she could weep, and release this awful tension inside her. But while the tears ached behind her eyes, they wouldn't fall, and so she leapt from the bed and paced across the floor, and at last, in desperation, yanked the stopper from the brandy and poured herself a glass. She closed her eyes as it burned down her throat and the fumes wafted through her head, and she thought of Somerton, the way his kisses tasted in the evening, when he had indulged himself in a glass after dinner. How his black eyes would soften just a little, and he would carry her to bed and call her his Markham as he made love to her. How sometimes the moonlight would come through the window at just the right angle, and gild his black hair silver, and she would run her hands through it and call him beautiful, and he would laugh and say she was a fool, a marvelous little fool.

Surely that was not the entire sum of her earthly happiness. Surely God could not be so unjust.

Luisa went back to the bed and lay back down, and this time the brandy fumes lulled her into a little more calm. Her eyelids drifted shut. Gunther would be back soon, with news. Gunther would tell her that Olympia and Somerton had been forced to go into hiding, that they couldn't send word, that they were nonetheless planning a . . . planning something . . .

"Madam! Your Highness!"

The whisper slipped urgently into her ear. A gentle hand shook her shoulder.

Luisa's eyes sprang open. "What's that?"

"Your Highness!" It was the maid Frieda. Her eyes were wide and blue. She looked quickly over her shoulder and back at Luisa. "You must come! Quickly, now! Before he returns!"

"Before . . . Herr Hassendorf . . ." Luisa shook her head to clear it. "What's happened? How did you get in here?"

"The housekeeper has copies of all the keys. I took yours from her chain. Oh, Your Highness, he will betray you. You must come. He is . . . he is with the conspirators!"

Luisa bolted upright. "Who's with the conspirators? Herr Hassendorf?"

"Yes! Oh, Your Highness, when I saw it was you . . ." The blue eyes turned wet. "You must come!"

The bottom fell away from her chest.

"But my husband!" she managed. "Where is he?"

"In the prison! He and your uncle, they were betrayed. They're in the prison beneath the castle. They've been questioned for days."

Luisa gripped her by the shoulders. "How do you know this? Tell me, Frieda!"

"My brother, he's a gardener there. He knows one of the prison guards, and he hears them at night, through the windows." She took Luisa's hand from her shoulder and kissed it. "Oh, please, Your Highness. You must do something. Everything, everything is terrible now, since the Brigade came in, after you left. They told us the richest burghers would be put in prison, and there would be no rulers, and the country's wealth given to the people, but instead . . ."

"Frieda, listen to me." Luisa's blood was running cool now, her mind sharp. "You must take me there, right away. Your brother, can he help me? Will his friend the guard let me in?"

Frieda wiped her eyes. "Yes, Your Highness. My brother would die for you. As would I. As would anyone in Holstein, except those traitors."

Luisa had no particular reason to trust this maid. She had trusted Gunther, and now he was apparently about to betray her. Or perhaps Gunther was loyal, and Frieda was the traitor. Frieda had come to take her to her doom.

But she had to make a decision. Whom to believe, whom to follow. And in the end, it didn't matter which one had betrayed her, Frieda or Gunther. She had to get out of this house and into the town. She had to search the prison, because that was where her husband probably lay. If this maid could take her there, she would take that risk. She had to. She had been waiting for nearly ten months; she could not sit a moment longer, hoping for someone else to save her.

"Quickly, then." Luisa leapt from the bed and found her hat and jacket. Her pulse thudded eagerly in her neck, ready for action. "You must do exactly as I say, Frieda. We've got to free them tonight, the duke and the prince consort, and take them somewhere safe. Do you know where we might go?"

"I think so, madam." Frieda brushed her apron and set her cap.

"Then let's go, before he returns. And Frieda?"

"Yes, Your Highness?"

Luisa took both her hands and kissed each one. "Thank you for your loyalty."

Frieda opened the door and locked it again behind them, and in minutes they were slipping out the back of the house and into the darkened street, toward the twilit hulk of Holstein Castle, and the prison beneath.

Holstein Prison. Her chest constricted in pain at the thought of her husband lying in a dank, half-lit cell, surrounded by criminals, guarded by ruthless traitors.

What were they doing to him there?

TWENTY-SIX

Holstein Prison

On the third day, he had given up trying to keep track of his injuries. They had all stitched together into a seamless garment of pain, after all; there was no use remembering that the searing agony on his left arm corresponded to the episode with the burning tongs on Monday afternoon, and the dull ache in his kidneys came as a result of an encounter with his questioner's meaty fists on Tuesday morning. Pain was pain. He endured it because he had to, because there was no alternative.

Except death. And he couldn't die yet, not while Markham needed him. Not while this pummeled husk of a body might, in clinging to life, still be of some use to her.

Of what use, however? That remained the central question. He'd known from the outset that betrayal of some sort loomed around the next corner, or across the next smoke-filled table; he avoided these sorts of capers—dropping oneself into a complex foreign affair, trusting people on local hearsay—for that reason. When he had accompanied Olympia to the first rendezvous, shortly after their arrival, he hadn't liked the look of the place, and he'd said so. Blocked lines of sight, no secondary escape, a regular box canyon of a beer hall.

I quite agree, said Olympia, *but we must start somewhere. And this fellow, at least, can be trusted.*

To his credit, Olympia's contact had looked as surprised as they were when the men at the neighboring table had risen from their seats and taken out their revolvers. He had fought hard, and ended on the sawdust with a bullet through his brain.

Somerton had taken out two men himself, and might have escaped were it not for the Duke of Olympia, who took an unlucky blow to his ribs from a flying chair and had to be rescued. Now here they were, rotting at the bottom of a loathsome German dungeon, questioned at regular intervals by men who had evidently been trained at the highest level. The torture always stopped short of actual incapacitation: not a broken bone, not a damaged organ, not a single significant laceration. Pain was the object, clear and precise and sublime. For whatever reason, they wanted him alive.

He hated to oblige them.

They would be returning soon. Time had taken on a vague elasticity since he had arrived here—had it been days? weeks?—but there had passed some hours since the last session, and they were due. The thin, cruel one came at night, and the genial, muscular one during the day. Or perhaps it was the other way around: How was he to know? Without a window, immersed in the dull and clammy air of this troglodyte world, laden with the mingled scents of effluvia, the cycles of sun and moon had no meaning.

Somerton stretched out one aching leg against the flagstones, starting with the swollen toes, one by one, and the metatarsals, and then the tarsals. He extended his calf in gentle movements, ignoring the searing pain, and then moved to the other foot. From down another passage came the distant sound of a carrying scream, cut short abruptly.

"Why the devil does he scream so?" murmured Olympia, a few feet away. "Hardly neighborly."

"Not all men have had the benefit of your training in such matters, Your Grace," said Somerton. His cracked lips hurt as he moved them.

"Bad form," said Olympia. "Damned bad form."

The effort of speaking was immense, but Somerton made it anyway. "Is she alive, do you think?"

"I should hope so, or this has all been a great waste of one's natural endurance."

"She will come to look for us, of course."

"Let us pray she doesn't succeed." A faint grunt and a clink of metal against stone, as Olympia shifted his weight. "Let us pray she did the sensible thing, and sent that wire to London."

Somerton rather doubted it, with the kind of doubt that sat like a stone ball of dread in one's empty belly. Better he should suffer a thousand times worse than this, better he should lose himself in an agony so profound as to transcend the ordinary boundaries of human experience, than Markham should fall into the power of the Revolutionary Brigade of the Free Blood. The contemplation of this possibility hurt far worse than the constant chafe of the manacles about his wrists, the daily inventiveness visited upon his skin and sinews.

Markham, and the possibility of a child growing inside her, begotten of their dreamlike weeks in the Fiesole sunshine. His Markham, their child.

"I do wonder, in my moments of leisure, why they take such trouble to keep us alive," he said.

"Because a dead man has no value, of course. An elementary principle. I'm surprised you should ask."

"But they hardly need keep us alive, to lure Luisa here."

"My dear fellow, this goes further than capturing the princess. A duke and an earl of Great Britain, of some practical and personal value to the Queen herself, are valuable sorts of commodities for a fledgling republic to own."

Somerton's mouth tasted of copper mixed with bile. He spat carefully into the flagstones to his left. He knew all this, of course, but it was useful to keep talking about sensible things. It kept the mind from drifting into the shoals. "We haven't told them who we are," he pointed out.

"But she knows. Dingleby knows. She must be back from England now, having failed to lure Stefanie back with her. She's on her beam ends, with two princesses safely married and great with child, outside the range of her influence. You and I are her last hope. The ripe plum, fallen into her lap." The duke spoke reflectively.

"Luisa will not allow herself to be used by the revolutionaries."

"Do you think not?"

"Nothing means more to her than her people, old chap. Her integrity is absolute."

The chains clinked again. "Obviously, my dear fellow, you haven't paid much attention to the way your wife looks at you."

Ah, God. Like a new gash, the pain tore through his ribs, infinitely deeper than the torture he'd endured in this prison.

"I smell a wager, Your Grace."

"Done. The stakes?"

"My best agent in Vienna . . ."

A gasp. "Von Estrich?"

"The same. To your chap in St. Petersburg . . ."

"You can have Kurikov for free, by God."

"That fellow in Sarajevo, then. The one who bagged the elephant last spring."

Olympia laughed. "Oh, ho. You heard about that? Very well, then. Since the stakes must be rich enough to mean something. Your Von Estrich to my Begovic, she turns up with bells on, army at her heels, weeping over your wounds."

"And I say she holds firm, wires the British Consulate in Berlin, and trades our meager lives in exchange for a Life Guards regiment to roust the anarchists out of her castle."

Olympia said nothing. The sounds of distant bustling drifted through the prison bars. Time for the next round of questioning, it seemed. Thin man or heavyweight? Somerton hoped the latter. He was stronger, but less inclined to wanton cruelty.

"What is it, old man? I can hear that feline smile of yours, all the way over here." Somerton rested his aching head against the wall.

"I don't know what you mean."

"You've got something up your sleeve, do you? I don't suppose you care to share it."

"No, I . . ."

The voices grew louder, and Olympia swallowed his words. Keys rattled in the lock, that familiar metallic sound that sent cold dread stirring inevitably in his blood, in anticipation of the trials to come. What would it be this time? Burning cigarettes? The tongs? Immersion of the head in ice water?

"Doctor here for the prisoners," the guard said tonelessly.

Sweet Christ. Not a *doctor*. This was worse than he thought.

He braced his arms in the manacles.

"A light, please, if you will," said a familiar voice, speaking in cultured German. "Not too bright as to hurt the prisoners' eyes."

The breath froze in his lungs.

A lantern appeared, next to the visitor's face, casting a dim glow across the ridge of a well-known regal cheekbone and the slope of a firm chin. A plaid hat came down low above a pair of eyes that, if he could see them well enough, if he could dare to examine them closely, would be warm and topaz-brown.

"They appear to be in very poor health indeed," said the doctor, and only Somerton could have heard the waver in that confident voice, the timbre in the vowels that meant its owner felt something.

He closed his eyes. The light really did hurt them.

There was a clink beside him, as the lantern was set down on the stones.

"Can you open your eyes, sir?" asked a steady voice, this time in English.

"Yes, Markham," he whispered, and cracked his eyes back open.

"Jolly luck," said Olympia. "I do believe I've just gained myself an agent in Austria."

L uisa was no doctor, but she could see that Somerton—and her uncle, too, blast his clever schemes to hell and back—had endured a horrifying ordeal this past week, while she had been slumbering among Frau Schubert's best down pillows back in Huhnhof. His eyes were swollen, his skin mottled, his lips crusted. He was hanging from a pair of manacles, chained high upon the wall, in such a way that his shoulders hunched at an unnatural angle, bearing his weight.

She touched his cheek, his lips, his forehead. He watched her intently. She turned her head slightly to the opening of the cell and said, in German, "Both prisoners must have their wrists released from the chains this instant, or I cannot answer for the consequences."

"But Herr Doctor! There are very dangerous men!" The guard was shocked.

"I have been sent from Herr Hassendorf himself to ensure these prisoners are well enough to continue questioning by morning. I will take any risk to ensure his orders are fulfilled to the strictest extent. Unlock these manacles at once." She used her most commanding tone, filling the walls with the force of her conviction.

The guard came forward, shaking his head, and took out his keys. "It's your funeral," he muttered.

He freed Olympia first, and then Somerton. Her husband slumped down the wall in relief, rubbing one wrist and then the other. She picked up his hand and examined it. The skin was raw where the metal had chafed it, day and night. "My God," she whispered, bending her head so the guard wouldn't see her expression. A tiny drop fell from her eye and landed on the inside of his wrist.

"Markham, don't," he said.

"What's the prisoner saying?" demanded the guard.

"That it hurts, of course. I'll need a large bucket of warm water, and soap, and lengths of toweling. The malignant animalcules must be cleansed from the wounds before putrefaction sets in."

"But I can't leave you alone with them, Herr Doctor! They'll eat you alive!"

"I assure you, I have treated more dangerous criminals than you have hairs on your head, and not one of them has offered me anything more than grateful thanks."

"But these two are . . ."

Luisa pounded the floor. "At once, sir!"

The guard scurried from the cell, clanging the door shut behind him.

"Not the brightest chap, is he?" Somerton said, in a voice she hardly recognized, so low and broken it belonged to another man.

She put her hands on his face and kissed his cracked lips. "Oh, my lord! What have they done to you?"

"Damn you for risking yourself," he whispered. "You damned marvelous fool."

"I suppose *my* suffering is immaterial," said Olympia. "Never mind. I'm merely an old man of fragile health and uncertain prospects."

"You're the reason we're all here to begin with," she snapped.

"I protest. *You* are."

"Can we not waste time on the pleasantries, if you please?" Somerton was testing his arms now, flexing each one, wincing as he went. "We only have minutes before that fool of a guard returns."

"Can you walk?" she said.

"There's one way to find out, isn't there?"

He braced one hand against the wall and drew his feet carefully beneath him. Luisa ducked under his shoulder and laid his other arm across her back.

"Thank you," he said, and straightened to his full height.

"How do you feel?"

He looked down at her with his dark eyes, in which burned a tiny, flickering reflection of the nearby lantern. "Tolerable," he said, in such a way that her toes curled in her boots and her brain relaxed in relief.

He was still Somerton.

"Able to stand over here as well," said Olympia, "if anybody gives a damn."

Somerton kept his gaze on Luisa. "Not particularly, though I suppose one's grateful not to have to carry your ancient carcass from the prison across one's shoulders."

"Take a few steps," she said. "Loosen your limbs, if you can."

"My dear, you will perceive the door to our apartment is still locked."

He was moving stiffly, supporting himself against the wall as he went, but he could stand. He could walk. She searched his face in the lantern-lit shadows, trying to gauge how hurt he was, but of course the expression on his fearfully bruised features remained stoic. His shirt seemed to be stuck to his back, and stained here and there with spots of blood.

She dug her fingernails into her palms. "I . . ."

He stiffened. "Quiet! He's coming back."

In perfect tandem, Olympia and Somerton dropped to the floor, lying as if mortally wounded. Somerton groaned piteously as the key rattled, as the hinges ground open.

"Here's your bucket, Herr Doctor. There's soap at the bottom."

She rose and took it from him. "Thank you," she said, and swung the contents into his face.

In the next instant, Somerton had leapt silently from the floor to swing a heavy fist into the guard's jaw, followed by a driving blow to his middle. The man crumpled without a word, only a pathetic small cry that ended in a squeak, smothered by the clank of his keys hitting the flagstones.

"Quickly," said Somerton. He scooped up the keys and handed them to Luisa, and bent down again to pry the service pistol from the guard's belt. He tucked it into the waistband of the trousers.

Olympia stepped out of the cell. "Which way?"

"To the right," she said.

"Are you quite certain?"

"Yes. My father never used this place; there's a modern prison just outside of town. My sisters and I used to run away from Dingleby on rainy days and play here. Now put your hands behind your backs, both of you." She started off down the corridor.

Somerton obediently put back his hands, as if held by restraints. Olympia did the same. Luisa leaned down and picked up the guard's baton and drove them forward and around the corner.

"Up the stairs," she said.

Olympia put his hand out to the wall and stopped.

"Are you all right?" she whispered.

"Yes." He lifted his head, put his hands once more behind his back, and climbed the stairs, one by one, as if borne down by a sackful of gravel.

She couldn't think about that. She couldn't think about what had been done to them, or the way Somerton's shoulders slumped forward, or the blood on his shirt, or the limp in his right leg, or the rotten smell wafting from both of them, unwashed and unloved. She would go mad if she thought about any of it. She would break down and cry, she would lose her calm control, and they would never get out of here alive.

"Hurry along," she said. "Turn left at the top of the stairs, and I'll unlock the door."

Marvel instead, she thought. *Marvel that these two men can walk, that they can react in seconds to the shock of your arrival, that they have been trained and honed for just such a moment as this.*

You will survive this. They will survive this.

They reached the door. Luisa reached between them and fumbled with the keys until she found one that fit.

"Where does this lead?" asked Somerton, in a low voice.

"To the outer prison corridor, and then to the hidden entrance, the one they used to use for political prisoners, according to the older servants." She swung the door open and urged them on.

The corridor was a long one, but it smelled fresher than the network of cells and corridors in the inner dungeon. Luisa breathed it gratefully into her lungs. In another moment, they would reach the tunnel to the secret entrance, which had given her so much delight in her youth, playing with her sisters, and now meant freedom.

She did not stop to wonder why the atmosphere of this corridor should be fresher, when the passage and entrance were both too inconvenient to be used in the ordinary course of prison business. She tested the handle and found it unlocked, and had just nudged Somerton's back to guide him and her uncle into the familiar bracken lit by a slim crescent moon, when the click of a revolver sounded through the clear night air, followed by the deep masculine voice of Gunther Hassendorf.

"My dear princess, how utterly predictable."

A noble effort," said Olympia, "if astoundingly unsuccessful. Would you stop rattling the bars, Somerton? You set my teeth on edge."

He whipped around. "I beg your pardon. I had rather hoped that you would face the prospect of public execution with a little less sangfroid."

Olympia waved his hand. "These are the sorts of misfortunes that happen in our business, my dear fellow. One must accept one's losses philosophically. We have been bested, that's all."

Somerton turned to his wife, who sat on the floor with her knees drawn up to her chest. Her jacket was gone, and her shirt was untucked from her trousers. "I will get us out of here, Markham. I swear it."

"You needn't speak platitudes for my sake, Somerton. I'm not a child. I recognize the reality of our circumstances."

"I will not allow my wife and my unborn child to die in a public square for the amusement of a set of bloody anarchist revolutionaries, Markham. *That* is reality."

She looked up at him with hopeless dark eyes. "There is no child, Somerton."

The world spun. He curled his fingers around the bar of the cage and stared at her. "No child?"

"I discovered the fact shortly after you left the farmhouse in Huhnhof."

"I see."

"So I've failed at that, too. I've failed to rescue my people, I've failed to rescue you. I suppose it's up to Stefanie and Emilie now, to carry the banner, except that I suspect they won't. Will they, Olympia? They never cared for duty the way I did." She put her head back into her knees. "But they will live, at least. They have their husbands and their babies and will probably go on to lead very lovely English lives."

Somerton looked down at his wife, curled up in misery. A giant helplessness opened up inside him: he, Somerton, who had never met the foe he couldn't vanquish, the ill wind he could not blow away with a rank puff from his scoundrel lungs. What could he say, in the face of this grief? What could he say to comfort his wife, his true and noble Markham, whose only fault was to have chosen her husband with such disastrously poor judgment?

He lowered himself next to her and touched her hair, her soft, shorn auburn hair that he loved.

"We'll have a daughter, one fine day, with hair just like this," he said.

She turned her face into his chest and sobbed.

He leaned back against the stone wall, every muscle protesting, every bruise and scar howling, and wrapped his arms around her. "A daughter, a son. Whatever the devil, really; it doesn't matter, as long as they're ours, Markham, yours and mine. We'll spend the springtime in England, if you don't mind all the blasted rain, and take them climbing in Wales to toughen them up. Children need a bit of toughening, in my opinion. The rising generation is entirely too soft."

He went on talking, until her sobs slowed down and she slept, curled up against his chest like a child, and eventually he slept, too.

He knew he slept because they were awakened together by a clang a minute later—or what felt like a minute, and must have been a few hours—and a female voice of such sharp command, such crisp efficiency, such wanton disregard for the ease of others, it could only belong to an English governess.

"Well! This is a fine predicament, Your Highness. I expected better of you."

Luisa bolted to attention. "Dingleby?"

Somerton's tired eyes flashed open. A tall and slender woman stood before them, flanked by guards, her features too shadowed to pick out properly and her hair pulled back in a strict governess knot. She was wearing a simple black dress and a pair of eminently sensible shoes, a detail he wouldn't ordinarily have noticed at first glance, except that he was sitting on the floor.

"Dingleby," said Olympia, rising to his feet. "My hat is off to you indeed. The student usurping the master." He made a flourish with his hand.

Somerton levered his aching body upward, still holding Luisa. "*This* is Miss Dingleby?" He lent his voice its most scathing tone of condescending disappointment. "*This* is a woman who sends a young lady off to be murdered most ignobly in a public square, for a pointless cause, to say nothing of the persecution she has visited on her charges over the past several months?"

"I regret the public square deeply," said Miss Dingleby.

"How comforting," said Olympia.

"It's true. I made my wishes known to Gunther, but I'm afraid my supporters in the organization have become few. Ironic, since I recruited Gunther to begin with, after his disappointment with Stefanie first planted those vital seeds of disillusionment with this archaic, creaking method of government we call a monarchy." She spread out her hands. "Still, I far prefer to work without the messiness of bloodshed. I believe he's making a great mistake, an act of barbarism that the world will condemn. But he sees things differently. *Propagande par le fait*, he says."

"Propaganda of the deed," murmured Luisa. "The dramatic act that rallies the masses to your cause."

"Nothing more dramatic than a public regicide," said Olympia. "Just look what it did for the French."

"I assure you, I've spent the last year protecting you and your sisters from Gunther's more violent tendencies. It was I who arranged your escape from Holstein last October, I who brought you to England and hid you from his agents. But he convinced old Hans that he was right, that the princesses had to be eliminated, and poof!" She snapped her fingers. "The fiasco at Emilie's engagement ball."

"Yes, yes. And you laid us low with typhoid, so you could make your escape back to Germany before I discovered your subterfuge."

"I didn't mean for Luisa to eat that cake," she said. "My deepest apologies for your illness, my dear."

Somerton growled, low in his throat.

She turned to him. "You don't believe me, but I've always defended their interests, haven't I? I made certain there were no further legitimate heirs. I've protected them from the Revolutionary Brigade for years. You've no idea the trouble I had, the recriminations when it all went wrong in England. There's nothing more I can do, I'm afraid. Everyone's turned against me." She spread her hands piteously.

"But your Brigade won't win, not in the end," Luisa said fiercely. "Stefanie and Emilie will carry on the royal line, and one day . . ."

"Rubbish. They will mind their own business and become proper Englishwomen, turning out babies like runner beans, year after year. As you should have done, my dear. I could perhaps have kept Gunther from seeking you out, but you had to return and play straight into his hands." She clucked her tongue. "Now he'll bring you out for the ritual sacrifice tomorrow, and I don't know how the cause will recover. Perhaps I shall emigrate to America and join one of the more pacifist groups there. Yes, I think I shall."

Somerton rose to his feet. "The cause? I beg your pardon. The *cause*?"

"Why, yes," she said calmly. "The reason for all this. The overthrow of an unjust political system, one that's oppressed millions, has been responsible for the deaths of millions. What other end could justify such extreme means?"

"There, you see," said Olympia. "There's the difference between my way of thinking and yours. I don't consider that the end does justify the means."

She turned to him. "Oh, that's splendid. And who was the one who taught me that the few must sometimes be sacrificed for the good of the many? It was *you*, Olympia. You who opened my eyes and trained my hands."

"The difference, my dear Dingleby, is that I don't advocate the killing of the innocent."

She shrugged. "Who among us is innocent? Every man who doesn't oppose injustice is complicit in it." She slipped her watch from her pocket and turned behind her. "Citizen?" she said, in German.

A tall uniformed man stepped up smartly. "Yes, citizeness?"

"It's time to prepare the prisoners. We shall need them in the Kirkenplatz in one hour. Alive, if you please." She turned back to Luisa and smiled. "Farewell, my dear girl. I've no doubt you'll do me great credit in meeting your end with the dignity and deportment it was my honor to instill in you. You may take comfort in the fact that your death will perhaps one day bring about the emancipation of mankind, if Hassendorf doesn't contrive to make an utter balls-up of the entire proceedings."

"Splendid speech," said Olympia. "I couldn't have said it more elegantly myself. Did you perhaps scribble a few words out beforehand, for the occasion?"

She laughed affectionately. "My dear Olympia. How I shall miss you. Citizen? The prisoners are yours. My train leaves for Rome in fifteen minutes."

The officer snapped to attention. "Yes, citizeness!"

Miss Dingleby walked from the cell, without a backward glance.

TWENTY-SEVEN

Every August of her life, Princess Luisa had traveled from Holstein Castle to the Kirkenplatz for the opening of the festival of St. Augustine, as had every member of the Holstein-Schweinwald-Huhnhof royal family since the Middle Ages.

She had never made the journey in a prison cart.

The morning breeze blew down from the mountains today, cooler and fresher than the end of August had a right to be. Luisa closed her eyes and drank it in, that familiar scent of wood and sweet water, of the Alpine stone she loved. Somerton's arm lay around her shoulders, absorbing the jolt of the cart. He hadn't said a word since they'd passed through the grim prison entrance a quarter hour ago, swinging around the back alleys of Holsteinton in this ramshackle covered wooden cart with its heavy metal bars, like a cage for animals. He sat against the back of the cart with her and stared with hard and unblinking eyes at Olympia's profile.

The cart bounced against a rut in the cobblestones, and Luisa opened her eyes again. The morning sun, pressing against the prison bars, cast long vertical shadows against the duke's face. Ahead and alongside, the prison guards marched in twos, about twenty of them, while the officer led the way on his large gray horse.

Olympia was crafty and vigorous for a man approaching seventy years, and Somerton had the strength and cunning of a beast of prey, but they were only two unarmed men—weakened, moreover, by a week in Holstein Prison—against twenty soldiers of the Revolutionary Brigade of the Free Blood.

"It's hopeless, isn't it?" she said softly.

"It's not hopeless. We wait for our opportunity to strike, that's all." Somerton's voice was deadly.

Olympia roused himself. "What's that? Hopeless? Nothing of the sort. A life everlasting stretches before you, pearly gates and flights of angels and all that. I, for one, am pregnant with anticipation. So many philosophical questions to be answered at last. But I confess I do have a rather more practical question for you, Luisa. It's been preying on my mind for some time."

"What's that, Uncle?"

"This business of a feast day. Don't you find it all rather unsuitably papist? Ought your people really to be celebrating such blatant idolatry, good, upstanding Protestants that they are?"

Luisa smiled. "St. Augustine is the patron saint of brewers, Uncle. We might have given up our Latin masses and our rosaries, but there was never any question of giving up St. Augustine's Day, here in Holstein."

"Of brewers! Ha. How remarkable. Yes, I see how it is." Olympia closed his eyes and leaned back against the cart. "Now that I think on it, Augustine was a bit of a Calvinist at heart, when all's said and done," he added, a moment later.

Luisa leaned into her husband. "He's mad."

"The cart's stopped," Somerton said.

So it had. Luisa sat up straight and looked about. It was difficult to see around the cart sides and the bars above them, and the street itself, a residential row, remained cast in morning shadow and still as death. Even the soldiers stood quietly at attention, without moving.

"What the devil?" the earl muttered, rising to a watchful crouch.

Where were all the townsfolk? In the square, no doubt. Luisa could hear the faint hum of people in motion, of voices and commerce, but it came as if through a tunnel, muffled and distant.

She curled her fists against the bottom of the cart. Next to her, Somerton's body radiated tension. His bruised face faced straight ahead, where the officer and his horse approached at a slow walking clop that echoed off the cobblestones.

The clopping stopped, followed an instant later by the brisk strike of boots on cobbles as the officer dismounted. The whisper of metal, as he unsheathed his sword.

He was going to murder them here. *That* was Gunther's plan, to bring their dead bodies into the square, the deed already accomplished, so that no popular uprising could save them.

No opportunity for escape.

The opening of the cart lay on the right side, opposite Olympia. Somerton shifted position, edging his big body around the corner, flush against the wall next to the door. He glanced at Luisa and made a movement of his hand. *Stay back.*

Olympia hadn't budged an inch. His face was shadowed, but she thought his eyes were still closed.

The officer's boots cracked confidently near. Somerton crouched on the balls of his feet now, braced by his fingertips on the wooden boards below. Like a burly black panther, ready to pounce.

The other soldiers stood in a ring around the cart, perfectly still.

Panic skidded across Luisa's brain, lightening the blood in her veins. She held fast to the sight of the waiting Somerton; she took his calm readiness into her skin.

This couldn't be it. This couldn't be the end.

What had she done to him?

Don't panic. Do *not* panic.

If she were going to die, she would die in dignity. She would die alongside her husband, who had sacrificed everything for her. His hair absorbed the light. His black eyes stared keenly between the bars of the prison cart. He meant to go down fighting.

I love you.

But it was too late to say it, hours and days too late. She should have said those words in Fiesole, in their little cottage with the white walls and the red tile roof, while they were lying naked and tangled and silent in the twilight. It would have been so easy.

I love you.

He might not have said them back to her. No, he probably wouldn't have replied at all. But at least he would know.

The footsteps stopped, a few feet away. Luisa braced herself against the wall.

An almighty metallic crash shook the cart, as the officer brought his sword down on the lock. The hinges creaked wildly open.

Somerton struck in a blur. He grasped the edge with one hand, swung himself around, and launched his big body like a missile through the opening and into the chest of the German officer.

Luisa scrambled after him.

"Run!" he yelled, but she couldn't run, she couldn't flee away from him.

He struggled with the officer, swearing loudly as they thumped and rolled together on the cobbles in a match with no rules. Oaths and protests rang from the paving stones. The man's hat flew off, and one of the soldiers stepped forward to pick it up.

But the match was unequal. Somerton was the bigger man, the aggressor, bloodthirsty and desperate, while the German fought a defensive game. They rolled again, and Somerton heaved his opponent on his back in a mighty growl. He lifted his arm to deliver the killing punch.

And held it there, aloft and astonished.

"I say," said the German officer, in a flawless gentleman's club English drawl, "you're looking rather rough, my good man. Do you mind lowering that meaty fist of yours, before somebody gets hurt?"

Behind Luisa, the cart groaned as Olympia alighted and stretched his body to the sun.

"Ah! Hatherfield, you old sport," he said, in the midst of a yawn. "Arrived at last."

We haven't much time," said the Marquess of Hatherfield, dusting himself off. He nodded to the doorway of the nearest house. "My wife's inside, dressed and ready. She has a change of clothing for Luisa. Your Highness?"

Luisa stepped forward, blushing pinkly along her cheek-bones, looking impossibly alluring in her stained shirt and trousers, her short auburn hair running in every conceivable direction. Somerton narrowed his eyes at the sight of her, having her hand kissed gallantly by the superbly handsome Hatherfield, whose golden brown hair picked up glints of sunlight in much the same manner of another young Adonis he knew and loathed.

"My dear new sister," he said, "I can't tell you how charmed I am to make your acquaintance at last. When Olympia's telegram summoned us from our honeymoon in Paris, I fairly leaped at the opportunity."

"Lord Hatherfield, the honor is mine. I'm sure you've made my Stefanie a very happy woman indeed."

"Southam, isn't it?" said Olympia. "You're the Duke of Southam now, my boy."

Hatherfield shrugged his shoulders. "To be perfectly honest, I still rather prefer Hatherfield."

Somerton stepped forward and held out his hand. "Your Grace." He couldn't quite keep the gruffness from his voice. "A pleasure."

Hatherfield turned and took his hand. "I look forward to profiting from your friendship, my lord. A great deal more comforting than your enmity, I daresay." He rubbed his shoulder.

"Now, go. We have only minutes before that grotesque revolutionary madman begins his puppet show and wonders where the puppets have gone."

He nodded to the doorway, where a lovely young auburn-haired woman was already bursting through the door with her arms held out. "Luisa!" she called.

In the instant before the two sisters crashed together, Somerton saw that the Duchess of Southam's belly curved gently with child. His gut clenched, stopping his breath.

"Ladies!" called Olympia. "No time for that now! We've a country to wrest back."

Ten minutes later, Somerton was shaved and dressed in a handsome pair of breeches and riding coat, a trifle short in the arms and tight along the shoulders. His bruised face he could do nothing about. He hurried out of the house to the cobbled street, where one of the soldiers handed him the reins to a large gray gelding, identical to the one Hatherfield—the Duke of Southam—rode. The soldier gasped.

Somerton turned.

His wife stood hand in hand with her sister, in the doorway of the house, wearing a silvery white dress that made her look as if she might float away. Her short hair was pinned back and topped by a small diamond tiara. The sun, rising now just over the tops of the buildings opposite, picked out the flame in her hair and turned her creamy skin to gold.

Around her throat lay the ruby necklace he had given her, sparkling brilliantly, a perfect match for the extraordinary ring of state on her right hand.

His knees, already weak, nearly gave way.

She was too beautiful. He couldn't bear it.

Somerton turned to Olympia. "Well, sir? Any more cards tucked into your sleeve, before we act? There remains one more princess unaccounted for."

Olympia shrugged. "I sent the Duke and Duchess of Ashland away on a honeymoon several months ago, on my own private steam yacht. I believe they were last heard from in Sydney. I've cabled, of course, but I haven't a clue whether they received the message. It's just Hatherfield in our corner, I'm afraid."

"Just as well," said Somerton. "I daresay Ashland would just as soon murder me as old Hassendorf. The small matter of having seduced his first wife."

"Cheer up, old chap," said Olympia. "If you're lucky, Hassendorf will get you first."

The crowd in the Kirkenplatz milled about restlessly, seething with rumor. Olympia, leading the procession, stopped where the street emptied out in the square and held up his hand.

The soldiers stopped obediently and formed a protective ring about the two royal couples.

Luisa heard a voice shout out above the crowd. Beside her, Stefanie made a sharp indrawn breath.

"It's Gunther, isn't it?" she whispered.

"I believe so," said Luisa.

How close had Stefanie and Gunther been, the two of them, that long-ago summer? Had they been lovers? The possibility had never occurred to her before; it was so far beyond her imagination. The Luisa of seven years ago would never have conceived of intimacy with a man before marriage, of relinquishing her priceless virginity to the mayor's son. In her most lurid conjectures, she had feared a kiss or two between her sister and Gunther Hassendorf.

But Stefanie's stiffened body told her otherwise.

Good God. How had this happened? Did Hatherfield know?

Luisa recalled the feel of Stefanie in her arms, hardly a quarter hour ago. The firm new roundness of her pregnancy had pressed into Luisa's belly, making her heart melt and her throat burn. The baby would be born in November, Stefanie had said, as they dressed together, talking at double speed, words tripping over one another as they tried to describe nearly ten months of separation. The baby. Stefanie was going to have a baby.

Somerton stood quietly on her other side, surveying the scene before them. She closed her hand more tightly around his fingers.

"Give us the princess!" someone called out angrily, from somewhere in the crowd.

"Yes, give us back our princess!" echoed another. "We know you've got her!"

Luisa's heart swelled against her ribs, with a pride she didn't know she owned. All those months of exile, that sense of crushing rejection. Thinking her people didn't want her, her country didn't want her. That they wanted *these* men, these anarchists, these revolutionaries.

And now this. *Our princess.*

Gunther was answering them, something she couldn't hear. He must be facing away from them.

"We don't believe you!"

"Give us back our princesses!"

The crowd took up the call, turning it into a chant. *Gebt unsere Prinzessinnen zurück! Gebt unsere Prinzessinnen zurück!*

Olympia moved briskly forward, into the square and the full light of the morning sunshine.

"Here are your princesses!" he bellowed, in German.

A stunned silence rushed across the crowd, from the near end of the square all the way to Holstein Cathedral, standing in majesty at the other. Tears stung Luisa's eyes at the sight of those proud Gothic spires, soaring into an eternal blue sky.

Olympia stood aside, and the crowd parted.

Hatherfield and Somerton led the two of them forward, she and Stefanie, before the shocked faces of the townspeople. Many of them she recognized, from one encounter or another. She smiled and nodded, as she'd been trained all her life to do. Somerton's hand was steady in hers, his body a bulwark against danger.

In the center of the Kirkenplatz stood the same platform, under the same oiled canvas canopy, she had known all her life. The festival always began at the official behest of Prince Rudolf, dressed in his ceremonial best, ringing the ancient brewer's bell that was brought out from the royal armory every year for the occasion. Speeches, singing, a prayer led by the bishop. She gazed out at the vendors' stalls, the young dancers in their traditional costumes.

This was Holstein. This was *hers*. Gunther, Dingleby, this band of foreign men who had dived in like vultures, to scavenge the wealth and commerce of her country for their own purposes: They had no business here.

With every step, she gained in confidence.

"Guards!" Gunther called out, into the silence. "Arrest them! Arrest the foreign agents!"

But the guards around the platform didn't move.

As she passed, people began to bow. One by one, the inhabitants of Holsteinton dropped to their knees in the cobbles, and then, in her wake, started up a cheer.

Her blood stirred. The tears welled at the corners of her eyes. She had endured months in exile, in order to win back their hearts. She had married a powerful man as her consort, in order to win back their hearts. She had tried to conceive an heir, in order to win back their hearts.

But she hadn't needed to, had she? She, Luisa, was sufficient by herself. She was their princess. No one else in the world could serve them so devotedly as she could.

On her right, Hatherfield leaned down into Stefanie's ear and whispered something. She laughed and whispered back.

They reached the platform, where Gunther had fallen silent. He gazed down at them contemptuously. He was wearing some sort of uniform, bright red in the morning sun, without trim or medals of any kind, except for a set of handsome brass buttons.

"Step down, Herr Hassendorf," said Olympia, in a booming parliamentary voice that traveled to the far ends of the hushed cathedral square. "Your time has passed."

Gunther straightened himself to his full impressive height. "I do not take commands from strangers."

"I speak for the people in this square. The people of this state." Olympia waved his hand. "Their wishes, I believe, are quite clear."

"Are they? And who are you, to speak on their behalf? An Englishman, by your accent. A foreigner." Gunther sent a quick nod into the crowd.

Somerton intercepted the nod. His body tensed next to her, thrumming with alertness.

"I am the Duke of Olympia, the brother of Princess Louisa, first wife of Rudolf and mother of his three daughters. I am the uncle of the princesses of Holstein-Schweinwald-Huhnhof, and I have brought them here to restore them to their rightful rule over this fair and persecuted land." Olympia had chosen his words carefully, and he spoke them with all the command of one of England's highest dukes. He towered over the crowd, literally and figuratively, and though Gunther Hassendorf stood above him on the platform, he seemed somehow diminished.

"The princesses! The princesses!" someone called out, and a hundred voices echoed him.

Gunther held up his hand, trying to silence them, but the chants only grew louder.

"You cannot turn back the clock!" he shouted. "An archaic system, propped up for centuries to oppress the masses, to . . ." The rest of his sentence drowned in the swell of voices.

Olympia pounded his walking stick into the cobblestones. "Move aside, Hassendorf! It's over for you."

Gunther made a frantic signal into the crowd.

In a flash, Somerton stepped before Luisa and Stefanie, blocking them both with his massive shoulders.

A loud crack shattered the air. Somerton staggered back, holding his arms out as a shield. Just before his full weight crashed into Luisa's body, Hatherfield lunged around the two sisters and caught him under the shoulders.

A patch of blood blossomed on the left sleeve of his jacket. "He's hit!" Luisa screamed.

"I'm all right." His voice was labored. "Just a nick. To the left, Hatherfield. The man in the navy jacket. His companion, too."

Hatherfield was already bolting into the crowd, scattering the townspeople in his path. Luisa bent over Somerton's arm. "It's not a nick! A doctor!" she called out. "A doctor for my husband!"

But the crowd was roiling with panic. No one heard, no one stepped forward to help.

"There's no time," said Olympia. "Can you walk, sir?"

"Of course, damn it!" snarled Somerton.

Olympia stepped between Stefanie and Luisa and took their arms. "To the platform, now!"

"But . . ."

"Now!"

Somerton took her other arm, and he and Olympia dragged the both of them up the steps to the empty platform, where the bishop cowered in the corner, next to the canopy pole. There was no sign of Gunther.

Olympia pushed her to the front of the platform. "Speak to them!"

"I can't!"

"You've got to! You're the princess. You've got to be the princess. You've got to show them, Luisa."

Somerton curled his arm around her elbow. "You can do this, Markham."

She stood there at the edge of the platform, her silver white dress rippling in the breeze, and stared down at the scene of chaos before her: men and women running, children screaming, the smell of sausages burning the air. A scuffle broke out near a cluster of vendor stalls. That man standing there by the cathedral door—was he holding a pistol, ready to shoot? She saw her father's body, Peter's body, white and still among the Schweinwald leaves; she looked down at her husband's blood-soaked arm, held stiffly by his side.

She had never felt more exposed.

"You can do this." Somerton's low voice in her ear. "Show them there's nothing to fear. I won't let anyone hurt you."

His solid weight filled the air beside her. His determined hand warmed her arm, impossible to doubt.

"Speak, my love. You were born for this."

She opened her mouth and filled her lungs with air.

"*Mein Volk!*" she said.

No one heard.

"*Louder*," her husband whispered.

"*Mein Volk!*" she called out. "My people! Calm down! There's no need to panic!" She turned to the guards, who formed a protective line at the bottom of the platform. Protective of her. Her blood warmed, sending confidence like an incandescent light through every vessel of her body. "Guardsmen! Ten of you to the left, ten to the right. Restore order to the crowd."

The men marched off at a fast clip, ringing the square.

She straightened. "My people! The guards are here. The shooter . . ." She searched the crowd, and picked Hatherfield's golden brown head in the eastern fringe, where he was holding a navy-suited man in an unshakable headlock. Relief flooded her. "The shooter has been apprehended! There's no need for fear!"

Somewhere, in that roiling mass of confusion, a calm began to spread. A few people stopped, and a few more. A young man drifted back toward the platform, gazing at her with an idolatrous half smile.

How she must look, standing up here in her silvery dress, and her hair catching the light. She must seem glorious.

She held out her arms. "Holsteiners! Show them we're not afraid. Show them we won't allow our fates to be determined any longer by an organization of half-mad zealots from abroad."

Her voice was carrying over the crowd now, from deep down in her chest, in the way Dingleby had once taught her.

The tide was turning. More people drifted back. Watching her. Listening to her.

Somerton touched the small of her back. She drew in another deep breath.

"My dear people, I have been in exile these many months, since a small group of evil men assassinated my father and my husband and assumed control of this state in the fear and confusion that followed. I have taken shelter in England, with my uncle the Duke of Olympia, and with this man, the Earl of Somerton, who has guarded my person and my honor with the utmost fidelity."

A stir of interest.

"I return to you now in hope of regaining the honor that was so briefly mine, that of ruling my beloved state, in which I was so fortunate as to be born and raised, as the inheritor of a most noble line of princes."

Another stir, louder this time.

She held up her hand. "But I will not do so against your will. I ask you, the people of Holstein-Schweinwald-Huhnhof, whether you would have me as your princess. Whether you wish me to lead you, in partnership with a new parliament of your own election, with all the zeal and devotion and ardor for justice in my power."

A low roar began to build, like a wave coming to shore.

She spread out her arms. "Will you, my beloved subjects? Will you allow me to return to your castle, to lead your government, as Princess Luisa of Holstein-Schweinwald-Huhnhof, daughter and heir of the great Rudolf?"

The roar built into a wall of sound, a continuous and joyous noise of approval, and Luisa's heart beat so madly, and her mind sang with such elation, that she hardly noticed that Somerton's hand had long since fallen away from her arm.

And it was not until the roar of approval changed to a collective and horrified gasp, that she realized something had gone dreadfully wrong behind her.

The pride in his heart hurt his chest, eclipsing the dull throb in his injured arm.

The Earl of Somerton watched his wife stand before her

people, glorious in the morning light, all beauty and eloquence and pure Markham dignity. He was dimly aware of the awed silence hushing the crowd, and then the growing swell of approval.

She's mine, he thought, incredulous, and then, the natural corollary: *I'm hers*.

Hers, her servant, body and soul.

All at once, his future opened before him. What he had been placed on this earth by God to do. He was here to protect Luisa, to guard her against all enemies, to serve and support her. To be her master, when, exhausted by the responsibility of command, she needed someone to command her; to be the captain of her guard, when she needed someone to execute her commands.

To give her relief. To give her what wisdom and cunning he possessed. To give her his great physical strength, to give her the sole use and pleasure of his body, to give her his fidelity and loyalty to the end of his life. To give her laughter and companionship and the children who would carry her legacy into the unknown future.

To *give*. He, who had only ever known how to take.

He tore his gaze away from her sunlit cheek and surveyed the crowd before them. Hatherfield was discreetly transferring two men into the custody of the guardsmen. The slyness of Olympia, summoning his new ally to the cause.

Hassendorf. Where was Hassendorf?

Somerton whipped around, and as he did so, an extraordinary sight caught the corner of his vision.

He came to a standstill.

A man strode toward the platform, a man unlike any other Somerton had ever encountered. He was six and a half feet tall, with short white hair that bristled from his head. The left side of his face was extraordinarily handsome, sculpted by the gods.

The right side of his face was missing an eye and half of a once sturdy jaw.

The Duke of Ashland.

The Duke of Ashland, whom Somerton had cuckolded fifteen years ago, thoughtlessly conceiving a daughter with his shallow and beautiful wife.

The Duke of Ashland, now married to Luisa's younger sister Emilie, who was supposed to be on an extended honeymoon on the far side of the world, on the Duke of Olympia's private, state-of-the-art, twin-screw propeller steam yacht.

But a cabled message might reach anywhere in the world in days, and a particularly fast state-of-the-art yacht, built for speed, might conceivably steam through the Suez Canal to the Venice railway terminus in a matter of less than three weeks.

Ashland held a revolver in his left hand. The other hand did not exist.

As Somerton watched in shock, rooted to the wooden floor, Ashland approached at a brisk march and raised his revolver.

Instinct gathered in Somerton's muscles, launching him between Luisa and the poised revolver, to shield her with his body.

But Ashland, breaking into a run, waved his empty sleeve in the other direction. To the back of the platform.

Somerton swiveled.

The Duke of Olympia was locked in struggle with Gunther Hassendorf, who held a lighted torch in his left hand and a wicked, long-bladed knife in the other. The duke, weakened by eight long days in the dungeon of Holstein Castle, was losing the fight, inch by inch.

Ashland had no chance of a clean shot.

Somerton moved his battered body into a run, just as Hassendorf caught his booted foot behind Olympia's exhausted leg and sent him tumbling to the wooden boards of the platform.

Without the slightest hesitation, Hassendorf leaped onto a chair, lifted his torch high, and set the canvas canopy alight.

The fire spread across the oiled cloth in an instant.

Somerton launched himself into the air, directly into Hassendorf's outstretched and unprotected middle. Together they toppled to the floor in an inhuman crash, Hassendorf bearing the brunt of Somerton's enormous weight. He stared up at the earl with bulging eyes and lifted his left hand.

Too late, Somerton remembered the knife.

He tried to twist his body to avoid it, but he was hopelessly entangled, hopelessly bruised, his left arm useless, and Hassendorf's other arm locked against his back. The liquid heat of the canvas overhead already singed his back. He closed his eyes and gathered every last atom of strength in his failing muscles.

A loud crash sounded in his ears, and Hassendorf's arms went limp.

Somerton staggered to his feet and turned. His ears seemed full of cotton wool. The Duke of Ashland stood before him, tall and avenging. The smoke still trailed from the barrel of his revolver.

"Thank you," Somerton mouthed.

And then he saw what lay beyond Ashland.

The canopy, billowing with flame as it drifted down on a horrified Luisa.

Noooo, he screamed silently.

Before he realized his own actions, he was running toward her, through the flames and smoke, the bits of ash. He found her shoulders and brought her down beneath him, taking the brunt of the fall on his knees, and covered her with his body as the flames scorched through his jacket.

Blackness fell, thick as pitch, seething with inhuman pain. He let himself sink inside the dark, and even as he drifted out of conscious thought, the pain went on and on, unstoppable.

There were hands on him, cloths beating his body, water drenching the searing agony, sweet and fleeting relief.

There was Luisa's voice—*alive, thank God, thank God*—calling him a fool, her darling fool, her love, don't die, don't leave me.

He opened his eyes, and her beautiful face was before him, wet with tears.

"Don't worry," he said. "I'll never leave you."

When he opened his eyes again, some untold hours or days later, he was in a bed, on his stomach, and someone was changing the dressing on his back. The pain of this act enclosed every nerve of his body.

The pain, in fact, had woken him up.

"Ah! There you are, my dear nephew," said the Duke of Olympia.

"You again." Somerton closed his eyes and ground his teeth together. "Where's my wife, damn it?"

"She's sleeping, and I refuse to disturb her. It's the first sleep she's had in forty-eight hours."

"When can I see her?"

"If the bishop has his way, not for a month at least."

At that, Somerton summoned the energy to lift his head. The duke was gazing down at him, curse the old scratch, from a chair pulled up next to the unconscionably soft bed on which Somerton lay.

"The bishop? What the bloody hell does the bishop have to do with it?"

"Because the Bishop of Holstein is the chap to whose unenviable lot it now falls, Somerton, to look after the eternal health of your black soul."

"The devil you say!"

"Indeed. And I daresay he rightfully suspects that if you were to lay eyes upon the fair Luisa, you would shortly contrive to bed her, whatever the extent of your injuries."

The attendant stripped off the last dressing, in a stroke of white-hot agony.

"And why the devil shouldn't I bed my own lawfully wedded wife? I bloody well nearly sacrificed my life for her sake! I've been thrown in dungeons, chased, shot, wrestled, and burned, and worst of all, I haven't had the pleasure of my wife's body in weeks. Weeks! By God, she won't be able to walk straight, by the time I've had my fill of her. And neither will I, if I know my Markham."

A gasp disturbed the air above his head.

A smile spread across Olympia's face.

"My very dear, very wicked fellow. I assure you, I applaud your conjugal enthusiasm without reserve. But . . ." He let the word dangle.

"But? *But?*"

The duke leaned close.

"But it seems the people of Holstein-Schweinwald-Huhnhof refuse to be cheated out of a royal wedding after all."

One month later

His Royal Highness, the Prince Consort of Holstein-Schweinwald-Huhnhof, crossed the threshold of the state bedroom and kicked the door emphatically shut.

"At last," he said. "I thought that chap with the pointed gray beard would go on bloody forever."

From the shelter of his arms, Her Royal Highness the Crown Princess kicked off one satin shoe, and then the other. "Bite your tongue. Herr Lowenbrau is the master of the brewers' guild and a very dear fellow. And like everyone else in the room—everyone in the entire principality, to be precise—he can't quite believe his good fortune in gaining such a brave and warriorlike consort to rule by my side."

"Well, he was the last man standing between my lavish royal wedding banquet and my lavish royal wedding night, and by God he's lucky to be alive." He cast his gaze about the room, the sumptuous furnishings and gilded crest work, falling at last on the massive canopied bed at the end of the room, atop a small dais, the pillows invitingly plump. "Good God. Is that my marriage bed or a damned stage at the theater?"

"We are, after all, supposed to be performing a public duty," said his wife primly.

He looked down at her blushing face, which had been kept altogether too distant from his own in the past few weeks. "Markham," he said, "let me make myself quite clear. I will execute whatever demands you make of me; I will cut ribbons and christen ships and make speeches until my ears bleed; I will know your enemies' thoughts before they can think them up themselves. I will pay the Americans with my own gold to keep Dingleby occupied with her new friends on the other side of the Atlantic. I have already allowed myself to be made patron of twelve different charities, including the Society for the succor of stray cats, God help us all. But in this room, in this bed, there are only two of us. Man and wife. Pleasing only each other. Do you understand me?"

"Quite." She smiled and looped her arms around his neck. "You can put me down now, if you like."

"On the contrary," he said, striding toward the bed, "I

promise you your feet won't touch the ground until morning, if I can help it."

She had already untied his starched neckcloth and was flinging it on the plush carpet beneath them. "No? But my feet so enjoyed touching the ground on our first wedding night."

"Hmm. Yes." He tossed her on the bed and tore off his priceless silk wedding coat, embroidered with the Holstein crest in at least a dozen places. "But I was a reckless young fellow then. With time—and a second wedding in Holstein bloody Cathedral, complete with trumpets and bishop and medieval bloody crown—comes respect for the proper decorum."

She laughed and held out her arms. Her lady's maid had already changed her clothing, from the voluminous ivory brocade gown that weighed nearly as much as she did, into a diaphanous negligee of fine Parisian silk and lace, through which the twin dark circles of her nipples were plainly visible and plainly aroused. "Decorum? The Earl of Somerton?"

Somerton, now shirtless, grasped the hem of her negligee and drew it up and over her head. Her creamy nakedness made his brain spin. He threaded his fingers through hers and urged her backward, into the mattress, his darling beautiful Markham, his own wedded wife, bound to him twice over. In a moment, he would boil over from the joy of it.

"I'll show you decorum," he growled, bending his head over her breast. "Just mind the skin of my back, if you please. What's left of it."

An hour later, he lay on his stomach, teasing his wife's silken hair with his fingers. It had grown out a bit this past month, curling around her ears now, shining and playful. He took up a few strands and kissed them. Her eyelids fluttered. "What was that?"

"I didn't say anything."

"Mmm. I thought I heard something."

"Not a word." He nibbled her shoulder. "The delirium of your pleasure, no doubt."

"No. No, I quite distinctly heard you say something. A few words only. Simple little words." Her eyes were still closed, but she was smiling. One hand traced along his side, carefully avoiding his tender back; the other lay draped above her head, a most voluptuous pose that was already stirring blood he'd thought must surely be quieted at last, after the recent thunderbolt between them. "*Ich . . . ich* something something."

"A hallucination, I assure you."

"Something with an *L*, I believe."

"An *L*, you say?"

"Perhaps, if I say them first, the words will jog your memory."

He lifted himself on one elbow and gazed down at her face, still flushed with release, smooth with contentment. An auburn curl whorled on her forehead, touching one eyebrow. He drew it aside. "Perhaps they will."

"All right." Her eyes opened at last, true and topaz-brown, meeting him without a flinch. "Husband. Scoundrel. Noble consort." She raised her hand to clasp his cheek and whispered to him with her true and noble lips.

The air turned into gold.

He bent his head, kissed her, and whispered back.

Ich liebe dich.

BABYLOGUE

Holstein Castle
December 1892

At three o'clock in the morning, as the snow landed softly on the ledge outside his bedroom window, the Duke of Olympia was awoken by his valet and told that a young lady awaited him downstairs in the state bedroom.

"A young lady, is it?" He threw off the covers and snatched away his nightcap from his whitening head. "At this hour? By God, she had better not be shrill."

In the hallway, he was forced to shield his eyes, for the castle was ablaze with light. A single loud crack from the cannon on the rooftop made him jump almost to the ceiling. "Damn it all," he said, "she'd better be comely as well, the hoyden."

"Yes, sir," said his valet, brushing hastily at the duke's dressing gown as he strode magnificently down the crimson hallway.

"How I despise these females who arrive in the middle of the night, demanding all manner of fuss and attention. It's frightfully common, don't you think? Vulgar, really." He turned smartly around the corner, where the hallway opened up into the second-floor gallery.

"Yes, sir. Common, indeed."

"Give me a plump, smiling, well-favored damsel who arrives promptly in the evening, just after dinner, when everybody is settled and content and ready for a bit of civilized entertainment before bed."

The duke strode across the gallery, sparing not a glance for the portraits on the walls, nor the fearsome six feet of ancient plate armor standing guard before the east wing, as it had once stood guard before the Saracens at Antioch. His slippers made scuffing sounds on the polished marble, until he reached the soft comfort of the carpeted corridor.

"Convenient, to be sure," said the valet, whose task it was to agree with Olympia's every pronouncement.

"Or better yet, give me a pretty young lad. Far less trouble and expense, and a good deal sturdier."

"Indeed, sir. Shall I make you up a toddy of some sort, sir, to recruit you afterward from your labors?"

Olympia came to an abrupt halt, several feet shy of the handsome louvered double doors of the state bedroom. He tapped his chin. A long peal of laughter rang out through the wooden panels, followed by an infant's wail.

"No," he said, "I think not. A double measure of neat Scotch should do very well."

The valet placed his hand on the door handle and opened the portal wide. "Very good, sir."

The Duke of Olympia swept through the doorway and into a scene of unprecedented debauchery. At one end of the room, Hatherfield was playing cards with an eight-year-old Lord Kildrake, who held an unlit cigar in his mouth and looked as if he were winning handily. Nearby, Lady Roland Penhallow sat beautifully on a red velvet sofa, deep in feminine conversation with Lady Mary Russell, the curiously dark-haired and dark-eyed daughter of the fair-featured Duke of Ashland, who himself stood propped like a masked six-and-a-half-foot white-haired Adonis at the mantel with a sherry at his elbow and his wife's burgeoning waist shielded possessively under his enormous hand.

That damned Emilie, breeding again. Hadn't she the good sense to find her husband a mistress?

A peal of laughter diverted his attention to the other end of the room, where Princess Stefanie was leading Ashland's strapping eighteen-year-old heir Lord Silverton in an impromptu demonstration of a Bavarian folk dance, while Lord Roland Penhallow kept perfect time with a pair of slim silver candlesticks on the back of a priceless Louis Quatorze chair. Upon that chair rested His Royal Highness the Prince Consort of Holstein-Schweinwald-Huhnhof, looking drowsily drunk and decidedly pleased with himself as he surveyed the pandemonium before him. A cello lay in an open case on the floor next to his feet. The bow dangled from one hand.

Olympia marched up and clapped him on the back. "Well, then, nevvy! Banished from the bedchamber, were you?"

Somerton nodded. "Was only trying to help."

"So it goes."

"A fine girl, however." He smiled happily. "Ginger, just like her mother. All well. They're resting now, of course."

Another determined wail sallied forth from the bedroom on the other side of the wall.

"Or perhaps not," said Olympia. "Was the travail a difficult one?"

The happy smile collapsed. "God, yes. Horrifying. Penhallow had to pin me forcibly to the chair, just before the end." A slow shake of the head. "I don't know how I survived it."

"I see. Scotch?"

"Brandy."

"Is there any left, by chance?"

"I doubt it," the prince said mournfully.

The bedroom door opened, and a fortyish woman in a neat uniform of dove gray slipped out to cast a disapproving glance around the august receiving room of the royal bedchamber.

Princess Stefanie dropped Silverton's hands and clasped her own together. "Oh! How are they, Nurse Muller?"

Philip set his cards carefully on the table, facedown, and stubbed out his cigar in the ashtray. "I want to see my sister! I want to see my sister!"

"You may see your newest little sister in the morning, your lordship," said Nurse Muller, in her English-trained voice of no nonsense.

"But it *is* morning!"

Lady Roland rose hastily from the sofa. "Now, Philip. You must do as Nurse Muller says."

"Out," said Nurse Muller. "All of you, out. You're making altogether too much noise, and it's long past Lord Kildrake's bedtime."

"Papa Roland said I could stay up," said Lord Kildrake. "And Father gave me this cigar." He held it up.

Nurse Muller looked horrified. She snatched the cigar from his fingers. "His Highness was not in his right mind, your lordship. Now, off with you. To bed in the nursery with your little cousins."

She made shooing motions with her hands, and one by one the members of the royal family tossed down the dregs of the remaining sherry, put away the candlesticks, and disbanded for the various bedrooms in the castle, as well as the royal nursery, which was filled almost to capacity at the moment in the overflow of visitors for the much-anticipated birth. Little Lady Stephanie Lambert and her cousins the Ashland twins— a more mischievous damned pair of two-year-old boys Olympia had never known—lay side by side with the cherubic Honorable Miss Florence Penhallow and her baby brother Phineas, while Olympia suspected that Princess Stefanie was headed upstairs to nurse the two-month-old ginger-haired Lord Hatherfield (like her sisters, Stefanie would insist on feeding the infants herself, despite the availability of several perfectly good wet nurses in the district) this very minute.

At the moment, however, and for the man now rising from the much-abused Louis Quatorze chair, the new little princess testing her lungs in the room next door was the only baby in the world.

Certainly, the principality of Holstein-Schweinwald-Huhnhof had been awaiting this moment for two anxious years. And judging from the often drawn faces of the baby princess's parents during that period, and those quickly shuttered gazes of longing frustration at the multiplying collection of cousins and half siblings, Olympia suspected that Leopold and Luisa had suffered more than one tragic disappointment along the journey to Her tiny Highness's arrival this snow-scented December night.

"Come along, then, Your Highness," said Nurse Muller, far more kindly. "They're both awake, and the little princess is eager to meet her father."

Olympia turned away at the look on Somerton's face, the passing expression of raw emotion, as if someone had placed a hand on his heart to count the measure of its beating.

"And Your Grace as well, of course," added the nurse, blushing just a trifle as she met his eye.

Olympia followed Somerton's broad silk back at a respectful distance. Over a quarter century ago, he had followed another nurse into this very room, in order to meet his recently arrived niece Luisa. The chamber hadn't changed much. The same stately furniture in blues and golds, the same priceless rug, the same window seat with its breathtaking view of the town and the mountains beyond, now hidden behind great shrouds of midnight damask. He paused just inside the doorway, so as not to interrupt the new parents.

The princess was at her mother's breast. Luisa looked up, and the smile on her exhausted face made Olympia blink rather forcefully. She said something to Somerton as he approached; Olympia couldn't quite hear what it was, thank God, for he despised all that mawkish sentiment that turned the air of the castle so distastefully sticky when all the husbands and wives were visiting together.

Somerton reached the bedside in a few long strides. He took his wife's outstretched hand, fell to his knees, and pressed his lips to her fingers.

At the foot of the bed, a small white and rufous corgi lifted his head from his paws and growled at Olympia, low and menacing. The duke rolled his eyes and went to stand near the window seat.

For God's sake, not Somerton, too. Was there no husband left alive in this palace who maintained a proper sense of reserve where his wife was concerned? Olympia opened the curtains a crack and observed the snowflakes drifting by the millions, the lights flickering ablaze all over the town, the faint sounds of revelry drifting up the hill to celebrate the birth of the longed-for heir to the throne.

Something tickled the corner of his right eye; he rubbed it quickly, before anyone noticed.

A weight settled into the cushion nearby. Olympia looked down at the slight man who sat there in a satisfied posture, thumbs in his pockets. The doctor, he remembered. He sat down next to the fellow in a friendly manner.

"Congratulations, my good man," he said, in German. "I understand the labor was a difficult one."

The doctor looked surprised. "Why, no more than most. A textbook delivery, in fact. The husband took the hour of crisis exceptionally hard, however."

Olympia risked another glance at the royal bedside, and nearly slipped off the cushions to the floor.

The prince consort was actually *holding* the baby. Holding his daughter in his arms, as if he were a nurse! Holding her as delicately and reverently as he might hold a first-class revolver, or a particularly promising new pup for his hunting pack. The candlelight bathed the princess's round new head in reddish gold. Her father touched her downy ginger hair with one finger and said something soft, something suspiciously like a croon. He turned to his wife and murmured a few words that made her smile broadly.

By God. What would come next? Did the old scoundrel plan to strap on a teat and nurse her himself?

Olympia shook his head.

"Is something the matter, Your Grace?" asked the doctor. "Such a fine portrait of a family I never saw before."

"Only reflecting how very unexpectedly one's schemes can turn out." Olympia rose to his feet and tightened the belt of his dressing gown. "It's almost enough to put one off scheming altogether."

He walked to the happy threesome, congratulated his niece and nephew on a most blessed event, and went back to bed.

Read on for a special preview of
an all-new historical romance ebook
novella from Juliana Gray

THE DUKE OF OLYMPIA
MEETS HIS MATCH

Coming Spring 2015 from InterMix

At Sea
March 1893

At half past six o'clock in the evening, the White Star liner *Majestic,* seven hours out of New York with a cargo of American heiresses, steamed past the tip of Cape Cod and into the open ocean.

His Grace, the Duke of Olympia, who happened to be crossing the threshold of the first-class saloon at that moment, felt the triumphant surge of the engines through the soles of his shoes and smiled. A casual observer—say, one of that multitude of well-bred faces turned hopefully toward the new arrival—might safely presume his smile was one of pleasure.

They presumed wrong.

"Is it quite necessary to accommodate so many Americans on board, Mr. Simmons?" he said to the first officer, by way of greeting.

"I am afraid so, Your Grace," said Mr. Simmons, who had excused himself from his companions and traveled across the length of the saloon at utmost speed to greet this particular passenger. "They have a great deal of money, you see, and a steamship of ten thousand gross tonnage is the very devil to supply and maintain. To say nothing of the cost of coal."

His Grace cast an arch gaze over the assembly. A general

impression of horsiness stole over him. "Can they not be stowed in steerage instead?"

"I'm afraid not, Your Grace," Mr. Simmons said earnestly. "Not when they've paid seventy-five dollars each for a state-room." He lowered his voice. "They do have a tendency to complain at ill usage."

An elegant clock ticked out the minutes in the center of the frieze above the doorway, but Olympia chose to slip a hand inside his snowy waistcoat and examine his pocket watch instead. He sighed deeply and said, "I suppose I shall have to talk to them."

As he might say *fornicate publicly with them.*

"My dear sir, I assure you I have taken the utmost care in selecting your dining companions. I have seen to the matter personally."

"You have, of course, included the names from the list I forwarded to you three days ago?"

"Of course."

The duke slipped his watch back inside his waistcoat and made a minute adjustment to the gleaming black lapels of his tailcoat. His voice was soft. "And you have destroyed that list."

"Yes, sir. Directly after I read it."

An earnest chap, this Mr. Simmons. The Bureau had assured him that the *Majestic*'s first officer could be relied upon for dis-cretion and loyalty—he had been used before, from time to time—and naturally he had no idea of the magnitude of the mission in which he was playing his little part. *A diplomatic matter,* they had told Mr. Simmons, and his keen brown eyes reflected an anxious gratitude at having been called to do his mite for Queen and country. His gaze traveled doggedly up Olympia's imperial six and a half feet to land at the ducal eye-balls, and his bony neck almost strained from its collar.

Olympia could only imagine Mr. Simmons's reaction if he knew the truth. That this little *diplomatic matter*, in fact, took the form of a female agent for the French government, known to have purchased a first-class ticket for this particular pas-sage, whose identity must be discovered before the papers in her possession could be delivered to her masters in Paris.

The duke smiled. "Good man. If you don't mind, then, I should like to—"

"Mr. Simmons! There you are."

A woman's voice, flat-voweled and large-nosed, invaded the cozy masculine air between them like a whinny from a dyspeptic American farmhorse.

Olympia turned his head and gazed down the sharp length of his nose to discover its source. He didn't have far to look. The voice's owner stood about four scant inches from his left elbow, broad of hip and black of hair, and her bosom stood out from her chest in such a prominent manner that Olympia wondered whether she might not have inspired the ship's builders when they were designing the prow.

As if sensing the scrutiny lurking behind the duke's nose, she turned, smiled, and fluttered a pair of insincere eyelashes. "Oh! I hope I haven't interrupted."

Mr. Simmons coughed delicately. "Not at all, Mrs. Morrison. May I have the honor of presenting to you His Grace, the Duke of Olympia. Sir, Mrs. Stewart Morrison of New York City."

Mrs. Morrison's eyelashes fluttered insincerely. "Good gracious! I had no idea. We are honored indeed, your lordship, to make your acquaintance."

Olympia took her offered hand between his fingertips and endeavored not to wince. "Enchanted, Mrs. Morrison. The honor is all mine, I assure you."

This time, the eyelashes fluttered with conviction. "How very kind, your lordship. I presume you are on your way home?"

"Indeed, Mrs. Morrison. I fear I have tarried far too long."

"How lucky you are. I do feel the greatest affinity for England. I almost feel as if I'm English myself, really. My friends all say so. They say, Portia, you were born in the wrong country. And it's true! I've always thought the USA so coarse and rough-mannered. Even as a child, I did. All my taste is for English things. English books, English furniture, English decoration . . ."

"How very flattering, Mrs. Morrison. Have you any particularly favorite corner of Albion?" *That I may be certain to avoid,* he added privately.

"Oh! Well, as far as that goes, I'm afraid I don't know much about Albania."

"I mean England, Mrs. Morrison."

"Ah. Yes. The truth is, your lordship, this is my first visit. But I'm sure I shall love every dear little blade of grass, every fragrant flower—"

"Every delightful patter of rain."

"Indeed, indeed! You *do* understand me. I declare I'll bless the rain that falls upon my head, your lordship, just because it's an English rain."

"We do maintain a large national reserve of sturdy umbrellas, however, should the repetition become tedious. The endless mornings of drizzle, interrupted by the afternoons of incessant showers."

She laughed and wagged her finger at his stiff white shirt-front. "Oh, I do *adore* the English sense of humor."

"I rather suspected you would, Mrs. Morrison. I fear, however, I am keeping you from your purpose."

"My purpose, your lordship?"

"You had, I understand, a question for my friend, Mr. Simmons."

Mrs. Stewart Morrison turned back to the first officer in surprise. "Yes! So I did, I believe. Mr. Simmons, I'm afraid we're going to need another seat at dinner tonight."

The face of Mr. Simmons turned a shocked shade of pale. "Another seat, Mrs. Morrison?"

"Yes. My daughter's governess will be taking dinner in the saloon, instead of her stateroom, as we'd planned. My daughter wouldn't hear of it, you see. She has such a warm heart, my daughter." This she addressed to Olympia. "Twenty years old, my daughter, and though my friends tell me she's the most beautiful girl in New York—which I put no stock in, your lordship, no stock at all, though I will concede she's a pretty girl, a very pretty girl—as I said, the most beautiful girl in New York, so my friends say, but for all that she's a dear, kind, loving girl, and she's always treated her friends the same, high and low. That's the sign of a good heart, your lordship, which as you know is the most important thing in the world."

"Indeed," said the duke. The scent of rat wafted past his nose.

"Anyway. I understand we'll be sitting together tonight, at the captain's table. I'll be sure to introduce you to my daughter, your lordship, so you can see for yourself. About her beauty, I mean. I'm sure I heard you were a connoisseur of beauty."

"What man is not?" said the duke.

A distant gong rippled through the air.

"If you'll excuse me," said Mr. Simmons, still pale, "I shall give the necessary instructions to the staff." He bowed and bolted.

"Well! There's the dinner gong. I guess that means you'll have to take me in, your lordship." Mrs. Morrison offered him a long gloved arm and a winning smile.

Olympia accepted the arm, as the price one paid for civilization. "With the greatest pleasure, Mrs. Morrison."

Miss Ruby Morrison unfolded her fan with an expert stroke of her wrist and peered over the edge. "He's at least seven feet tall. Possibly eight. And his hair is quite white."

"He is a tall man, to be sure, my dear," said her companion. "But not ill-favored."

"He's ancient."

"*Ancient* is a monument of classical Athens, Ruby. Not a vigorous man of sixty years."

"Sixty-eight, Mother says. And you can't deny his hair is white."

Under the guise of admiring the plasterwork surrounding the saloon's vast lantern skylight, Penelope cast another glance at the Duke of Olympia. He stood near the entrance, speaking to Mrs. Morrison with the withered expression of a man who holds all British civilization upon his sturdy shoulders. She'd heard the stories about him, of course. That he was one of England's most powerful dukes; that he had the constant ear of the queen herself. That he was immensely rich, that he had—over the decades—enjoyed any number of infamous mistresses, that he had sired at least one natural child from them. That he was a widower, a confirmed bachelor, and a man of impeccable prestige, despite his history of immoral dalliance—a duke could pull off that sort of thing, of course. But she hadn't expected him to be quite so . . . well, *handsome* wasn't the word for it, was it? As well might you call the Man of the Mountain handsome, or Genghis Khan. He was simply colossal. "White hair is the natural consequence of the passage of time," she said, returning her attention to the purse-lipped Ruby. "And I rather think it suits him."

"He's half a century older than I am. Mother can't possibly be serious. Besides, he's already rich. Why does he need a fortune from us? It's nonsense." Ruby rapped her fan back into a stick and turned her elegant silk back to the Duke of Olympia and his ancient white hair.

"True, he doesn't need a fortune," said Penelope, still gazing dukeward from the corner of her eye. "But he does need an heir, a proper heir of his own body. Both his sons died early, and the dukedom will pass to a grand-nephew, whom nobody knows."

At the words *heir of his own body*, Ruby looked as if she might be ill, right there atop the polished first-class floorboards. "I would rather *die*. Die, I tell you. That old man."

"Nonsense. I imagine he knows his matrimonial business better than most gentlemen half his age. A certain discreet lighting is all that's required. No, you're simply determined to dislike him, because of Robert. I think if you give him a fair chance—"

"He's nothing to Robert. Don't even *begin* to compare them."

"Compare a stockbroker to a duke? I should say not."

"Robert is the handsomest man in the world, and the dearest, and he adores me. While this . . . this . . . *duke* of yours"—she pronounced the word like an epithet—"no doubt recalls the Battle of Waterloo. What on earth would we talk about?"

Penelope paused. "Miss Austen, perhaps?"

"He probably knew her personally." Ruby tilted an obstinate chin at the heaven from which Miss Austen watched tenderly over her, the patron saint of unmarried young ladies.

Well. Ruby had a fair point. The august Duke of Olympia *was* far too old for a glittering twenty-year-old American beauty like Miss Ruby Morrison. The very idea of a union between them struck Penelope as distinctly unwise, to say nothing of . . . well, my goodness, she wanted a word . . . distasteful. That was it. *Distasteful.* No, she couldn't blame Ruby for blanching so perilously at the thought of married life with a man old enough to be her grandfather.

But like the doomed six hundred, theirs was not to question why. Penelope had done that once—questioned why—and found herself delicately uninvited from the Washington Square mansion of her first cousins the Schuylers, her bags packed and her train ticket purchased, and two distant relations later she had landed here, under the thumb of Mrs. Stewart Morrison, her late husband's mother's second husband's second cousin, the end of the line. She had a roof over her head, and a decent clothing allowance, and a first-class berth on the RMS *Majestic*, bound for Liverpool, and having faced the prospect of no roof and no clothes and no berth at all— what was she fit for, after all, at her age? You couldn't start a profession at age fifty, at least not a legal one—she was now more than willing to ride obediently into the mouth of Hell, even if Mrs. Morrison had most assuredly blunder'd.

Another quasi-accidental glance across the room, where His Grace was offering Mrs. Morrison the ducal arm, looking rather like a Great Dane magnificently enduring the attentions of a vociferous Yorkshire terrier.

Yes. Most assuredly blunder'd.

"Good Lord. He's coming," said Ruby.

"No great surprise. Your mother *did* arrange the seating." With the skill of a master strategist, Penelope thought, to say nothing of a strategic bit of civil bribery.

"I can't endure it. They'll make me sit by him."

"Do compose yourself, my dear. It's only dinner. And I assure you, His Grace is likely to prove the most interesting dinner companion in the entire ship, if you can set aside your prejudices and simply enjoy his company."

Ruby's mouth formed a stubborn moue. "I would far rather sit next to Robert."

"Well, Robert remains at his desk in New York, so you had best put him out of your mind."

"You have *obviously* never been in love," Ruby said, in bitter tones. Her high forehead took on a single tragic line across the middle which, combined with the moue, created the distinct impression of a young child about to execute a monumental tantrum.

The words hit Penelope like a fist to her chest. She grasped Ruby gently by the elbow and turned her in the direction of her approaching mother. "Be polite," she said. "Be brave."

And the great glory of Ruby—the miracle of her, really, considering her creamy young beauty and her indulgent upbringing and her impossible mother—was this: She straightened her back and transformed, in the passage of an instant, from a stubborn child into a lady.

Penelope took a single step back, as belonged to a distant widowed relation who had reached a certain age. She allowed the duke to take in the miracle of Ruby: her iridescent skin, her honey-blondness, her mouth like the bow of a particularly strong-fisted Cupid. Her graceful waist, the swell of her youthful bosom. Her well-trained voice, rounded and lowered and molded by the experienced hands of the very best Swiss finishing school. (Penelope herself had attended that school, thirty years and a stock market crash ago, and she thanked God the lawyers couldn't take *that* away from her at least, they couldn't reach into her throat and take away her beautifully fashioned voice.) When Mrs. Morrison made the ecstatic introduction, and the Duke of Olympia made some rumbling courteous reply, Ruby held out her slender hand and said, as if she were quite accustomed to meeting dukes, "How kind of you, Your Grace. The honor is all ours, of course."

And then the duke said something else, and a brief silence floated in the air, and Penelope realized that his words had been directed at her.

She turned her surprised gaze from the curve of Ruby's cheek to the man standing before her.

"Oh!" said Ruby, before her mother could open her mouth. "This is our dear cousin Mrs. Schuyler, who was kind enough to agree to take the voyage with us. Though I do wonder if she'll repent her generosity by the time we sail past Nova Scotia."

"Mrs. Schuyler." The duke fixed his eyes on her, and a rather queer sensation overcame the sensible Mrs. Penelope Schuyler, who had borne so much misfortune with so much fortitude, who had carried on regardless beneath a thick layer of aplomb.

She felt as if someone had just painted the world a most extraordinary shade of summertime blue.

She was too far away to offer her hand, tucked as she was in the shadow of Ruby. She inclined her head politely instead. She was an American, by God, and she didn't curtsy to dukes. "Your Grace."

The Duke of Olympia's eyebrows lifted, as if he were expecting more. But what was she supposed to say? That she was honored to meet him? She couldn't quite remember.

She must be a little unstrung, she realized, a little thrown off by the intensity of color in the ducal pupils. She'd never seen a shade quite like that, certainly not in the center of a magnificent face like that. Ruby was wrong: The duke wasn't eight feet tall, or even seven, but he did stand a good three or four inches above six, towering physically and metaphorically above them all. Up close, his hair was more silver than white. He was remarkably lean-waisted and broad-shouldered, a man who evidently didn't choose to lounge with the other aging dukes in the leather-scented quiet of the club library, snoozing away his remaining afternoons over crisp sheets of newspaper. No, he radiated vigor. He was made of energy. His stomach lay quite flat beneath his white silk waistcoat. His evening clothes fit him elegantly. In short, he wore his six and a half decades with remarkable ease, and Penelope was trying to work out why and how he effected this almost youthfulness, and was just concluding that it had something to do with his lack of whiskers, when she heard Ruby laugh.

"She's not usually so tongue-tied, Your Grace. I think you've got to stop glowering at her like that."

"I beg your pardon," said the duke, making a little bow. "I must have been lost in thought. A consequence of my ancient years, I suppose."

"Oh, no, your lordship," said Mrs. Morrison. "Not ancient at all. Isn't that right, Ruby?"

Ruby laughed again. "Mama, *Your Grace*. Not *your lordship*. Because dukes, we presume, are just chock-full of divine grace. Isn't that right, Your Grace?"

"In truth," said Olympia, with a single pat to the watch pocket of his waistcoat, "a simple *sir* will do. Or *duke*, if you must."

"What do your friends call you?" asked Ruby.

The look he cast her was not the slightest bit amused. "I

have no friends, Miss Morrison. But my family, when they deign to address me by something other than a vulgar epithet, call me Olympia."

"How very intimate," Penelope said, under her breath.

The duke's eyes shot back to her. "We *are* English, after all."

The gong sounded over the end of his sentence. Penelope wondered at its temerity.

"Dinner at last," said Mrs. Morrison. "I believe we have the honor of sitting with you, your . . . your . . . that is . . . Duke?"

The Duke of Olympia turned to the elegantly set table before them, snowy of linen and gleaming of silver. The captain's table, toward which the captain himself was now advancing, resplendent in uniform and whiskers.

"I fear I shall perish from the pleasure," said His Grace, with a sigh.

A small white rectangle of a letter lay on the carpet, just inside the stateroom door. Penelope bent and picked it up.

Miss Ruby Morrison, the envelope proclaimed, in calm black handwriting.

She held it out to Ruby, who was just entering behind her. "For you."

"For me?" Ruby's eyebrows arched upward. She took the paper between her fingers and opened the flap of the envelope.

Penelope proceeded to the small washstand, where she unscrewed her garnet earrings—a gift from her husband, deemed too insignificant for the lawyers to bother with—and began to remove the pins from her heavy dark hair. John had always loved her hair. Her skin might be taking on lines, and her bosom no longer resided at quite the same height, but her hair remained thick. And her eyes were bright, she thought, staring intently into the mirror. Not so luminous as Ruby's wide hazel man-traps, perhaps, but then she wasn't trying to trap a man, was she?

No, of course she wasn't. At her age, in her lowly condition. The idea.

She glanced to the side, where Ruby's reflection hovered over her shoulder. The Cupid lips had formed into a pink-rimmed *O*, slightly parted in the center.

"Something interesting?" Penelope asked.

Ruby's mouth closed. She looked up, smiling, and folded up the paper and stuffed it back into the envelope. "Not really. That awful Miss Crawley we met at tea wants to go walking with me tomorrow morning."

"Walking where?"

"The promenade deck, I suppose. If the weather holds." Ruby stifled a yawn. "My goodness, I'm exhausted! What a great effort it is, talking to a duke all evening. Watching every word."

"*You?* Watching your words?" The last pin came free, and Penelope picked up her brush.

Ruby laughed her tinkling young laugh. "Well, comparatively speaking, of course. He wasn't so bad, I'll admit. But I'm not going to let Mother marry me off to him."

Penelope set down the brush and turned around to unbutton Ruby's dress. "Don't get ahead of yourself, my dear. After all, before you can claim the glory of refusing the Duke of Olympia's hand in marriage, he first has to offer it."

R uby was dead right about exhaustion, however. Whether because of the duke at dinner, or the cold salt air on deck, or the previous week of frantic preparation, Penelope couldn't even remember drawing up the covers and falling asleep in her berth.

She only found herself startling awake into the dark room, some unknown time later, under the distinct impression that something—or someone—was moving about the cabin.

Three intrepid princesses find themselves targets in a deadly plot against the crown—until their uncle devises a brilliant plan to keep them safe...

How to Master Your Marquis

A PRINCESS IN HIDING ROMANCE

Princess Stefanie, the most rebellious among her sisters, is appalled to find herself masquerading as a drab clerk for the most honorable barrister in England. But her dull disguise turns out to have its privileges—namely, the opportunity to consort unchaperoned with her employer's exceedingly handsome friend, the Marquis of Hatherfield...

PRAISE FOR THE NOVELS OF JULIANA GRAY

"Gray makes one of the best trilogy debuts in years, proving she is a literary force to be reckoned with."
—*Booklist* (starred review)

"Juliana Gray is on my autobuy list."
— Elizabeth Hoyt, *New York Times* bestselling author

julianagray.com
facebook.com/julianagray
penguin.com

M1416T0114

*Three intrepid princesses find themselves targets
in a deadly plot against the crown.*

FROM
JULIANA GRAY

How to Tame Your Duke

England, 1888. Quiet and scholarly Princess Emilie has always avoided adventure, until she's forced to disguise herself as a tutor for the imposing Duke of Ashland, a former soldier disfigured in battle. When chance draws them into a secret liaison, Emilie can't resist the opportunity to learn what lies behind his forbidding mask.

The duke never imagines that his son's tutor and his mysterious golden-haired beauty are one and the same. But when her true identity is laid bare, Ashland must face the demons in his past to safeguard both his lady—and his heart.

"Juliana Gray has a stupendously lyrical voice."
—Meredith Duran, *New York Times* bestselling author

julianagray.com
facebook.com/JulianaGray
facebook.com/LoveAlwaysBooks
penguin.com

M1348T0813

FROM

JULIANA GRAY

A GENTLEMAN NEVER TELLS

Six years ago, Elizabeth Harewood and Lord Roland Pen-hallow were London's golden couple, young and beautiful and wildly in love. Forced apart by her scheming relatives and his clandestine career, Lilibet and Roland buried their passion beneath years of duty and self-denial, until a chance holiday encounter changes everything they ever knew about themselves . . . and each other.

But Miss Elizabeth Harewood is now the Countess of Somerton, estranged wife of one of England's most brutal and depraved aristocrats, and she can't afford the slightest hint of scandal attached to her name. When Roland turns up mysteriously at the castle where she's hidden herself away, she struggles to act as a lady should, but the gallant lover of her youth has grown into an irresistibly dashing and dangerous man, and temptation is only a single kiss away . . .

PRAISE FOR JULIANA GRAY

"Juliana Gray has a stupendously lyrical voice
unlike anybody else."
—Meredith Duran, *New York Times* bestselling author

"Juliana Gray is on my auto-buy list."
—Elizabeth Hoyt, *New York Times* bestselling author

julianagray.com
facebook.com/JulianaGray
facebook.com/LoveAlwaysBooks
penguin.com